Vol

D0196492

Secrets

Satisfy your desire for more.

Reviews from Secrets Volume 1

"Four very romantic, very sexy novellas in very different styles and settings. ... The settings are quite diverse taking the reader from Regency England to a remote and mysterious fantasy land, to an Arabian nights type setting, and finally to a contemporary urban setting. All stories are explicit, and Hamre and Landon stories sizzle. ... If you like erotic romance you will love *Secrets*."

— **Romantic Readers** review

"Overall, for a fan of erotica, these are unlike anything you've encountered before. For those romance fans who turn down the pages of the "good parts" for later repeat consumption (and you know who you are) these books are a wonderful way to explore the better side of the erotica market. ... *Secrets* is a worthy exploration for the adventurous reader with the promise for better things yet to come."

— **Liz Montgomery**

America Online review

"These are romances, not just erotica, which contain love as well as delving into the secret depths of fantasy and sexuality."

— **Tanzey Cutter**

Reviews from Secrets Volume 2
Winner of the Fallot Literary Award for Fiction

America Online review

"*Secrets, Volume 2*, a new anthology published by Red Sage Publishing, is hot! I mean *red hot!* ... The sensuality in each story will make you blush—from head to toe and everywhere else in-between. ... The true success behind *Secrets, Volume 2* is the combination of different tastes—both in subgenres of romance and levels of sensuality. *I highly recommend this book*."

— **Dawn A. Long**

Erotic Readers Association review

"I think it is a fine anthology and Red Sage should be applauded for providing an outlet for women who want to write sensual romance."

— **Adrienne Benedicks**

Reviews from Secrets Volume 3

Winner of the 1997 Under the Cover Readers Favorite Award

"An unabashed celebration of sex. Highly arousing! Highly recommended!"
—**Virginia Henley**, *New York Times* Best Selling Author

"*Secrets, Volume 3* leaves the reader breathless. Each of these tributes to exotic and erotic fiction offers a world of sensual pleasure and moral rewards. A delicious confection of sensuous treats awaits the reader on each turn of the page. Sexy, funny, thrilling, and luscious, Secrets entertains, enlightens, and fuels the fires of fantasy."
— **Kathee Card**, *Romancing the Web*

"*Secrets, Volume 3* is worth the wait… and is the best of the three. This is erotic romance reading at its best."
— **Lani Roberts**, *Affaire de Coeur*

"From the FBI to Police Detectives to Vampires to a Medieval Warlord home from the Crusade — *Secerts Vol. 3* is SIMPLY THE BEST!"
—**Susan Paul**, Award Winning Author

Reviews from Secrets Volume 4

"*Secrets, Volume 4*, has something to satisfy every erotic fantasy… simply sexsational!"
—**Virginia Henley**, *New York Times* Best Selling Author

"Provacative…seductive…a must read! ★★★★"
— *Romantic Times*

"These are the kind of stories that romance readers that 'want a little more' have been looking for all their lives without crossing over into the adult genre. Keep these stories coming, Red Sage, the world needs them!"
— **Lani Roberts**, *Affaire de Coeur*

"If you're interested in exploring erotica, or reading farther than the sexual passages of your favorite steamy reads, the *Secret* series is well worth checking out."
— **Writers Club Romance Group on AOL Reviewer Board**

Reviews from Secrets Volume 5

"*Secrets, Volume 5*, is a collage of lucious sensuality. Any woman who reads *Secrets* is in for an awakening!"

—**Virginia Henley,** *New York Times* Best Selling Author

"Hot, hot, hot! Not for the faint-hearted!" — *Romantic Times*

"As you make your way through the stories, you will find yourself becoming hotter and hotter. *Secrets* just keeps getting better and better."

— *Affaire de Coeur*

Reviews from Secrets Volume 6

"*Secrets, Volume 6* satisfies every female fantasy: the Bodyguard, the Tutor, the Werewolf, and the Vampire. I give it Six Stars!"

—**Virginia Henley,** *New York Times* Best Selling Author

"*Secrets, Volume 6* is the best of *Secrets* yet. ...four of the most erotic stories in one volume than this reader has yet to see anywhere else. ... These stories are full of erotica at its best and you'll definitely want to keep it handy for lots of re-reading!"

— *Affaire de Coeur* Magazine

Reviews from Secrets Volume 7

"...sensual, sexy, steamy fun. A perfect read!"

—**Virginia Henley,** *New York Times* Best Selling Author

"Intensely provocative and disarmingly romantic, Secrets Volume 7 is a romance reader's paradise that will take you beyond your wildest dreams!"

— *Ballston Book House* Review

"Erotic romance is at the sensual core of Red Sage's latest collection of short, red hot novels, *Secrets, Volume 7*."

— *Writers Club Romance Group* on AOL

Satisfy Your Desire for More... with *Secrets!*

Did you miss any of the other volumes of the sexy Secrets series? At the back of this book is an order form for all the available volumes. Order your Secrets today!

Jeanie Cesarini

MaryJanice Davidson

Alice Gaines

Liz Maverick

Volume 8

Secrets

Satisfy your desire for more.

SECRETS Volume 8

This is an original publication of Red Sage Publishing and each individual story herein has never before appeared in print. These stories are a collection of fiction and any similarity to actual persons or events is purely coincidental.

Red Sage Publishing, Inc.
P.O. Box 4844
Seminole, FL 33775
727-391-3847
www.redsagepub.com

SECRETS Volume 8
A Red Sage Publishing book
All Rights Reserved/December 2002
Copyright © 2002 by Red Sage Publishing, Inc.

ISBN 0-9648942-8-9

Published by arrangement with the authors and copyright holders of the individual works as follows:

TAMING KATE
Copyright © 2002 by Jeanie Cesarini

JARED'S WOLF
Copyright © 2002 by MaryJanice Davidson

MY CHAMPION, MY LOVE
Copyright © 2002 by Alice Gaines

KISS OR KILL
Copyright © 2002 by Liz Maverick

Photographs: Copyright © 2001-2002 by Greg P. Willis; email: GgnYbr@aol.com

Printed in the U.S.A.

Cover design, layout and book typesetting by:

Quill & Mouse Studios, Inc.
2165 Sunnydale Boulevard, Suite E
Clearwater, FL 33765
www.quillandmouse.com

Contents

Taming Kate

⁂

by Jeanie Cesarini

To My Reader:

I was in the mood for a cowboy and since *this* cowboy would be my very first…*Secrets* provides the perfect place to explore my mood, a place where stories indulge sensual fantasies and deep dark desires. So, dearest reader, hop on and let's go for a red-hot ride west, to a town called Love where just about anything can happen…and does.

Her Family Tree was a Shrub

Kathryn Roman stared at the telephone receiver, then brought it back to her ear with a chuckle. She'd been on this phone so much while launching the new ad campaign for Simply Seductive fragrances she was beginning to hear things. "Forgive me. Could you please repeat that? Kitty left me what? I thought you said *brothel*."

"I did," the masculine voice confirmed over the line. "The late Ms. Romanov left you sole ownership of Katia's Palace, a brothel in Love, Nevada. I'll make the records of material assets available when you come to town. We have some issues involving the inheritance taxes to discuss…"

The lawyer, whose name had flown right out of Kathryn's head, droned on, his words forming a western-edged buzz that echoed in her ear without making a bit of sense.

Kitty had owned a brothel?

A brothel?

Kitty Romanov, bless her soul, had been a little old lady who'd kept a condo in the same Central Park West hi-rise where Kathryn had lived all her life. For the past seven years, ever since Kathryn's mother had died in fact, Kitty had become a late-night-ice-cream-and-sigh-at-old-movies buddy. Someone Kathryn had considered a friend.

Not a full-time friend, by any means. Kitty hadn't been around long enough to be a full-time anything. She'd only stayed one week a month in New York. The rest of her time she'd spent playing one-armed bandits and soaking up the dry Nevada air. Or at least that's what she'd led Kathryn to believe.

"A brothel, Mr.—" What was the man's name? "Sir. Obviously there's some mistake. This isn't the Old West."

"There are legalized brothels in the state of Nevada, I assure you, Miss Roman, and Kitty Romanov was the proprietor of one of the most renowned."

Kitty had been a *madam*?

The idea alone seemed absurd, even more so when coupled with the image that sprang to mind of Kitty, swirls of coiffed white hair piled high on top of her head, juggling a poopie-scooper in one hand while fighting to get her trio of fluffy Maltese dogs into their twelfth floor elevator.

Kitty had been a character to be sure, and Kathryn had been genuinely sorry when she'd passed on not long after celebrating her eightieth birthday. But a *madam*?

"If Kitty did own a brothel…" Even the words sounded stupid. "Why would she leave it to me?"

"Ownership of Katia's Palace passes to the oldest female of the Romanov family."

Kathryn sank back in her leather chair and issued a sigh of relief that sounded shakier than it should have. "There has definitely been a mistake, Mr.... *Carter*." That was his name. "You've confused me with someone else. My name is Roman, not Romanov."

"No mistake, Miss Roman. I'm aware of the circumstances surrounding your name." She heard no emotion in the lawyer's voice, not even a hint of censure, yet Kathryn felt the hairs on the back of her neck tingle.

"If you know that I go by my mother's maiden name, then you should also know I have no living family."

The silence on the other end of the line turned those few tingling nape hairs into fully-fledged raised hackles.

"Miss Roman." His voice held a note of caution, as though he held an open can of worms and was prepared to dump them right onto the lap of her lined silk skirt. Kathryn knew the tone and braced herself. "I'm aware that you and your mother reverted to her maiden name after her divorce from your father. Apparently you weren't aware she also legally changed her name from Romanov to Roman at that time. The records are on file with the court."

Kathryn inhaled sharply. Her thoughts spun wildly out of her grasp, like a box of puzzle pieces dropped on the floor. Her mother had legally changed her name? Why? So she wouldn't be connected with the family business?

It fit. It *definitely* fit. Kathryn's high society mother would never have tolerated a legalized prostitution skeleton in her closet without slamming the door tight and sealing it in with the safest security system money could buy.

Kathryn's mother had been a respectable matron of New York's elite, hosting charity functions for all the right causes, never stepping an elegant toe out of line. She'd educated her only child at all the best schools, debuted her to society with the finest parties, had done everything by the letter—everything except open her heart and allow her daughter to get close.

"You're telling me I was related to Kitty?"

"She was your great aunt. Your grandmother's sister."

Great aunt? Grandmother? Kathryn's fingers tightened around the receiver until her knuckles grew white. She'd never had a clue these people had existed— the ultimate irony, given how often she'd longed for a family during those lonely years of her youth. Having a great aunt like Kitty visit her boarding school just once would have done wonders.

"I surmise that my news has come as something of a shock," Mr. Carter said.

Something of a shock? That was *something* of a mild understatement. Shaking her head, Kathryn forced her attention back to the matter at hand. "I'm sorry. You were saying?"

"I'll fax the preliminary information to your office today for you to review. When can you make it to Love, Miss Roman? Business decisions need to be made immediately—"

"I can't leave New York right now. I'm in the middle of launching an ad campaign that requires my undivided attention. But I readily admit you've taken me by surprise. Why don't you just fax me that information? I'll bring myself up to speed, confirm the details of my mother's name change and get back with you."

"Fine, Miss Roman, but certain decisions regarding the business require immediate—"

•

"I'll get back with you, Mr. Carter. Good day."

Kathryn's hand shook as she settled the receiver back in the cradle. Unable to sit still any longer, she launched to her feet, found her favorite spot in front of the floor-to-ceiling windows that cornered her office.

"Kitty, why didn't you ever tell me?" she asked aloud, her voice echoing emptily above the drone of the air conditioning.

Folding her arms across her chest, she willed the heat of the midday June sun that baked the city outside to ease her sudden chill.

How she'd longed for a family, a sister, a brother, an aunt...someone she could feel connected to, someone to giggle with, commiserate with or even cry with. Someone other than her mother, who'd always done her best in rearing Kathryn, but who'd never allowed a drop of emotion to crack through her veneer of proper deportment.

A smile tugged at her lips at the incongruity of caftan-loving Kitty sporting the same bloodlines as Kathryn's own designer silk suit mother. Imagine them running into each other in the hallway. Kathryn's mother would have fainted, before she uprooted every last stake and relocated to Boston.

Nevertheless, Kathryn had liked Kitty. They'd had fun together, had feasted on pints of Haagen-Dazs wrapped in dishtowels and had laughed themselves silly watching old comedies. They'd even remarked upon the similarities of their last names, yet Kitty had never told her the truth.

She'd had a great aunt, and she'd never even known it.

Now she had a brothel. The trade off seemed lopsided in the extreme. What on earth was she going to do with a brothel?

Kathryn gazed around her office, fashionably decorated with corner windows that overlooked the city, where she created multi-million dollar advertising campaigns that sent businesses spiraling off in new and exciting directions. She was a new partner in one of the most respected advertising firms in the country. Imagine, her running a brothel.

Her smile faded. Like her mother, she'd obviously missed whatever gene had made the women in their family capable of running a business that involved sex and men. Her track record with the gender was beyond abysmal. Her fiancé's words when he'd broken their engagement were chiseled in her head.

I need a woman with fire, Kathryn.

Those genes must skip a generation. Or in her case two.

What on earth was she going to do with Kitty's brothel?

Kathryn would have to do something, simply out of respect for Kitty. Unfortunately, she didn't have the time or the brain cells to hash through the problem at the moment. The Simply Seductive campaign demanded all of her attention, and if that wasn't enough, she'd have to track down the documents confirming her mother's name change...and work through her feelings about having discovered and lost a great aunt all in one phone call.

She'd had family. For a little while at least.

Turning away from the window, Kathryn returned to her desk, doing exactly what she always did when life got too complicated to deal with—work.

Life's as Crazy as Popcorn on a Hot Skillet

Six Weeks Later

"Belt up, city girl." On-the-Wing Joe shot the command over his shoulder in a crusty voice. "We're heading down."

Belt up? Kathryn wasn't only belted; she white-knuckled the seat to stay attached during this hour-long ride from hell.

Squeezing her eyes shut, she staved off one more round of queasiness as the engines whirred and the plane jerkily dropped another dozen feet. What insanity had possessed her to fly into Love on a commuter plane that typically hauled copper miners into the area?

Here was a classic example of how trying to save time would wind up costing her some. If she could walk straight once this plane—*hopefully*—landed, she wouldn't be up for much except hiding in a dark room with a washcloth on her pounding head.

Forget about blowing into town, meeting with the mayor and lawyer, and blowing out again by Friday. She'd lose even more time traveling back to the city and a real airport, because she would *not* be making the return flight with On-the-Wing Joe.

Chancing a glance as the plane jerkily descended another twenty feet, Kathryn caught the pilot squinting myopically and suspected he couldn't see the terrain through the windscreen, let alone read the numbers and dials on the instrument panel.

No problem, Kathryn told herself, taking a deep breath. She could handle anything. This would be the first and only time she'd have to act on behalf of her family, and she planned to act with dignity.

Dignity did *not* mean arriving in Love and beelining straight for the nearest bathroom to lose the remains of the bagel she'd eaten back in the Big Apple.

"Looks like the posse's here to welcome you, city girl."

"Posse?" she croaked out, loosening her grip on the seat to lean into the aisle and peek through the windscreen. "Don't posses hang people?"

On-the-Wing Joe gave a rusty chuckle. "Don't think the folks down there are gonna be inviting the Palace's new owner to a necktie social. Every man in this county and the next, and his daddy and granddaddy, has lost his virginity to one of the princesses. They'll want to stay on friendly-like terms, if you know what I mean."

Kathryn did indeed and swallowed back a curt retort. What business was it of his if she planned to turn over management of Katia's Palace to the town as soon as she could sign the papers?

"Are we landing in that field, Joe?" she asked incredulously as the plane's gears gnashed louder than the noisy engines on the snowplows back home. "There are people down there. It looks like a riot."

"Naw, city girl. They're here to welcome you. We Nevadans are friendly folk."

Kathryn leaned back and gazed out over the wingspan as they approached, confirming with one glance what she'd suspected since first boarding this death-trap—On-the-Wing Joe's eyesight wasn't nearly what it should be.

A large group circled the field, following the path of the plane as if sucked into its air stream. Some held signs high. Welcome signs? Kathryn didn't think so. As a "city girl," she'd developed the ability to spot trouble in large crowds.

"They don't look very friendly."

"Aw, pshaw. They're giving you a special Love welcome."

If a special Love welcome involved a crowd that looked about as happy as fans at Shea Stadium the last time an ump had called Mike Piazza out, Kathryn would have to agree. But she didn't get a chance to comment as the plane touched down with a bump and a thud and the gears whined shrilly.

Whispering a mental prayer of thanks to be in one piece, Kathryn popped the clasp on her seatbelt, stretched her legs, and caught sight of one of the "welcome" signs.

Historic landmarks need to be preserved, not closed.

Closed? Who was planning to close a historic landmark?

Katia's Palace is part of Love's History.

Uh oh.

"Don't open that door, Joe!"

He swung a puzzled glance her way, his grizzled brows drawn tight in a frown. "What's the trouble, city girl?"

This cornpone still didn't realize the mob was here to lynch her. She pointed out at the sea of bobbing cowboy hats and handmade signs swarming the plane. "Look out there."

Joe obliged, and she saw surprise, then understanding dawn on his craggy face. "Well, now, would you look at that? Your arrival sure did stir up a hornet's nest. What'dya do, city girl? Put the princesses on vacation?"

Kathryn assumed the princesses were Kitty's...*employees.* "I didn't put any-one on vacation. In fact, I haven't spoken with anyone except the mayor—"

Joe's bristly brow shot clear up to his hairline. "Now why would you be talking to Mayor Barclay? Aren't you fixing to step into Miss Kitty's place and run the Palace?"

"Of course not," she snapped.

Joe shot a nervous glance out the window. While the crowd wasn't eye level with the cockpit, the picket signs were.

Don't leave the princesses homeless!

Joe gave a decided shake of his head. "You sure are stepping into a pile of dung."

Kathryn didn't intend to step anywhere, least of all into that angry mob, but options were limited. Did she tempt fate by heading back into the sky with a pilot who couldn't see?

"Can you get us back in the air, Joe?"

"Not unless you want me to run down a few of these folks."

She sank back into the seat with a huff, avoiding another sign that popped into the window's view and read *The Royal Fraud!* feeling as though the confines of the plane were shrinking as the grumbling and catcalls outside grew louder.

"What's this all about?" she asked rhetorically, but Joe obliged her anyway.

"Don't know, city girl. Except if you've been talking to Mayor Barclay then you might have headed down the wrong mine shaft. The Mayor sold his saddle to get elected and his ideas about what's best for Love have got most folks gritting their teeth like they could bite the sights off a six gun."

Kathryn could only stare, brain cells churning to comprehend the man's language. She recognized Mayor Barclay's name and could only surmise that selling saddles to finance his mayoral campaign was *not* a good thing.

"Well, here comes Trey Holliday. He'll see you through."

"Trey Holliday?"

"He's the ranching vet, the Palace's overseer, too."

Overseer? Now that Kathryn thought about it, she remembered seeing a signature on some paperwork Kitty's lawyer had faxed to her. She couldn't remember the name. One thing was clear, though, Trey Holliday commanded a great deal of respect with Love's townspeople. The crowd parted like the Red Sea had for Charlton Heston in her favorite Easter film.

And out strode a real live, honest-to-goodness cowboy.

Kathryn's mouth popped open. Trey Holliday looked as if he'd emerged straight off the silver screen. One of those old Westerns that always left her sighing and wishing they made real men like that nowadays.

Tall and broad-shouldered, he strode along with a sort of loose-limbed grace that lent him an aura of authority. He nodded politely and responded to what she assumed were greetings, and faces that had worn expressions reminding her of snarling street dogs now wore relieved, even pleased smiles.

The cowboy *was* pleasing to look at.

His jeans slung low on trim hips, and his boots kicked up little puffs of dust with each step. With his checked cotton shirt and plain leather vest, Trey Holliday was as different from the men in Kathryn's world as if he'd just appeared from a different century.

Even Joe seemed relieved to see him, and before she could object, he flung open the cockpit window. "Well, hey there, Trey. I'm right glad to see you."

"The lady in there with you?" asked a deep male voice, a strange combination of Western twang and throaty richness.

"Sure is. Get those folks back and I'll let you in."

"Joe, don't—"

Before Kathryn cleared her seat, a metallic lock clicked and the cowboy pulled open the door. While he lowered the steps, Kathryn could only see the top of his Stetson. The breath seemed stuck in her throat as he propped one booted foot on a rung and tipped his head back to gaze up at her.

He couldn't have been much older than she was, maybe thirty-two or three, but his face was all hard lines to match his hard, outdoorsy body, a study of character in every inch of weathered skin the color of freshly tanned leather, or at least what Kathryn imagined freshly tanned leather would look like if she'd ever seen any. Crinkles fanned outward from his eyes when he grinned, which appeared to be a familiar expression, given the depth of the grooves.

As his gaze moved over her, assessed her with a glance that made her feel the caress of his deep brown eyes like a warm breeze, Kathryn stood riveted to the spot, felt the breath dislodge in her throat when his smile widened.

"Trey Holliday, ma'am." He touched the brim of his hat politely. "See you're in a spot of trouble here."

She forced a tight smile. "A pleasure, Mr. Holliday. But I don't understand what's happening here. These people must have been misinformed. I don't plan on closing Katia's Palace."

"Call me Trey," he said genially. "Are you planning to turn over management?"

"I am, but I'm turning it over to the town. Katia's Palace is part of Love's history."

"Yes, ma'am, it is. And most folks around here believe it needs to be preserved. Others, though, think it's standing in the way of Love's future."

A chill zipped along her spine, whether from the niggling suspicion that much more was going on around here than she knew or the intense way this cowboy kept staring at her, Kathryn couldn't say. Instead she asked, "How's that?"

"The brothel zoning ordinance limits the town's population. The mayor and his supporters want the brothel closed down to attract developers into the area so they can build a mega-mall."

"With a twenty-four screen cinema," Joe piped in.

Kathryn ignored him and faced the cowboy. "Are you telling me if I turn over management of Katia's Palace to the town, the mayor will close the doors?"

The cowboy nodded.

She sank down to the edge of the seat. "I've walked into a turf war, haven't I?"

That quirky half-smile never wavered. "You have, ma'am."

Kathryn let her face flop into her hands, a gesture of despair that had the bonus of blocking out sight of the cowboy.

What had Kitty been thinking to bequeath a brothel to a New York City ad exec? An ad exec who didn't know the first thing about romance? Kathryn couldn't seriously entertain the idea that Kitty thought she'd run the place. They may have only known each other for the past seven of Kathryn's twenty-eight years, but Kitty had known work took precedence in Kathryn's life. She'd remarked upon it often enough.

Was that what Kitty had been counting on, that somehow Kathryn's business experience might ensure the brothel's future?

Quite simply, Kathryn didn't have enough information to formulate an opinion. The opinion she'd already formulated, though, was if all families were this much trouble, she understood why her mother had run far away from hers.

"Ma'am?"

Inhaling deeply, Kathryn forced herself to meet his gaze. "Are those the...*princesses* out there?"

The cowboy shook his head. "The townsfolk. The princesses can't leave the Palace while they're on duty, except to visit the doctor for their medical exams."

"How long is 'on duty'?" she asked.

"Three weeks."

Something of her horror must have shown on her face, because the cowboy frowned and changed the subject.

"I can get you to the Palace safely."

"Those people want to roast me alive, Mr. Holliday."

"Trey."

"Trey. I'm not leaving this plane." She glanced at the myopic cornpone and placed her fate in God's hands. "Joe, take me back to the airport."

"Now?" Joe asked, none too cheerfully. "I was heading for Sadie's. It's Wednesday and she's fixing meatloaf."

"I'll buy you your own cow," Kathryn said. "Just get me out of here."

The ensuing silence spiked her heartrate, then her temper when On-the-Wing Joe said, "If Trey says it's okay."

"You won't be needing your own cow tonight, Joe. If you get a move on to Sadie's, you'll miss the dinner crowd." The cowboy flipped the brim of his hat back to reveal a thatch of wheat blonde hair in such contrast with his tanned skin that his brown eyes seemed to melt into warm molasses. "The way I see it, ma'am, you've only got two choices. I can carry you to my truck, so the first glimpse this town gets of their new madam will be of her backside propped over my shoulder, or you can walk on your own two feet. Lady's choice."

"Excuse me? How...dare you," she sputtered, unable to form a coherent reply, but outraged enough to try.

The cowboy smiled, a full-fledged smile that drove two pencilpoint dimples into his cheeks and made his eyes twinkle. "You're no bigger than a nubbin'. I'd be pleased to carry you."

A nubbin? Kathryn didn't have time to ponder this new and strange land where people spoke an incomprehensible language before the cowboy stepped up another rung on the ladder.

Leaping from her seat, she backed away. "I don't need you to carry me, cowboy."

His smile faded, but that stupid grin replaced it, playing at the corners of his mouth, and making her feel as though she'd just purchased a twenty-dollar Rolex from a street vendor.

"You'll walk then?"

Slinging her purse over her shoulder, Kathryn fixed a stony expression on her face. "I'm not going anywhere until I see the sheriff. Surely this town has a sheriff."

Trey Holliday nodded casually, inclined his head toward the window. "He's right over there. His deputy, too."

Before Kathryn had a chance to register that the sheriff and his deputy appeared to be chatting with the protesters rather than making any attempt to disperse them, the cowboy shot forward and whipcord arms threaded around her.

Kathryn gasped as he brought her hard against him and then hoisted her up over his shoulder, as easily as though she were no bigger than—what had he said?—a *nubbin'*.

Her bottom bumped the plane's ceiling and she found herself imprisoned by strong arms as he carried her down the steps to the sound of Joe's laughter.

Enter the Tenderfoot

The reluctant new madam of Katia's Palace had better sense than to create a fuss by kicking her legs and throwing him off balance. Though judging by the way the townsfolk hooted and hollered, Trey guessed they would've enjoyed the show.

Some made some rather promising suggestions for what he might do with this pretty lady once he got her back to the Palace. Trey couldn't see the lady's face to know what she thought of their ideas, but reckoned the way her body went all stiff was a pretty good indication.

Figuring he'd made his point that he wouldn't help her turn tail and run from town, he planned to set her back on her feet once they reached the edge of the crowd. A plan that changed quick enough when her teeth sank into his ribs.

"Damn." He instinctively slid her off his shoulder and blessedly, every curvy inch of her body rode down his, distracting him from the pain.

Looked like he wasn't the only one with a point to make.

"You got a pootin' pony there, Trey," Chester McGee, owner of the Bar M commented. "She'll have you cinched by the last hole if you ain't careful."

Trey didn't get a chance to reply before the lady took a few unsteady paces away from him and yelled, "Sheriff."

Rubbing the tender spot below his ribs, Trey smiled at the lady, greeted Sheriff Luke and his son, the town's deputy.

"Yes, ma'am," Luke said.

"I demand protection from this man until I can secure a restraining order."

Luke rocked back on his heels, stroked his chin and regarded the lady thoughtfully. "From Trey, ma'am? Why would you be needing protection from him?"

"He assaulted me."

"I didn't see any assault." He turned to his son. "Did you, Jess?"

Jess only shook his head and Trey bit back a smile at the lady's obvious outrage. Her pretty eyes flashed blue fire, just like a lightning bolt.

"You have an easy two hundred witnesses here, Sheriff." She swept a hand around in a gesture that was no less elegant for its impatience. "If you and your deputy were temporarily blinded, I'm sure any of these people can tell you what happened."

Luke cupped his hands around his mouth and yelled, "Any of ya'll see Trey assault this lady?"

With every denial issued in his defense, the lady became more stoic, more remote. Old Minnie Crocker said, "I saw the lady assault Trey," before turning to him and advising, "Better give yourself a tetanus shot. Wouldn't want you catching anything." Trey reckoned the lady just might explode.

"Let's go to the Palace," he said. "We'll work out everything there."

She fixed him with that lightning blue stare. "I'm not going anywhere with you."

"Trey here's your overseer, ma'am," Luke said. "I suggest you go talk things out with him. He knows best what Kitty wanted for you and the Palace. You have my word that Trey'll treat you with respect."

Kate scowled, clearly disbelieving that she could take Luke's word on anything.

"My truck's this way." Trey motioned to a field beyond the edge of the crowd.

A war raged in those blue eyes. Kissable lips narrowed into a line straight with displeasure. But Trey sensed the instant she made her decision, the slight flare to her nostrils, the lift of her dainty chin. She spun on her heels and swept into the crowd as regally as a queen.

Trey followed up the rear, far enough to stay clear of the lady's claws, yet close enough to step in if more trouble brewed. To the townsfolk's credit, though, most just gawked, and Trey right along with them.

Lady Kate, as he'd dubbed her the instant his eyes fixed on her pretty face with those big eyes and shiny black hair, was something of a sight. In her sleek blue suit, she stuck out like a mustang in a herd of muleys, a city girl lifted right off the shiny cover of a magazine and plunked smack dab into a crowd of rumpled denim and dirt-scuffed boots.

He liked the contrast. Her sleek suit hugged her slim curves in a way rumpled denim never could. And she did have the sweetest little body.

More petite than he'd pegged her from Kitty's accountings, he'd somehow imagined that a woman who dealt in the multi-million dollar advertising business should have been taller, more aggressive. While Lady Kate might have thorns, the top of her head didn't quite reach his shoulder. Even in high heels that made the going over the dusty summer ground a mite slow.

But the lady didn't let that trouble her in the least. Sweeping along with her head held high, she measured each step as if she was walking along a satin runner in some fancy hotel.

Trey liked her spunk.

He got her to his truck without further incident, but no sooner had he slammed the door behind her than folk started firing off questions faster than grease jumped on a hot plate.

"You'll set her straight, Trey, won't you?"

"You won't let her toss out the princesses, will you?"

"Tell her what'll happen if she closes the Palace."

Trey wound his way around the front of the truck. "You've got my word I'll explain the situation to the lady," he assured them. "In the meanwhile, calm down. We'll work something out."

Judging by the doubt on their faces—and he'd known most of these people his whole life—they didn't believe him. After meeting the lady who controlled the Palace's fate, Trey wasn't so sure he blamed them.

"Keep the faith, Cody." Kicking in the clutch, he shifted into first. "And let me know how Tilly's doing with the colic."

Gunning the engine, he sped off toward town, watching the crowd recede in the rearview mirror. He had a good ten minutes to start over again with this stubborn lady, but as luck would have it, she took the initiative and saved him the trouble.

"I won't talk about anything with you, cowboy, unless you promise to keep your hands off me."

"Agreed. You talk and I'll keep my hands off you."

She eyed him doubtfully, as though gauging whether he was a man who made promises he didn't intend to keep. Then she nodded, clearly deciding to take him at his word. "Those people put a lot of faith in your abilities. How long have you been overseer for Katia's Palace?"

"Since my father died. The job came along with the Tex's Sweet and has passed from owner to owner ever since Tex Justice brought himself a real Russian Princess to run the brothel back in 1916. My father bought the place when I was two."

"The Tex's Sweet? If memory serves, that's the ranch that leases the property to the brothel."

"Memory serves." Though he couldn't help noticing how the new owner of said brothel didn't look happy about sitting across from the man who held her lease. "It's an honorary post. Lending a hand to the madam, keeping an eye on the princesses, making an appearance when customers get out of hand."

"A bouncer?"

"When someone needs bouncing."

She fixed her gaze on the view through the windshield, a vista that encompassed summer green valley and snow-capped mountaintops with miles of bright blue sky in between. What did a woman raised around buildings so tall she could barely see the sky think about all this nature?

Trey couldn't guess from her expression. Her delicate profile might have been whittled from white pine. Whatever else Lady Kate might be, she was surely in control of her emotions. He'd bet his last biscuit after a day in the saddle that she didn't let her hair down nearly enough.

Not that she had much hair to let down. That shiny black mass only fell to the middle of her neck, but it was cut full in one of those kicky styles that waved around her face and swung whenever she moved her head, surely as slick as spring water to the touch.

"No chance you'll run the Palace like Kitty wanted you to?"

"Not a chance, cowboy."

Well, he'd agreed not to touch the lady for her promise to talk. But raking another appreciative gaze over silky black hair and full red lips made just for kissing and Trey reckoned he wasn't much in the mood for talk, anyway.

The Stampede

When the cowboy wheeled off Love's main road and pointed to a road sign, Kathryn sat up in her seat and assumed her best boardroom expression. She wasn't going to let him know he'd rattled her the tiniest bit.

She could handle him and she could handle Katia's Palace. She'd listen to what he had to say about turf wars as a courtesy and then come up with a viable alternative. No problem. She may have to extend her trip a few days, but she'd manage.

"Are you ready, pretty lady? The Palace is at the end of this road."

Her breath slowed expectantly as he wound along a narrow forest path, cut off from the rest of the world before opening onto a bright valley, where a Spanish-style villa sprawled in the shadow of a towering ridge.

"Well, what do you think?" he asked. "It's a Russian princess's Western palace."

The place did have a palatial presence. Perhaps the sheer size of the sprawling villa lent to its splendor. Or the way it nestled between the valley and the ridge as if springing from the ground in a burst of quirky grandeur.

The cowboy drove around the building and wheeled into a parking space with a laugh. "And it's your family home."

"I can see Kitty here," she grudgingly admitted.

But Kathryn couldn't ever see her mother stepping foot inside. Krystal Roman had been a woman much more at home with the high-ceilinged condos of Manhattan and the Mid-Atlantic summer homes on Long Island Sound. And sex? To Kathryn's knowledge, her mother had never even had sex after doing the deed that had conceived her. At least, Kathryn had never met any love interests on trips home from school.

"Tex Justice built this place for the Princess Katia."

"Was he the princess's pimp?"

The cowboy winced. "Legal prostitutes are a whole different breed from streetwalkers, Kate."

"The name's Kathryn," she said abruptly when a blush crept into her cheeks. "So what makes them different? They have a physical address? Or their rates?"

The cowboy circled the car, opened her door and stared down at her with a hard-edged expression. "Respect."

His answer cut straight to the point, and his steely tone left her no doubt he wouldn't tolerate any confusion on the issue. She stepped out of the truck and immediately put distance between them, squelching the ridiculous feeling of embarrassment that she hadn't made the distinction herself. Romanov blood might run in her veins, but she'd been reared a Roman through and through. Neither *streetwalker* nor *legal prostitute* had been words ever spoken in her home.

The cowboy led her toward the ornate double-doored entry, looking so stoic she wondered if he'd finally accepted what she'd known since Kitty's lawyer had first called—this world was not hers and never could be.

Steeling herself mentally when he held the door wide, Kathryn swept past the cowboy. One step inside and the open expanse of the sunny outdoors gave way to carved woodwork, tiled floors, and ornate gold stenciling that made her feel as if she'd stepped inside a world of wealthy Spanish grandees from another century.

Elegant, expensive and beyond extravagant, the entrance room of Katia's Palace reminded her of a mansion on the Cape rather than any brothel she might have imagined. Two arched doorways with fanned windows splintered sunlight across the room and flanked a full-length portrait of a very beautiful woman, dressed in what Kathryn recognized as an early-last-century gown. The woman welcomed visitors with an enigmatic smile.

"That's the lady herself. You resemble her a lot."

The cowboy's observation wasn't lost on Kathryn. Staring up at her ancestor's portrait, she forced herself to ignore the heat of his gaze and the sensation of being crowded by his big-bodied nearness. He hovered somewhere above her right shoulder, invading her personal space.

Kathryn didn't like the feeling one bit. With every breath she inhaled his man/leather/outdoorsy scent, an unfamiliar combination she found rather unique, and…well, *male*.

The men she'd known all her life would never have dreamed of leaving their clubs without first showering and making themselves presentable for polite society. By comparison, the cowboy was so much more earthy, real…*neanderthal*, if she judged by his manner of getting her off the plane.

"Your eyes." He touched a rough fingertip to her temple.

Surprised, she could only stare as he traced the line of her cheek to her jaw, riveted by his melting gaze and the appreciation in his expression. She got the distinct impression that he couldn't resist touching her, and her breath hitched, a funny little fluttering sound that emphasized their closeness.

"Your delicate features, too." His finger trailed upwards along her chin and brushed her parted lips. "You're a very beautiful woman, Kate."

Kathryn.

The name shrieked in her mind, but she couldn't force the correction to her lips. Not when the slightly salty flavor of his skin created such an unfamiliar intimacy between them that Kathryn only managed to respond by staggering back a full step, desperate to break the connection.

"You agreed to keep your hands off me."

"I agreed to keep my hands off you if you agreed to talk. I don't care much about talking anymore."

Surely he didn't mean…Clutching her purse like she did when awaiting a taxi late at night, she held it close, an anchor, a shield, or a weapon if necessary. But when that crazy half-grin kicked up the corners of the cowboy's mouth, Kathryn felt annoyed she'd provided him an easy source of amusement.

"Katia was a tiny woman, too." His deep voice bridged the distance she'd placed between them with its rich timbre. "Just like you, Kate. Like a china doll."

"The name's Kathryn, and size notwithstanding, I can't think of anyone less china doll-like than me."

She'd earned the reputation as a competent businesswoman in her world, and better he know that up front, especially if he planned on sneaking touches to catch her off guard. He should also know she wasn't stupid. She wasn't falling for his gentle-the-wild-horse routine, either.

Before she had a chance to tell him a shrill screech had her pivoting in the direction of the sound.

"Trey, why didn't you come in? We've been waiting—"

A very pretty blonde skidded to a halt in the middle of the room, eyes growing wide when she noticed Kathryn. "Ohmigosh, you're *her*." With that, she spun around and shot from the room like a bolt, yelling, "She's here. She's here."

The cowboy folded his arms over his chest and watched the blonde's retreat with a smile. "Take a deep breath, pretty lady, because we're about to be rodeoed. Ready to meet your staff?"

Kathryn opened her mouth to correct him—the princesses were not her staff, nor would they be—but the thought flew out of her head entirely, when the blonde's reaction to seeing the cowboy suddenly struck her.

Every man in this county and the next, and his daddy and granddaddy, has lost his virginity to one of the princesses.

Trey Holliday had been raised in the shadow of Katia's Palace. He kept an eye out for the place and had probably sampled each and every princess who'd ever worked here. He may have been Kitty's taste tester, for all Kathryn knew, which would certainly explain the fond smile driving pinprick dimples into his cheeks at the moment.

Kathryn didn't have time to dwell on what she thought about that, or why the observation had even popped into her head, before a racket the decibel level of an elevated train—or a stampede of wild bulls, if she wanted to get into the spirit of things—erupted down the hallway.

Drawing herself up to full height, Kathryn adopted her best walking-into-a-boardroom-full-of-men expression and refused to flinch when women stampeded into the room.

She barely had time to take in the remarkable collection of blondes, brunettes, and redheads, when a tall black woman, who resembled the striking Grace Jones, demanded, "Why aren't you letting us work?"

"Excuse me?" Kathryn edged near the cowboy, recognizing the woman's battle stance and not sure whether a special Love welcome might also include pummeling the accidental madam.

"Gwendolyn," the cowboy said. "Didn't anyone ever tell you you'll catch more flies with honey than vinegar?"

"I'm not interested in catching flies. I impose order around here remember? And right now we need a good dose."

Kathryn wasn't quite sure what to make of that remark, but everyone else in the room seemed to understand, and her gaze slipped to the riding quirt the woman tapped agitatedly against the palm of one tapered hand.

"You really going to shut us down for good?" a pixie-haired brunette asked.

"Now let's all just calm down and give Lady Kate a chance to catch her breath. I haven't explained the trouble yet."

Lady Kate?

Kathryn wasn't inclined to correct him as he took her arm and led her through the crowd and down the hallway into a formal dining room, furnished with antiques as exquisite as those she'd seen on her last trip to Christie's.

Over the next hour, and several cups of coffee to which the cowboy had added draughts of something called "bottled courage," Kathryn was brought up to speed.

In a nutshell, the trouble involved varying viewpoints about the town of Love's future. The cowboy had been right when he said the brothel's zoning ordinance forced the town to stay within a certain population. Mayor Barclay and his ilk wanted the brothel closed to attract developers to the area, while the cowboy, most ranchers and the rest of the townsfolk opposed the mayor's plan.

The lease with the Tex's Sweet Ranch meant land usage was restricted. Katia's Palace could only be run as a brothel. If Kathryn agreed to let the town manage the Palace, Mayor Barclay and his council could and would cease operation, which meant the land would revert back to the cowboy.

Like On-the-Wing Joe had said, she'd stepped right into a pile of dung.

But Joe hadn't counted on Kathryn's business experience. "Cowboy, you've got to run this place."

"No can do, pretty lady. Running a ranch takes up most of my time."

The cowboy couldn't give up the ranch to run the brothel, because he owned the land the brothel sat on. What a mess. "You can hire someone like Tex Justice did. I don't know if you can manage a princess, but . . ."

"I already got me a lady to run it." He stared at her meaningfully.

Damn, the cowboy was going to be stubborn. A suffocating sort of alarm constricted her throat as she stared around the table, where a host of pretty faces looked to her for answers. Hopping to her feet, Kathryn paced, brainstorming alternatives before panic got the better of her.

She didn't feel obligated to these women. Not really. But she couldn't just ignore the fact that Kitty had cared for them. She'd cared for Kitty. And she couldn't deny a certain sense of sadness that she'd been so cut off from the Romanovs, echoes of the little girl who'd desperately wanted a family no matter how unsuitable their trade.

"I'll just have to find someone to manage this place, then," she finally said. "Someone who wants to run the Palace."

"You won't find anyone, ma'am," the fresh-faced blonde princess said. "The mayor will make sure of that. He's got most of the town council in his pocket."

"Dale Barclay is mean enough to eat off the same plate with a snake," the pixyish princess said. "Most people don't want to cross him."

"Yet you want me to take him on?"

"I'll protect you, pretty lady." The cowboy smiled.

Kathryn scowled.

"The mayor won't mess with Trey," the sultry brunette said. "That's why he's been doing all his dirty work behind the scenes. Kitty told us you could handle him."

Kathryn exhaled sharply, collecting her racing thoughts to find some way to translate into words what these people didn't seem to understand. "Forgive me, but you all are missing the point. I have no desire to take on Mayor Barclay. This isn't my fight, my town or my home, and it never will be. All I can do is promise not to turn over management to the mayor and attempt to find another manager."

"But Kitty wanted you to run the place," the blonde said.

"Not an option." She spread her hands in entreaty, ignoring a pinprick of guilt for going against Kitty's wishes so completely. "Kitty knew that, which is why she sprung this on me *after* she died."

"You are one heartless bitch, Lady Kate," the tall black woman said. "I'm glad Kitty's not here to find out she put her faith in someone who can't live up to her expectations."

"Here, here." The glamour queen saluted with bottled spring water.

Kathryn stared around the table of accusing faces, shocked by their animosity, relieved to be standing so she could lock her knees against the weakness that made them tremble.

Who were these women to judge her? She didn't even know them. She hadn't asked to be left in charge of their futures, and she'd offered as much help as she could. Worst of all was the cowboy's dark eyes, staring through her as if wondering what Kitty had seen that he was missing.

Why did she even care?

Swallowing past the tightness in her throat, Kathryn faced them all with her best I-will-not-back-down boardroom stare, refusing to be intimidated because everyone in this room obviously knew a great deal more about her than she knew about them. "Kitty had no right to tell you to expect miracles from me. I wish you all the best of luck."

Turning on her heel, she strode across the room, hoping she could find her way to the door, because she had every intention of walking straight to town. She'd meet with the lawyer and then hole up in a dark hotel room. One glorious migraine echoed in her head, and she'd forgotten her medication. Surely there was a pharmacy in this hick town.

Kathryn hadn't even passed beneath the arch of the dining room doorway before another accusation brought her to a halt.

"You're just going to walk out that door and let Trey keep footing the bills?" one of the women—Kathryn wasn't sure which one—said, sounding astonished.

That got her attention and she spun back around to recognize the glamour queen sliding her chair back from the table.

"Gwen's right," she said. "You're not half the woman Kitty thought you were."

A chorus of agreements erupted only to be stifled just as quickly by the cowboy. "Pull in the claws, ladies."

His warning worked on every woman in that room. Except Kathryn. "What are they talking about? What bills?"

Sliding his chair back, he rose to his feet in a leisurely motion of fluid strength that drew lots of appreciative gazes.

Kathryn's included, before she realized she gawked right along with the rest of them and fixed her gaze on the Gothic iron chandelier overhead.

"The princesses split their earnings with the Palace fifty/fifty," he explained. "When they don't work, they don't get paid. I've been covering their lost wages."

Kathryn rubbed her temples to stimulate her memory and dull the ache throbbing there. "I just didn't realize this was a problem. Do I need to sign something to reopen? What was that paper you faxed me, cowboy?"

The paper she obviously hadn't paid close enough attention to. And she couldn't even blame her lawyer—he'd tried to tell her to get out here and reopen the place, but she'd flat out refused, not wanting to be forced into operating the business even temporarily.

"A letter about the reopening. Nevada law requires the manager—the madam—to be on-site while we're open for business."

He didn't smirk, but several of the princesses did, and Kathryn got her first taste of swallowing a bitter pill.

"Mayor Barclay is looking very tempting about now," she admitted, wondering if she could turn the place over and still live with herself. Maybe if she sold her condo and moved into another building where she wouldn't see Kitty's face every time she stepped into the hallway?

"Well, now that we're down to it, there's a problem with that, Kate." The cowboy braced his hands on the back of his chair and faced her with a mildly apologetic grimace. "Legally you can't do anything with the Palace when it's not in the black. A provision of the property lease with the Tex's Sweet."

"So I owe you money?"

The cowboy nodded.

"A lot?"

"Reckon it might be to some folks."

The pixyish princess shook her head. "He's paid me almost three thousand in lost wages already."

The ensuing chorus of numbers had Kathryn totaling a sum that had her drawing deep breaths to stave off hyperventilation. She'd had no idea *princesses* earned so much. And remembering Julia Roberts in *Pretty Woman* only called to mind the cowboy's definition of the differences between legal prostitutes and streetwalkers.

Surely there'd been other expenses, as well. A place this size must cost a bundle to operate, Kathryn knew. But the amount she owed him really didn't matter. Anything over the few thousand she kept in a conventional savings account for emergencies was an amount she couldn't pay.

The money her mother had left her would be tied up in trust until she was thirty, which wouldn't help her put Love, Nevada and Katia's Palace behind her for another two years.

Letting her eyes flutter shut for the briefest moment, she rallied the courage to admit the truth. "The exact amount doesn't matter. My money's tied up at the moment."

The cowboy smiled a smile that made Kathryn's heartbeat slow to a crawl while she waited for him to make his move.

She didn't wait long.

"I don't want your money anyway, pretty lady. I promised Miss Kitty I'd encourage you to take over."

"You go, Trey," the glamour queen said, raising her hand for a ringing high-five with the blonde.

This time the sultry brunette raised her spring water and clinked bottles with the pixie-haired beauty in salute.

The cowboy shrugged, plainly unfazed by their approval. He just locked that intense gaze on Kathryn until her heartbeat stopped crawling and halted altogether.

"You mean *coerce*, don't you?"

"*Encourage*," he repeated, and the warmth in those molasses-dark eyes promised he'd encourage her in ways she'd never dreamed of. "I just need a chance to convince you."

"Where's the phone?" Panic expelled the words right through her suddenly dry mouth. "I need to talk to my lawyer."

The cowboy nodded obligingly. "Bring the lady a phone."

One of the princesses complied, Kathryn wasn't sure which, because she was too busy forcing her rattled brain to remember her own calling card number. Then she began the battle of making her shaking hands press the right buttons.

Damn, damn and double damn, she mentally cursed while dragging the telephone through the doorway to hide from the chattering princesses, all of whom had rushed into the cowboy's corner as though he were a prizefighter contending for a belt.

There had to be some way out of this mess. But the conference call with Kathryn and Kitty's respective lawyers quickly proved that Kitty had backed her into a neat little corner with her legal agreements, restrictions on long-term leases, and high-handed overseers. Had Kathryn not signed the agreement six weeks ago...but she'd decided to see the transfer of Katia's Palace through.

Kitty had known her well enough to guess she'd feel obligated. Or had she simply counted on her being interested enough in her family to get involved? Either way, Kitty had set her up, big-time.

Why? Surely eating the last of the macadamia nut during *Breakfast at Tiffanys* didn't warrant this sort of retribution. Then something Kitty said not long before her death echoed in Kathryn's memory.

You need to make time in your life to relax and have fun.

That's what her legacy was all about. From beyond the grave, Kitty was forcing Kathryn to leave the high-powered lifestyle she'd never approved.

Slamming the receiver down onto the cradle, Kathryn dragged the phone cord back into the dining room.

"Well, Trey Holliday," she said in a voice a cross between hysterical laughter and growl, "I don't have the money to pay you back, so what do you want?"

"For you to run the place."

"I can't do that." Had she been in her right mind, Kathryn would have been mortified that she'd stamped her foot to emphasize her point. "I have to be in my office on Monday."

"Then go."

"But I'm legally responsible for this place now. I'm liable for any expenses you incur and if the princesses can't work...."

The cowboy rocked back on his heels, clearly amused by her panic and untroubled by the sea of bright gazes around the table, bouncing between them like spectators at a tennis match.

He flashed her a smile that was the embodiment of all those bad boy grins she'd ever seen on the silver screen. "Seems to me you only have one choice then. Work off your debt."

A silence fell as complete as a blackout in Manhattan. Everyone stared at her, waiting, and Kathryn's worsening migraine had to be dulling her senses because a good minute passed before she realized they were all awaiting *her* reaction.

"Work off my debt?" Kathryn noticed the meaningful glance he slanted at the table and the amusement of those seated there. The Amazonian princess handed her a brochure. In slowly dawning horror, Kathryn scanned the page.

Princesses' Menu

Straight
In-dates
Three-way
Half-and-half
Fetishes
Bondage
Submission
Role-playing
Dominance

Exciting Extras

French	Meal-in-bed
Striptease	Erotic Videos
Water Play	Manual Stimulation
Massage	Lingerie Modeling

$200.00 House Minimum

By all rights the bagel she'd eaten for breakfast should have been long gone, but it roiled uneasily in her stomach. She sank back against the wall, not wanting to show any weakness to these bullies, but the ache in her temples grew ferocious.

"Are you insane, cowboy?" she finally choked out. "You expect me to become a...a—" His molasses gaze warned her to choose her word very carefully— "*Princess*?"

"You can service the clients, or you can service me," he said in that rough silk voice. "Lady's choice."

Kathryn had barely strung all his words together in her aching head before the room receded from view.

Code of the West

A sadist fired a blowtorch inside Kathryn's head, and she dared not move while her stomach churned, unsure whether its contents wanted to come up or stay where they were.

The moist cloth on her head appeared like a cool breath from heaven and a sigh escaped her, a pathetically grateful sound that resembled more of a whimper.

"You feeling okay, Kate?"

The cowboy.

No, she wasn't okay. Not with her head aching like a train had run through it, the memory of her whole sorry situation crashing along at a hundred miles per hour.

"What...wha—?" The words didn't resemble any sounds she recognized, but the cowboy must have understood what she was asking because he said, "You fainted."

Fainted? She'd never fainted in her life. Had he hit her on the head? She tried to sit up and face her enemy.

Unfortunately, sitting wasn't in the game plan. Neither was opening her eyes. Someone had left the drapes open, and the sunlight streaming through the windows seared through her eyelids like a laser. She could barely lift her head off the pillow. She was at this man's mercy.

"Should I have Jed call the doctor?"

Who was Jed? Did she even care? No. Not when she heard worry in his voice. She sighed deeply, gratified he sounded genuinely concerned. As much as she wanted to blame the cowboy for this blinding ache in her head, she recognized a migraine. The mother of all migraines, apparently, and she'd had enough bad ones to compare it to.

"No." A croak.

She'd be fine if she could just rest for a bit. Though she wasn't sure where she was, she was definitely horizontal. She wouldn't try to open her eyes, just lay here and not move...

The next time Kathryn approached awareness, the migraine had abated enough to make some sense of her surroundings and the first thing that struck her was that she was lying someplace soft and comfortable—a bed?—and she was naked. *Naked?* Yes, definitely and completely without a stitch of clothing.

Disbelief drove her to sit up, or try to, as a blast of pain hindered her best effort. Then the bed sank as though someone sat beside her.

Kathryn's stomach pitched with the motion, but before she could demand directions to the bathroom or question whether or not she might actually make it there, strong hands slipped beneath her shoulders and lifted her.

Suddenly she was cradled between hard thighs, could even feel a suspicious bump beneath the seam of jeans pressing lightly between her bare shoulder blades.

The cowboy.

She tried to pull away, but he held her firmly, which given her current state, didn't require much effort.

"Shhh. Relax. You're still as white as biscuit dough."

He guided her head back against his tight stomach, and Kathryn was too weak and too nauseous to fight. She lay as limp as a rag doll against him, moaned when he massaged her temples.

Relax?

"My…clothes," she croaked out.

"You don't need them. I wanted you to be comfortable."

She'd be more comfortable *in* her clothes, but she couldn't rally the strength to tell him that.

"Migraine?" he asked.

Who was this man? And, better yet, when had she time-traveled into another century, a time when it was okay for a man to strip a woman without her permission?

She almost refused to answer him out of pure defiance but couldn't quite see what defiance would accomplish, except letting him know he'd rattled her. Letting him think she was used to lounging around in the buff between strange men's legs, might level the playing field a bit.

"I get them sometimes." Rather, she got them often, but Kathryn wouldn't admit that.

"Kitty told me. Stress."

The assurance in his voice irked her. "Not stress."

"I may be a vet, pretty lady, but I still had to go through med school. You move quicker than a road agent on the dodge. Trust me, stress."

In her current state, Kathryn couldn't even contemplate translating that remark. "In English, please?"

He chuckled, a warm rich sound that should have driven a spike through her brain, but surprisingly didn't, which meant she was definitely on the mend.

"You don't relax enough."

"No time."

His warm fingertips stroked her head with just the right amount of pressure to soothe, not hurt. "Make the time."

Easily said by a man who'd only known her two hours, but arrogance aside, she did have to admit he had a magic touch.

The black clouds in her brain slowly receded, freeing up enough brains cells to wonder why he'd undressed her. Was he trying to shake her confidence so he could bully her into his ridiculous proposition? If he was, he had another thing coming.

"Just tell me what you want." Good, she sounded stronger.

"I want to prove Kitty was right about you, that you belong running the Palace."

"And you expect to prove that by forcing me to have sex with you?"

"Not exactly." His throaty chuckle made her bristle. "I want to make love because I'm attracted to you. I'm asking you to work off your debt because I can't see another way to keep you here long enough to seduce you."

Kathryn wavered violently between being more offended than she'd ever been in her life to being absurdly excited that this cowboy wanted her. The conflict made her head pound all over again.

"As long as you're in the Palace, the princesses can return to work and you won't run up any more debt. As far as paying off what you owe me goes, I'll tell you what I like and pay fair market price. You have my word."

The word of a cowboy. Wasn't that sacred? The code of the West or some such nonsense she'd seen in a movie once?

He sounded so reasonable, so civilized, and a strange voice inside urged her to go for it, to drop everything and tempt fate once in her life. A few days of sex the likes of which she'd never had before, she'd pay off her debt, sell Katia's Palace, and head home with her reputation no less for the wear.

Beneath the Western drawl and corny similes, the cowboy was attractive in a Marlboro-man sort of way. How hard could it possibly be to please him? He said he'd tell her what he liked…and he'd know because he was a man who'd had an entire brothel at his disposal since the day he'd lost his virginity. Maybe even before.

Kathryn gulped and the brunette's earlier accusation echoed in memory.

You're not half the woman Kitty thought you were.

"Forget it, cowboy."

Leading a Filly to Water

Taming Kate wouldn't be easy, but Trey looked forward to the challenge.

"Why don't we get you feeling better before we lock horns, pretty lady?" He knew an ailing woman when he saw one, and though she put on a brave show, he figured she still hurt.

"I'm on a time limit. We've got to come up with some sort of resolution and fast." That pretty mouth of hers thinned, a sure sign of stress.

This wasn't where he wanted her to go. "Let's not deal with tomorrow just yet. You don't want to rush right to the end of your visit and miss all the fun of getting there."

"The fun?" Her eyes closed, her lashes forming silky half moons on her pale cheeks. "Fun isn't part of this equation."

"It will be. I plan to surprise you."

"I hate surprises."

He supposed she would. Surprises meant veering down unexpected trails. That'd surely mess with her schedule.

"You may hate them, but you've been handling them pretty well, I'd say. Especially being attracted to me. I'll bet you never expected that when you hopped on Joe's plane."

"Whatever gave you the idea I'm attracted to you?" she scoffed. "We just met."

"And we're already in bed. First surprise." He traced the curve of her clenched jaw, rewarded by the goosebumps spraying up her arms. She might hiss like a rattler, but her body told the only tale worth listening to.

"I'm beginning to wonder if any of your lovers ever took the time to woo you right." When she jerked her face away indignantly, he caught her chin between his thumb and forefinger and urged her back. "I know when a woman's attracted to me."

"All that training with the princesses?"

So his friendliness with the princesses bothered her. Trey had moved farther down the trail than he'd reckoned. "I might have an edge."

"Not with me you don't. Now why don't you answer my question? How are we going to fix this? I don't want to leave the princesses in a bind, but you're not leaving me a choice."

"You have no choices, Kate. Even if you're willing to abandon the princesses and turn over the Palace to Barclay, you can't until you're square with me. You already said you don't have the money to pay."

A fact that plainly outraged her, judging by the way she tried to leap off the bed. But Trey had anticipated her move and countered by wrapping both his legs and arms around hers.

"Let me go."

"No." The games were over. "Kitty believed you belonged here, and she asked me to show you why. I gave my word."

"Damn it, cowboy," she hissed, squirming like a hog-tied calf and in the process touching every inch of him with her creamy skin. "This isn't the wild west. This is assault."

"Not if you stop fighting."

"I'll have you arrested."

"Not if I don't let you up."

That got her attention, because she sucked in a sharp breath and stopped fighting. Trey used the opportunity to drive home his point by thumbing the undersides of her satiny breasts. "You won't be sorry."

"You're, you're...*molesting* me. This will be rape."

"Trust me, Kate." He couldn't swallow back a chuckle, which started her struggling all over again. "Rape won't enter the picture. I'm not much for fetish sex and I promise you'll want me as much as I want you before we make love." He grazed his thumbs over rosy nipples that had already hardened into greedy little points. "I know when a woman's wanting."

She struggled. He only held her tighter until she gave up.

"Give Kitty a chance," he murmured in a tone he used on scared critters. "Give me a chance."

Her chest heaved, driving those pebbled tips right into his hands. He obliged with another caress that made her suck in more air. No matter how hard Kate fought, she couldn't deny her body's response.

"Why was Kitty so convinced I'd be happier being a madam than I am in New York with my own career?"

Beneath her resentful words, Trey heard the question she didn't ask: *didn't she approve of what I'm doing with my life?*

To reassure her, he loosened the vice grip he had around her upper body, smoothed his thumb along the stubborn curve of her jaw as he pondered his answer.

There were any number of ways to bridge the distance with her, but only one he thought she'd respect. The truth.

"Kitty told me all about you, Kate. *Kathryn and I* did this. *Kathryn and I* did that. She thought you were the strongest Romanov woman yet, a fireball who accomplished anything you set your mind to. She admired and respected you. But she worried about you, too."

Trey watched a tiny frown play between her brows. A certain vulnerability shone through Kate's prickly hide like a sunbeam on a cloudy day, and he found that he liked feeling warm.

"Don't you want to know why Kitty worried about you?"

When she stubbornly refused to answer, he scooted farther down on the bed, hauling her up until his erection sat squarely between her sweet cheeks and he could rest his chin on the top of her silky head.

"She thought you were too comfortable being alone, that you worked too much and didn't live enough. She wasn't sure if you'd been taught how."

"So she wants you and the princesses to teach me?"

Her tone was pure resentment, but at least she'd stopped fighting. "Something like that."

Her black silk hair felt as cool as spring water against his cheek, and he breathed deeply, liking the taste of her fresh scent in his nose and mouth. "She didn't want you living your whole life without love."

When she stiffened slightly, Trey knew he'd made the right choice, allowing her to face away from him and keep her expressions, and her pride, to herself. She resisted showing him any sign of what she perceived as weakness, and not having love in her life was clearly a sticking point. He had to show her that sharing her emotions wasn't weak, and to do that she had to trust him.

But getting Kate to trust him might be a problem, if he couldn't control his own emotions. Right now lust topped the list. The warm curves of her breasts taunted him, just a hairsbreadth below a hand that itched to touch, to roll those tight peaks between his thumb and forefinger until they speared toward his hand again, eager.

He wanted to hear this pretty lady moan softly with pleasure and the power of that want stiffened his erection.

"When you say that Kitty wanted me to have love in my life," she whispered into a silence that had grown thick and charged with sex. "Are you talking about companionship love or romantic love?"

If he was reading her right, she didn't want to fall in love, with him or anyone else. "There are all kinds of love and Kitty wanted you to know them all. She didn't want you going through life thinking no man could satisfy you better than your vibrator could."

"Damn Kitty. Damn *you*, cowboy." She tried to jerk away, but Trey held her firm.

"Don't judge Kitty too hard for betraying your confidences, Kate. She was only giving me ammunition to work with."

"Now you're telling me what to think, too," she hissed.

"You're a woman who deserves to know pleasure." He pressed his erection against her backside. "You've got me aching with want, pretty lady. I'm ready to pleasure you."

She shot her head back, catching him in the chin hard enough to make his teeth thunk together. "I won't be coerced into sleeping with you."

But that breathy quality to her voice suggested the idea wasn't as offensive as she'd have him believe. And that was exactly the response Trey had been hoping for. He skimmed his palm down her smooth belly, was rewarded when her muscles twitched.

"I'm not giving you a choice, Kate."

"This is ridiculous."

"What's ridiculous? That I want to make love to you? Or that Kitty thought you needed love in your life? What's the worst that would happen here?"

"All I'm doing is proving to you and everyone else I'm not cut out to be a madam."

Trey heard the note of despair beneath her frustration and realized there was more to Kate's refusal than met the eye. "Why are you so convinced you can't take Kitty's place?"

"The passion genes skipped a few generations in the Romanov family, all right, cowboy? Trust me on this."

"Trust you on what? Are you telling me you're not a passionate woman?"

"As a matter of fact, I'm not. No passion. No fire. Not a spark."

Trey blinked. He heard her expressionless tone, felt her tension in every curve that had gone rigid against him, but he still couldn't believe what he was hearing. Her beautiful breasts had stretched taut, her nipples puckering into needy rosebuds that aimed for his hands. Where in all creation had she gotten this notion?

One glance at the set to her dainty jaw told Trey she wasn't about to answer that question even if he asked politely. In fact, she was so stubborn; he didn't think she'd hear a word he had to say, even if he spoke the gospel truth.

Kitty had told him all about her ex-fiancé but Trey had never imagined she would take the idiot's criticism to heart. Kitty had flat-out said the man had been blaming his own bedroom deficiencies on Kate and Kitty had been a madam long enough to spot a sidewinder from a mile off.

But what could he possibly say to Kate to convince her?

Nothing, plain and simple. Kate wouldn't listen to him, but she might listen to her own body. Might not have much of a choice, if he played his hand right. And right now his hand wanted to play…he speared his fingers into the silky hair between her legs.

"Don't," she cried, but her protest cut off in mid-gasp when he found that silky little nubbin peeping through the folds of her soft skin.

"I can't imagine why you don't think you're a passionate woman, but I aim to show you different."

She was either struck speechless or feeling a good bit of something that twisted her tongue into a knot, because she didn't reply. He took her silence as another step toward consent and stoked her soft woman's skin until she shivered.

"I suggest we start with an in-date," he said quietly. "It's a long party that costs a bundle, but we'll have time to get to know each other. I want to know all about you."

He ran a hand slowly down the length of her bare arm. "You're not shying from me now. You might enjoy letting me touch you like this."

His answer was a slight arching of her hips, so slight, he wondered if she even guessed he'd noticed. He did, and he continued to stroke her, slow and steady, a touch designed to gentle, to reassure. To drive him crazy with trying to control himself. Trey usually scratched his itch when the need arose, and with the way he ached right now, denial might not be his best event.

But taming Kate would make the wait worth his best efforts. Her slender legs stretched out between his, shapely and pale, her creamy curves all begging to be touched and her breasts…rosy-tipped and full, he knew this woman would be worth rallying every ounce of patience and skill he could muster.

She was passion in the flesh, though she may not have discovered that about herself yet. But she would soon. She hadn't broken away, though he held her only with one hand resting lightly on her belly, while the other entertained itself—and her, he thought—between her thighs.

He enjoyed the feel of her response, the way her sex grew moist beneath his fingers. He sank the tip of his finger into her heat, just enough to make her shiver and to feel her hot, wet walls clench greedily.

"Feel that?" he whispered against her ear, was rewarded with another shiver. "You may think you're not passionate, but your body's singing a different tune. Are you so sure you want me to stop?"

She was silent so long, he'd have thought she'd fallen back asleep if not for the thready rise and fall of those beautiful breasts. Finally she said, "I don't know if I can do this."

"Why?"

"I've never made much time for this sort of thing."

"You don't have to *do* anything. I'll be in charge."

"So basically I'm just supposed to lie here and let you do as you please."

"Basically." He prodded his erection into her backside again, sank his finger a little deeper. She sucked in a broken breath, a gratifying sound that told him he'd shocked her, that he had her. She was going to give in. "All you have to do is stop fighting. I'll tell you what I want. All you have to do is obey my commands and enjoy yourself."

Taking the First Sip

Obey his commands?

Was this man insane? And just what would happen if she disobeyed? Was disobeying even an option, sandwiched as she was between his erection and the hand he worked his magic with? Disobeying would mean finding the energy to break away and Kathryn wasn't so eager to disturb the unfamiliar languor that made her melt back against the cowboy like her body had dissolved into a hot puddle.

She'd pleasured herself before, but that pleasure had only been the barest fraction of this intense sensation, a sensation that perhaps should have frightened her given her nudity and the fact that this cowboy was a stranger.

Kathryn didn't feel frightened, though. She didn't feel much beyond amazed that *a stranger* could coax such a red-hot response from her usually tepid body.

Did she really want to disobey him? Or did she want to take the chance that Kitty had been right about her? If she'd never learned how to relax and have fun, wasn't it possible she hadn't learned how to experience pleasure either, that a spark of fire smoldered inside her, waiting to be stoked into a flame?

The cowboy certainly seemed to think so. But the cowboy also claimed he wasn't much for fetish sex, yet here he was suggesting she *obey his commands*, which smacked of serious fetish sex in her estimation.

Once Kathryn had accidentally surfed across a pornographic website that had literally taken possession of her computer, windows popping up of men and women in black leather and studs engaged in all sorts of shockingly dominant and submissive acts.

When all else had failed to stop the images from popping up on her screen, she'd freaked, finally shut off the power without backing out of the operating system. She'd begged the network administrator from work to erase all remnants of those sites from her hard drive, on the off chance she died and someone happened upon them while packing up her things for charity. Was that kind of graphic roleplaying what the cowboy wanted?

Tipping her head back, she gazed up at him, saw no hint of a threat, or any other strange obsession in his sun-weathered face. He looked relaxed, easy, as though he'd asked her nothing more out of the ordinary than to pass the salt. His lack of emotion when she felt so shaky and vulnerable annoyed her. "You're crossing the line."

"What line is that?"

"The socially acceptable line."

He contemplated her intently, a frown wrinkling his blonde brow. "I don't believe I am. You're a strong woman who has already made up her mind about the Palace and what we do here. I'm just asking you to come at it from another angle."

"You're asking me to trust you."

"Is trust a problem for you?"

"You're a stranger."

"I'd like to change that." His fingers moved over her sex in sleek swirls, an intimacy she shouldn't have allowed him, yet couldn't seem to deny. That realization irritated her, too.

"Would it help if I promised to respect you?" He flashed that quicksilver grin, and those dimples peeked at her from his tanned cheeks. "But I think you already know I do, otherwise you wouldn't be lying here letting me touch you like this."

His finger probed a little deeper, just to make sure she noticed exactly how intimately he touched her. Her sex yielded up one slow, aching throb.

She'd *never* felt anything like this before, an incredible ache as though her insides begged for his touch. The cowboy was right. If she'd questioned her safety, she would still be screaming. While he might have Kitty's reference to vouch for his character, he'd asked her to step into uncharted territory.

What if he was wrong about her?

I need a woman with fire, Kathryn.

She'd admitted the truth about her broken engagement to Kitty late one night while they'd been sobbing over the movie *Camille*. Kitty had said something about men who weren't fit to shoot when you wanted to unload and clean your gun.

While remembering that statement in reference to her ex still made her smile, Kathryn remembered more vividly what Kitty had told her afterward. She'd said that some women just needed the right man to get them in the mood.

Kathryn had scoffed, but deep down, in a barely-acknowledged place, she'd nursed the hope that some day the right man would come along and she'd know what it meant to…*want*.

Could the cowboy be that man?

Just hearing him talk about her submission had started a fluttering deep inside, like a thousand butterflies that had munched their way through a pound of espresso beans. Not exactly a flame, but she couldn't deny the situation excited her. His touch made her achy and needy in a way she'd never felt before, not from her own sexual explorations, which had been her only orgasms to date—hardly worth the name compared to what she was building toward right now.

If the possibility of a real orgasm wasn't enough reason to take a chance, the cowboy's impressive erection was. He had a physical reaction to *her*, a compliment to a woman who'd been accused of having no fire. This man had a bevy of beauties who made love for a living at his disposal, yet he wanted *her*.

And like he'd already pointed out, what was the worst that could happened? If Kathryn turned out to be a disaster in bed, she'd just hop on a plane and head home, leaving the cowboy to convalesce in the willing arms of the princesses. She'd be off the hook and no one would be the wiser. Except for her. She hadn't realized how much she didn't want to be a disaster.

Perhaps her headache placed her in the pitifully desperate category. Or maybe the cowboy's touch had just bewitched her, but either way, lying sandwiched between his thighs seemed as natural as his fingers caressing her skin. She wanted to trust him. She wanted him to be right.

"I shouldn't be surprised that Kitty charged you to get me to take over this place," she murmured in a thick voice. "Only Kitty would try to manipulate me from the grave. But what's your deal, cowboy? What do you get out of all this?"

"Besides making love with a beautiful woman?"

She sighed. "If you only knew who you were talking to, you might not be so eager to take on the job. *Fire*. To date, my personal reserve only flares in the boardroom."

His laughter rumbled deep in his chest. "I think we can find something that sparks your kindling, pretty lady."

"Do you really think so?" she asked a bit hysterically. "Until right now, I didn't even know I had kindling."

"Enough to start a forest fire, I'd say." Another rough-velvet chuckle burst hotly against her ear.

Grinding his erection into her bottom, the cowboy found that tiny bundle at her core and applied a slow, steady pressure, so exquisite her sex clenched in reply.

"Looks like we found a hot spot." His deep drawling voice reflected his satisfaction.

He had indeed. This ache, while unexpected, held such promise, a natural sort of potential that prompted her to spread her legs a bit wider to savor the sensation, so intense, Kathryn thought she might be content to lie in this man's arms forever.

An outrageous thought, to match this outrageous situation.

"I want to make you feel good," the cowboy whispered against her skin, a breathy declaration that made her shiver in reply. "Let me."

Let him? she thought wildly. Could she stop him? Kathryn could barely think beyond the need to arch into his touch, to foster this desire he'd ignited in her.

"I'll fulfill my promise to Kitty." His finger sank deeper inside her, a slow, wet stroke that made her ache. "And I'll help you discover who you are. Trust me, Kate."

He sounded as though he had no greater aspiration. Kathryn couldn't deny him, or herself in that moment, not while he caressed her most intimate place, a slow, knowing rhythm that made her sex gather in long, exquisite pulls.

Yet she couldn't seem to speak the words that would give him so much power over her, either. She simply closed her eyes, spread her legs wider and hoped he understood her silent invitation.

"I'll take that as a yes."

Yes.

With his chin resting on top of her head, he took control, using his palm to ride that sensitive gathering of nerves in exactly the right place, coiling the tension inside her tighter. She gave way to the sensation, eager to follow where it led and soon found herself rocking against his hand to meet his strokes, needing, *wanting* to increase the pressure.

Had Kitty been right all along? Had she just needed the right man to help her find her own sexuality?

Kathryn couldn't say, but she hoped, *desperately* hoped, that Kitty had been right. Yet she couldn't dwell on whether the cowboy was the right man or not. Not now. Not with him touching her so intimately. Not unless she wanted to freak out all over again and wind up in bankruptcy court with her name splashed all over the tabloids as *The Madam Who Wasn't*.

She breathed deeply to clear her thoughts and focused on the cowboy instead, noticed all sorts of little things about him. The quiet whisper of his breathing when he inhaled, the soft, slow release. She followed the rise and fall of his chest, an expanse of muscle that created a warm cushion beneath her. His hard thighs flanked hers, his strong torso and broad shoulders sheltering her body in a way that made her feel strangely protected, possessed.

When he drove his finger deeper, starting a hot thrusting that wound her insides tight and demonstrated he could make good on his erotic promise, Kathryn began to hope.

Her heart raced. Her skin grew flushed. She tried not to think about lying naked in this stranger's arms, her bottom swaying against his tanned hand, her breasts jiggling with her shallow breaths.

Whatever sight she presented seemed to arouse the cowboy. His chest heaved. His erection prodded her bottom like a length of hot steel. And somewhere beneath the restless stirrings of her body, the knowledge that she affected him so physically fueled her hope, made her eager to experience this passion he offered.

And the cowboy knew, oh, he knew better than she knew herself, exactly how to build the pressure, increasing the friction of his palm, using his fingertip against that magic spot deep inside until the sounds of her body's response smacked wetly with his every thrust. And when the work-rough fingers of his other hand cupped her breast, plucked at her nipple, Kathryn almost came off the bed.

He held her down.

Sensation coiled through her with a blinding intensity, wound her so tight inside, she squeezed her eyes shut hard and barely dared to breath. She was on the edge, a place she only recognized from the climaxes she'd had before, vague echoes of what she felt right now, a place she never imagined as this powerful, persuasive.

She didn't care that she bore down on this stranger's hand with no shyness, didn't care that a stranger knew her body better than she knew her own. She only wanted to know what lay beyond the edge, wanted to experience the freefall into pure sensation.

"Say my name, Kate." The cowboy's warm velvet mouth dragged along her shoulder. "I want to hear you say it."

So simple a request. He didn't say he wouldn't bring her to fulfillment unless she did as he asked, but the implication was there. In the way he held the pressure of his hand steady, left her hovering on the brink. Such a simple request.

"Trey," she whispered, the taste of his name sweet on her tongue. "Trey, please."

And with his hand buried between her thighs, his finger deep in her heat, he lifted her back against him, the exquisite pressure just enough to send her over the edge, the tension unfurling in the most intense orgasm she'd ever had.

Blazin' New Trails

Kathryn must have dozed, because when she opened her eyes again, the bright sunlight in the suite had faded along with the nauseous soreness around the edges of her brain. She felt warm, relaxed, *sated* in a way that seemed impossible after a migraine that had made her faint.

The cowboy was exactly where she'd left him, except that the hands he'd so expertly stroked her with earlier now only cradled her close. She thought about playing possum, not wanting to disturb the languor of the moment or face the man responsible, but a sleepy yawn gave her away before she'd begun.

"Feeling better?" His voice was a gravelly murmur in the twilight-soaked quiet.

"Much."

She found his erection where she'd left it, too, snug up against her bottom, patiently waiting.

"How long have I been asleep?"

"A few hours."

"Did I spoil your plans?"

"Can't have much fun with a headache." His nose nudged her ear, a playful gesture that while not overtly sexual, brought to mind the intimacies they'd shared. "Too hard to concentrate. Besides, I've been entertaining myself."

His fingers grazed along her arms to emphasize his point, and a crazy little tingle sizzled through her in reply.

"Priming the well, have you?"

"The term is 'priming the pump,' city girl, and yes, I have."

He'd done a good job, Kathryn decided. She was aware of everything about him, from the possessive way he held her to the warm strength of his hands on her arms. When he transferred his touch to her hips and skimmed his fingers along the sensitive place that joined hips to thighs, her sex yielded up one slow throb that held the memory of his power over her.

She sighed. Her thighs parted without her consciously willing them. But instead of obliging her, the cowboy suddenly removed his hands and slid out from behind her, leaving her spread wide on the bed, cold and confused.

When his booted feet hit the carpeted floor, she rolled over, jerked the comforter over her and sat up in a hasty attempt at some dignity. "Was I supposed to resist?"

Pivoting around on a boot heel, he rose above her, tall and broad and masculine in a way that left her feeling as though she was no bigger than an ant crawling across Lady Liberty's feet.

"You did what you were supposed to do."

"So you're leaving?"

He reached out, his callused fingertips caressing her jaw, tilting her face upward to meet his gaze. "I've got to check in with my foreman and call Cody Wilson about his mare. I'll head back over for dinner after you've had a chance to settle in and make some calls. Take care of your business, Kate. I want your undivided attention."

He didn't *ask*, Kathryn noted, suspecting this was her first glimpse of the differences between a request and a command. His wishes. His timetable.

A half grin twitched at the corners of his mouth. "You're supposed to say 'yes, Trey.'"

"Oh," she said, not a little flustered. "Yes, Trey."

He smiled, a real smile now, one that drove the pencilpoint dimples deep into his cheeks and made him seem so attractive in that rugged sort of way. So male. So unfamiliar. So very potent with those challenging dark eyes asserting the sexual power he commanded.

Her body still echoed with the aftereffects of the intimacies he'd taken, a mass of vulnerable achy sensations that jabbed her with the reality that she was in over her head. The rules of his game were far beyond her comprehension.

"Joe should have dropped off your bags by now. I'll have them brought up and send one of the princesses to help you dress for dinner."

She nodded, though she needn't have bothered, since he obviously hadn't been waiting for her permission.

His hand slipped from her face, and he strode to the door, retrieving his hat from the telephone stand and planting it firmly on his head. "I'll be back soon." He paused, his broad shoulders filling the doorway as he turned back to her. "Get ready to become my princess."

His words hung in the distance between them, a challenge, a command, and surprisingly, his words made her eager…to please him? To run screaming? Kathryn couldn't say, but she knew what he was waiting for and said, "Yes, Trey."

His dark eyes flashed. He brought those skilled fingers to the brim of his hat in a polite goodbye before turning on his heel and departing. Kathryn watched him leave, heart pounding with a strange mixture of trepidation, excitement, and, yes, even embarrassment at the highhanded way he'd left her lying naked on the bed, *wanting*.

Leaping to her feet, she prowled the suite, barely noticing the tasteful mahogany furnishings or the attractive combination of greens and golds that adorned the rooms.

So this little scenario was all about what the cowboy wanted. Okay, she got that part. But how did she feel about serving his needs? Kathryn paused, considering, and realized she wasn't apprehensive at all, wasn't really offended by the idea either, just taken aback, out of her element.

She was used to being in control, of her actions, her emotions, her environment, and here the cowboy challenged her to give the control over to him.

Someone leads and someone follows, Kitty had once said while watching Fred Astaire and Ginger Rogers dancing across the screen. *It's the natural way of things.*

Then she'd pointed out that following could be harder than leading. Fred and Ginger danced the same dance, but Ginger danced every step backwards. He led; she followed and together they were awesome. There was a lesson in there somewhere, Kathryn was sure, but all she could find was a question: why had she never considered following before?

Veering out of the bedroom she pondered the answer in a tasteful sitting room decorated in pseudo-Victorian, formal, but not fussy or feminine. Had she been frightened? Of getting close? Of being hurt?

Glancing at a framed photo, Kathryn recognized the three white furballs in the picture, realized she stood in Kitty's suite. Of course the cowboy would bring the new madam to the former madam's suite.

She stared at the Maltese dogs, all impeccably groomed with bows in their white hair. Pink for the mother and blue for her two sons. Kathryn smiled. Kitty had loved her pooches to the point of obsession, a fact proven by their portraits of honor on her vanity.

Kathryn's own college graduation photo resided there as well but noticeably absent was the first photo she'd ever given Kitty—her high school graduation picture, which Kitty had admired from the full-size portrait.

I'm sorry I didn't know you then, Kathryn. You're a beautiful young woman with such fire in your eyes.

Kathryn had framed a smaller photo and presented it to Kitty as a gift, and she'd never again looked at her portrait without remembering Kitty's words—even after her broken engagement when she believed Kitty must have been mistaken.

Glancing around the room, she wondered what had happened to that photo, more sentimental, she believed, than the one currently residing on the vanity.

A knock brought Kathryn out of her thoughts. "Come in."

The door cracked warily and the blonde princess popped her head inside. "Lady Kate, it's me, Phoebe."

"Hi, Phoebe." Kathryn forced a welcoming smile and filed the name Phoebe away in long-term memory. "Please, call me…Kate." She might as well run with the dual identity thing. If she thought of herself as a different person, she just might get through whatever the cowboy had in store for her.

Phoebe kicked the door open with a sandaled foot and hauled in what Kathryn recognized as her garment bag.

"Oh, here, let me take that."

"No need." Phoebe walked straight through the sitting room to the bedroom. "It's not heavy. You weren't planning on staying long, were you?"

Kathryn followed, recognizing the accusation in Phoebe's voice. Not anger, she thought, but hurt.

"I wasn't," she answered honestly. "But as I'm sure you've heard, my plans have changed. I'll be extending my stay a bit."

"Trey told us." Stretching up on tiptoes, she fumbled to fasten the garment bag over the back of the closet door.

Kathryn came to her aid, lifting the bag to help the girl, who wasn't much taller than her own five feet, three inches.

"We've taken care of Kitty's things, so there's plenty of room in the closet for your stuff," Phoebe said. "Whatever's left in the room is what Kitty wanted us to leave for you."

"Oh," Kathryn said, surprised. "You mean like the furnishings?"

Phoebe laughed merrily. "Technically everything in the Palace is yours, Kate. But I meant clothes. Kitty wanted to leave you some things to get you started."

Peering into the closet, Kathryn glanced at the first item hanging there—a red beaded sheath dress hanging neatly in a clear plastic garment bag.

You should wear red, Kathryn, Kitty had once said. *It would look lovely with your vivid coloring.*

Kathryn could only stare, afraid to reply when her emotions skimmed so close to the surface.

"They're not hand-me-downs." Clearly misreading Kathryn's expression, Phoebe quickly pulled out another boutique garment bag, then another. "They're all brand new. She'd been shopping for a while. We all took turns driving her into the city on our off weeks." She smiled fondly. "Kitty knew she was nearing the end and wanted everything to be perfect after she'd gone."

Kathryn stared at the bright colored fabrics of the gowns in the closet, such a contrast to her own wardrobe of dark solids and neutrals at home, and again she could hear Kitty's voice through the years.

You're such a lovely girl, Kathryn. I'd love to see you celebrate your beauty and youth.

Kitty had seen so easily through her, and had cared—so much more than Kathryn had ever realized. Now she was gone. Leaving behind her brothel, her belongings and—Kathryn watched Phoebe rummage through the clothing—the people she'd cared about.

"What happened to her dogs?" she finally asked.

"They've been in such a sorry state since the funeral, Gwen's been letting them sleep on her bed."

The idea struck Kathryn as a bit inconsistent with her impression of the Amazonian princess with the riding crop, but she didn't comment.

"You should wear this tonight." Phoebe slipped a flesh-toned sequined sheath from its protective cover. The sequins shimmered when the light hit them, a striking rainbow of translucent color. "Trey'll be on his knees."

"I'm the only one who'll be on my knees tonight."

Phoebe gave a bright laugh. "Then all the more reason to wear this."

She seemed so earnest that Kathryn couldn't help but smile, reminded of days long ago in her school dormitory, when she and her schoolmates would spend hours deliberating the right clothing and cosmetics for their monthly co-ed dance with the boys from St. Peter's School.

"Trey said it'll be a bit before he gets back, so you've got some time to make yourself pretty." She backed out of the closet, then turned around before Kathryn had a chance to follow. "Don't let Trey take advantage of you. He's old hat and you're new to this game. If you have any questions about the menu or the prices, just ask. We'll all help you."

Kathryn appreciated the sentiment, yet her doubts must have shown clearly in her expression, because Phoebe added, "Trust me. The princesses stick together at the Palace. Always have, always will." With a decided shake of her pale blonde head, she swept though the door. "I know you may not have gotten that impression, but you threw us a curve. Bottom line is you're our madam as long as you're here."

Kathryn issued a very unladylike snort. "I'm not sure I'll make a very good...madam."

"Why ever not?" Phoebe looked genuinely puzzled. Then she rolled her eyes. "Oh, lord, don't tell me Gwen was right. You're not a virgin, at your age?"

"No, of course not."

Her denial hung in the air for long moment before Phoebe sniffed haughtily. "There's nothing wrong with being a virgin, Kate. Trust me. I lose my virginity at least twice a week."

This was the absolute last thing Kate expected to hear and for a moment she could only stare. Then a laugh burst unbidden from her lips. "Think the cowboy will have mercy on me if I pretend I'm losing mine, too?"

"You don't want Trey's mercy, Kate. You want every ounce of that man's lust. Trust me. Mmm-mmm." She paused in the bedroom doorway and gave a contented sigh. "The flesh-toned gown and no virginity. Trey'll be on his knees and that's exactly where you want him. Got it?"

"Got it," Kathryn said, in spite of her growing sense of amazement that she was making jokes about having sex with the same man Phoebe apparently knew very well. Twelve hours ago, jokes like this simply wouldn't have been possible.

Phoebe looked genuinely delighted and disappeared from the bedroom with a bouncy step. Kathryn watched her go with a smile. Life had certainly taken a turn since breakfast. All because of Kitty. Kitty, who'd done the outrageous and bequeathed her a brothel. Kitty, who'd cared enough to push her beyond the confining boundaries of her safe little world.

Plucking the flesh-toned gown from the closet, she hung it on the outside of the bathroom door. "There you go, Kitty. The least I can do is go along for the ride."

And when she picked up the phone to postpone her departure, Kathryn felt more relaxed than she had in a very long time.

Grinning Like a Jackass Eating Cactus

After arranging to have their meal sent up when he called, Trey made his way back to Kate's suite. When she didn't respond to his second knock, he let himself in and heard the shower. Grinning, he strode into the bedroom, wondering how Kate felt as she stood beneath the pulsing showerhead, water pouring over that sweet body of hers. Was she washing away the sickness? Or prettying herself up for him?

Trey hoped both, because just the thought of the night before them sent a downswell of blood south. He'd showered already, though he'd been mightily tempted to share that pleasure with her. And he would, as soon as they'd traveled farther down the trail to knowing each other.

He planned to get to know Kate very well. He wanted her. Leaving to check on Cody's mare and clear off his own plate at the ranch hadn't been as simple as putting on his John B. and walking out the door. Not with Kate rubbing her sex against his hand like a purring barncat.

When Trey saw a sparkly gown hanging on the outside of the bathroom door, the hangar keeping the door from closing properly, he decided right then and there not to deny himself some waterplay, even if he didn't think Kate was ready for him to get wet.

Setting his saddlebag on the floor by her dresser, he entered the bathroom. A double sink vanity claimed an entire wall beneath lighted mirrors, and he walked past, noting the array of toiletries efficiently arranged on top.

Efficiency and control. Kate sure did have her fill.

He stopped in the doorway of the adjoining room, the sight before him catching him by surprise like the onset of a Nevada sunset, a sight that still awed him, though he'd lived his whole life here.

Her face turned up to the shower spray, the water jetting over her delicate features, streaming down the curves and valleys of her naked body, glossing her in clouds of mist.

All sleek curves and creamy softness, she was the kind of woman a man claimed to quench his fires, a woman so sweet she raised his protective instincts, too. Her hair was a smudge of midnight behind the glass shower door, the fine points of her body all softly blurred, veiled as though he viewed her through a morning mist on the range.

Trey's pulse kettled in his veins like a bucking bronc, an adrenaline kick that made him dig his palm against his crotch to curb his response. No such luck.

Sinking onto the commode, he braced his legs apart to ease the vice of a troublesome seam, and sat back to enjoy the show.

Kitty had known he'd react to Kate like a virgin walking his first princess line-up. She'd been one talented madam, and her fine old hand had snared Kate into coming to the Palace and had backed him into making her stay.

She'd manipulated them both, and Trey couldn't say he was sorry. His needs were sparking like a brushfire in a drought season as he watched Kate lift her sleek arms to rinse her hair. He wanted to touch her, to explore every nook and cranny of that body God must have designed to tempt a man to eternal damnation with a smile on his face.

Though she was slightly built, she wasn't half-starved and frail like so many women. She was curvy and womanly, a woman created to touch. Even her motions were graceful, almost lyrical beneath the rush of water and the hiss of steam. With that water flowing over her in streaming ribbons, Trey could imagine her bathing in a sunlit pool under a mountain waterfall.

Awed, he watched as she bent slightly to soap a long leg, revealing the slim line of her back, the smooth turn of her pale backside, a quick flash of darkness between her thighs. His cock swelled painfully in response, and he squirmed on the commode lid to ease the pressure of that damned seam.

He was of half a mind to strip off his clothes and join her, but guessed he'd pushed his luck enough. Kate was a filly who needed a firm, but gentle wooing, and he aimed to take the reins and woo her proper.

Though he'd never been much for playing domination and submission games, filling his needs with more playful antics, he recognized Kate needed to let go of her almighty control. She was wound tighter than a twirl-twizzler roping his first calf and didn't look like she'd loosen up any time soon on her own.

He could help her with that, though it went against his grain to push her. He'd settled on using gentle force for the time being. Kate was an intelligent woman. She'd see the importance of what she meant to the Palace and what the Palace could mean to her soon enough. And once she did…well, then he could only hope for the best.

He'd have done his part and shown her the way, and, lord, was he eager to show her the way. *Too* eager, because when she spread her legs to the water in a seductive dance, the sooty splash of color between her thighs sprang words to his lips before he realized that talking would only end his private show.

"I want you to shave for me."

She reared around so quickly Trey thought for sure she'd slip and he'd wind up toting her back to bed unconscious again.

"Jeez, cowboy. You scared me half to death." Her hands were pressed to her chest, not to cover her pretty breasts, but as though she tried to keep her heart from galloping right out of her skin.

"I won't bite, pretty lady." He wrestled back a smile. "But I've got a hankering to taste your sex soft and smooth under my tongue."

Trey's heartbeat speeded up in time with the pulsing rush of the shower as he awaited Kate's response. She seemed frozen in place, the only change was the rapid rise and fall of her chest, and he wondered whether she was honestly mulling over her reply or simply shocked into silence.

Then, through the steamy glass, he detected a pink flush that started above those nice firm breasts. "Yes, Trey."

Those words shot through his body like a flash flood. "You can knock off a hundred dollars for the show."

"I thought there was a two-hundred dollar house minimum?"

He smiled. The lady learned quickly.

"I'll pay."

Slowly she lowered her hands from her breasts, and she reached toward the soap dish.

Trey's breath hitched as she rolled the bar of soap between her hands. Hiking a foot onto the edge of the tub, she bent slightly, making her breasts plump forward invitingly.

Her hair fell forward over her face, concealing her expression, but the rosy tinge creeping up her neck deepened, a soft focus blush prettier than any sunrise over the ridge.

Propping his elbows on his knees, Trey leaned forward, too, closing the distance between them, aroused by the way her breasts swelled when she took a heavy breath and rolled a soapy hand between her thighs, long, lingering caresses, designed to draw and hold his gaze.

They did. His blood pumped when she spread her thighs, leaving herself open to his gaze, reminding him of how she'd felt earlier, pressing that soft mound into his palm, urging him to stoke the fire inside her.

He wanted to touch her now. To thread his fingers through that soapy dark mass, feel the power of knowing it was his hand she responded to, he who made her purr silkily in his ear.

Shifting uncomfortably on the commode again, he watched as she parted the dark silk lips of her sex with pale fingers, thighs spread wide, torturing him with images of driving himself deep inside her. Feeling her sweet softness welcome him in that way had his cock straining in his jeans like a bronc in a chute.

The razor appeared in her hand, and she guided it over her skin, carving away the lush thickness in clean strokes. Water rinsed the remnants away, down her thighs in tufts of dark silk.

Trey had to anchor his hands on his knees to force himself not to slide open that glass door and join her. Watching her performance assaulted him with a lust he'd never felt before. Knowing she sought to please him excited him in a way he'd never explored before, a way he could become mighty used to.

The thought was new and startling. Trey liked being the center of Kate's thoughts, liked it with a dark sort of hunger he'd never felt before. Liked it enough that he fought a hard battle to sit still and just watch, when he wanted to feel her sleek moist body spread hot and willing beneath him.

"Come on out now, Kate. I want to watch you dry off."

"Yes, Trey."

Those words again, soft breathy bursts of sound that undermined his restraint, affected him with an intensity he had to wrestle to control. The steady pulse of the showerhead seemed to mock his best efforts, then the silence, as she flipped the water off. Awed by the sight, Trey watched as she rallied the courage to face him, a visible struggle that stiffened her spine, drew back her shoulders before she slid open the door and stepped out.

He wasn't a small man, and the quarters proved tight for her to maneuver around him, but he was too enamored by the sight of her dripping curves to leave his perch on the commode and give her more space.

Not when she was only inches away, so close he could smell the light flowery scent of her skin, see a bead of water roll over her hip and disappear into the curve of her inner thigh.

Dragging a towel off the rack, he held it out. "Here."

With a trembling hand, she took it, brought it up against her without ever meeting his gaze.

He sat back, fascinated by her struggle, waiting.

Her flush revealed she fought a war within, but he thought she might be winning, because she hiked her painted toes onto the rim of the commode seat between his legs, drew the thick towel up one shapely calf and launched a well-aimed attack on his senses, worthy of the two-hundred dollar house minimum.

Her hand trembled as she worked the towel lazily up her leg, each stroke buffing her creamy skin and directing his gaze a little higher toward the juncture between her thighs that flashed teasing glimpses of her freshly shaved sex, full pink lips slightly parted and pouting at his inattention.

Keeping her gaze lowered to her task, she dragged the corner of the bath towel into the valleys between each painted red toe, her full breasts jiggling with each stroke, kicking his heartbeat into a gallop.

Something about the smile tugging at the corners of Kate's pretty mouth suggested she was very aware of the effect she had on him, and very pleased. But still she avoided his gaze as she slipped one foot away, only to replace it with the other and begin the sexy show all over again.

Trey's breath came in arrested bursts, his every sense rushed with *her*. The sight of her sleek skin, feminine curves moving in a graceful swirl of motion that kicked off faint whiffs of her freshly-scrubbed skin, forced him to wedge his hands under his thighs to keep from gathering her into a naked wet bundle on his lap. Each breath of her slightly floral scent gnawed away at a little more of his restraint, until Trey was left asking the question: *what fool put him in charge?*

Ride for the Brand

Kathryn knew nothing at all about the cowboy except that he temporarily controlled her fate and was used to an entire brothel servicing his sexual needs. He knew so much about her. Kitty had shared not only the details of her life, but her deepest, darkest secret.

I need a woman with fire, Kathryn.

The cowboy knew, yet he'd told her to put on this sexy little show, knowing she wasn't any good at sexy shows. He'd told her to please him, and *she had*.

That hungry expression on his face and that bulge in his crotch were so reflective of his pleasure that Kathryn found herself not nearly so intimidated by her naked performance as she might have been. The effect left her feeling feminine and appealing in a way she'd never felt before.

Knowing the cowboy was in control, knowing she really had no choice in the matter was…well, *liberating*. Her task here was to keep that smile on his face and that bulge in his pants. Inhibitions and worries faded in the quest of her goal.

She wondered what a psychologist would say about finding such freedom in submission, then decided she really didn't want to know. She'd never approached anything before in her life with such an utter lack of control and, combined with that rapt hunger on the cowboy's face, Kathryn found herself spurred to a boldness she'd never imagined herself capable of.

Dragging the towel around her shoulders, she dried her back and neck with one swipe, then let the towel drop to the floor in a wet heap. "Would you hand me that lotion, please?"

The cowboy glanced askance at the vanity, zeroed right in on her favored sweet pea body cream and grabbed the tube with one sure shot. Blonde hair fell over his brow as he turned back to stare at her, his potent dark gaze demanding everything she had to give, and then some.

He was such a big man, those hard chiseled features and miles of rugged broad shoulder sucking up all the space and air between them. "I'll do the honors, pretty lady."

That gravelly whisper threaded through her, made her intensely aware of all her bare skin in contrast to his fully clothed self. He'd apparently showered and shaved while he'd been away and somehow his fresh shirt and knife-creased jeans made him seem primed for a night of sex as if he'd shown up on her doorstep with a bouquet of fresh flowers, a polite and very sweet gesture.

But there was nothing sweet about his stare. The heat in those dark eyes made her nipples gather tight and Kathryn suffered through another flush as he glanced right at the greedy peaks that had the temerity to tighten even more.

Judging by his smile, the man was clearly pleased he could affect her with no more than a glance. She wondered exactly what he'd do if she told him to keep his hands to himself, she'd lotion her own body, thank you very much, but found she wasn't willing to test that particular boundary yet. Not when the testing would mean denying herself his special brand of magic.

With a steady hand he squeezed the fragrant pink lotion into his palm, a sharp contrast to the way her insides trembled when she propped her foot between his thighs.

He glided his callused hands along her calves with strong, sure strokes, as though he'd performed the service on a thousand women before. Such innocuous attention shouldn't feel so...*possessive*, yet something about the way he worked his way steadily upward, as though he desired to touch her and needed no permission to do so, made her feel very possessed.

Kathryn savored the unfamiliar feeling. Gone was any uncertainty of consequences, any struggle of wondering if she was crazy to give herself to a stranger, even a stranger who could make her climax like he had. He'd simply take what he wanted and she found that thrilling in a dark sort of way.

With his gaze lowered to his task, he gave her a view of the top of his head, the wheat-blonde strands bleached pale from the sun, and she savored the simplicity of wondering what his hair would feel like, when she would get a chance to find out.

Not just yet, apparently, when he slid his work-rough hands along her thigh, kneading the lotion into her skin, tantalizing her as he edged closer and closer toward her newly bared sex.

She'd never realized how much that fine cover of pubic hair had protected her until the cowboy traced his tanned fingers over her, sweet pea lotion slicking callused fingertips against oh-so-sensitive skin and creating a friction that made her suck in a surprised breath.

The sound seemed to hang in the steamy air between them and the cowboy peered up from beneath his brow, his melting gaze raking every bare inch of skin along the way.

"This spot is definitely a winner." His lotion-slick fingers separated her sensitive folds, found that intimate knot of nerve endings and squeezed gently. "Can you feel my touch better freshly shaved, Kate?"

Kathryn felt his touch straight to her toes and grabbed his shoulders to hang on while she rode out the sensation.

"Yes, Trey," she managed on the edge of a breath.

Shaving had made a difference, even in contrast to the feel of his hands on her most intimate places only a few hours earlier. Her sex ached, that tiny core swelled with the need.

He rubbed his thumb in lazy circles, occasionally catching that responsive core between his thumb and forefinger and shooting another molten wave through her.

She grew woozy. Her breasts grew heavy, her nipples ripe for his touch. Her thighs began to vibrate with the intensity of her need and he must have noticed how he overwhelmed her because his free hand snaked around her waist and pulled her forward just before her legs gave way.

"Come here, pretty lady." He forced her to straddle his lap, spreading her sex wide. His hand unfurled beneath her, his rough palm rasping her tender skin with a breathtaking amount of friction before his thumb started up that dreamy rhythm again. "Tell me what you want, Kate?"

King Cowboy was actually asking? Kathryn glanced at him, surprised, but judging by that hooded expression, he was only interested in exercising some more control over her body. Not too difficult of a task. Her body had become slave to his touches and she barely recognized the sight of herself, naked and vulnerable, before this fully-dressed stranger. The clean scent of his freshly scrubbed hair filling her nostrils, his tanned face level with her breasts.

His hard mouth poised just inches before a beaded nipple.

"I want…Oh, Trey. I want to feel your mouth on me."

This was the scene from some erotic fantasy and when he dipped low to her breast, caught her nipple with a swirl of his tongue and a hot pull of his lips, Kathryn never wanted the fantasy to end.

She moaned, *loud*, and gave in to her desire to touch him. Threading her fingertips through the heavy strands, she anchored his mouth against her breast, shivered as he lavished hot attention on first one nipple then the other.

"Think we found another spot, pretty lady." He glanced up at her, dark eyes molten with a look of such hungry pleasure that she let out another sigh.

With his thumb tracing those crazy circles and his mouth sucking greedily on her nipple, Kathryn felt the tension inside her shooting into warp speed even faster than before. Her sex clenched in needy spasms and heat pooled low in her belly.

She wanted to experience that soaring ride to climax that she had earlier, wanted to know that her body's response hadn't been a one-shot deal. Only this time the cowboy kept the pressure steady, bringing her to each new peak, only to leave her there, waiting, aching, *wanting*.

She finally realized he had his own agenda this time around and it obviously wasn't about bringing her to fulfillment. Perhaps earlier had been a teaser, a means of convincing her to play this game. But now, now it was obvious the cowboy wanted to lift her to new heights and leave her hanging there to enjoy the view.

"That should do it," he whispered, withdrawing his mouth from a nipple.

She wanted to ask what he was talking about, but in the face of this urgent sense of loss, speech completely failed her. She could only stare, breathless, as he reached into his shirt pocket and withdrew a handful of gold jewelry.

"I brought you a present."

He captured her gaze and she saw pleasure in the dark depths, and something else entirely. He seemed almost…*eager*, she decided, and sensed that her response to his gift was somehow important to him.

He poured a golden chain into her palm. At first she thought he'd given her a necklace, but quickly realized this was like no necklace she'd ever worn before. The fine gold links made up a very long chain and three tweezer-like clamps were fastened at various intervals.

"What is it?" she asked.

"Hang on. I'll show you." He slipped his arm from around her waist and she braced herself steady on his lap as he lifted the chain and unfastened one of those shiny gold clamps.

"What is—" her jaw dropped open when he aimed for one of her nipples.

"Trust me," he said with a smile and latched that mean little clamp right onto a tender peak.

Kathryn gasped at the pinch, not quite pain, but not far from it. "Whoa, cowboy."

"Too tight?"

She breathed deeply, gave the sensation a chance. "Depends. What am I supposed to feel?"

He fastened the second clamp to her other nipple, then gave a tug that stretched her nipples tight. Kathryn gasped.

"I don't want you to hurt, but I want you to be very aware of how aroused you are. Are you?"

"Yes, Trey." But there was still a third clamp dangling from the chain and she eyed it skeptically. "And where, pray tell, does that go?"

He flashed a dimpled smile that flustered her by its sheer devilry. Patting her thigh, he motioned her to stand. "Hop up and I'll show you."

With a sort of morbid fascination, Kathryn did as he asked, then forced herself not to shy away when he slipped his hands between her thighs.

"Oh, no."

He coaxed that intimate knot that was distended and oh-so-sensitive from its fleshy hiding place. "Oh, yes."

He tightened the clamp gently and before she had a chance to even register the feel of that pain/pleasure pinch, he lowered his head and laved his rough-velvet tongue over her vulnerable bud.

Kathryn jumped away, knees shaking, breasts jingling, mouth emitting a sound that was a cross between a moan and a sob.

"I like the idea of you wearing my brand," the cowboy said earnestly. "You'll remember how I make you feel with every breath you take."

He wasn't kidding. Her breath came in tight ragged heaves, each one causing the chain to pull and the clamps to tug at her nipples, at her clitoris. The wild, urgent pounding deep inside left her hovering somewhere between *aching* and *desperate*.

She stared at the cowboy's satisfied grin and decided that she really had stepped into a new and strange land today. A land where Kathryn Roman, tireless junior partner to one of the country's top advertising firms became Kathryn Romanov, madam, branded by Trey Holliday, cowboy master.

Her sex gave one hard throb of pleasure.

Luck of the Draw

Trey retreated to the doorway to get a bird's eye view of Kate as she applied make-up. Leaning over the vanity, she peered into the mirror, her every move a study of creamy curves and liquid grace.

Gold chinked softly with her movements and he found himself riveted by the sound, by the sight of the chains swaying from her breasts, a narrow V that trailed over the smooth expanse of her belly. Her nipples had hardened to the size of small red grapes, ripe for his attention, and he found himself chomping at the bit to taste her again.

She aroused him in a way that tested his restraint—a first time in his memory. A princess named Sadie had taken his virginity long ago and she'd skilled him in the arts of self-control for many long steamy nights before declaring him ready to tackle loving. Kate was proving to be as apt a pupil as he'd once been and he was very pleased with the way the night progressed, the way she responded to him.

Something about her fierce independence challenged him to rein her in like a mustang, not to break her, but to test that strong will to see how far she could go. She'd come so far in such a short time already. Challenging him about her fees, and…he glanced at the gown hanging from the door, choosing clothes from her new wardrobe to please him.

He ran his fingers over the shimmery gown. "Nice choice, but you can save your pretty dress for later."

She gazed at his reflection in the mirror. "I thought we were having dinner."

"We are. We'll eat in your suite."

Those big blue eyes swept down over his own clothes and she frowned. "Oh, I see. I get to waltz around butt naked like your obedient little love slave."

"I like seeing you naked. You've got a fine body.

Though she pointed that dainty chin high in the air, Trey could tell by how hard she worked to look unmoved that she liked when he called her pretty. She needed to admit how much she liked it, too.

Moving toward her, he ignored the wary light that flared in her eyes when he caressed a finger along the cleft of her heart-shaped backside. "You've got a body made for admiring, and touching."

Goosebumps skimmed along her creamy skin like a breeze over the range and he ran his finger along her cleft again, just enough to separate those sweet cheeks and make her blush at the liberty he took. "No sense denying the obvious, Kate, you like when I touch you." He met her reflection in the mirror and smiled. "There's nothing wrong with that."

"Maybe not," she said saucily. "But it's going to cost you, cowboy."

He trailed his finger upwards along her spine, was rewarded this time when she shivered. "That's what makes this the perfect arrangement. I'm willing to pay."

Retreating, he sensed her staring after him as he grabbed his saddlebag from the bedroom. Withdrawing a leatherbound journal, he turned to head back into the bathroom to find that she'd followed him.

She stood in the doorway, natural and at ease, gold chains dangling, seeming to have overcome her nerves about displaying all her lovely bare skin.

"Another present," he said, presenting her the journal. "For keeping track."

"How much am I into you for?" She flipped through the pages, eyes growing wide. "Oh, no. I really had no idea the princesses made this kind of money. It'll take me forever to pay you off."

"That all depends."

"On what? Trust me, cowboy, nothing I know how to do is worth this much money."

He laughed, liking the bite of her humor. "Leave that for me to decide, since I'm the one paying."

"You're going to knock off two thousand bucks to spend the night with me?" she asked incredulously.

"For an in-party." He flipped back to the front of the journal and plucked out a house menu. "An in-party means I have your undivided attention for as long as I want you tonight. We can negotiate for the extras. Speaking of, you'll need to mark down that two hundred for the shower show."

She shot him a look that suggested he'd gone plum loco, but Trey saw her pleasure, too, in the slight straightening of her shoulders, the way she stood tall with pride. Unless he was way off the mark, Kate liked that he wanted her.

And there was something so inviting about knowing that, about her yielding her strong will to his that made her trust so much more worth the earning.

A love slave. Trey had never thought much about having one before, but then, he'd never met Kate in the flesh before.

"Are you hungry, pretty lady?" At her nod, he said, "I'll give a call then, because I'm starved."

He let his gaze trail over her, telling her without words that he was starved for a lot more than food.

The Cowboy's Lady

Kathryn discovered she wasn't hungry for food, after all. Her appetite seemed focused on the man who sat across the table, growing distinctly more ravenous with his every steamy glance. The perfect gentleman and dinner companion, the cowboy entertained her with tales of the Palace and Tex's Sweet, seemed intent on engaging her in conversations that compared life in Love to the life she knew in the city.

She found him a very intelligent man, which she supposed shouldn't come as a surprise given his various occupations. His wit had a dry edge that made her laugh often, and combined with his quicksilver smiles, she found their meal passing in a blur, the wine the only memorable course. Every sip chased away her inhibitions about sitting naked across from a fully dressed man, chased away nerves about what would come on her first in-date.

The cool air on her bare skin and the heat of the cowboy's glances combined to make her...*ready*. Her breasts had grown heavy and swollen, the clamps squeezing her nipples just enough to make them ache, yet not grow numb, the clamp between her legs making her squirm on the chair. She'd grown moist and achy and eager to find out what he had planned next.

"A tour of the Palace, I think," he said to her surprise. "You didn't officially reopen, but now that everyone knows you're here, they'll be lining up at the door. Place is probably full already. Do you feel up to an appearance? Has that headache gone?"

The last thing she wanted to do was play temporary madam. She didn't want to think about the responsibilities Kitty had saddled her with, didn't want to worry about how she was going resolve the problems. But to Kathryn's amazement, she found she didn't want to think about leaving the cowboy either. She'd much rather focus on easing this hungry ache he'd started with his skilled touches and possessive demands.

"Let's get it over with." The sooner they toured the place, the sooner they could be alone together again.

The cowboy stood, circled the table and extended his hand. "Then let's get you ready to meet your fans."

She slipped her hand into his, thrilled at the way he tightened his fingers around hers, a simple touch that shouldn't have amplified her awareness of him, but did.

"Fans?" she said. "I think Joe used the term 'posse.'"

The cowboy chuckled. "Now it's not that bad, Kate. Everyone's just disappointed you don't want to stay."

She wanted to ask if the cowboy would be as disappointed when she left, but couldn't bring herself to. Somehow his answer mattered, when it shouldn't, and she refused to fuel the flames of this absurd obsession by...well, obsessing.

Just because the cowboy made her feel sexier than she'd ever felt in her life implied no exclusivity on his part. The man was simply fulfilling his commitment to Kitty. That he was obviously enjoying himself in the process was only good fortune.

He led her into the bedroom, slipped the gown off its hanger. "Lift your arms."

"Cowboy," she said. "I have nothing on but your brand."

His dimples flashed. His dark gaze twinkled. "I know. I like knowing you're naked under all this finery."

His gaze held hers and arousal zipped through her at the pleasure she saw in those sparkling depths. "Yes, Trey."

His strong hands guided the gown over her head and down her body. The beaded fabric chafed her bare skin, a tantalizing friction that fired her sensitive nerve endings and increased that needy pulsing between her legs.

She'd only touched up her lipstick and fluffed her hair when the cowboy declared her perfect and with her hand in his, she went to greet her guests.

The cowboy hadn't been far off the mark when he'd said the Palace would already be filled with eager guests. And one glance into that busy dining room clued her in on why he'd had their meal sent to Kitty's suite. The princesses weren't the only employees the Palace's new madam would have to contend with. The place screamed *thriving business.*

The bar teemed with Stetsons, creased slacks and dress boots. Kate realized with surprise that, like the cowboy, these men had obviously dressed for their night out. Visits with the princesses were clearly taken seriously around Love.

One young man with a bouquet of roses left the bar to greet them. He inclined his head at the cowboy. "G'evening, Trey."

"This is Jess," the cowboy said, shaking the man's hand.

Jess handed her a bouquet of fresh roses with baby's breath, as Kathryn recognized the man who presented them as the town deputy. A peace offering, she suspected.

"I'm pleased to meet you, Lady Kate."

Lady Kate. Word sure got around quickly in Love.

"Thank you very much, Jess. They're lovely."

Two spots of red actually bloomed high on Jess's cheeks, and Kathryn realized he was actually blushing. With a head full of shiny black hair and bright blue eyes, he was a handsome young man, probably not much older than twenty.

Jess rocked back on his boot heels and smiled a shy grin. "Just wanted to say howdy and that I hope you decide to stay," he said, before beating a hasty retreat.

Kathryn watched him fade back in with a group of other young cowboys, lifted the roses to her nose and inhaled deeply. "He was very nice. Does he come here often?"

The cowboy frowned. "He's sort of connected to the place."

"Is he?"

"His full name's Jess Romanov."

Kathryn nearly dropped her roses.

The cowboy reached out to steady her bouquet, looking slightly uncomfortable. "Your cousin."

"I didn't know I had a cousin," she said dryly, wondering what else the man knew about her but had neglected to mention.

"Kitty's brother had four kids. Your mom was the oldest."

Burying her face in her bouquet under the pretense of enjoying the fragrant blooms, Kathryn schooled her expression, unwilling to let the cowboy know how much his news affected her.

Her mother had been a part of a family.

"My mother was supposed to run this place after Kitty, then," she finally asked. "Do you know what happened?"

He nodded. "Let's get through with your well wishers and we'll find a place to talk."

With a strong hand on her elbow, he steered her into the crowd, not allowing her time to wonder how many other family members she had floating around and knew nothing about. Within seconds, they were rushed by men of all ages and over the sea of heads, she could see Adoreé dancing on a raised platform, a seductive dance comprised of spangly scarves and bare skin.

Kathryn shook hands and smiled, quickly realizing that she may as well have worn the cowboy's brand outside her evening gown because every one of these men seemed to think they needed the cowboy's permission to talk to her. He dutifully introduced each and every one, as though their deference was his divine right. Kathryn supposed in this strange new land it was.

At one point she managed to scoot close to the cowboy and whisper, "You're just full of surprises tonight. I didn't realize the Palace had a stage, either."

He shrugged. "Some of the princesses enjoy dancing. Not all, but Adoreé spends her fair share of time up there."

And just where did the glamorous Adoreé rank on the cowboy's list of favored princesses, Kathryn wondered? She didn't ask, just followed him through the crowd, a smile plastered on her face, abandoning any attempt to place names with faces. As preoccupied as she was with the way her body ached, she didn't stand a prayer.

When they broke free of introductions and well wishes, the cowboy led her into the entrance room, which unlike most of the other rooms she'd seen so far was fairly empty.

Looping his arm through hers, he led her toward Katia's portrait, away from the doorman and the arriving guests.

"Glad to have you, Lady Kate," one man called out.

Kathryn waved absently. "These people were ready to lynch me this morning. Now I'm getting flowers. What's the deal?"

"You reopened," the cowboy said simply, plucking the bouquet from her grasp and handing it off to a passing waiter. "Take these to the kitchen and tell Jed to fix them up and send them to Lady Kate's room." When the waiter departed, the cowboy said, "Okay, Kate. What do you want to know?"

"How many other cousins I have roaming around would do for starters."

"Your mother had one sister and two brothers and they have fourteen children between them."

"I have *fourteen* cousins?" she asked incredulously. "I never had a clue."

All her life she'd yearned for a family. Now she'd found one in the unlikeliest place—a place overseen by a cowboy who was fast occupying too much time in her thoughts. The man hadn't been joking when he'd said he would surprise her. And judging by his expression, he wasn't exactly sure how she'd take his surprises, either. Worry creased his brow and his mouth had thinned to a tight line.

"Do you know why my mother left?"

"Kitty told me she fell in love and married very young and the man she married turned out to be more interested in her connection to the Palace than he was in raising his family. He behaved poorly and forced your mom into a messy divorce. Kitty thought your mom blamed her involvement with the Palace. She wanted a different life for you. She left Nevada and never looked back."

Kathryn didn't know what to say, had no grasp on the emotions rioting inside her, except that the scenario made sense. Her mother had been a very strong woman and if she'd made up her mind to put the Palace behind her…"Did they just let her go?"

The cowboy seemed to know she referred to the rest of the sizeable Romanov family and shook his head. "To my knowledge your aunt and uncles spent years trying to break the ice with her, but…well, she never warmed up and then she died." He slipped his hand over hers and squeezed reassuringly. "I know they went with Kitty to her funeral."

"Oh," was all Kathryn could say. On the day when she'd felt most alone in her whole life, she'd had family around her and had never even known. She peered up at the portrait of Katia, silently asked, "Was my mother right to protect me? Am I better off without them?"

Those bright blue eyes stared back, just as silent, but Kathryn's mind filled with memories of late nights with Kitty and how she'd always looked forward to the last week of the month when Kitty would arrive in the city with her pooches, how much less lonely her life had seemed during those weeks.

She also remembered a young man who shyly welcomed her with roses, a young man with striking blue eyes and black hair so similar to hers…so similar to the woman's in the portrait.

"Tell me about Katia, cowboy," she finally said. "How did a Russian princess wind up running a brothel and siring such a crazy family?"

My family.

He followed her gaze to the portrait, his smile seeming to approve her handling of such bittersweet revelations. He tightened his grip on her arm possessively and steered her away.

"Story starts when a lawman from Texas came to Nevada hunting a cattle rustler and winded up settling in White Pine County as sheriff. Love wasn't much more than a miner's camp at the time, but he took a liking to it and set himself up here."

Kathryn didn't have the heart to point out that Love didn't strike her as much more than a mining camp now, but she said nothing, just ran a finger along the filigreed edge of a Tiffany wisteria lamp as they passed an antique buffet.

"The mines were booming in copper ore, and the miners were growing wealthy. But they played as hard as they worked, and Tex could barely control them. He decided they needed sex to vent their energies and the closest brothel was East in Ely, too far away to give them the sort of constant exposure to women he thought would civilize them."

With the gentlest pressure of their linked arms, the cowboy brought her to a halt in front of glass doors that opened onto the panoramic view of the ridge.

"Tex's first brothel was in town, above the saloon, but the idea took real good hold and the stable of ladies grew until the manager couldn't run the brothel and his business."

"He needed a madam to keep the ladies in line."

The cowboy nodded.

"So how did a Russian princess land the job?"

"Our princess was the Tsar's illegitimate niece, and given the trouble the royals were having at the time—" He fixed a doubtful gaze upon her. "I assume you learned about the Russian Revolution in all your fancy schools?"

"I did, indeed," Kathryn assured him. All her mother's money had gone for something, at least, and she bit back a smile because he seemed relieved that her "fancy schools" hadn't left out what he clearly considered a basic.

"The royal family couldn't openly acknowledge Katia and feared their enemies would find out about her. They set her up for a new life here in America."

"And she ended up as Tex Justice's madam?" Kathryn asked incredulously.

"Their enemies already knew about her and murdered the Cossacks who were charged with her protection at the same time the royal family was executed. Katia managed to escape and Tex got her purely by chance, when he came across her being sold as a slave. He bought her."

Kathryn stared at the night-draped spread of juniper and pinions that ascended the ridge both saddened and impressed by Katia's story.

"The Palace isn't what you expected, is it?" he asked, his voice a low whisper.

"Not at all," she admitted. "In my head I envisioned an Old West saloon. This really is a palace."

"Katia had a liking for Spanish Colonial and the Sears catalogue. Kitty added some, but it's pretty much the same."

"It's so open, so homey."

"It is a home. To quite a few people."

It seemed an intimate sort of admission, and she wondered if he was referring to himself as much as the princesses. When he guided her toward the magnificent antique organ and reached up to retrieve a small oval frame that sat on top, Kathryn could feel the heat of his body close to hers, and the clamps that dangled from her nipples seemed to suddenly grow heavier.

"The Princess used to play this organ." He held a faded picture up for her perusal. "Here she is entertaining at a party. If I'm remembering right, Tex brought it back from a trip East as a birthday gift."

Kathryn recognized the woman in the miniature as the woman in the portrait and realized the cowboy had been right. Katia had been a tiny woman, a fact not readily apparent in her portrait, yet obvious as she sat in front of the enormous organ. She was very beautiful. Though her image had been captured in profile, her easy smile and spirited expression shone clearly.

This woman had been her great-grandmother, a woman who, like Kathryn herself, had had a family that she hadn't been a part of. Had she been as lonely as Kathryn had always been? What had she endured before being purchased by Tex Justice's friend and brought to Nevada?

She appeared happy. What had she found at Katia's Palace that had made her seem so content? Kathryn peered around the elaborate room that had weathered close to a century with its sturdy wood floors and unmistakable attention to detail, and suspected she knew the answer.

"Did Tex build this place for her?"

"He did. Cut and carved each and every timber himself from the forest up the ridge."

Her great-grandmother had found love in Love, Nevada. And though Kathryn had never even known this woman had existed until six weeks ago, she felt a smile touch her own lips.

"Come on, Kate," the cowboy said. "I want to show you something."

He linked his body close and led her through another door that led to a dim hallway. She could hear the even threads of his breathing and the thud of his boots as they stepped from the thick carpet onto a polished wood staircase. At the top, a room opened before them and Kathryn found herself looking out over the bar through a wall of dark glass.

"What's this?"

"The madam's private showroom."

"Oh my." The room was lushly furnished for entertaining with cushioned sofas, a private bath and a small bar that occupied the opposite corner.

The cowboy must have sensed her uneasy curiosity because he said, "I don't know what else Kitty did in here, city girl, but she could get a bird's eye view of the action from this window without anyone knowing she was watching."

"I suppose that makes sense from a security angle."

"Mmm-hmm." Slipping his arms around her, he steered her in front of him, rested his chin on the top of her head and forced her to stare out over the crowd in the bar below. "Look at them, Kate. It's all about wanting. There's nothing shameful in a healthy need, nothing wrong with a healthy appetite. These boys want sex. The princesses want to give it to them. It's consensual. Respectful."

Judging by the happy crowd she saw socializing below, Kathryn would have to agree. She recognized several of the princesses in the crowd, chatting with various men, all dressed elegantly in evening formal wear. Adoreé entertained others with her sexy striptease, enjoying the lusty responses from her group of admirers.

As the cowboy had said, there appeared to be nothing shameful in a dose of healthy wanting. *Wanting.* That's what she was, and she remembered again what Kitty had said about some women just needing the right man to get them in the mood.

The cowboy felt like the right man.

Kathryn rested back against him, liking the feel of his strong arms around her. His brand had her entire body pulsing with a need to feel his hands on her. Adoreé's sultry dance was having an effect on her as well.

A beautiful woman, Adoreé was all long graceful lines and sleekly tanned skin. She danced with an easy rhythm that suggested sex in each rolling motion, in each well-timed graze of fingers along firm thighs, over the mound of her sex. The beaded halter top only covered enough of her breasts to hint at the hue of her nipples below. It had been tied loosely so her breast swayed as she shimmied around a pole, and revealed her toned bottom clad in nothing more than a matching g-string.

Cowboys crowded around her, their dazed glances and goofy smiles revealing just how much they were enjoying the show, and Kathryn remembered performing for her cowboy in the shower, how his appreciation and the desire in his eyes had made her feel cherished. She'd coaxed that same needy expression on his handsome face, wanted to again.

As though the cowboy sensed her restlessness and read her thoughts, he asked, "What do you want, Kate?"

His deep voice filtered through her, made her shiver. "I want to know why I respond when you touch me," she said softly. "I want to feel you inside me."

A low growl was his only reply before his hands rounded the curve of her shoulders and found the gown's zipper. Soon the fabric parted and the gown fell away, a beaded puddle at her feet, leaving her clad only in strappy high heels and the cowboy's brand.

Sweeping her into his arms, he waltzed her into motion, the only music the sounds of their breathing, their heels shuffing softly on the polished wood floor.

Her sensitive nipples brushed the cowboy's shirt, the fabric tugging on the clamps and sending firebolts of sensation through her. With one hand he held hers, but the other he cupped around her bottom, shaping the skin with his hot fingers, anchoring her against that bulge swelling in his jeans.

She'd never felt so free as when his hands were equally free to roam over her skin, to explore, and Kathryn sighed, a contented, purring sound just before the cowboy's mouth descended on hers, devouring hers, an intimacy, a pleasure, he'd not yet allowed her. His rough velvet tongue swept through her mouth, exploring every hollow with a bold thoroughness that spoke of a man who liked kissing. Hot hungry kisses. Slow leisurely kisses. Needy reckless kisses. Kisses that stole her breath with their wildness.

She'd never known a kiss like his before, a kiss that made her melt against him with a gasp. Her tongue tangled with his, yielded to the sparks raining through her, to the need to meet his tongue stroke for stroke, to make him gasp, too.

Suddenly their dance ended and he held her rooted to the spot, one hand snaking behind her to cup her head and draw her further into his kiss. Emboldened, Kathryn slid her hands along his broad back, felt the muscles gather beneath her fingers, realized that though he had much more skill at schooling his reactions, he was as affected by her as she was by him.

There was a certain intensity about him that reminded her of a summer storm, the moments between the blinding flash of lightning and the crash of thunder. The rigidity in his muscles, the way he braced his booted feet apart to lock himself into place and create a strong shelter for her naked body hinted of the power of his need.

She wanted to know, *needed* to know that his desire was as powerful as her own. Slipping a hand between them, she molded her fingers around the hard length of his erection safely restrained behind sturdy denim.

He didn't stop her when she fumbled with the button of his fly, just rocked back on his heels so she could slip her other hand between them and kissed her harder. Carefully Kathryn unzipped his pants, coaxed him from the parted denim and quickly discovered the mystery behind that absurdly large bulge.

"Sheesh, cowboy," she whispered against his lips as his erection sprang free, thick, perfectly shaped and proudly erect.

He chuckled. "I've never had any complaints."

"No doubt." She slipped her hand around him, filled her palm with his scorching heat, but the cowboy caught her lower lip between his teeth and nipped gently. "No touching me, Kate. I'm the one doing the touching right now."

She wondered why he denied her the pleasure of serving his needs, when he played master to her slave. But her role in this game wasn't to argue, so she slipped her hands around his waist and shimmied up to cradle that heat against her bare belly.

Suddenly his mouth blazed a trail of fiery kisses down her exposed throat and he forced her to arch backwards over his arm as he blazed that trail down...*down*.

Wrapping his fist in the chain that dangled from her breasts, he gave a slight tug that stretched her nipples and made her eyes flutter closed helplessly. Then his mouth was upon her, his tongue laving the sensitive tips, swirling and rolling, his jaw abrading her skin, a rough contrast that shot fresh showers of sparks through her.

All she could do was hang on and try to breathe through the intensity of her arousal, anchor her hand against his erection to prove she wasn't the only one about to erupt into flames.

He drew a swollen nipple into his mouth, one long hard pull that made her cry out.

"You respond to me because you're my woman, Kate." His words gusted hotly across her skin, his utter conviction, the possessiveness of his declaration jarring Kathryn from her daze. "I've been waiting for you a long time. Now you're mine."

The need in his voice made him sound as though he had indeed been waiting forever, but that couldn't be. They'd barely known each other a day.

Perhaps he sensed he'd distracted her, or maybe he was just so in tune with her physically he anticipated her reaction, but the cowboy drew upright to stare at her with an intensity in his dark eyes, an earnestness in his expression, that revealed he meant exactly what he'd said.

This man wanted to do more than play games with her.

Every inch of her naked skin seemed to blast out a warning. She was far too exposed, far too vulnerable. She pulled away, an instinctive reaction rather than a conscious one. Just as the cool air seared her wet breasts, his low growl told her she'd overstepped a boundary.

With a movement so sudden she jumped, the cowboy lashed those whipcord arms around her, twisted her around until she faced away from him before she'd even thought to resist. With his body, he crowded her against a winged chair, forced her to bend over until she lay draped across the arms, the muscles in her legs stretching, her bottom boldly exposed to his view.

Kathryn realized rather belatedly that she was playing games she knew nothing about with a stranger she barely knew. He'd been very respectful so far, but they hadn't discussed any parameters. She had no clue how far he would go. He'd said he wouldn't make love to her until she asked him to, but when he kneed her thighs apart, she half-expected to feel the heat of his erection prodding against her.

She should have recoiled at the thought of being taken forcibly, but to her utter mortification, Kathryn felt a dark thrill instead, a sense of profound disappointment when the cowboy only sank his fingers into her buttocks and hiked her bottom even higher into the air.

The lips of her sex separated, exposed to the cool air. The chain stretched taut, tugged on the clamps.

"Cowboy," she issued a warning that sounded more scared than warning as she pushed herself upright only to have him restrain her with a hand in the small of her back.

"The name's Trey, Kate. Use it and knock off another five hundred dollars for a half-and-half."

Kathryn couldn't remember exactly what a half-and-half was, but experienced a surge of pure rebellion at his highhandedness. Craning her neck, she caught him sinking to his knees behind her, his face level with her bottom and got a pretty good idea of what the first half involved.

"Trey," she croaked out, but the next sound out of her mouth was a gasp as he nipped the tender flesh inside her thigh.

She jumped. He spread her cheeks wide, his wicked tongue lashing out over her aroused sex, one bold wet stroke that traveled from her swollen clitoris back to where he had no business traveling.

"Trey!" his name rode out on the edge of a low moan as she shivered from head to toe.

He didn't reply. He didn't stop. He only began a well-aimed assault of his mouth on her most intimate places. His tongue tasted and teased her satin folds. His teeth tested the clamp, exploring her with a thoroughness that declared he had every right in the world to do so, as though he'd waited a lifetime for the privilege.

Some barely functioning part of her brain warned Kathryn she was in over her head here, that the cowboy was playing games with more far-reaching consequences than she knew. Though reason declared she should stop before getting in any deeper, she couldn't seem to murmur a single syllable that would distract the cowboy from his fiery attentions. Not when his attentions felt so delicious, so...*right*.

What she wanted didn't seem to matter anyway, because the cowboy had already decided he knew what was best for her. Right now *best* involved his tongue sinking into her heat, making her sex seize in hot wet spasms, making her abandon all thoughts of resistance. She arched her hips back with short thrusts.

The cowboy knew exactly what she needed. Sliding his hand between her thighs, he braced his palm beneath her, the heel of his hand riding against the clamp as he lifted her higher so his tongue penetrated deeper.

A liquid heat washed through her, and she had no choice but to abandon herself to it, though she found herself gasping and straining against him, combining her efforts with his to lift her even higher . . .

His tongue slid from her sex and trailed back to invade her nether parts. Kathryn cried out at the unfamiliar sensation, the insistent pressure that warred with her body's natural response to resist. But he didn't relent, just kept up that steady pressure, not quite intrusive, just *there*, until she writhed back against him, mindless to feel him inside her.

She exploded without warning, a huge engulfing burst that wrenched a moan from her lips. Clutching the arm of the chair, she hung on as fire poured through her. With his face buried between her cheeks and her bottom riding against his tongue, the cowboy rode out each clutching spasm until she caught her breath in broken sobs.

She tried to rally the energy to lift herself off the chair, needed to see his face, desperately needed to know that such a detonation of the senses was normal, but she hadn't moved before he was on his feet. His powerful body was suddenly bending over hers, his rock-hard erection riding against her moist sex.

"Do you want me, Kate?" he asked in a throaty whisper.

"Yes, Trey."

With one deep thrust he sank into her heat. He slid his hands around her, grasping her breasts, using them to pull her up enough so her hips arched back and drove him even deeper.

His low growl resounded in her ear as he reared back, a gliding stroke that carried him almost out completely. Then he thrust back, stretching her, filling her, blinding her with a pleasure she'd never known existed, an intensity far beyond her comprehension, her control, that made her body begin to vibrate with such violence only his hands and the chair kept her from dissolving onto the floor in a heap.

She only knew that she didn't want him to stop, would have begged for his next silken stroke, and the next...

Then she came apart again.

Kathryn had no idea how long had passed before she felt the cowboy pull out. A sob caught in her throat, her sense of loss overwhelming when her body reacted so far beyond her control, her emotions pushed so close to the surface she didn't know whether she might laugh on the next ragged breath, or cry.

She was only vaguely aware of the cowboy's hands on her as he lifted her, rearranging her boneless body until she sat curled up in the comfortable chair. She couldn't find the strength to open her eyes, didn't care she must look like a pathetic heap, barely able to hold her head upright.

She heard the cowboy's heels rap across the floor, then a warm weight settled over her, enveloping her, coaxing her to snuggle within the soft folds of…a woolen throw, she decided.

She forced her heavy eyes open and found herself face-to-face with the cowboy's rock-hard erection. He was pulling his jeans back up, frowning as he shifted his hips to tuck that impressive equipment, still shiny from her body's juices, into his jeans.

Her warm yummy feeling drained away. She'd been so wrapped up in her own pleasure she hadn't realized the cowboy hadn't reached his own fulfillment. He'd annihilated her. She hadn't satisfied him.

His gaze flicked up, and he must have recognized her stricken look, because he abandoned his impossible task and knelt before her, turned his handsome face up to hers. His dark eyes were so earnest, her heart seemed to swell in her chest.

"I don't expect you to understand, Kate, but I can't make love to you until you're mine. Not just while you pay off your debt, but forever."

She gave a broken laugh, a ridiculous, hysterical sound that proved she was about to lose the fragile grasp she had on her emotions. "Forever? We haven't known each other a day."

"You haven't known *me* a day."

"I don't understand."

"I know." He stroked strands of hair from her cheek, such a tender gesture she didn't know what to make of him or his revelation. "Don't think about it now, Kate. Now is for enjoying how you feel." He gave her a goofy half-grin. "No fire? I don't think so."

It was the goofy half-grin that did it. The goofy half-grin that made a huge knot expand in her chest, forced tears to her eyes and pushed her emotions right over the edge.

One strangled gulp and she was crying, deep wrenching sobs that welled up from her soul in watery bursts, overwhelmed her with the knowledge that this stranger, a cowboy from a hick town called Love, had cared enough to help her find her fire.

She didn't know why, couldn't even rally enough energy to ask. But he did. She didn't know how she knew, but she did. And as if women dissolving into hysterics after multiple mind-blowing orgasms was the most natural thing in the world, he got to his feet and half sat on the arm of the chair, gathered her against him and let her weep her heart out on his broad chest.

As Crooked as a Snake in a Cactus Patch

Kathryn awoke the next morning to find herself alone in the madam's private showroom still curled up in the chair. Both the cowboy and his brand were gone, though she had no memory of him removing her clamps or leaving. All she had left was the memory of his hands and his mouth taking her to incredible heights and the glorious aches of a woman who'd been thoroughly and skillfully loved.

She decided that perhaps waking up alone was for the best. Her head was a muddle of thoughts she was best left alone with for the time being, but she couldn't help wondering if the cowboy would come back today, hoped he would.

Gazing through the wall of glass to the bar below, she found the Palace empty, the brass fixtures shining, the chairs neatly stacked on the tables and bar, as though a cleaning crew had made a late-night appearance.

After performing her morning ablutions in the private bath, she shimmied back into the beaded gown, which the cowboy had laid over the sofa, and prepared herself to face the new day as a changed woman from the city girl who'd arrived yesterday on the flight from hell with On-the-Wing Joe.

Though she had no clue what temporary madams did during the daytime, she decided not to try and puzzle it out without caffeine. An even bigger problem than her schedule loomed on her horizon—a phenomenon called a shadow migraine, which was a debilitating echo that typically followed a headache the size of the one she'd had yesterday.

After foolishly forgetting her medication in the frenzy to make this trip, Kathryn could only get her blood flowing to hopefully minimize the pain that would soon make an appearance. She didn't relish fainting again. Especially not when the cowboy wasn't around to catch her.

But she wasn't going to think about Trey Holliday right now. Not when just the thought of his smile, his strong arms and his twangy accent made her heart ache and her blood pound and her nipples tingle as though he'd awakened a hunger that was going to need constant feeding.

So, feeling as weak as a newborn—a feeling she couldn't entirely attribute to yesterday's ferocious migraine—she left the madam's showroom and made her way down the stairs.

The trail to the kitchen proved easy to find by following the scent of frying bacon. A wiry old man with a head full of grizzled hair stood over the stove, but no sight of the cowboy.

"Good morning," she said, glancing around the huge room, which resembled a food service prep area of a restaurant more than a kitchen. But there was a frilly curtain adorning the window over the sink and a table on the opposite wall, which lent the place a homey air.

The man turned around and sliced a beady black stare her way. "So you're the new boss. Care to tell me if we're keeping the doors open, ma'am, because everyone around here needs to get laid real bad." As an obvious afterthought, he wiped beefy hands on a white apron that was dingy from too many bleachings and extended one in greeting. "The name's Jedidiah. Most folks around here call me Jed."

Kathryn covered the distance between them. "Pleased to meet you, Jed. Most folks around here call me Kate. I'm afraid I can't answer your question just yet, but I hope you won't hold that against me. I seriously need a cup of coffee."

Jed's eyes sparked, his bushy brows drawing together like a hairy gray caterpillar, giving Kathryn the impression he wouldn't hold anything against her just yet.

Motioning to a sturdy wooden table in the corner of the big kitchen, he said, "Take a seat, Kate. I'm fixing up breakfast for myself. The folks around here won't start showing up for another hour yet. Want to join me?"

"Thank you. I'd like that. Just coffee for me, please." She wasn't awake enough to decide if she had an appetite and wasn't sure if food would set off another headache. So far she was holding her own.

After seeing Kathryn comfortably settled at the table with a mug of steaming coffee, Jed slid bacon and sunnyside eggs onto a plate and joined her.

"Are you the gourmand responsible for my delicious meal last night?" she asked in an attempt to make conversation that didn't involve an explanation about when she'd officially take on the job as madam. The truth was she barely remembered the meal, having been far too preoccupied with her own nakedness and wildfire responses to the sexy cowboy sitting across from her.

"I'll take that to mean you liked your supper," Jed said, tucking a napkin in his collar and reaching for a piece of bacon. "If you settle on staying, you'll have to tell me what a tiny thing like you eats. Can't be much more'n a rabbit does."

"I eat enough to keep me vertical." Kathryn shrugged and sipped her coffee.

Jed gave a bark of laughter that made her jump. "Well, I reckon you're right about that, Lady Kate." Cramming the bacon into his mouth, Jed stood and crossed the room. Pulling open a stainless steel door, which appeared to be a walk-in freezer from the icy steam blasting him, he disappeared for a moment only to reappear with a pint of ice cream, instantly recognizable as her favorite, Haagen Daz.

"Butter Pecan," he said. "Kitty told me what you liked, so I stocked up. Got Swiss Chocolate Almond and Macadamia Nut, too, for when you're in the mood for something different."

What was it about a pint of ice cream that made a lump stick in her throat, a lump not so different from the one she'd nearly choked on last night when the cowboy had held her in his arms and let her cry? It had nothing to do with this grizzled old man she'd never met before, welcoming her to the Palace with her favorite treat. Nothing at all.

But she found herself thanking Jed anyway, relaying the tale of the time she and Kitty had resorted to sucking out the last drips from a pint of Macadamia Nut with a cocktail straw.

His laughter told her he was very pleased with her response and for some reason Kathryn couldn't fathom, she was pleased to have put the smile on his face.

When barking erupted from somewhere beyond the kitchen, Kathryn spun around on her chair. "Kitty's pooches."

"Tell me you've got coffee, Jed," a raspy voice said as the Amazonian princess burst into the kitchen with three familiar white Malteses scampering around her ankles.

"Malted, Hambone, Lambchop." Kathryn sank to her knees, opened her arms to the hyper dogs who scrambled right up onto her lap as though no time had passed since their last visit.

That stupid lump in her throat started to choke her again.

"The brats are used to waking up at the crack of dawn with Kitty," Gwen said. "They haven't realized yet that the rest of us keep late nights."

"There's coffee in the pot, darlin'," Jed said, spearing an ample forkful of eggs into his mouth.

Gwen helped herself while Kathryn sat on the floor, petting and kissing the pooches, keeping her head lowered not to let the others see her blinking back tears. More than anything she'd seen since her arrival in Love, the pooches brought home to her just how much she missed Kitty.

Kitty had brought something to her life that Kathryn hadn't known had been missing. And only now realized how much she wanted someone in her life who cared.

Hambone curled in a tiny ball on her lap. She rubbed her nose on the top of Lambchop's head and scratched Malted behind the ears, absorbing the thought that there were other people in this town who might grow to care for her. People like the cowboy and Jed. And family like Jess, who'd welcomed her with a shy smile and fresh flowers. If she did nothing else today, she wanted to find out more about her family.

She listened absently as Gwen filled Jed in on the events of the past night. How Adoreé had had her heart broken yet again in her never-ending search for a rich husband. How two men had gotten into a fist fight over Phoebe and Jess Romanov had broken up the fight himself and then snatched Phoebe for the night from beneath both men's noses.

When she reached for her coffee mug from the table, she found Gwen getting up.

"Might as well work out," she said. "Got to keep this body the stuff that fantasies are made of." Grabbing her coffee mug, she glanced down at the pooches. "Come on, brats. Let's go."

But Kitty's pooches had obviously decided they'd found a comfortable place to stay and weren't following the direction. To Kathryn's surprise, Gwen didn't accuse them of conspiring with the enemy. She just rolled her eyes and asked, "Will you keep them with you for a spell, Lady Kate?"

"I'd love to."

"When you're over them, just bring them back to Jed. He'll know where to find me."

Kathryn nodded, and couldn't help but feeling she'd passed some sort of test for the Amazonian princess to trust her with her charges.

After Gwen had left, Jed refilled Kathryn's coffee mug and said, "Don't let Gwen there put you off. She's got a heart of gold under her knife-sharp airs. The Palace here's the only home she's ever known. She gets overprotective."

It is a home. To quite a few people. Kathryn remembered the cowboy saying. Could the Palace be a home to her, too?

She was still mulling over the question an hour later after emerging from a hot shower to dress for the day. She chose a long floral skirt and cashmere sweater, the most casual of the outfits she'd brought. She hadn't given a thought to her attire when she'd packed for the trip, but now her suits seemed so out of place. She hadn't even packed a pair of slacks or flat shoes. In her mind this trip had been all about business.

It was turning out to be so much more.

The pooches were clearly at home in Kitty's suite and she left the closet to find them all sound asleep, each curled up in a tiny white ball on his and her own pillow under the large bay window that looked out over the ridge.

Kathryn didn't have the heart to wake them. Instead she pressed her nose to the bouquet of roses, which had been placed in a crystal vase on the dresser and inhaled deeply.

Orgasms, ice cream and roses. She could get used to this. Had Kitty known that when she'd bequeathed the place to her?

She thought you were too comfortable being alone, that you worked too much and didn't live enough. The cowboy had said. *She wasn't sure if you'd been taught how.*

Gazing down at the photos beside her college graduation photo, Kathryn knew beyond any doubt that if nothing else, Kitty had had her best interests at heart. Did the cowboy?

Where was he today? Had her hysterics last night turned him off? For a man used to having the princesses at his beck and call, her meltdown must have seemed tedious. The one time she'd tried to touch him, he hadn't been interested. Did he find her sexual inexperience just plain boring?

And why did that thought depress her so completely?

Retrieving the cowboy's journal from the dresser, she curled up on the bed, opened the book to take a closer look at exactly what expenses he'd been covering these past six weeks.

Salaries. Medical bills. Utilities. The usual stuff. Totals that seemed entirely uninteresting compared to her column—in-date, waterplay….

The phone rang. Kathryn reached for it quickly, hoping not to disturb the dogs, felt a zing of disappointment when she heard Jed's voice on the line and not the cowboy's.

"What's up, Jed?"

"The mayor's here to see you, Lady Kate," he said. "I'm holding him and his cronies off at the door, but he's planted himself there like dry rot, says he won't leave until he talks to you."

"His cronies?"

"Don't wolves travel in packs in that big city of yours?"

Great. "I'm on my way. The dogs are sleeping, Jed. Will they be okay if I leave them?"

"In Kitty's suite?" He gave a sharp bark of laughter. "They're home. Just leave them and come on down."

Kathryn replaced the receiver in the cradle, took a deep breath and headed down to tackle her first official duty as temporary madam of the Palace.

Mayor Barclay was a slick looking cowboy dressed all in black with a string tie and an ornate silver belt buckle. He did indeed have cronies—two physically fit men dressed similarly in black, flanking him on both sides like bodyguards.

"Ms. Roman," he said, striding forward to greet her the minute she stepped through the door. "I'm glad to meet you in person. I'm sorry we're forced to conduct business on the doorstep, but the staff here has refused to invite me in."

The staff, indeed. Looked like everyone had turned out to line up along the porch like some bizarre sort of honor guard. Obviously some of the princesses had tumbled straight from bed to join the party and Gwen, who'd clearly been in the middle of her workout, glowered at the men, her formidable curves bathed in sweat, making her look like she was headed into battle more than ever.

Kathryn supposed she should feel better that so many people from the Palace had turned out, though she suspected their interest stemmed more from curiosity to find out if she'd sell the place out from under them rather than any interest in providing her back up against these men. Except for Jed, who'd sidled right up behind her, clutching a wooden rolling pin like he might have held a shotgun.

"There's no need, Mayor Barclay. I'm sure we can conduct our business quickly."

His smile never wavered as he motioned to one of his bodyguards, then accepted a clipboard holding papers she guessed were the contracts for the sale.

"I was expecting you at city hall yesterday to conduct our business."

She held the man's gaze steadily, wouldn't pull any punches. "As you may be aware, half the town met me at my plane yesterday, bringing several new concerns regarding the management change to my attention. I saw no point in meeting with you until I'd investigated their claims."

This clearly wasn't what Mayor Barclay wanted to hear but he managed to keep his smile in place. "Ms. Roman, I'm sure I can answer all your questions satisfactorily. I know you're pressed to return to New York."

While that had definitely been true, as Kathryn glanced back at the honor guard of sleep rumpled and sweaty employees, she realized that twenty-four hours had changed her priorities. Yesterday, she'd been thinking only of herself. Today...well, today she felt a need to think about a few others.

"I'm not prepared to ask my questions yet, nor to sign your papers," she said in her best boardroom tone, a tone the mayor apparently understood as his smile grew more strained. His bodyguards, too, as they moved a step closer.

Jed's burly chest was suddenly brushing her shoulder. Kathryn heard a sudden squeal of tires and absently glanced at the parking lot to see a shiny black and white sheriff's car jolt to a sudden halt. The mayor's reinforcements? Just what she needed.

"Now, Ms. Roman," the mayor said, not a little condescendingly. "We had all the details worked out before you ever stepped foot in Love. There's no need to go changing our agreement now."

She could see how Mayor Barclay might appeal to some people with his polished looks and slick smile, but Kathryn knew his type too well to buy into his reassurances.

"You misled me into believing that the town would preserve the Palace, not close it for business. Until I investigate my options, I won't sign any papers. I have nothing else to say."

The mayor snatched the hat from his head and his big-toothed smile faded. "I heard about how Trey had to carry you off the plane yesterday. Don't tell me he's already made you his whore. I thought you had more sense than that or I'd have met your plane myself."

"You didn't meet her plane because you knew that crowd would have lynched you, Barclay," Jed ground out. "You may have tricked folks into believing you were the right man to put in office on election day, but they've sobered up now."

Before the mayor got a chance to reply, he was jerked right off his feet by the scruff of his neatly pressed collar. He stumbled and landed in a cloud of dust on the sidewalk. His bodyguards went down with two muscled thuds beside him.

"I'd say you owe the lady an apology, Barclay." The sheriff, a brawny, rugged looking man with silver shot black hair, scowled down at him. "Best get it out of your mouth before my fist goes in it."

Kathryn glanced up at the men who stood over the mayor and his bodyguards with fists clenched and realized the sheriff and his posse weren't the mayor's reinforcements after all. She recognized Jess, noticed the similarities in appearance to the sheriff and their companion, and suspected what she hadn't yesterday—these men were more Romanov men.

Her family.

In a flash, the sheriff had hauled the mayor back up while Jess and his companion held the bodyguards down. Just as he'd promised, the sheriff planted his big fist square with a sickening crunch. The mayor's head snapped back and he staggered, would have gone down had the sheriff let him go. But he swung the mayor around, hauled him right up in front of her.

"Apologize, Barclay."

"My apologies, ma'am," the mayor said through a bloody lip.

Kathryn held his angry gaze with a stoic one of her own, not quite sure how to respond when faced with a scene straight from an old *Ponderosa* rerun. Noble cowboys protecting the lady from a black-hearted villain. If she wasn't so amazed, and yes, touched, she might have laughed.

"Now get on." The sheriff shoved the mayor toward the gate, threw his hat after him.

The mayor staggered, then shot to his feet like a bolt, grabbing his hat and shoving it back on his head. "You'll be hearing from my lawyer, sheriff, and you, too, Ms. Roman."

Jess and his companion escorted the men through the gate.

Kathryn didn't answer, was too busy staring at the sheriff, who was just as busy staring at her. "Thank you," she said and she meant it. Not only for tossing the mayor off the property, but for abandoning her to the cowboy yesterday.

"No need for thanks, little lady. I'm your Uncle Luke and I'm always glad to chase away any sidewinders who bother you."

His words hung in the air between them, a promise. She didn't know how to respond, only knew that she was touched in a way she'd never been touched before.

Kathryn may not have known what to do, but her uncle did. He opened those burly arms to her and said, "Haven't given you a hug since you were in diapers, little lady. Come 'ere."

His smile was so genuine that Kathryn didn't think twice. She stepped right into the big circle of his arms, rested her cheek against his broad chest. "Hi, Uncle Luke."

He stroked her hair with a beefy hand and said gruffly, "Glad you've come home, Kate."

The Round-up

Jed corralled everyone back inside for breakfast. Her uncle looped his arm through hers and escorted her back inside, saying, "We're having a dispute between the sheriff and mayor's offices this term and you've landed right in the middle."

"So I've heard," Kathryn said, gratefully accepting a mug of coffee from Jed as Jess and his companion filed through the crowd into the kitchen.

She greeted Jess with a smile. "My roses are opening beautifully this morning."

"I'm mighty glad you like them, ma'am."

"I understand I have you to thank for breaking up a fight last night."

"Just doing my job, ma'am."

She wondered if spending the night with Phoebe was part of his job description, too, but found that the thought of this red-cheeked cousin honing his skills with the lovely young Phoebe only made her smile.

"This here's my oldest son, Tanner." Uncle Luke wrapped an arm around Jess's companion's shoulder. "He used to pull your hair when you were a little 'un. Course, he wasn't much older himself at the time."

Tanner was a tall, strapping man, another cowboy like all the men in Love, with his boots and hat and polite smile.

She shook his hand in greeting. "I assume I don't have to protect my head from you anymore."

He gave a hearty laugh, patted her hand reassuringly. "No, you don't, Kate. In fact, I came to help your head today. I grew up to be the town doctor. Trey told me about your headache and asked me to drop by and see if you were feeling better this morning."

"Oh, that was...nice of him."

"So how're you feeling? Any aftereffects? Some people suffer from shadow migraines the following day."

"I know. I usually get them."

"Took your medication?"

"No. In my rush to make this trip, I forgot to pack it."

"What do you usually take? I can prescribe it for you."

She met the concern in his big blue eyes, not just doctor beside manner, but what seemed to be a real desire to help. "Thanks, Tanner, but I think I'm going to be just fine today. If I were going to have another headache, I'd have it already, which is really very odd, now that I think about it. My migraines are usually very predictable."

"Maybe it's just a side effect of small town living. We're pretty relaxed around here. Not much time for headaches and sickness. Keeps my schedule manageable."

Kathryn chuckled, but couldn't help remembering the cowboy's words about making more time to relax. After that off-the-Richter-scale migraine yesterday, she by all rights should be suffering today. She wasn't. In fact, she felt great.

"What are we going to do 'bout the mayor?" Jed joined them. "Can't do to have him strong arming Lady Kate here."

"Don't worry about Barclay, Jed," her uncle said. "I'll head over later and have a talk with him. He won't mess with Kate if he knows he'll have to take on the Romanovs, too. No walking through the door and fighting like a man for that one, not if he can sneak in though the back." Her uncle scowled. "We need to be worrying about how he's got the council and all those new folks who've moved into the new subdivisions on the outskirts of town sold on closing the Palace."

Kathryn glanced through the curtained window above the sink. The daylight revealed a silhouette of a ranch house up on the ridge. Was that the cowboy's place?

"The man's slicker than an oil spill," Tanner was saying. "It's hard to go up against someone who works like that. He's got folks panicked that the Palace is the root of all evil and that spending money at a supermall will keep their kids from becoming sex maniacs. He's won over those suburbanites, all the soccer mamas. They're plum fierce protecting their young 'uns."

"What's the Palace done to counter?" she asked curiously.

They all turned to gaze at her, clearly not understanding the question.

"The media," she explained. "Advertising, promotion to offset these negative views of the Palace."

They all stared blankly, which answered Kathryn's question. "For all its evils, the media can be put to constructive use on occasion, gentlemen. Sounds to me like you need a media blitz of the facts. Spell out how the Palace's zoning forces the town to stay within a certain population and how closing it to attract developers into the area will mean zoning changes that will not only skyrocket the population but invite other adult entertainment businesses to set up shop here. Let the people decide which is the lesser of the two evils. Then schedule a town meeting with an ad hoc committee to address everyone's concerns and come up with a—"

"Whoa, whoa, Kate," Uncle Luke said, his mug poised at his mouth. "You're right. *We* know the facts and anyone who hasn't been snowed by Barclay knows them, too. But not everyone else. We need to put all the cards on the table, sway some folks to our side. I'm thinking there's enough of us who see Barclay for the snake he is to convince a few more."

"It's a great idea," Jess said, his shy smile filling Kathryn with more satisfaction than she'd ever gotten from her work on the Simply Seductive campaign.

"I think it could work," Jed agreed. "Now the only thing we need is someone who knows how to run a media circus."

They all turned to look at her.

She ignored their looks. "What about the Palace's lawyer?" she asked brightly. "He was very helpful. I'm sure he can hook you up with a reputable firm."

"That lawyer is my nephew Sam," Uncle Luke said, looking as though he had no intention of letting her side skirt the issue at hand. "He's another cousin of yours. His mama's your Auntie Kay. She's chomping at the bit to see you, but we decided to honor Aunt Kitty's wishes. She wanted us to wait until you got to Love and Trey settled you in."

Kathryn buried her nose in her mug, stoically refusing to blush and let these men know why Kitty had been so determined for the cowboy to *settle* her.

"This is a family business, Kate," Tanner said, his bedside manner firmly in place.

A family business. She remembered wondering why Kitty had bequeathed a brothel to a New York ad exec and realized, as she gazed around at these men, that Kitty had left her the Palace to bring her home to her family.

Was she insane to think about returning to New York? In one visit to Love she'd found the family she'd always longed for, orgasms that she'd only dreamed about and a cowboy named Trey who wanted to possess her *forever*.

"I, uh, need to talk to the cowboy."

"Trey?" Uncle Luke asked.

She nodded.

"You got his cell phone number, Jed?"

"I'd rather go see him if that's possible." She wanted out of the Palace to clear her head and collect her thoughts.

"Where do you reckon he'd be about now?"

Jed glanced at his watch. "This time of day he'll be out riding the range."

Uncle Luke glanced at his sons. "We'll have to ride to find him then."

"Ride?" Kathryn asked. "You mean as in on the back of a horse?"

"No." Jess shook his head in horror, blue eyes growing wide. "Lady Kate, don't tell me you don't ride?"

Kathryn had no intention of disappointing her cousin. "Of course I ride, Jess," she said with a smile. "In Manhattan we ride in taxis. I can corral one from a block away."

Bucking Off a Man's Whiskers

Since Kathryn hadn't packed anything suitable for riding, Phoebe, who was close in size, provided a change of clothes. Dressed in a pair of jeans, boots and a flannel shirt, Kathryn felt like she'd stepped off the cover of a dude ranch promotional brochure.

The men in her family approved the change.

"Now you don't look nearly so much like a city girl," her uncle said as he hoisted her up behind Jess.

Though Jess wasn't a small man by any stretch of the imagination, he hadn't bulked up to his father or brother's dimensions yet, either. With her weight, they combined to make an acceptable burden for a horse.

They rode in the direction of the ridge with Uncle Luke picking her brain about ways to effectively use the media to present the facts about the mayor in a way that would portray the best side of the Palace and still have a G rating.

Kathryn tossed out ideas and charged her cousins with remembering them. Brainstorming sessions only happened once, and with everything cluttering her mind right now, she'd never recall a thing she'd said.

But then as they rode out on the cowboy's land, Kathryn found herself falling silent to admire the gorgeous spread of juniper and pinion trees along the lower ridge. Mountain streams cut down from the forest to slice through the range where cattle grazed. With the clear sunny sky, the land was as different from the close gray streets of New York City as though she had actually landed on another planet. How had Kitty left this open sky filled with sunshine for the slushy snow and leaden skies of New York as often as she had?

The answer was simple: Kitty had left because of *her*.

And before she had a chance to absorb yet more evidence of Kitty's love for her, the cowboy appeared over a grassy slope, silhouetted by the brilliant blue sky, just like out of a scene from a romantic Western movie. He sat astride a…brown horse. She had no idea of the different breeds, except to say that this one looked huge, even from this distance.

"Well, here's Trey now," Uncle Luke said.

Instead of riding out to meet him, her uncle just waved, then dismounted in a fluid leap for such a large man. Coming straight to her, he grabbed her around the waist and helped her slide from the back of Jess's horse.

"You're leaving?" she asked when her feet hit the ground.

"You don't need us anymore," Uncle Luke smiled. "You go hash things out with your cowboy, Kate. He's a good man."

Damn, and here she'd been thinking her secret was safe, but the smiles on her handsome cousins' faces convinced her they all knew why Kitty had wanted the cowboy to *settle* her.

"Thanks for the lift." She waved as they rode off.

Kathryn watched the cowboy ride toward her, stared agog as he drew near and two things became obvious—his horse was indeed huge and just the sight of him made awareness roar through her louder than car horns blaring in the Holland Tunnel during rush hour traffic.

A muscular display of man and beast, he rode naturally, as at home on that horse with the sun sparking on his blonde hair, sweat trickling down the corded muscles of his neck as he had sitting at the head of a table, trying to negotiate a compromise between a dozen angry princesses and one stubborn ad exec.

Kathryn forced herself not to shy away as he reined his horse to a stop close by, shoved the hat back from his brow and raked that warm gaze over her. "Howdy, Kate. How are you feeling today?"

"Fine, thank you."

He nodded appreciatively. "You're sure looking fine."

"Thanks." She smiled, so aware of the way his gaze caressed her, and the way her heart beat quicker in response.

"So what can I do for you today, pretty lady?"

"I want to make love with you, Trey."

He leaned back in the saddle, considered her with that small smile still playing around his mouth. "You do, do you? That's a big step."

She nodded, drawing a deep breath before she trusted herself to speak. "I think I've found everything I've ever wanted here. I need to understand where you fit in."

He didn't move. The breeze calmed on the air and the myriad sounds of the herd grazing lazily around them faded. Even his horse seemed unnaturally still, watching her with those big rolling eyes. Kathryn's lungs constricted around a breath as he waited, wondered. Would he take this chance on her?

Then she thought she noticed the faintest softening of his mouth and…"I want to make love with you, too."

And before she'd even caught her breath he swung off his horse and was lifting her onto the saddle.

"I'm taking you back to the ranch house." He swung up behind her, fixed his hard thighs around hers, took up the reins. "I want to make love to you in a real bed. My bed."

And they were off. The horse pounding over the range in a rumble of hammering hooves and churning muscle. She relaxed her body to move with the horse's rhythm, her back riding against the cowboy's chest, her bottom rocking steadily against his crotch, which responded to her presence with a gratifying increase in dimension.

He buried his face in her hair, nuzzled her neck with teasing kisses. She responded to his touch as though every nerve inside her had been tuned to his signal. Her breasts grew heavy and tight, her sex pulsed with achy little bursts that the seam of these jeans only whetted.

But he didn't touch her, only pressed on with his mouth, nibbling on all the tender places of her neck until she marveled that he could focus such lavish attention on her and still control his horse.

When they reached the crest of yet another gently rolling slope, the cowboy stopped his horse to let Kathryn take her first glimpse of Tex's Sweet ranch.

A variety of buildings bordered a corral, where several cowboys worked with horses in a scene straight off of a television rodeo. She recognized the main ranch house by its size, because like the Palace, the house sprawled over the landscape as bold in its southwestern simplicity as if it had sprang up from the earth.

Though the scene before her revealed a busy, working ranch, with the horses, a tractor hauling dirt and cowboys loading what appeared to be fencing into a pickup, Kathryn found the scene somehow tranquil, so different from the don't-look-up pace of the city.

Maybe it was all the fresh air and wide-open spaces. Or maybe the cowboy's look of pride as he identified the various outbuildings: the stables, the cookhouse, the bunkhouse and the blacksmith shop that made Kathryn fall in love on the spot. But fall in love she did. She had the absurd image of herself learning to ride in that corral, of kissing the cowboy goodbye on that porch before he rode off into a pastel-streaked sunrise to begin his workday.

The image was so incongruous with everything she'd ever known, everything she knew about herself that Kathryn might have laughed, if not for the wary expression on the cowboy's face.

"You like it." It wasn't a question.

"I do." She didn't even need to say the words because the cowboy's satisfied smile mirrored all the pleasure she felt.

With a snap of the reins, he plunged them down the slope into the thick of the Tex's Sweet ranch. He dismounted in a burst of masculine grace that made the pulsing little ache between her legs give an odd clench, then dragged her down into his arms. And held her there.

She blushed when whooping war cries and several variations of "All right, Trey!" greeted them from the cowboys milling around the place, but her cowboy only smiled, scooped her into his arms and carried her into his house as if she was a young bride on her wedding night.

He didn't give her a chance to admire his home or, indeed, even to notice the furnishings as he strode surefooted from one room to the next and up a flight of stairs, until he'd reached a bedroom. He kicked the door shut behind him.

A huge four-poster bed with what she suspected was a hand-sewn quilt occupied the center of the room. The rest of the furnishings were simple, only a dresser, a chair and a thickly-woven Native American rug, but there was a huge fireplace on one wall, while the other framed floor-to-ceiling glass doors that opened onto a balcony.

Once at the windows, the cowboy loosed his hold beneath her thighs and she slipped to her feet, shimmying full-bodied against him on her way down. She stood still, not willing to break the moment, wanting to savor the feel of her body against his, his warm breath gusting against her hair.

She pressed her cheek to his chest and gazed through the glass doors. She expected to see the cookhouse and the other outbuildings, but found herself staring at only a breathtaking vista of land, and…"Is that the Palace?"

"Tex added this room after bringing his princess home so he could see her, even when he couldn't be with her."

"That's so romantic."

"What would be even more romantic," he whispered against her ear, "would be for you to undress for me."

"Yes, Trey." She stepped out of his arms with a smile.

With no hint of shyness and only an amazing feeling of contentment, as though stripping for this man brought her more pleasure than anything she'd ever accomplished in her life, Kathryn unbuttoned the flannel shirt, shimmied the tight jeans down her legs and stood proudly for her cowboy to admire.

"God, you're beautiful." He reached out to cup his fingers along the satiny underside of a breast and she felt the heat of his touch sizzle straight to her toes.

She wanted to feel him naked against her, know how their bodies fitted together, knew an eagerness that made her reach for his vest. "May I, Trey?"

"Absolutely, pretty lady."

With her gaze lowered to her task, Kathryn shoved the vest over his shoulders and down his arms, unbuttoned his shirt with trembling fingers as she exposed his muscular chest.

He may have become intimately acquainted with her body during the past twenty-four hours, but she'd never seen much more of him than he'd showed her when he'd shoved his pants down his hips to take her in the showroom last night.

Now Kathryn savored each inch of his tanned skin, the dusky blond swirls of hair nestled into the cut ridges of his chest, the powerful arms that had held her so possessively.

He had to help her with his boots, though she promised herself that she'd be thoroughly versed in removing cowboy boots before long. Dragging his jeans down his trim hips forced her onto her knees and suddenly she was mouth level with that incredible erection.

"May I, Trey?"

"Nothing would please me more, pretty lady."

The pleasure in his voice inspired her. Leaning forward, she pressed her breasts against his knees and swirled her tongue along his hot length. She felt his muscles gather with that one stroke, knew a sense of heady satisfaction that had her running her hands along his hard thighs, cradling his heavy scrotum in her palm and drawing him into her mouth with a sigh.

The sight of his erection had stung her last night, as had the realization that he'd brought her to climax so thoroughly, while she'd left him to suffer the effects of unsatisfied arousal. Kathryn wanted him to lose control today. She wanted to know him completely, wanted to watch his handsome face sharpen with his pleasure, wanted to hear that throaty low growl as his body exploded inside hers.

And she seemed to be making headway toward fulfilling her wish. His muscles quivered, his erection swelled with her moist attentions and when she arched her throat to take him into her mouth even deeper, slipped her hands into his firm butt cheeks he emitted that throaty low growl, threaded his fingers into her hair and dragged her to her feet.

But she only remained upright for a second. Then she landed on the soft mattress and the cowboy was suddenly beside her, gathering her in his arms, pulling her against every hot hard inch of his body.

His mouth caught hers, all fire and need, and they were kissing, a bit desperately, as though they'd waited far too long to be together again, tongues tangling, breaths clashing. His hands raked the length of her body with such fierce tenderness that Kathryn longed to feel him inside her.

He didn't resist when she swung her leg over his, straddled him, using her hand to stroke that magnificent erection against her passion-wet folds. He growled again, a needy sound that did much to build confidence in her ability to drive him wild. He rocked against her, created friction against her hand, driving in just enough to prove that the feel of him inside her last night had been no figment of her imagination.

She wanted nothing more in that moment than to please him, to prove she could stoke as many fires in him as he stoked in her and with a boldness she hadn't known she'd possessed, she slipped her free hand between them, balanced herself with a hand on his chest and sat up. Right onto his erection.

He groaned. His hot gaze flew up to hers, surprised and so very, very pleased that she sighed and began to ride him with the same commanding mastery that he'd shown when riding his own horse in from the range.

He met her stroke for stroke, building tension inside her until all she could do was grab the headboard for leverage as she drove her hips down to meet his thrusts, gasping for air, because she could barely breathe past the building tide, each hard thrust carrying her higher.

When he sank his fingers into her bottom to step up her pace and ground out, "Oh, god, Kate," she felt the first hot rush of his climax, felt her own rushing up to meet it.

Kathryn wasn't exactly sure when she'd collapsed against him, didn't remember him tugging the quilt over their bare bodies, but she knew with a certainty she'd never felt before in her life that if she ever had to dream about how it would feel to be completely and thoroughly adored, cherished and *loved* by a man, she'd feel exactly the way she did right now with their hot bodies pressed together, hearts racing, breaths coming ragged in the stillness.

But she had to be mistaken, because she'd only known the cowboy for little more than a day.

You've only known me *for a day*, she recalled him saying last night in the showroom. *Don't think about it now, Kate. Now is for enjoying how you feel.*

The time had finally come to start thinking.

But before she could reason out about how best to broach the subject, a framed photo on the dresser caught her eye, a familiar frame that seemed out of place in this man's bedroom.

Without a word, she slipped out of the cowboy's arms, drawn to the photo, needing to know if by some fluke they'd owned two so similar. He let her go.

And Kathryn knew before she even reached out to take the unusual tri-gold frame in her hands, before she even dropped her gaze to the picture, that she'd find her own face staring back at her from her high school graduation photo.

She stared down at herself, a fresh-faced girl swathed in black velvet and pearls, a girl with so many dreams and such hope for her future. Had she come close to living up to her hopes? Or had she closed her heart like a fist, tried to cut emotion and people from her life just like her mother had?

One lonely beat of her heart told the truth.

Clutching the frame in suddenly shaky hands, she turned to the cowboy, to ask the only other question that needed asking, and found him propped up on an elbow, watching her intently.

She never even had to ask.

"I'm in love with you, Kate," he said simply. "I have been ever since Kitty came back from your mama's funeral and told me all about a beautiful little spitfire who faced the world with her head high and so much dignity that no one could get close."

Kathryn hadn't felt like that at all during her mother's funeral. She'd felt broken, needy and all alone in the world. Her mother may not have been much for overt affection, but she'd been Kathryn's only family and losing her to cancer so young had come as a huge blow.

"I don't know what it was about you…" His warm eyes reflected both amusement and amazement. "You were clear across the country, living a life I had no ken of, but you touched me somehow. Deeply. When Kitty showed me that photo, I just knew exactly what I wanted in my woman."

"But you didn't know me."

"Well…" He shot her that goofy half-grin, looked a bit sheepish. "I knew a lot about you. And I fantasized a good bit about the rest."

Fantasized? She shook her head, trying to clear it. *She* was this man's fantasy?

The very idea of no-fire Kate being any man's fantasy—let alone a man who had a stable of princesses vying for his attention—struck her as so ridiculous that she could only stare, and struggle to control her runaway heartbeat.

But she had to know. Good, bad or otherwise, she had to hear the truth from his mouth. He'd done things to her that she'd never dreamed of letting a man do. He'd brought her to pleasures that she'd never imagined existed. She had to know, because what he thought mattered.

The breath caught in her throat. Her heartbeat slowed to a crawl. She clutched the photo frame, needing something to cling to, an anchor against the uncertainty that raged through her. And then she forced the words past her suddenly dry lips. "How does the reality hold up to the fantasy?"

He swung his long legs over the edge of the bed, rose to his feet in a muscular burst of grace that took her breath away even though she wasn't actually breathing, because her breath had already locked tight in her chest, waiting, just waiting.

He strode to her, completely unfazed by his bold nakedness. He plucked the frame from her hands, set it carefully back on the dresser.

Slipping his hands over her jaw, he tilted her face up to his and the truth she saw in his expression brought tears to her eyes. "The reality beats anything I ever fantasized about, Kate, and trust me, I have a pretty vivid imagination."

She gave a watery chuckle. She just bet he did. After all, he'd been reared with a palace filled with princesses just clamoring for chances to help him explore that imagination.

And he wanted her.

"So…so what happens now?"

His molasses eyes softened and he stroked his thumbs along her jaw, so tenderly she felt her heart issue its very own sigh.

"I ask you to stay in Love with me."

"As the Palace's madam?"

"I think you're a very bright business woman. I have no doubt that you can get the Palace back on track and work out a situation that'll meet everyone's needs. I'll help you."

Kathryn had had a few thoughts along those lines already, inspired by discovering that the Palace was actually a family run business. And it just so happened that she had *lots* of family around town who might be persuaded to help her work up a new way to run the place. Kate would dearly love devoting her talents to the marketing end and living on this ranch and making babies with her very own cowboy.

"I don't know what the future will hold for us, Trey, but I'd like to take it on together."

He smiled that sexy grin that made her blood ignite, and said, "Nothing would please me more."

Slipping her arms around his waist, she melted against him. "Then we'd better get busy. I've got a lot of debt to work off because I plan on running up a whole lot more."

About the Author:

Jeanie Cesarini is a multi-published author who believes in paying attention to the characters that whisper in her head. Or shout, *as was the cowboy's particular case. This hero wanted his story told so Jeanie said, "Yes, Trey," and obliged him.*

To check out more of her sensual **Secrets** *stories and other red-hot romances, visit her website at* http://www.jeanielondon.com.

Jared's Wolf

by MaryJanice Davidson

To my reader:
When I wrote *Love's Prisoner* for **Secrets VI** and introduced Michael and Jeannie Wyndham, I was overwhelmed by your response. All your wonderful letters and phone calls boiled down to one request: more Wyndham werewolves! Your wish is my command. I hope you like Moira and Jared as much as you liked Jeannie and Michael.

Chapter One

Moira smelled him before she saw him.

She had been strolling through the rose garden, which sounded nice but was actually chilly and miserable, being mid-winter on Cape Cod. She shivered among bare branches, because she couldn't bear to watch her pack leader nuzzle his mate for another second. Which made her feel like a jealous cow. Which only contributed to her misery.

She was a werewolf. A good one, in fact, but that didn't mean she didn't get lonesome just like a regular person. It wasn't that she didn't adore Michael and Jeannie Wyndham. She would have killed for them. She *had* killed for them. They were her sun and moon and, like lovers, they established her world. She accorded her pack leaders the respect due an alpha male and female, but more than that, she loved them as friends.

But she was alone and likely always would be. Her mother had mated with a human and it had brought her nothing but pain. She had wanted more for her daughter. Moira had promised her mother she would settle only for absolute happiness in a mate. Fine and good, except it pretty much doomed Moira to a solitary life. Which, for a werewolf, was usually a disaster.

It was one thing when Michael had been a loner, too. Once Jeannie arrived (or, as Jeannie put it, "was kidnapped"), things were exciting for several months. Helping the new non-werewolf alpha female settle in had been one surprise after another. There had been no time to be lonesome.

Now Jeannie had given the pack a marvelous girl-child, had made her home with the werewolves, and never gave a thought to her old life. No conflict in that time, while good for the pack, meant there'd been nothing to distract Moira from her troubles.

Michael's utter happiness with his mate only made Moira more acutely aware of her own loneliness. She loved them, but could watch them snuggling, smell their lust, only so long before she needed to walk, or snivel in self-pity.

The pack, Moira thought grimly, was no place for loners. Werewolves were enormously social and tended to mate for life as soon as possible. Loners got into trouble, and a loner who got into too much trouble went rogue. Rogue was bad. Very bad.

She shivered, remembering Gerald. He was the only rogue male she had ever run across and, by God, he was enough. Gerald was on her mind because his estranged eldest, Geraldine, had just left Wyndham manor after a brief visit. After Gerald had been driven out, Geraldine had remained loyal to the worthless bundle of fur. Since no pack would welcome a rogue, the two had wandered the country for years. Admirable loyalty, but the price the poor girl had paid! Her father had been dead a year and Geraldine still roamed.

No, a werewolf alone did more harm than good, and she had no business begrudging Michael and Jeannie their happiness. Better to leave the house and take her poor attitude with her. Thus, the rose garden in February. Thus, she would probably catch a cold from skulking in the sparse snow—and serve her right! Thus, there was a stranger on the grounds.

Her thoughts derailed in sudden confusion as she sniffed and caught the scent again. Stranger, yes. Male. Not pack. Probably a reporter; Michael Wyndham was a charismatic, handsome billionaire frequently courted for interviews. Now that he'd married and had a daughter, "journalists" (her lip curled) constantly tried to get a picture of the baby for *People* magazine.

She would find the man and escort him off the grounds; the Wyndham estate was private property. Her woes aside, there was, as always, duty. She turned to search and saw the stranger about fifteen yards away.

She was suddenly furious with herself because he wouldn't have crept up on her, downwind or not, if she hadn't been busy drowning herself in an ocean of pity. And she was also amazed, because he looked…well, amazing.

The stranger, who was rapidly approaching, had dark blonde hair pulled back in a ponytail. He was quite tall, easily a head taller than she was, dressed in jeans so faded they were nearly white, and a black duster which swept past his knees. And his eyes…his eyes were the color of the ocean on the first day of winter, dark blue and filled with restrained fury. She caught his scent again: clean and crisp, like freshly ironed linen. Male linen. Incredibly gorgeous, highly masculine linen. Linen she could wrap herself in, sink her teeth into…

Her mouth popped open, both at the man's sudden appearance and his exceptional good looks. He was the handsomest non-pack member she'd ever seen. Too bad she had to kick him off their property.

He opened his mouth and she spoke, too; they said in unison, "You can't be here."

They reacted in unison, too: "*I* can't be here?"

Moira stared at him, almost afraid to speak, and heard him say, "I'm really sorry. It's incredibly dangerous here. I'll try not to hurt you."

His unbelievable speed so shocked her, she let him hit her. He struck her with the flat of his hand, just below her chin, hard enough to knock her back into the frozen ground, hard enough to render a human unconscious.

Instantly, he was lifting her into his arms, carrying her away like a demented bridegroom. Demented and blind—he hadn't noticed she hadn't been knocked out.

Outraged, she seized his nose and twisted. He howled and dropped her; her butt thudded into the dirt. He clapped both hands to his face, but not before she saw she had given him a nosebleed. Good.

"That hurt." She flipped to her feet and growled, literally growled. She could feel the fine hairs on the back of her neck come to stiff attention. If she'd been in her wolf form, her fur would have been standing out in bristly spikes. "You're an interloper, a trespasser, a creep, and this is private property."

"This is a derrible blace," he warned nasally, still clutching his nose. "You cad be here." He seized her elbow with a bloody hand and tugged. She set her feet and didn't move. He pulled harder. She kicked his ankle and heard the 'crack' and his groan at the same moment. "Lady, for Christ's sake, I'b drying do save your life here!"

"My life doesn't need saving, moron, idiot, twit. Get your degenerate hands off me or I'll snap your spine."

"Fuck it," he muttered. He let go of her so abruptly she staggered. Then he stepped back, pulled out a gun, and shot her in the throat.

Jared watched the gorgeous blonde topple over and had to fight a sigh of relief. Cripes, what a balls-up! He hadn't thought she'd ever go down. His own damned fault—he was so worried about really hurting her he'd gone too easy. Hadn't had the heart to give her a really firm slam. And he'd paid the price: his nose was still streaming blood. The tranquilizer had worked (thank goodness for the Boy Scout motto!), but now what?

After years of research, of greasing palms, of knocking skulls together, of doing anything to get the information he needed, finally, *finally*, he had the murdering bastards cornered. His reconnaissance trip had instantly been cut short when he'd run across the woman. He'd been watching the Wyndhams for weeks and had their routine memorized…this was the time of day when the grounds were usually deserted. But there she was—obviously she hadn't read his recon notes—right in the line of fire, looking at him with those big eyes, probably getting ready to inflate those pipes and screech like a banshee.

Who would have thought a five foot nothing girl with eyes the color of pale violets would be so hard to knock out? Who would have thought she'd pack such a wallop?

Who would have thought he wouldn't be able to stop staring at her?

He knelt, pulled the tranquilizer dart out of her throat, and checked her pulse. Nice and strong. Weirdly strong. It was as if she was in a light sleep, not a drugged unconsciousness. If he didn't know for a fact that werewolves were all men, he'd wonder…

He picked her up, surprised again at how light she was. His dirty laundry weighed more. Now what to do with her? He couldn't leave such a delectable morsel lying around for anyone to nibble. Besides, if she had the freedom to wander Wyndham's grounds, she was probably a source of information. Perhaps a slave to the werewolves.

Anger swelled at the thought of this little sweetie at the beck and call of those monsters. Well, he could help her, and she could certainly help him. When she woke up, he'd pump her for whatever info she could provide.

The thought of pumping the blonde brought a surge of heat to his groin, which annoyed the hell out of him. You've got a dirty mind, buddy, he told himself. Just because you haven't gotten laid in a while…

He started back toward his truck. Wyndham and his pack of murdering dogs weren't going anywhere. His sister had been waiting too long in her grave for vengeance. He'd get the information he needed, see blondie on her way, and come back to avenge his sister.

God help anyone who got in his way.

Chapter Two

Moira opened her eyes and said, "I'm going to rip off your skin for that."

Beside her, the idiot-twit-jerkoff who'd shot her jumped in surprise. She heard the 'thump' of his book hitting the floor, and sat up.

And nearly fell herself, as a wave of dizziness slammed into her. She quickly shut her eyes, and groped for the edge of the bed. "As soon as I get my hands on you. Death. Agony. Screaming. I foresee all of these happening to you. Perhaps several times."

He had picked up his book, and now she felt cool hands on her, easing her back. "Take it easy, cutie. The trank packs a punch."

"Believe me, schmuck, putz, moron," she said. "You don't know what a punch is."

"You shouldn't even be awake yet," he soothed.

She seized his wrist, twisted, ready to crush the bone into splinters, already hearing his screams...

"Cut that out, it tickles."

"Dammit! How long am I going to have the strength of a newborn?" She had meant to shout thunderously. Instead what came out was a pitiful wheeze.

"Probably for the rest of the day." And did the lout have the gall, the temerity, the *nerve* to sound apologetic? After punching her and shooting her and trespassing?

"Why were you trespassing?"

She opened her eyes and took in the room at a glance and a sniff: cream and white bedroom, south-facing window, double bed, wool blankets, hardwood floors in dire need of a waxing, mothballs in the closet, cedar lined wardrobe. And *him*, sitting on the lone chair, holding his book (*Vengeance for Dummies*) and looking at her with honest interest. His dark blue eyes were thoughtful, and bracketed with laugh lines. As if he ever laughed. His hair was down from the ponytail; the sandy strands brushed his shoulders.

"I'm glad you asked," he said. Unfortunately, she'd forgotten the question. "That's a bad place. Do you work there? Do they force you? It doesn't matter. You don't have to go back, sweetie."

"Thanks, *sweetie*." Ugh. Had this oaf been sent to warn the Wyndhams about something? Alarm pierced the fog produced by the drug. "Is Michael in danger? Or Jeannie?"

His face didn't change, but his lips went white. And his scent...it shifted so quickly it nearly burned her nostrils. Acrid smoke. The smell of danger, the smell of hate. "How long have you known him?" he asked slowly, pleasantly. "Wyndham?"

Be careful, Moira. "Forever," she said shortly. "He's my boss." *And a whole host of other things you'll never, never understand.* "And if he's in trouble, you've got to tell me. And if you're bringing trouble to him or his, I'll kill you."

"God, you're beautiful," he said softly, which was not the usual response to a death threat. "You should see how fierce you look. He's not worth that kind of loyalty. If you knew what he was…"

If you knew what I am… She was starting to get really, really angry. Oh, for a full moon right about now! It wasn't just the humiliation of being snatched practically from her front yard. It was that he was an ordinary man, nothing special at all, and he had made it look *easy.* "Who are you?" she practically snapped.

"The UPS guy. But we were talking about you, cutie."

"We were not." She felt like leaping from the bed and throttling the information out of him. "And you haven't answered my question."

"Well," he said with maddening reason, "you haven't, either."

Like that, is it? Think you can outsmart me, monkey boy? We'll see.

"My jaw," she said, "hurts like hell." She made her eyes go big; blinked pathetically. "Why'd you hit me? I wasn't doing anything."

Monkey boy had the grace to look embarrassed. "Sorry," he muttered. "I didn't want you to raise the alarm. Besides, you don't want to be there, anyway, hon. It's a bad place. It's going to get a lot worse, too."

Moira wasn't listening anymore. Her head was clearing, though her body still felt as limp as overcooked pasta. An alarming series of facts was ripping through her brain.

Fact: this man managed to get on the grounds without anyone spotting him until he was on top of her.

Fact: he knew how to fight.

Fact: he had come armed.

Fact: he had drugged her, taken her away, and no one knew, and no one had stopped him.

Fact: he didn't like Michael.

Fact: he seemed to like her.

Fact: she had to stop this man.

Fact: she couldn't do shit until she had her strength back.

Fact: she couldn't let him *leave* until she had her strength back. More, she wouldn't leave, not until she better understood exactly what he represented for her pack.

Conclusion? Nakedness was in her future. Possibly quite a lot of it. He was a man and she had, quite frankly, a nice rack. He'd take one look at her tits and forget everything except his name. She'd buy recovery time and pump him for all the information she could.

It was annoying: she could count on one hand how many times she'd gotten laid in the last two years; she was extremely selective. Or, as her friend Derik put it, "weirdly frigid". Now she had to expend precious energy to seduce this human.

Moira was not a promiscuous woman by any means…not, in fact, strictly a woman at all. A pack animal first and forever, everything she was, did, and said was shaped by that knowledge, that identity. When the leader was in danger, the pack was in danger.

When the pack was in danger, she'd do whatever it took.

"My head," she whispered, breath-soft.

"What?" the idiot said, bending closer.

Fighting the urge to shriek, "Gotcha!", she put her mouth right near the cup of his ear and murmured, "My head hurts soooooo much…may I please have a glass of water?"

"Oh. Sure. I'm sorry, I should have…" Moron Boy moved away, and she couldn't help staring at the exceptional way his butt filled out the seat of his jeans. Yes indeed, the world-class ass had a world-class ass. She wrenched her thoughts back on a more business-like track…then remembered his butt sort of *was* the business at hand, at least until her metabolism blasted the last of that hateful trank out of her system.

The idiot came back with a glass of water, which she promptly spilled all over her blouse. "Oh, it's cold!" she squealed, inwardly groaning—Derik would be laughing his head off if he could see this—and outwardly shuddering as her nipples came to stiff attention. What's-his-face had been helping her sit up, and nearly dropped her back into the pillows. "Do you have a shirt I can borrow?" She fumbled at the buttons of her soaked blouse.

Jared blinked, taking in Moira's smooth, pale skin as she stripped the wet fabric away. He wondered if she had a fever. He wondered if *he* had a fever. He knew who this little cookie was. He'd taken her prints while she'd been unconscious, scanned them into his laptop, and found out her name over an hour ago. Technology was swell.

Moira Wolfbauer, place of residence: Wyndham Manor. Place of business: Wyndham Manor. Employer: Michael Wyndham. But she'd tried her hand at social work just out of college, lucky for him, and thus her prints were on file. Mother deceased, father unknown. He'd pretended to know none of this, of course, and began a gentle interrogation, and hadn't been pleased to hear how protective she was toward the Wyndhams.

Obviously fond of the asshole, what was she up to? She'd threatened to kill him, had assaulted him, and was pulling off her blouse and—yep, there went the bra—a frothy, lilac-colored concoction that exactly matched her eyes.

All right.

It would take more than a wet blouse to distract him.

He was Jared Rocke and he would have his vengeance. He was Jared Rocke and she had the nicest rack he'd ever seen, all creamy white skin with nipples the color of wild roses. He was Jared…uh…Rocke…and…

"Aren't you cold?" he asked hoarsely.

"Extremely," she whispered, her hands on his shoulders, pulling him down, her mouth by his ear, her small white teeth sinking into his earlobe, and the sensation shot straight from his ear to his groin.

He groped, seeking a blanket to cover her, and instead his hands found the delicious firmness of her breasts. She arched against him, her tongue in his ear, and his mouth found her throat. She wriggled delightfully, tugged at him, and then his shirt was sliding off his shoulders and floating to the floor.

Her wriggling had been to good effect; she was nude, he was nude, their clothes a tumbled heap on the floor. Her soft skin made for an erotic contrast against the wool blankets, and for a moment all he could do was stare. Her violet eyes were huge, dominating her face, the arched golden brows above them making her look sweetly surprised. Her short hair was a delightful muss of tumbled blonde curls, curls so light they were almost silver, and her limbs were slim but strong-looking. Her nails were short, almost brutally so, and he had time for a quick, analytic thought: They're short because she bites them all the time. He wondered what a cookie this cute had to worry about. Men probably fell over themselves trying to take care of her.

Then she opened her arms and he fell into her embrace, and that was the end of his analysis. For the first time in years, thoughts of vengeance fled his mind as he buried himself in her creamy softness.

Moira braced herself for the oaf's full weight, but to her surprise he caught himself on his hands and came into her gently, almost carefully. His hand caressed her messy hair, and then his mouth came down on hers, his tongue skimming across her teeth and, when she obligingly parted her lips, probing her mouth. His taste overwhelmed her, all smoky masculine heat, and she gasped.

She'd never mated with someone who wasn't pack. This was partly out of self-imposed obligation to her mother and partly out of pure concern. She had always, in some part of her subconscious, worried about hurting an ordinary man. And really, wasn't that her problem? She had promised her mother she wouldn't mate into the pack...but couldn't bring herself to mate with an ordinary human. Now here she was, buying time, and he didn't seem so ordinary, this man, and his hands, what his hands were doing, that didn't seem all that ordinary eitherrrrrrrrrrr...

"Oh!" Her hips bucked. He moved, kneeling beside her, and his thumb settled back atop her clitoris, his fingers spread and resting against her thighs, barely touching, almost *not* touching, but moving so slowly and delicately that she could almost...feel it...and it was driving her crazy. Meanwhile, he had reached for her breast, was pinching her nipple between his thumb and forefinger, hard enough to almost hurt. Between the throbbing of her nipple and the light, delicate, feathery touch between her legs, she was halfway to a climax. Ridiculous! He'd been touching her for less than a minute. She wasn't a goddamned windup doll. She didn't even *like* him. She didn't even...she didn't...she...she felt a flood of heat between her legs and reached out.

She found him, hard and hot and long, and squeezed, and his eyes tipped up and he stared blindly at the ceiling, the muscles in his neck standing out in rigid relief. He turned his hand and his thumb was now wiggling inside her.

Moira reached for him again but he kept that maddening distance, almost as if he were afraid to be too close to her. She opened her eyes wide, and in the afternoon light had a postcard-perfect look at him, at the way the light bathed him, made him seem more tan than he was. She could see the muscles moving beneath his taut flesh and, reaching up, felt the tension in his abdomen. He was holding himself back, rigidly so, and she wondered why. She could smell his urgent lust and it kindled her own; she knew he wanted to shove her down and bury himself inside her until they were both screaming. So why did he hold back?

More, she wondered how she could have gotten caught up so quickly in what had started out as a stalling technique, an act she had been prepared to dislike, or at least find dull.

He smiled at her, reached for her, cupped her chin in his hand. They stared at each other and Moira forgot to breathe, so amazed that there could be such a tender, perfect moment between strangers.

Then he eased her over, onto her stomach, and nudged her thighs apart with his knee. She could feel his thumbs on either side of her spine, pressing, soothing, and instinctively arched into his touch. Then she felt a silky firmness, and realized he was dragging the tip of his cock down her spine, between the cleft of her buttocks, and pausing at the opening of her vagina. She waited expectantly, but he paused. Bent. Murmured.

"I'm Jared."

She said nothing, just surged toward him.

"And you're Moira."

The bare tip of him was teasing her nether mouth, almost easing inside but not quite, and she swallowed a groan. His fingers were on her, spreading her wide for him, but still he didn't enter, still he lingered.

"Say it, Moira."

"Jared." The word was nearly wrenched from her. "You're Jared."

He chuckled, deep in his throat, almost a purr. "Nice to meet you."

He pushed forward and was almost—almost!—inside her, but not quite. She began to shake. Had she imagined she'd have the upper hand in this seduction? Had she really?

"Please…"

"Moira, we're going to have a nice long talk when I'm finished." Coming inside her now, the full, engorged head pushing, pushing. "About you…" Another inch. "the company you keep…" Another. "And your boss." Abruptly he was gone from her, and she could have cried. His finger replaced his cock, dipping, teasing, feeling her slippery wetness, and then he was stroking the tight bloom of her anus, gently rubbing the rich core of nerve endings there. She made a surprised sound which escalated to a muffled shriek as he slowly pushed his finger past that tight muscular ring.

"Easy."

"Don't." She tried to scramble away—she had never, no one had *ever*—but he nudged her again and she couldn't get the leverage she needed. When he was up to the first knuckle she felt his cock at the mouth of her vagina, and there was no gentle easing this time, this time he was instantly inside her, while his finger slid around slowly, out just a touch and then back in, no big dramatic strokes, just an overall pressure and gentle wriggling. She could feel him everywhere, filling her up, taking everything…

"Yes, we'll have a nice long talk," he said, his voice so gritty she could scarcely understand him. He pulled out and his finger stilled; she was reasonably certain her heart would stop. "About your unfortunate choice of associates." He slammed all the way in.

She screamed.

She screamed into the pillow as he thrust, rocked, as he took her again and again, one hand on the small of her back, one hand…doing things inside her, doing things no man had ever…and always his cock, throbbing and huge and a terrible thing, doing his bidding, ignoring her pleas, her cries, just shoving and thrusting, and it was a terrible thing, a terrible *wonderful* thing, because somehow the tables had turned, she wasn't using him, he was using her.

She would kill him. She would kill him for making her scream. She would kill him if he stopped.

"Moira," he groaned. He wouldn't let her move, wouldn't listen to her cries, but his hands on her were gentle. "Moira, ah, *God*." His tempo increased, he slammed into her, the bed moved, she braced herself and shoved back as hard as she could, because she could sense it, feel it, her orgasm was on the horizon, was almost there, and another finger joined the first inside her, stretching her, and that was enough, that tipped her over.

She tried to throw back her head and howl, but all that escaped was a wild groan as she bucked against him. She felt him clench behind her, felt his seed pour into her, could actually feel the temperature change as he heated her up from the inside, and came again, so quickly and fiercely that white spots danced on the edge of her vision.

He pulled out of her, away from her, and she collapsed, alone, on the bed. She lay on her stomach for long moments, shaking from the aftereffects of the most cataclysmic sex *(with a human! a human!)* she'd ever had, then finally rolled over and looked at him.

To her surprise, he'd pulled on his jeans, had sat down in the chair and was watching her with hungry interest, the way a wolf watches a limping fawn. She could still smell the musk they had made. Could smell herself, on him.

"Now," he said, smiling, and she didn't much care for that smile, not at all, "let's talk about your boss."

Chapter Three

Moira sucked in her breath in a startled, hurt gasp. "You...you were using me."

He blinked. "Well, you were using me first. In fact, you sort of gave me the idea."

She glared. She felt like a fool—where did she get off, accusing him of anything? She sounded like a brat. Well, she couldn't help it. Right now, she *felt* like a brat. He was right, but that didn't make accepting it easier...or lessen the hurt. However, she would eat her own eyeballs before letting him see how she felt. "Yes, that's true, I did start things," she said slowly. "It's just as well, since you apparently enjoy forcing women to get them to do what you want."

Score! Bright color jumped into his cheeks. Suddenly she felt a bit better. It was hard to feel triumphant, thought, when her thighs were still throbbing from what he'd been doing to her. For a while—a teeny, tiny while—she'd forgotten all about the pack, about this man being a threat to her leaders. It just...just went completely out of her head. She could count how often this had happened on one finger. Yesterday, she would have been able to count it on no fingers.

Jared cleared his throat, obviously piqued to see her interest was elsewhere. "Now...where were we? Oh, right. Your scumsucking boss. You—"

"I'm not telling you spit about Michael Wyndham, you cretinous globulous fornicator, and you can just—stop laughing!"

He'd thrown his head back at "globulous" and was still chortling, despite her specific order to the contrary. He finally stopped and looked at her admiringly. "Has anyone ever told you how you insult people in threes? Cretinous-globulous-fornicator? Schmuck-putz-moron? Anybody mention this before?"

"Yes. Michael Wyndham, for one." That wiped the smirk off his face. "I don't know what you want with him or his, but he's—"

The brother I never had.

"—my dearest friend and not only am I *not* going to tell you things about him, I'm going to put you to the floor if you go near him with harmful intent."

Of course, now *Michael* would be laughing at the thought of her defense, because a pack leader who couldn't fight off intruders wouldn't be a pack leader very long. Still, her pride demanded some sort of action.

He shook his head at her. "You poor kid. You have no idea what he is, do you? I suppose you're fooled by a pretty face."

"I wasn't fooled by yours," she said coldly. He grinned. It made him look years younger. It made him look nice. When he most assuredly *was not*.

She sat up suddenly, testing herself, pleased to find she wasn't dizzy. In a bound she leaped out of the bed and stood on the floor, fists planted on her hips. Jared's gaze lowered to her breasts and she could practically hear his I.Q. dropping. Pretty soon his mouth would fall open and a silvery line of saliva would start tracking down his chin. "I'm *out* of here, schmuck, putz, idiot. I don't appreciate being kidnapped and drugged and—er—seduced—"

"Technically," he pointed out mildly, "you were the one to introduce sex into the equation. I was just—er—a willing pupil."

"Details. Anyway, stay away from the Wyndhams, or I'll pull off your ears and you can use them for cufflinks." With that, she whirled and marched toward the smell of Comet cleanser…presumably the bathroom.

It *was* the bathroom. Excellent. Shutting and locking the door behind her, she ignored the laughter coming from the bedroom. Moira had always been the shortest person in any room and was used to people—*men*—laughing at her fierceness. The laughter usually stopped when they had to spit out their back teeth to avoid choking.

It was time—past time—to get the hell out of Dodge. She didn't trust herself to remain around The Insufferable One. When he laughed he threw his head back and she thought about nibbling on his throat, licking until she tasted his sweat and—oh, yes, it was time to leave.

She spotted the window above the toilet and opened it. *Three stories up— hmmm. Big house.* She could easily get to the ground, but there was the small problem of being naked. Not that she cared—no werewolf cared—but she was supposed to pretend to care. A lot more humans lived in this town than werewolves, even here, the seat of Michael and Jeannie's power.

She snatched at the shower curtain—a silly thing with imprints of grinning ducks, and were the little bastards mocking her? They were!—and tugged it down. There was a paft-paft-paft! sound as the curtain hooks disengaged, but she didn't hear approaching footsteps. Good.

In a flash she wrapped it around herself, a sort of plastic, duck-laden toga. Wriggling through the window with a minimum of grunting, she dropped to the porch roof, about twenty-five feet straight down.

And fell through it.

That wasn't in the plan, she thought, dizzy with surprise. *Stupid old Cape Cod houses with shoddy porch roofs! And are those splinters in my…aarrgh! This day is never going to end.* She slowly climbed to her feet and heard Jared thundering down the stairs.

She ran.

Chapter Four

Moira limped into the combination dining hall/family room at Wyndham Manor (or, as Derik called it, Carnivore Central). For a moment she just watched them, drinking in the cozy domestic scene. She'd brought chaos and bad news (and splinters) with her, and was loath to disturb them.

Derik, her oldest friend, was deeply engrossed in a back issue of *Martha Stewart Living*. He was tall, broad, rippling, muscular, etc., etc., and made a quiche like nobody's business. His Chilean sea bass, served on a bed of sautéed spinach, could make grown men weep. Derik was convinced Ms. Stewart was a cleverly concealed werewolf, and read each magazine to tatters, looking for clues. When the article on steak *tartare* came out, he was sure she'd made a fatal slip.

Jeannie and Michael, her pack leaders, were stretched out on the carpet in front of a crackling fireplace. Baby Lara was lying between them. She would carefully extend a bare, pink foot (a foot that looked quite a bit like a pork chop with toes), giggle while her mother tickled it, then would withdraw, and slowly extend the other foot for her father.

Jeannie had settled in, if not seamlessly, at least with minimal trouble after that first hellish week. Moira often wondered if Jeannie thought of her old life. She'd never had friends to the manor, and never talked about her family. It was almost as if she hadn't really come alive until Michael had—almost literally!—swept her off her feet.

Moira felt the usual envy crawling up from the back of her throat, and fought it down. She was happy for Michael. She was. And she adored Jeannie. It was just…hard to take sometimes. That was all. They were so happy, and she'd just had the best sex of her life with a man who was trying to pump her for information.

She delicately cleared her throat ("Ah-CHEM!"), gratified to hear the yells of dismay. After the bruising her pride (and bottom!) had endured today, she was grateful to be surrounded by family.

Jeannie, her best friend and the pack's alpha female, was yelling the loudest. The leggy blonde rushed over to her, holding baby Lara and raking Moira with her piercing, blue-eyed gaze.

"What the hell happened to you?"

"Glah!" Lara added, waving a chubby hand.

Moira caught the baby's hand, kissed it gently. Lara had her mother's lungs, and her father's charisma. With a headful of dark, glossy curls and eyes the color of good cognac, she was a striking infant.

Michael took her in at a glance—bumps, bruises, smelling of sweaty sex and plastic, tired and pissed off. "Who should I kill?" he asked calmly.

"Are you okay?" Derik asked, hurrying over to join their small group..

"Only my pride has been savaged." She felt the shower curtain start to slip and adjusted it. "But probably permanently." Directly to Michael and Jeannie: "Can we talk?"

"Don't pull that," Derik protested. A broad-shouldered blonde, he and Moira had often been mistaken for siblings. Except for the fact that he towered over her, they looked a great deal alike, although Derik's eyes were the green of wet leaves. "I want to hear what happened, too. Start with, 'I went for a walk,' and finish with 'then I walked in wearing a ducky shower curtain'."

"Not now," she said, and hated it, because Derik really *was* like a brother to her, and she had no secrets from him. He'd informally adopted her as a littermate when she'd come to live at the mansion after her mother's death.

But the pack leader deserved to hear about the threat first—Jared had named Michael specifically. Michael would decide who to tell, after. "Come on, you guys. This shower curtain is itchy."

Jeannie unceremoniously handed Lara to Derik. The baby yelped in protest, then shrieked happily as Derik tossed her four feet in the air. "Later, Moira," he called after them. As in, *You'll be telling me the whole story, right?*

"Later, Dare." She used the nickname he'd had since they'd been small. The man would do anything if you triple-dog-dared him.

She marched into the soundproofed den and waited until Michael shut the door. Then she told them how she'd spent her afternoon. She left out nothing, save for how astounding and wonderful the sex had been. She was feeling very guilty about that.

Michael's eyes were thoughtful, distant. "Huh."

"'Huh', he says." Jeannie shook her head in annoyance. "Let's go back to the house and find out what this Jared's problem is." Moira could see every one of the woman's protective instincts was aroused. "Or have him arrested."

"For?" Michael asked mildly.

"Trespassing." She was scowling, but leaned into him for comfort. The scowl eased as he gently rubbed her shoulders. "Being a flaming asshole. Rape."

Moira coughed. "Uh...it wasn't exactly..."

"Never mind semantics! He's out to get you, Mike. I won't have it, I tell you I *will not have it!*"

Moira didn't say anything. Jeannie had become one of the family, and was so utterly fearless, it was often hard to remember she wasn't a werewolf. This was hardly the first time someone had come gunning for Michael. He controlled an admirable fortune and had three hundred thousand werewolves at his back. He was a tempting target.

"I really think we need to go over there and fire a warning shot into his spine," Jeannie continued. Michael was still rubbing her shoulders, and she raised her hands and closed them over his, gripping tightly. "Fix him somehow. Neutralize his ass."

"What do you propose we do, dear one?"

"Um, hmm, I'm not sure, let me think, how about...*lock him up!*"

"Then he skips bail and he's out and about with a hidden agenda. No."

"You're insufferable. Must you always think of every stupid little thing?"

He smiled at her. There weren't many people who dared speak to Michael Wyndham in such a way. The pack had been deferring to him since he was in training pants. He loved his wife's sharp tongue. "Every stupid little thing? I thought of going after you, didn't I?"

"Har, har."

His smile faded and he looked right at Moira, who'd been watching their interaction with undeniable longing. "Moira, will you go back?"

"Of course." She had figured out the problem as quickly as Michael had. Obviously Jared was a dangerous man…but was he alone? What exactly did he want, and why? And how far was he going to go in order to achieve his goal? Did he want to bring down just Michael, or Jeannie and baby Lara? The entire pack? For what purpose? When? She cursed herself for not having thought of this before jumping out the window. But there was time to make up for it. "Let me get changed and I'll leave right away."

"Leave?" Jeannie's fingers were twitching and Moira could tell, just tell, her friend was wishing for her gun. "Why?"

Moira started sidling toward the door. When the Wyndhams fought, chandeliers shook and foundations cracked. And Jeannie, a good woman in all things, was still a human. She would never be pack, and could never truly understand their motivations. She'd get it intellectually. But she would never feel it.

"Moira is going to go back to that house, and stay with Jared, and get all the information out of him she can, however she can." Michael said this with admirable calm, then waited.

Jeannie's eyes widened and seemed to actually bulge. "Stay put!" she snapped at Moira, who was tentatively reaching for the doorknob. "Moira, you don't have to go."

"Really, I'd be more comfortable up in my room—"

"I meant back to *him*."

"Of course I have to. We need to know what he's up to. And I'm in a unique position—he thinks I'm a cute bimbo twit. Also," she added, ignoring the rush of heat to her cheeks, "he likes fucking me."

Jeannie gaped at her, then swung toward Michael. "Michael, don't make her go! She doesn't have to—to whore for us."

Moira laughed, then clapped a hand over her mouth.

"Werewolves don't whore," he said, fighting a smile of his own, "and I'm not making Moira do anything. She only came here as a courtesy, you know. To—how d'you put it? Keep us in the loop." He glanced at her over the top of his wife's head and they shared a moment of perfect understanding.

"It's not right," Jeannie said stubbornly.

"Protecting us? Your daughter? Our friends?"

"Well…okay…" She exhaled sharply, puffing blonde strands out of her face. "I feel stupid having to say this out loud, but she shouldn't have to sleep with him."

"It's a sacrifice I'm willing to make," Moira said, straight-faced, but her cheeks felt very warm now. Michael looked at her sharply, and arched a dark eyebrow.

"Moira," he said, "can take care of herself. It's not like you to moralize, Jean."

Jeannie looked from her husband to her friend. She looked at them the way one might look at a new form of life: with superstitious awe.

After a long moment, Jeannie shook her head. Usually the difference between their cultures and species didn't seem so great, but today the gap yawned. "You'll do as you please," she told him, "you always do. But expecting Moira to put herself in danger for you, to have sex with a bad guy for you...that's going too far. It's—" She glanced at Moira and stopped. Moira was staring at her with a total lack of comprehension. "Oh, forget it. I'm obviously the only one who's got a problem with this. Fine, knock yourself out, have a grand old time, don't forget to write."

She marched across the room, punctuating her exit by slamming the door. Michael turned and looked at the couch. "It's about as uncomfortable as it looks," he mournfully informed Moira. "What a pity I'll be sleeping there, probably for the rest of the week."

Who are you kidding? Try a month. Moira smiled wanly. "It's actually a little flattering—if she didn't think so highly of me, she wouldn't have such a problem with me going back. But I can't think of how to explain it to her...why it's *not* a problem. Why I have to do it...in fact, why I should be halfway back to the house already."

"Yes, but first this. You've got to be really careful. Not just for your own sake. If Jared gets too close..." He smiled, showing his teeth. They looked very white and very sharp and might have fooled someone slow to notice the smile didn't reach his eyes. "I'd hate for my wife to have to shoot another bad guy on my property. The noise might wake the baby."

"He won't get close to them. And even if he did," she said matter-of-factly, "it will be very hard for him to harm my lady and my future sovereign while I'm chewing on his spinal cord."

Now the smile did reach his eyes. "Oh, Moira. Have I told you how much I love you today?"

They laughed together, like littermates.

Chapter Five

Jared told himself to stop worrying about Moira.

Impossible.

Which was annoying, because he had far more important things to worry about. His sister's murder had been too long unavenged. He was in place at last, ready to strike, a blonde, blue jean wearing hammer of vengeance.

But instead of oiling his guns, practicing his sleeper hold and making sure his revenge T-shirt was clean—in general, fantasizing about blood and screaming and other good stuff like that—he was fretting about blondie.

He didn't dare go back out to the porch. Every time he saw the hole in the roof and the scattered debris on the floor, he cringed, an action frowned upon by the Marines and the varied underworld types who'd helped him prepare for this week. She had been so desperate to get away from him that she'd flung herself out the window! She had been so desperate to get away from him she had fled on foot—with nothing more than a duck-laden shower curtain covering that lovely bod! As each hour passed he felt more and more like a Grade A jerk…and more and more frantic with worry.

He'd canvassed the quiet neighborhood, with no luck. She'd probably holed up somewhere to nurse a thousand wounds (and a million splinters). Probably dying! All because of—

The doorbell rang.

Jared blinked. No one in town knew who he was, it was too early for Girl Scout cookies, and was there still such a thing as a Welcome Wagon?

Had *Wyndham* sent the Welcome Wagon?

As was his habit, Jared fretted while he cleaned his guns. So he actually held a freshly oiled Beretta. It was a moment's work to slap a full clip in and slide a load into the chamber. Still barefoot and shirtless from his earlier (incredible, wonderful, marvelous lovemaking) tryst with (beautiful, gorgeous Moira) blondie, he padded to the door. By the time he reached it, the delicate tapping became an insistent pounding. Jared flung the door open, his gun already leveled.

At Moira's forehead.

"You're a limited man," was all she said, walking past him. Carrying a suitcase, no less. He stared. He couldn't help himself. She looked as pretty as a spring daisy, wearing a yellow dress which made her eyes seem a darker lavender, almost purple. The hem of the dress stopped a modest inch below her knees, which did nothing to disguise the fact that she was walking around on a world-class pair of stems.

The back of the dress plunged in a deep V, showing off creamy white skin.

"Well," she said, when it was obvious all he could do was gape at her, "I'm back."

"Huh?"

She rolled her eyes and muttered something under her breath. "I... said...I'm...back..." she enunciated loudly, as if he was feeble or deaf. Right now, he *felt* feeble. "I'm staying with you until we get this mess straightened out."

He had the dim feeling he was in the presence of a greater intellect. And awesome tits! He shook his head, hard. Focus, moron, he ordered himself. "Mess?"

"Yes. You're here to do something wretched, horrid, awful, to my friend and boss, Michael Wyndham. I'm here to talk you out of it."

Now he was focused, laser-sharp. "No chance."

"Why?"

"He—he's a monster. He killed someone I loved."

Not a blink from blondie. Not a twitch, not a fake show of sympathy. Just a cool, "No. He didn't."

Jared was surprised, both at her assurance and her inference. And frankly, not hearing her ooze sympathy was something of a relief. Women were either scared shitless of him, or felt sorry for him. Neither was conducive to horniness. And he didn't want Moira's pity. He especially didn't want her fear. It was very important she not be afraid. He couldn't bear it if she flinched back from him.

Jesus, why the hell did he care? Why should it matter if she was scared shitless of him? It would just make his job easier. And how could she defend the monsters so quickly, without knowing any of the details?

"Maybe not him," he said at last. "But one of his dogs."

At 'dogs' her upper lip curled, revealing lovely white teeth. He plunged ahead, unable to believe they were having this conversation. He was explaining things to the woman who worked for the man who **murdered his sister**! "Whatever or whoever, Wyndham is responsible. I don't give two fucks for the details. He's the boss dog. So he's going to tell me where I can find the dog responsible."

"I'll be glad to help you find out who hurt the person you cared for," she said quietly, hefting her suitcase and starting toward the stairs, "but you're wrong about Michael. Totally utterly completely wrong. I'll be around until I can convince you of that."

He watched her climb the stairs, silent. After a moment he wrenched his gaze from her legs and forced himself to think. His gut told him Moira was one of the good guys. His brain screamed exactly the opposite. But he was not the world's greatest thinker, as his father, training instructors, and commanding officers had pointed out on several occasions. He was alive today because he'd listened to his instincts and ignored his brain. He'd be a fool to ignore his gut now, when he was so close.

Moira was a veritable treasure trove of information. Not that she planned on telling him shit. His admiration, already high, went a notch higher. She was a safe, and if he cracked her with just the right tools, he'd get the gold.

After a while he unloaded the gun, put it away, and went up after her.

Chapter Six

"So...what? We're roomies?" Jared asked

"Yes." Moira unpacked the suitcase, shoved her clothes into the empty bureau by the window. And tried very, very hard not to show how pleased she was to see him again. She wasn't the first woman in her family to feel like this, she remembered with excitement and despair. Her mother, too, had been torn between desire and duty. Except her mother had been human, and her father a beta werewolf who left to form his own pack. Left her mother, pregnant and alone in a city by the sea. If not for Michael's father taking them in...

There was a lesson there: love made you stupid. On her deathbed, her mother had praised her former lover, who'd planted his seed one night and then left to better himself. Moira loved her mother, but hated weakness.

"I appreciate what you're trying to do—I think," Jared was saying, sounding confused—as usual. "And I'm glad to see you're all right. In fact, I'm pretty interested in hearing the tale of your trip back to the mansion. And what you did with my shower curtain—I bought a new one, by the way, in case you need to—uh—freshen up. But I'm still a little confused."

"I'm not surprised."

He ignored the sarcasm. "What exactly do you do for Wyndham?"

"I'm his accountant."

"His accountant."

"Yes."

"Uh...you don't look like an accountant."

"Obviously I do, because I am one." 'Accountant' was understating it a bit. She had a Master's in Business Finance, another Master's in International Business Relations, and (this one had been for fun) a Master's in Japanese Literature. "What does your accountant look like?"

"I don't have an accountant," he admitted. "I made about eight grand last year."

Eight grand! She'd signed off on that much for the birthday celebration the week Lara had been born. Heck, her Christmas bonus had been almost twice that. "Hmm. The revenge business isn't terribly lucrative?"

He smiled, which, annoyingly, she felt down to her knees. "That's about right. You know, Moira, if you're going to stay here, we should probably set up some ground rules."

"Such as...?" Here came the tiresome human stuff...he'd sleep on the couch, they'd draw up a bathroom schedule, they'd *talk* out their *feelings* in a really really *constructive* way. He'd explain about how difficult it was to be a modern man when all he really wanted to do was cry and share his enlightened consciousness with some poor bitch, and she'd pretend not to be semi-conscious with boredom.

She squared her shoulders. She would endure much for Michael and Jeannie and Lara. Torture. A physical beating. Sharing feelings in a constructive way. "I'm hearing what you are saying," she said, obediently quoting *Redbook*. "What rules?"

"Well," he said, and she noticed—how had this escaped her?—that he was unbuckling his belt. Now he was sliding his jeans down his long thighs and he wasn't wearing underwear. Now he was kicking the jeans in a pile, pulling his shirt over his head and yanking the band out of his hair. He grinned and then they were flying backward and landing on the bed, his cool nakedness pressed against her, warming her through the thin fabric of her dress. His hair tickled her chin and smelled like wild perfume. "The first rule, I think, is that we should be naked, pretty much all the time."

She laughed. She couldn't help it. Then she was laughing into his mouth as he kissed her. Her hands raced over him, greedy, and he was groping her with about as much finesse. She didn't care. Something about his scent drove her right out of her mind. She thought his first rule was a fine one.

Their thoughts:

He wants to hurt the pack.

She works for the monsters.

But in this moment of clean lust, logic had no force. The only thing that mattered was skin on skin, mouth on mouth. Preferably for hours.

There was a purring riiiiiiip, and then her dress was in pieces. "I'll care about that," she said, panting, "later."

"I'll buy you a new one." He issued a low growl, and then his mouth was on one of her nipples, and then, even better, his teeth were.

"That dress was worth one tenth of your total earnings last year."

"God, I love it when you figure out percentages in your head," he moaned. She could feel his beard stubble between her breasts...on her stomach...between her thighs. "Now talk to me about IRA rollovers and 401(k)s."

She started laughing so hard she lost her breath entirely. Which was all right, because at that moment his tongue darted inside her, and she wouldn't have been able to breathe anyway.

Her hips bucked against his mouth and he reached up, seized her waist, and shoved her back firmly against the mattress. All the while his mouth busily explored between her legs, his lips sucking and kissing and his tongue was probing. Moira heard herself scream.

He pulled back abruptly, leaving her teetering on the edge, and she screamed again, this time in frustration. She scrambled toward him, but he caught her elbows and flipped her. Her face hit the pillows as she was forced down on her stomach.

"God, you have the *most* luscious ass," he groaned, and she felt his hands on her, his fingers kneading her skin, hard.

Hard enough to mark my flesh, she thought with black excitement. Her blood was up so high she literally saw red; the room before her was cloaked in a red haze. Her tongue felt thick in her mouth.

She flipped back over, and grabbed him, and he laughed at her. But he quit laughing when she locked her ankles behind his back and forced his pelvis toward hers. Women had superior lower body strength anyway, and besides, she was probably twice as strong as he was, possibly three times.

He let her do it. In fact, he helped—put his hands between her thighs and gently held her apart, so that when she levered her back up off the mattress to meet him, his cock slid inside her without pause. Right up to the hilt.

They stared at each other for a long moment, then started rocking together. Her legs were still wrapped around him but now he was holding her, too, holding her and kissing her deeply while they thrust against each other, while the bed squeaked out their rhythm.

Now his mouth was on her neck and he was gently biting her throat, then greedily sucking her flesh. *His mark*, she thought again, and spun away into orgasm.

A moment later, so did he. Through a gaze slitted with pleasure, she watched his eyes roll back, felt him stiffen all over.

"Christ," he managed, right before collapsing on her.

"Yes, indeed," she replied. She started to push him off her, but he clung like a lamprey. "For heaven's sake, I need to get up and wash."

"No," he muttered sleepily. "Keep my smell on you. For a while."

A reasonable request. One she liked too much. She started to get up, but his arm tightened across her waist like a bar. She could have snapped it at the elbow, but didn't. Instead she nestled up next to him, and fell asleep.

Chapter Seven

Moira snapped awake in the dark. Where the hell was she?

"Don't. Don't. Don't."

Everything locked into place: she was in Jared's rented house. His stirring had awakened her. And what on earth was wrong with his voice? He sounded like a boy, not a man in his prime.

"Don't be dead. Oh, Jesus, don't…don't be. Dead. Dead. She's dead. My sister's dead! *Somebody help me!*"

She reached out a hand, too late. He sat up so abruptly the back of his head banged into the headboard, flung his arms out hard, belted her right below the eye. It didn't slow him down, or even bring him fully awake.

He lurched from the bed. She pressed a hand to her now-throbbing eye and forced her pupils to dilate. Suddenly what had been dark became light, and she got a good look.

The big, badass werewolf hunter stumbled around the room, hoarse sobs locked in his throat, compulsively rubbing at his hands. "Everywhere." His voice broke. "There's blood and it's just…oh, it's everywhere. Renee, my poor Renee."

He collapsed to his knees and scrubbed at the imaginary blood. Moira watched, horrified. In his recall of the night he found his sister's body, Jared had made the scene all too real for her. She could almost smell the blood.

What are you staring at him for, fool?

She was out of the bed in a bound and actually found herself stepping around the imaginary pool of blood. She bent to him. "Jared, love, it's a dream."

"Renee. Poor Renee. She fought and he…he…and I was too late. If I'd gotten home just half an hour earlier…"

You'd be dead, too. "Renee's out of her pain, dearest. Come back to bed."

"I can't—bed?"

"You're dreaming, Jared. It's just an awful, awful dream. Renee knows you tried. Renee knows you loved her—love her still. You've given your life up for vengeance, isn't that so?"

"It's…yes." Sounding stronger now; the boy's voice was leaving. The man was coming back.

"Lie down with me." She pulled him easily to his feet, although he had twelve inches and fifty pounds on her. She brought him back to bed as she would have led a child. "It's all right."

"No," he said, already slipping back into sleep. "It's never going to be all right."

About that, you may be right.

"Watch out, Moira. They're werewolves. I know it sounds incredible." He yawned, snuggled against her shoulder. "But they're the monsters from the fairy tales. Wyndham and his dogs."

"I know," she said softly. Thinking: *Oh, what will you do when I tell you I'm one of the monsters?*

And why did she care?

She was awakened by a delicious tickling between her breasts, and cracked one eye open to see Jared, nibbling her cleavage. It was still dark out—not even five o'clock in the morning.

"Did your mother wean you a bit too early, Jared?"

He snorted, the sound muffled against her flesh. "Very funny. Let's take a shower. My mouth tastes like a dead rat shat in it."

"Thanks for the visual. You should write for Hallmark—yee-ouch! Well, you should. And why are we getting up?"

He wouldn't look at her. "Can't sleep," he muttered. "Every time I fall all the way under, I—I wake back up. C'mon."

A few minutes later, morning ablutions completed, he was soaping her all over while the scalding shower beat down on them. Moira groaned aloud from the sheer pleasure of it. Her motto had always been, if it doesn't turn your skin bright red, it's not a shower.

They weren't talking about his dream. She wasn't sure he even remembered stumbling around the room, washing his dead sister's blood off his hands. She decided not to bring it up.

"You're probably the smartest woman I've ever met," he informed her out of nowhere, rinsing her breasts off again, then lathering his hands and running them over her slippery flesh. "And definitely the prettiest."

"Where'd *that* come from? And thank you. You're probably right. About the smart thing, I mean."

"And so modest!"

She shrugged under the water. "My whole childhood, I was my mother's doll. Little, blonde, cute. Something to be dressed up and fussed over. All she talked about was my looks. So it was all people talked to her about. I was a smart child, really smart. So *I* talk about *that*. My looks are boring."

"They're certainly not boring, cutie," he said, "but I can see how that would have been a major pain."

"Yes, it was. Sorry to digress into 'poor Moira's poor childhood' silliness." She shrugged, embarrassed. "Also, I think my breasts are clean enough."

"They're filthy," he solemnly informed her. "Really. Yech. I won't rest until I can eat off them."

She felt her lips twitch. "Indeed." His hands felt marvelous on her skin. She enjoyed the sensation for a moment, then went back to his earlier, most interesting comment. "The smartest, huh?" The pack took her brains for granted, and men who didn't know her didn't care that she was smart. She found it refreshing and marvelous to run into someone who noticed her brains, commented, and thought she was just fine. "Really? I mean, you must have known a lot of women." *Given your boudoir skills, I would guess thousands.*

"Mm-hmm," he said carelessly. "You've probably got twenty, thirty I.Q. points on me, easy." He sounded as threatened as if he was telling her she had two, three cup sizes on him, easy.

Opening her eyes wide, she ignored the stinging spray. "And that doesn't bother you?"

"Hell, no." He shrugged, water bouncing off his broad shoulders. "Everybody's good at something."

"Well." She chose her words carefully. This was one of the most interesting conversations she'd had in a while. "I'm definitely book smart. You're more...tricky, like. In a lot of ways, that's better than having a head for numbers."

"I know," he said casually.

"Now who's being modest?" She goosed him and he slapped her hand away.

"Careful, I almost maimed you with my incredible reflexes."

"Oh, sure."

His smile faded, and suddenly he looked through her, not at her. Just like that, he was somewhere else. "I was always good at fighting. Busting skulls, that stuff. I got in lots of fights as a kid—I mean, guys were *always* following my sister around, Renee, her name was..."

"I know."

He stopped talking. His hands stopped moving on her body. His eyes were narrow, blue slits. "How d'you know?"

"You dreamt about her last night. You were calling her name."

"Oh." She couldn't tell if it was the heat of the water or embarrassment at his vulnerability that made his face redden. "Okay. Say, I didn't hurt you, did I? Sometimes the nightmare...it makes me thrash about a bit. Sleepwalk, too."

"No," she lied. Of course she'd had a spectacular black eye during the night. And of course it had healed by morning.

"Oh. That's good." She pumped shampoo into her palm and started washing his hair, running her fingers through the long strands. He arched unconsciously beneath her touch for a moment, then continued. "Anyway, I'd get into fights to keep the boys respectful, you know? And my dad, before he died he signed me up for all these martial arts classes, and boxing, that kind of stuff. To keep me out of trouble—he figured if I was punching people in a class after school, I'd be too tired to get into fights. By the time I graduated high school I could pretty much kick anybody's ass. The Marines really liked having me around."

"I'll bet. That's why you took it upon yourself to find Renee's killer. It was your job to protect her. And when you couldn't, that last time, the least you could do..."

"Yeah."

They were silent, and then Jared rinsed his hair and started running his soapy hands down her back, started kneading her buttocks.

Moira thought, his *body* is his weapon. He's been using all those fighting skills to track down his sister's killer like a bloodhound. That's why he got the drop on me so easily. My whole life, I've taken my physical strength for granted. I couldn't do a karate chop if someone held a gun to my head. He's not an intellectual, and he doesn't have circus strongman strength. He's cunning, and quick, and can sneak up on people with no trouble.

He's more like a wolf, she realized with a bolt of excitement, than I am.

Could this man be the one? She would never worry about accidentally hurting Jared; he could take care of himself. Certainly it was no problem if he were to accidentally hurt her…she was a fast healer, and pain was, at times, almost a friend to her. Best of all, most wonderful of all, he absolutely didn't care that she was an adding machine on legs. That alone made it worth staying with him.

Her excitement derailed abruptly when she recalled one simple, devastating fact: he had no clue what she was. And once he found out, he would at least walk—run!—out of her life forever. Unless he considered her responsible for his sister's death, too.

How, she wondered forlornly, had the tables turned so quickly? Yesterday she would have seen him dead. Today tears sprang to her eyes at the thought of him leaving.

His hands were still stroking, still soaping, and she could feel his erection against her stomach. He pressed her close to him, holding her tightly.

"Moira, Moira," he whispered, his words almost lost under the thrumming of the shower, "a guy could fall in love. But if you're holding out on me…" He came into her, hard, a brutal shove, and she bit back a cry of mingled pain and pleasure. "…you'll live to regret it."

She didn't doubt it.

He picked her up, pulled her legs around him, and held her easily, pinning her against the slick tile like a butterfly to a board. He shoved, shoved, shoved, and it hurt, she wasn't ready for him, and she *loved* it, loved being used roughly. Had she really disdained coupling with a human because she thought they were weak? She had thrice his strength but, without leverage, could only take it. Take him. His length filled her up, took her over, he was deep, so deep. He was shoving angrily but his hands were gentle; she had a flash of intuition

(*he's angry because he wants me so badly…wants me but doesn't quite trust me*)

and then could only concentrate on what he was doing to her. She squirmed against the tile. "You're hurting me," she whispered.

"I know." He gently tongued her earlobe…then bit it.

Now his thrusts came easier because her body was easing his way, was flooding her with wetness. "Damn you," he whispered, his eyes gleaming, "I never wanted this to happen…ahhhhhhhhh…"

"I'm sorry," she gasped.

"You feel so slick, so sweet. I'm really close. I'm going to come and… you're…not."

"Don't you dare!" was as far as she got before she could feel him pulsing inside her. Abruptly, he pulled away, leaving her shaking with need.

"Jared…"

"What the hell are we going to do, bright eyes?"

"Jared…"

"It's a simple question, Moira," he said patiently, giving her nipple an impudent tweak. Oh, how she hated him. "A guy could fall in love, but I've got to keep my priorities straight."

His fingers. His fingers, between her legs, finding her throbbing clit. Stroking it, rubbing it. Even squeezing, very, very gently. Her legs trembled, threatened to spill her to the tile. Her head rolled back and forth against the shower wall. "You're smack in the middle of a mess, gorgeous, and I don't envy you at all. The question is, what are you going to do about it?"

"Please. Please. Please." The word was wrenched out of her, *shoved* out. "Please, Jared. Don't make me beg."

"But, sweetheart," his mouth very near her ear, "you *are* begging."

She moaned, lost. He took pity on her, knelt, gently spread her apart and lapped, lapped, lapped. She came at once, a shallow spasm that did nothing, that left her wanting him inside her, her need for him a bestial craving. "More," she gasped, demanded, urged. Begged.

He wordlessly led her from the shower, both of them dripping wet. Bent her over the tub. Took her again and again, until the room rang with her screams, until her legs wouldn't support her any longer and she collapsed to the floor, still feeling the spasms from her last orgasm.

Without a word, he lifted her to her feet, dried her with a big, fluffy towel, and tucked her into bed as if she were a precious treasure. Left her to nap.

Humans are weak, was her last thought before spinning into sleep. *In a pig's eye.*

Chapter Eight

When she woke, hours later, she was alone in the bed and utterly ravenous. The smell of frying bacon filled the room, filled her head, and she hurriedly pulled on some clothes and flew down the stairs.

She burst into the kitchen just as Jared slid three eggs onto a plate laden with bacon, toast, sliced tomatoes, home fries, and sausage links. "Morning, sunshine. Do you want some—" Snatching the plate away from him, she sat at the table, grabbed a fork, started shoveling. "—breakfast?"

"Nnnnf."

He grinned down at her. "God, you are the perfect woman. Super smart, awesome in bed, and you eat like a lumberjack." He ruffled her curls. "A sexy lumberjack."

"Mmmfff nnnggg mmmm," she said, or something like that. She swallowed. "This is good. Thanks very much. Being hungry does nothing for my manners." Human manners, she amended silently.

"I can't believe you're not throwing food at me." He turned back to the stove. "After this morning."

"Yes, yes, very non-PC, you beast, it's over between us, hate you forever…salt?"

He turned, blinked at her, then shook his head and nodded toward the salt shaker.

"What, I have to get up?" she complained. "You're standing right there."

"Cripes, you've got nerve!" He whipped around, exasperated. "You know, technically you're my prisoner. I mean, I *did* kidnap you."

"Yes, and then you lost me." At his scowl, she added, "Plus, you're standing *right there*. Besides, you and I both know you'd eat your own feet before hurting any woman. So spare me the 'you are my prisoner, fear me' crapola. And pass the damned salt! Please."

"I'll do it," he said, smirking, "if you'll show me your tits." He paused, obviously braced for shrieks of feminine dismay at his crude request…and nearly fell onto the frying pan as her T-shirt hit him in the face.

"Salt."

"Right." He fetched it for her, gave her left breast a friendly squeeze, and returned to his eggs.

"Thank you. Now there's bacon grease on my nipple."

"I'll take care of that for you," he said, scooping eggs onto another plate. He snapped a glance at her over his shoulder, and winked. "Later." He sat down across from her and fell to.

"Great. You could just pass me a napkin, you know."

"Spoilsport."

They ate in friendly silence, until Jared finally asked, "Do you remember last night?"

"Vividly."

"I mean...my dream."

"Yes." She stopped mopping egg yolk with her toast and looked up. "I'm very, very sorry about your sister."

He looked at her thoughtfully. She noticed he hadn't pulled his hair back in a ponytail, and had to keep brushing back the sandy blonde strands, keeping them out of his face. "And afterward. What I said afterward...I'm pretty sure I told you they're werewolves. Over at Wyndham's."

"Yes, you did." She answered his unspoken question. "I already knew."

Thunderstruck silence, followed by, "And you *work* for them?"

"They're my family." *Get it? My family? Don't make me say it, Jared. Figure it out.*

He shoved his plate back, stood, started pacing. She unobtrusively pulled his half empty plate toward her. Ah, two pieces of bacon left...

"Jesus, if I didn't know for a fact that all werewolves are male, I'd be really worried about—"

"*What?*"

"Don't try to deny it, pretty spy. You know, I had to take a long and very fucking strange road to get to this house, this town, and on the way I met some exceedingly weird people. And heard some strange shit."

"Werewolves are all men." She could barely get the sentence out without giggling. "Who told you that?"

"I paid good money for that information," he said proudly. "And I got it from an honest-to-God werewolf. I watched the beast change...into a bigger beast. And when the moon went down and the sun came up, he told me all about werewolves."

All about bullshit, more likely. "How'd you get him to talk?"

"I was resting the barrel of my shotgun against his testicles while we played Twenty Questions."

"Yes, that would do it." *So he'll never guess the truth about me. Not unless I tell him outright, or show him. So: good? Or bad?* Moira practically squirmed at the odd dilemma. Good for Moira-the-werewolf, because her main goal, always, was the pack's safety. Bad for Moira-the-woman, because this put more distance between her and Jared.

And why did she *care*?

He looked nonplussed at the way she hadn't been horrified to hear about the shotgun, and the testicles. That, in fact, she seemed to hardly be paying attention to his revelations. He resumed pacing. "Which is why you shouldn't be working there. What if one of them *bites* you, for Christ's sake? I didn't think to ask if a woman could get infected that way..."

"You're worried one of them will bite me?" She kept her voice calm, deliberately reasonable, unworried, in contrast to his violent emotions. His anger, coupled with fear for her, burned her nostrils. He was worried about her. She was annoyed and pleased at the same time.

"You might wind up...I don't know..."

"I do know. The biting thing is an old wives' tale. You're a werewolf or you're not. It's a whole different species, Jared, not the measles. Not something you catch."

He digested that, and she could practically hear the wheels turning in his mind. Could see the thought on his face: *Why would she lie? No reason, ergo it must be the truth.* She couldn't help but be warmed at this sign of trust between them. Never mind why would she lie…why should he believe her? And yet he did.

"A hundred years of bad movies are wrong?"

"Not to mention a thousand years of folk lore." Moira suddenly remembered the time she and Derik were kids and had gone to see *An American Werewolf in London.* They had laughed so hard they were kicked out not forty-five minutes into the movie. "The truth is always much more boring than the fable it grew from."

"What if one of them kills you?"

"Never, ever happen."

"Bullshit. Put down that piece of toast, it's mine."

"You left your plate," she protested.

He threw up his hands. "Can we stay on track, please? One of them *has* killed, you don't deny that, right?"

"Right. But tell me why you think Michael knows who killed your sister."

Jared blinked, surprised at the abrupt question, but answered readily enough. "Everything traces back to Wyndham manor, to your boss. Ev-er-ee-thing. The police even had a suspect, but the guy got away clean. He worked there, lived there, probably even had a family there. Then I got close, and he was smoke. Wyndham told the cops he didn't know a thing about it, which was just about the biggest lie since 'this won't hurt a bit'. The suspect worked for Wyndham practically his whole life."

"Was this…about a year ago?"

"How'd you know?"

"I'm just trying to figure out the timeline."

"The name I had was Gerald somebody," Jared confirmed.

Oh shit, oh shit, oh shit. She strove to look thoughtful, rather than horrified. This was good news and bad. Good news because Gerald was dead, and thus unlikely to be murdering anyone else's sister now that he was so much meat in the ground. Bad because Jeannie, Michael's wife, had shot Gerald. Multiple times.

Of course Michael had denied knowledge of Gerald's whereabouts. He couldn't very well tell the police the truth: that Gerald was beneath the White Ivy rose-bushes on the south lawn and, oh by the way, officers, would you like some tea before you haul my mate away in chains? She's pregnant, so make sure she takes her pre-natal vitamins in prison.

"I think I can help you," Moira said slowly. She had no idea what to do. Tell Jared everything and trust him to keep Wyndham secrets? Ha.

Tell him nothing and neutralize him? Hit him when his guard was down and bite the back of his neck until his strong heart stopped beating and his gorgeous eyes closed forever?

I've got a crush on the idiot.

Moira knew her limitations. She was intelligent—okay, *that* wasn't a limitation—but numbers were her game. She had no gift for leadership or strategy. That was Michael's job. She was a foot soldier, plain and simple.

Jared needed to hear about Gerald, but not from her. From Michael and Jeannie, and no one else. Would Jared follow her to Wyndham manor, unquestioning? Just trot right on over to what he assumed was the belly of the beast?

Ha.

"There's something on the back of your neck," she said sweetly.

"What?" He brought his hand up, brushed ineffectually. She put her hand on his shoulder, gently turned him around, and punched him at the base of his skull with her knuckle. Jared obligingly dropped without a sound, and she caught him on the way down.

I'm going to hear about this one for a while, she thought grimly, slinging him over her shoulder like a sack of toys.

Chapter Nine

He opened his eyes and saw he was surrounded by monsters, in a living room or den of some sort. Michael Wyndham, Moira, and Wyndham's hottie wife, Jeannie, were all bending over him, their faces like concerned moons. He was lying on a couch, and could hear the cheerful crackle of a fire nearby.

"You…bitch!" He sat bolt upright, then clutched the back of his neck, which was incredibly stiff. "Aarrgghh! What'd you hit me with, a piano?"

"I'm sorry, Jared." Moira-the-Judas had the nerve to look abashed. She blinked her big purple eyes at him and spread her hands helplessly. "I had to bring you here—we have things to tell you—but I didn't think you'd come if I asked."

"So you coshed me over the head with an iron and kidnapped me?" His hand slid down and around, but his holster was empty.

"Don't get too far up on that high horse of yours," Jeannie Wyndham said dryly. "You did the same thing to my friend yesterday." She waved his gun at him. Jared felt alternately nervous and aroused to see such a pretty woman handling his weapon so comfortably. "My *best* friend. And since you kidnapped my friend and are here in town solely to hurt my husband, you look stupid trying to sound outraged."

"Jeannie," Michael said quietly.

"Well, he does."

"Give him back his gun, please."

"Speaking of stupid." Despite her comment, she popped the clip, ratcheted a bullet out of the chamber, and gave him back all three, absently puffing a hank of blonde hair out of her eyes as she did so. He was so surprised he nearly dropped them on the floor.

"Will you listen?" Wyndham asked quietly. The guy had funny eyes—dark brown, ringed with yellow, dog's eyes, monster's eyes—but his voice was deep and soothing. Too soothing. Jared knew there were people in the world who could make you like them. It was a talent, like being able to raise only one eyebrow. Even knowing all he did about Wyndham, Jared still wanted to shake the guy's hand and hear what he had to say. Watch it, he warned himself. "Mister—ah—Moira?"

Moira cleared her throat. "Sorry. We should have done this right away. Jeannie and Michael Wyndham, this is Jared…uh…" She flushed. "I never did get your last name."

"And after all we shared," he said mockingly, and was gratified to see her blush deepen.

"Knock it off," Jeannie snapped. "You're still on my shit list, buddy-roo. I don't know *why* we're all tip-toeing around you. As far as I'm concerned, you're the bad guy." She smirked at him. "And you know what happens to the bad guy in books and movies, right, Jerked?"

"It's Jared," he said, and to his surprise he had to fight a smile. "Jared Rocke." Jeannie's eyes widened. "Rocke? Your last name is Rocke? Oh my God, that's the silliest name ever."

Wyndham was looking heavenward, as if for divine intervention. "Jeannie…"

"Seriously. It's like a bad romance novel. 'Jared Rocke brooded darkly before sweeping Shanna Silverington into his strong, rugged embrace.' Barf. What's your nickname? Rocky? Rocco? Double barf."

Incredibly, Jared could feel himself relaxing. He sensed no menace from any of the three—of course, he hadn't sensed menace from Moira before she'd bashed him with a serving tray, either. Still, Moira was so contrite, and Wyndham so polite, and Mrs. Wyndham so refreshingly rude, it was hard to stay tense. And what the hell did *that* mean? That Moira was right? The monsters weren't all bad?

He coughed to cover his confusion. "My nickname in second grade was Jared Poopypants, for an incident I refuse to go into, no matter how long you and your husband torture me. Creditors call me Mr. Rocke. My friends call me Jared. I don't know what you guys are," he added truthfully.

"Let's find out," Michael said genially. "Something to drink, Mr. Rocke?"

"Barf," Jeannie said again, but went to the wet bar.

"Yeah, I'd love a beer," he admitted. "And a bottle of aspirin."

Wordlessly Moira stepped behind him, and then he felt her kneading his neck with her small, supple fingers. By the time Jeannie handed him an ice-cold, foamy beer, his neck felt much better. "I'm still pissed at you," he muttered.

She bent to whisper in his ear. "I know. You can take it out on me later. At the house. In your room." Her mouth was hovering outside the cup of his ear and his dick was paying close attention to the conversation. "Do you know any rope tricks?"

"…your sister."

"Mr. Rocke?"

"Jared," he said automatically, trying to shake off the surge of excitement Moira's words had brought. Talk about the wrong place and time! "It's Jared."

"Thank you. I'm Michael, and you've met my wife, Jeannie. I was saying how sorry I was to hear about your sister."

"You'll be even sorrier when you hear the stuff I've been able to dig up."

Michael sat across from him holding a tumbler half full of Scotch. Moira declined a drink, staying behind Jared and gently rubbing his neck, and Jeannie sat next to her husband with a glass full of milk. At Jared's stare, she mumbled, "Still breastfeeding."

For some reason that made him laugh out loud. It seemed to emphasize the wholesome attributes of the room they were in, the pleasant people he was talking to. Death had no place here…not where women breastfed well-loved babies and potential girlfriends promised bondage games.

"I guess Moira can tell you what's been going on as well as I can," he said, because he wanted to hear what Moira had to say about the situation.

She ruffled his hair in response and started to speak. She spoke for quite a while, finishing with, "…and Jared's been tracking the killer. I think—I'm sure—it's Gerald."

Wyndham and his wife looked at each other. Jared was still trying to figure out why he hadn't loaded his gun and killed everyone. Except Moira. Probably except Moira—he still couldn't believe she'd gotten the drop on him so easily. He couldn't believe he was still thinking about the clothesline coiled neatly in the garage! 'Rope tricks', she'd said. Jesus.

The woman—Jeannie—had thrown him off-guard, that was why he was off his stride. She was about as adorable as Moira, and what a temper! She hung around werewolves all day—was married to one!—and hadn't been killed or mutilated or anything like that.

It was sure something to think about.

Then there was his pretty, purple-eyed Moira. She was hiding stuff from him, but he was seeing it less as duplicity and more as loyalty. There was nothing he admired more than loyalty...hell, loyalty to his family had brought him here. It was all pretty damned confusing. He hadn't counted on it becoming confusing. It had seemed pretty fucking black and white just a few days ago.

"Gerald probably did kill your sister—and I'm very sorry," Michael said.

"Really really sorry, Rococo," Jeannie added. "I don't know what I'd do if something horrible happened to Michael or Lara."

Sympathy from the dogs—well, the dog and his wife—he hadn't expected. He had to look away from the genuine kindness on their faces. Liking the dogs was not in the plan. No, sir.

"I only met the man twice...and the second time I killed him," Jeannie added candidly. Jared looked back in a hurry.

"Jeannie..."

"Michael, we've got to tell him." She took a big slug of her drink, and went on passionately, unaware of her milk mustache. If I go to jail, I go to jail...but I don't think Jared's the type to rat out the killer of a killer."

"No, ma'am, I am not. Why don't you tell me what happened."

"Yes, why don't I? Okay. Gerald was this disgusting horrible werewolf—and no, that's not redundant, so don't say it. Although it's an opinion I had myself not too long ago," she added, giving her husband a formidable frown. "Anyway. This jerkoff was a wife beater, a puppy kicker, a daughter smacker. And he got the idea in his head that his wife was giving him too many girl babies...he really wanted a son. Never mind biology and X chromosomes and that any idiot knows that sperm dictates the baby's sex..."

"Honey..."

"Right, right, I'm staying focused. I *am*. Anyway. He kills his wife—nice, huh? And my husband decided the guy's ass was grass, except Gerald's daughters—he had three—intervened on their dad's behalf. Begged for his life. So Michael felt sorry for the girls and banished Gerald from the pack. So he went away and did whatever rogue werewolves do.

"Then, when I got pregnant and turned up here, Gerald snuck back to town and tried to kidnap me. He got onto the grounds during a full moon and hurt a lot of people, so I shot him. The end."

"And when was this?"

"Almost a year ago."

Jared shook his head. "That's not right. There have been six or seven murders since then. Same M.O. I've been researching every murder that matched my sister's."

Moira turned to him, surprised. "A serial killer? I thought you were focused on your sister."

"I started out focused on one death. Then, when I started digging, I realized there was a lot more going on."

"All the murders happening during a full moon," Michael said.

"Yes. That's how I knew it was one of you..." Freaks? Monsters? Degenerate killers? "...people."

Michael let that pass. "And do the victims all look alike?"

Wyndham, Jared realized with growing excitement, knew something. "Yes. They're all between five foot two and five foot four. They've all got long dark hair parted on the left, and blue eyes. Very pale skin." Jared watched Moira's eyes widen with understanding. "What is it, babe?"

"You've just described Gerald's late wife," she said, almost gasped. "That's exactly what she looked like!"

"But Gerald's dead," Jeannie protested. "Nobody's got any reason to kill women who look like his wife."

"Are you sure he's dead? I mean...he's a werewolf."

"Yeah, that's right." Jeannie replied, nodding. "A werewolf. Not a living god."

Michael coughed modestly. "Well..."

"Shut up, honey. Werewolves are perfectly mortal. I put multiple bullets in Gerald's head. He's deader than the dodo bird, trust me, Rocky."

"Well, his daughters aren't," Moira said quietly. "Maybe we should go have a talk with them. Don't they still live around here?" Then she froze. Everything within her locked for a long moment; shock had rendered her incapable of moving, even blinking.

"Moira...Moira!" Jared shook her arm lightly. "What is it? What's the matter?"

She gulped. Looked at Jared, then at Michael. "Geraldine," she said hoarsely. "Geraldine killed Jared's sister. Geraldine killed them all."

Uproar. But Jared said nothing. Just kept his gaze on Moira while she continued. "Remember, Michael? She was here early this week. Passing through town," she said. She's a loner, a drifter...Geraldine—"

"Geraldine, named for her father," Michael said with deadly quiet. "Geraldine, the eldest. The son Gerald wanted more than he wanted anything. How long did he pour poison in her ears, I wonder? How long has she been killing her mother over and over again, to appease her father, himself a year in his grave? If we can track her movements...match them to the deaths..."

"Oh, she can't!" Jeannie protested. "You guys are wrong. And it's *not* me being humanly naïve, it's not. You're wrong, is all...it's not Geraldine. She was *in this house*. She played with my daughter, for God's sake. She's the sweetest thing, even nicer than Moira."

Moira, who knew herself to be far from nice, just shook her head numbly. And Michael, who'd seen Moira tear apart two armed men once upon a time, simply said, "Gerald did not kill those women. Geraldine did. And you know it, Jeannie...just give it a minute."

"No," she said stubbornly, but a species of frightened doubt drifted across her face. "She didn't do this. I've had her in my home, and she didn't do this thing."

"That may be true, ma'am," Jared said politely, but he was standing up, "but appearances can be deceiving. As everyone in this room probably knows. I'm going to go check it out. Bye."

"Not by yourself, you're not," Moira said, and was on her feet and after him in an instant.

"Indeed," Michael said. *He* was on *his* feet.

Jared spun. "No way. This isn't yours."

Michael and Jared were now chest to chest, and Moira saw with dismay that her leader's shoulders were up and he was leaning far forward, almost looming over Jared, although the men were close in height. The classic stance of a werewolf defending his territory. "You're wrong about that, Jared. In fact, the plain truth is, this isn't *yours*."

"Tell that to my sister. Where were *you* when one of your damned out-of-control dogs was ripping my sister in two?"

Moira winced.

Michael's eyes—a weird gold color—went even more yellow. His mouth thinned and turned down in a sorrowful bow. "Exactly. That's why this—this ungodly mess is mine. For your sister. For all the other sisters. I was asleep at the switch. Now I have to fix it."

"Um, hello?" Jeannie tapped Michael on the shoulder. "Any reason you both can't go? I mean, don't get me wrong, all this chest-beating and me-boss batcrap is enthralling, really, but don't we have a murderer to catch?"

Michael unhunched. Jared turned to look at Mrs. Wyndham, who stared back with raised eyebrows. "She's right," he said after a long moment. Moira sighed with relief.

"She often is," Michael said fondly. "What a pity it appears to go straight to her head."

"What a pity you're going to bed with a fractured skull, pal." But Jeannie smiled as she said it, and the tension in the room ratcheted down several notches.

Chapter Ten

Who would go and who would stay turned out to be a moot point as Geraldine had a job. "Which I s'pose we should have thought of," Jeannie commented.

Interestingly, Geraldine was a cemetery caretaker. According to her supervisor, the job was seasonal and Geraldine attended to it when she was in town. "Sure I gave her the job," he replied to Michael's questions. "Felt sorry for her. Nasty business with her dad, eh?"

By necessity, Geraldine's hours were flexible. As she could be at work or at home, the two couples split up. Michael declined to let the rest of the family in on the problem, preferring instead to leave Lara in the pack's protection.

"If we can't handle this ourselves," he explained, "we deserve to get eaten. And if we *do* get eaten, I want to know Lara's safe."

"Yuck-o," was Jeannie's only comment.

Based on what the cemetery supervisor had said, the group felt sure Geraldine was most likely to be at work, so Michael and Jeannie took that address. On that issue, Michael would not budge.

"Arrogant asshole," Jared growled, jerking the car into reverse and squealing down the cemetery entrance—backward.

"Yes."

"Pushes people around all damn day."

"Yes."

"Wife seems nice, though. In a scary kind of way."

"She's beyond marvelous."

He grunted. "How come you didn't mention it?" He brought the car around. Tires squealed. Gravel flew.

Moira, nigh-invulnerable werewolf, tightened her seatbelt. "What?"

"No. I mean, how come you didn't tap me on *my* shoulder like Mrs. Wyndham tapped Mikie? And suggest we both go find Geraldine? I mean, you're super-smart. You must have figured it out. After all," he added with a grin, "you weren't suffering from testosterone overload like me and Michael."

Shocked, Moira replied, "That wouldn't have been my place." A beta female, thrusting herself between two alphas squaring off? Moira's mama didn't raise no fools. "Besides, I figured out who murdered your sister. What…did I not reach high enough for you? Are you implying I'm an underachiever?"

He had the grace to look abashed, and quickly changed the subject. "Listen, when we get there—"

"I am *not* staying in the car."

"Yes, you are. I'm not having anything happen to you, too."

Touched by his concern, it was a long moment before she could speak. When she did, she told him a bald truth: "I'm not having anything happen to you, either."

He smiled at her. "Guess we're fucked, then."

"Guess we are." As far as romantic declarations of love went, this one left much to be desired. *So how come you can't stop grinning, you twit?*

Jared pulled into Geraldine's driveway sedately enough, and Moira noticed he had a pleasant look on his face. "That's right, Geraldine, nothin' to worry about out here," he muttered, still smiling inanely as he shut off the engine. "Just a fella who wants to ask you a couple of questions…nothin' to get excited about…"

"Jared, really." Moira didn't try to hide her exasperation. "Now I'm definitely not staying in the car. You need me for this. You've got this silly idea in your head that because the full moon isn't until tomorrow night, Geraldine is harmless. I can assure you that's not the case. Soothing words and silly grins aren't going to put her at ease. She's going to know what you want the minute she gets close enough to smell you."

He had been nodding politely during her lecture, but now smirked. "And me without my Old Spice. C'mere, sugar."

What on earth was wrong with the man? she thought before he grabbed her and pulled her close. She would have imagined he'd be a bundle of nerves, this close to confronting his sister's killer—

Probable killer, her ever-logical mind interjected.

—but he practically whistled in contentment.

"Listen, weirdo," was as far as she got before his tongue plunged into her mouth. With anyone else this kiss would have been an alarming development. Since the tongue belonged to Jared, it was actually a quite enjoyable development. Yes, indeed. Most pleasant. Especially the way his lips were so soft, the way he kissed and licked and nibbled and—

CLICK.

—handcuffed her to the steering wheel.

Moira sat stock-still for a thunderstruck moment. Then, heedless of the lurking Geraldine and the quiet neighborhood, she shrieked. "What did you *do?*"

"Uh. Moira. Not so loud." He rubbed his ear. "I don't have to answer that question, do I? It's—what d'you call it—rhetorical."

She tugged experimentally. She couldn't get over the fact that he'd ruthlessly distracted her and then shackled her like a dog.

When she spoke, her voice was quite calm, but Jared looked at her warily anyway. "You carry handcuffs in your car?"

"Hey, I was a Boy Scout before I was a Marine."

"Boy Scouts carry handcuffs?"

"Okay, well, I'm out of here." And he was…he was opening the car, getting out, standing up. "Sorry, honey. But no way are you going anywhere near that killer. Not while I'm still breathing."

"Something which can be rectified!" she shouted. He winced and shut the car door. "And I'm a killer, too, you moron!"

He snorted, then turned and started for the house.

Moira fumed inside the car. Oh, it would serve him right if she stayed docilely put while Geraldine cuisinarted his entrails. For two cents, she'd do it.

Yeah, right.

"Lord, love has made me a fool," she mumbled aloud. Inwardly, she added, *I have fallen in love at last. With a man who has spent his entire adult life hunting my kind.* She normally got quite a kick out of irony. Not today.

She gave the handcuffs a hard yank. Metal groaned, but didn't break. She pulled again, and slipped her hand out of the now too-wide handcuff loop, then smacked it irritably, watching the cuffs swing from the steering wheel.

Well, that was that. No way would Jared be able to overlook that little feat of superhuman strength. One way or another, this would all be over tonight.

One way or another, this would all be over tonight. Jared expected to feel hot exultation, but instead only felt relief. Relief, and the hope that there could be a future with Moira after this was behind them. Assuming she would speak to him ever again.

Well, he didn't care if she gave him the silent treatment for a damn year, if she was safe. *Ten* years. He'd take furious over dead any day.

Jared paused on the porch, unsure what to do next. Ring the doorbell, he supposed, and look into the woman's—Geraldine's—eyes and see if he could find murder there. He hadn't counted on the dog being a woman. He hadn't counted on a lot of things when he started this strange journey.

He heard a light thump behind him and turned just in time to see Moira's sneakered foot slip up and out of sight as she pulled herself up on the porch roof.

He ground his teeth. Christ, the woman was a damn monkey! He should have known someone that smart would have learned how to pick a lock…probably kept the picks in her hair as barrettes or whatever. Now she was on the roof, probably finding an open window…aarrgh!

He raised a fist to pound on the front door when it suddenly jerked open, hard enough to blow strands of his hair back from his face.

An enormously tall woman stood before him, grinning. Her hair was the color of damp dirt, as were her eyes. She had incredibly white teeth, which made her smile hard to bear. Quite thin, her collarbones stood out clearly against the yellow T-shirt she wore, a color which accentuated her sallow complexion. She wore faded jeans with old stains on the thighs and knees—mud? Blood? She was barefoot and he saw her toenails were long enough to curl over the tops of her toes. He wondered in a distant part of his mind if she clicked when she walked on a wooden floor.

She looked cruel and hard, so he was unprepared for her soft, sweet, lilting voice: "Hello. Can I help you?"

He stared at her. His back itched where his gun was pressing against his flesh. "Uh…yeah. My name is Jared Rocke. Uh—" Why have you been killing women who look like your mama? How have you been able to fool the Wyndhams for so long? Are you aware you're the most frightening thing I've ever seen, and I used to live in Miami? "You're Geraldine Cassick, right?"

"Yes, of course." The woman's smile widened, if that was possible. Jared nearly shuddered. He had no idea how this woman had been passing herself off as human for so long. "Rocke. How's your dead sister? By the way, your cunt of a girlfriend isn't fooling anybody."

At "your dead" he reached for his gun. At "by the way" she slapped it out of his hand so quickly he didn't see her move, and didn't realize she'd cut him with her nails until later. At "isn't fooling" she seized his shirt collar and yanked him inside her house, shoving him hard enough to send him sliding across the hardwood floor, where he fetched up against the wall with a sickening thud. For a half second he thought the top of his head had fallen off. White stars exploded before his eyes.

"Now I'm *really* gonna kick your ass," he groaned, hoping his vision would clear soon.

"I'm terrified," she said in her weirdly cute, feminine voice. Her dad must have hated that voice, he thought dazedly, especially when he wanted a boy so bad. "Actually, I'm relieved. I can get rid of you and get back to business. I did *not* like having you sniffing up my backtrail, Roque."

"It's Rocke. You were waiting for me."

"Of course I was!" she said. She crossed the room with terrifying swiftness and squatted down to look at him. He could see two—no, three—of her heads, floating around him in a shaky semicircle. Her six eyes were gleaming, fanatical. "Where better than to hang out and wait for you than here, where Michael-king-shit-werewolf and his monkey bitch live? My home, where I know everyone and they know me and oh, isn't it terrible about my dad, but *you're* all right, Geraldine, you poor, poor thing."

Jared shook his head, desperate to clear it. Ten seconds ago he'd been standing on her porch. "Just in case I hadn't already figured you were off your fucking rocker," he informed her in a croak, "I think I've got it now."

She ignored him. "Except, Jared, you were *supposed* to kill *them*." Geraldine's tone became sweetly reproachful. "You were supposed to come to me *first*, because you figured my father had been doing the killings, and I would have told you the killer was *Michael*! But you—did—it—all—backwards." Each word was punctuated by a brisk, hard shake.

"It wouldn't have worked, nutjob," he managed, fighting to loose himself from her grip. Cripes, she was barely holding him, but her fingers felt like steel. He smashed his palm into the underside of her jaw, but her head barely moved. "You shouldn't have framed a dead man, Geraldine. That's where you took a wrong turn."

"I'm going to kill that half-breed cow you've been fucking," she informed him with conspirational tenderness. "I can smell her all over you. She actually let you touch her? Let a nasty, smelly, monkey *touch* her?"

He tried to bring a knee up, hard, into her belly, but she shifted easily. She started choking him, throttling him almost absent-mindedly while banging his head against the floor. "Mm—not—smelly—" was what he managed before things started to go dark around the edges.

Suddenly her grip relaxed, and he sucked in painful breaths. Geraldine's face was, as if by magic, slashed in four long streaks, bleeding. So much blood, it rained into his face, spattered his shirt.

"Half-breed is all right," Moira said, and he realized she was directly above them. Geraldine whined, clutched her face and scuttled back, blood pouring through her long-nailed fingers, pattering to the floor. "It's tactless, but accurate. Calling me a plump herbivore is not. Also," she added, glancing down at him, "I'm not speaking to you. But I *will* save your ass."

"—get—out—of—here—"

"Oh, shut up. And you," she said to Geraldine, stalking toward her, "are a nasty, smelly, wretched creature. Look at you. You look like you're going to Change any second. Feeling the stress of the coming full moon, Geraldine? How rude of you to show it."

"You're surprised by how I look," Geraldine hissed back, flipping to her feet. "That's because you never saw me. No one has ever! Seen! Me! Not your precious Michael or his bitch-dog or Derik or Mother or—my—my—"

"I don't care, Geraldine. It's too bad you had an unendurable childhood, but what gives you the right to kill? Worse, kill helpless humans? Nothing. Those women did nothing to you."

Jared watched the two women circle each other. They moved strangely—more like big cats than an accountant and a cemetery caretaker. He rubbed his eyes and looked again. Everything hurt, his throat was on fire and he was seeing two Moiras and two Geraldines, but he still couldn't look away. He noticed they were very careful about where they put their feet. It was almost like a dance or ritual—something very old, something stylized.

"No," Moira was saying, "those poor women did absolutely nothing to deserve their fate."

"They did! They—"

Moira went on, implacable. Her voice rang with truth and scorn. "You've shamed us all. You're crazy, but part of you knows. Part of you *knows* everything you are is wrong, and everything you've done. Your father—Gerald—was the worst creature I've ever known. But that doesn't excuse *you*."

"Don't you talk about my father. You're not fit for him to piss on."

Moira shook her head. Her outrage had fled; now she just looked terribly tired. "You fooled us for a long time. But it's over now. You're not killing anyone tonight."

"Wrong, half-breed." Geraldine leapt. Moira dodged, pivoted quicker than thought, and sent her small foot into Geraldine's side. Jared's eyes widened; the 'crack' was very loud. Amazing! In between collecting college degrees for the hell of it and running the Wyndham finances, his Moira had apparently found time to get a black belt in karate.

Incredibly, Geraldine ignored the pain of broken ribs. He couldn't believe it, but she was still moving, and moving quickly—she spun and regained her center as rapidly as an adder. Too quickly for him to follow, both women were literally at each other's throats, locked in a brutal battle.

He tried to get up. He tried. And again. But…too hard, everything hurt, his head was spinning, everything was so fast, how did Moira adjust to things happening so fast? It was almost as if she, too, possessed that same inhuman speed and agility, as if his Moira was one of the…

Geraldine howled and all the hairs on the back of Jared's neck came to rigid attention. It was every bad or frightening sound he had ever heard, times ten. Everything that was in him wanted to run from the sound, get the Hell out and never, never come back. The part of his brain devoted 100% to survival was wide awake and screaming at him to leave.

As if in response to the unearthly noise, Moira had made a final, desperate leap, and now she was—God, was she biting Geraldine? Her teeth were fastened at the juncture between Geraldine's neck and shoulder. The killer shrieked again and drove an elbow back into Moira's stomach. Moira grunted and held on. Geraldine's fist came up in a blur and then Moira was tumbling away. Geraldine pounced, quick as a cat.

Jared crawled toward them. He had no idea why. He sure as shit couldn't help Moira in his condition. But somehow he was on his knees and he crawled, crawled. He saw Moira's hand come up, try to shove Geraldine away. Saw her claw for Geraldine's eyes. He crawled faster.

He wouldn't let this bitch kill another woman he loved.

He groped for his pants leg, for the small pistol in the ankle holster. Geraldine hadn't known about it, or hadn't cared. It was practically a toy, anyway. A one-shot Derringer. His Marine buddies would laugh themselves into hernias if they saw him with it.

He stopped crawling. He heard another wet snap and didn't know whose bone had broken. Moira was kicking Geraldine away, turning, trying to get distance. Geraldine was giggling through a mouthful of blood. Jared found the pistol…and dropped it right out of his bloody grip.

"Geraldine," he croaked, "your daddy died screaming."

That got her attention; she snapped her head around so fast he practically heard it. Her eyes were huge; the irises looked like gold-flecked mud. "What? What did you say, monkey?"

"Which word didn't you understand, cow, goat, uh—mammal with extra stomachs?"

"Ruminator," Moira suggested faintly, trying to get to her feet and failing. He could see the bulge in her left leg, below her kneecap. He'd heard her bone break.

The monster would pay for that. "Ruminator, thanks, babe. Oh, Geraldine?" Groping, groping. Got it. Hang on. "After Moira and I settle your hash, we're gonna find your dad's grave and fuck right on top of it." Hang on. "That's not gonna be a problem, is—uurrggh!"

Geraldine had jumped high in the air—impossibly high, his rational mind had trouble believing this wasn't a fantastic illusion—and landed squarely on top of him. That was fine. That was perfect. "Bite me, dog," he growled. "Let's see those pearly whites."

Her head swooped toward his, ready to tear out his throat. *For my sister. For my love.* He could smell Geraldine's breath: rank, meaty. *This is the last thing my sister saw. Oh, God, help me now.* He brought the Derringer up, jammed it into her mouth so hard he felt teeth break. Had time to register the killer's almost comical look of surprise before he pulled the trigger and blew the back of her head off.

Geraldine fell forward, onto him. He screamed, in horror and despair and rage for the dead. "Moira!" he roared.

Somehow, Moira heaved the corpse off him. And that's about when everything went black.

Chapter Eleven

Jared opened his eyes, and Moira shrieked.

"Owwwww!"

"I'm sorry," she said at once. He could see she was quite pale. Her eyes dominated her face and their color was deep, nearly purple, startling and mesmerizing at once. "I'm just really, really happy you're awake."

"Amen, sister." He started to sit up, hardly able to take his eyes off her, then just as quickly gave up and flopped back onto the bed. "Argh, even my hair hurts. Is it dead?"

"Yes."

"Where am I?"

"Wyndham Manor. Also known as Dogs R Us."

"Funny girl." Jared glanced around the lush bedroom, which was roughly the size of his last apartment. Sunlight streamed through the west window. It was late, then. They'd gone to Geraldine's before lunch. "Geraldine. God, what a mess."

"That," Moira said tartly, "is an understatement. FYI, none of the others can face you right now. They're so embarrassed they didn't see this before. Years ago."

"They shouldn't be." Jared paused. Yes, he had really said that. Weirder, he'd meant it. Blaming the dogs—err, Moira's employers—had become habit. Bitter, but comforting in its familiarity.

But ten minutes with Geraldine had changed his mind about a lot of things. She'd been so fast, so ruthless. So inhuman and, at the same time, heartbreakingly victimized. "You guys thought you solved the problem when Gerald was killed. Who could blame you? You wanted the nightmare to be over. I don't think there's blame in that."

"Ha!" Moira's tone was bitter, and Jared could see she would be blaming herself for a long time. She, who prided herself on her fine intelligence, hadn't noticed the killer living four miles from her bedroom. A difficult pill to swallow. He doubted Moira would do so gracefully.

He almost smiled. Christ, he adored her. She could have been killed—they both could have—but she never quit. She looked as innocent and delicate as a Hummel figurine, but had the temper of a wolverine and the tenaciousness of a pit bull. With rabies.

His thoughts derailed in sudden confusion. Geraldine was dead. His sister was avenged. Now what? Settle down with Moira? His life had been about vengeance since…well, since forever. Would there now be room for other things? Was it pos-sible? The idea was as wonderful as it was terrifying. Vengeance was a cold blanket, but he'd been able to wrap himself in it for years. Was there room now for more?

"I just don't understand how she held together so *long*," Moira muttered. She made a small fist and thumped her leg in agitation.

"I don't know how werewolves blend in with *any* humans," he said frankly.

Moira shook her head. "It's necessary. It's a skill learned early. What you saw—that wouldn't have fooled anyone. I think Geraldine was tired. She was tired, she wanted to be done. She quit holding herself together and stayed in her little house and waited for it to be over."

Jared thought back to the look on Geraldine's face when he shot her. Surprise, and…relief?

He would have bet his gun collection on it.

"By the way," the love of his life interrupted his thoughts with heavy sarcasm, "Mister-I-can-take-on-a-werewolf-in-her-prime-so-stay-in-the-car-Moira, you're not moving from that bed for a week. Among other things, you've got a nasty concussion and cracked ribs."

"I've got…" Memory returned; he lunged forward. "How's your leg?"

"Lie back down." She gently pushed him back against the pillows. "My leg?"

"It broke. I heard it break. Maybe we should take you to the hospital. Has Wyndham called a doctor?"

"Wyndham set it for me. You know, it wouldn't hurt you to call him Michael. Stop trying to get up." She sat down in the chair next to the bed, and propped her leg up on the mattress. The swelling was nasty, but Jared couldn't see the lump of broken bone any longer. Her leg was tightly wrapped in elastic. Not plaster.

"Huh. I guess it didn't break."

"Jared."

"Lucky for you, sugar, because that could have been nasty."

"Jared."

"And by the way, you must have had some kind of adrenaline rush in that hell house. You were tossing Geraldine around like she was made of paper. It was like watching the Hulk. A short blonde Hulk."

"*Jared.*"

"And I'm not staying here, cutie. Not even for you." He tossed the blankets back. "This place creeps me right the hell out. I'm heading back to my place, and I'd love it if you came with me. In fact, I insist on it. I need a sexy nurse to take care of me."

She was staring at him. Why was she looking at him so strangely? Part of him knew, part of him was pulling back the veil so he could see. He willed the under-standing away. "Moira? Come on, let's book. What do you say, babe?"

"I can't do that."

"Sure, it's easy. We'll scoot down to the truck, hop in, make a quick stop at the Colonel's—I'd kill another werewolf just for some fried chicken—"

"*I'm* a werewolf."

He didn't blink. "No."

Her eyes widened. For a minute he thought she was going to fall out of the chair. She'd clearly been braced for any reaction except calm denial. "Yes, I *am*. I'm a werewolf. Tonight when the moon rises I'll be hairier than the drain in the locker room at the YMCA."

He calmly folded his arms across his chest. "No."

She leapt to her feet. Her cheeks were flushed, her forehead burning like a lamp. "Jared, stop it! You know I am, you *must* know. I'm a werewolf."

He shouted, although it hurt his head like hell. "I'm not having this discussion, no way, uh-uh, count me out, folks." Of course she wasn't. It was impossible. They were the monsters. She was Moira. *Ergo*, nuh-uh, not happening, no way.

She bellowed so loud he feared for the mirror across the room. "**I'm a werewolf!**"

No slouch in the vocals department, he roared back, "The hell you are!"

Moira's temper snapped. "Of course I am, you idiot! *Adrenaline rush?* Come on!"

"Science is on my side."

"Bullshit is on your side. You would have seen it before now, if you'd allowed yourself."

"You are *not*," he repeated stubbornly.

"I am, so, a werewolf."

"You're just saying that so I don't think they're all scum. Which, by the way, they are."

"They aren't, and I am one."

"No, you're not."

"*How can you say that?* You can only fool yourself for so long."

"Because I can't care about one!" he roared. "That's absolutely impossible and *not in the plan!* You're not you're not *YOU ARE NOT!* You leap around like a monkey because you've got a gymnastics background, you heal quickly because— I dunno, you've got a super immune system—you don't get tired but big deal, one of my buddies can go for three days without sleep, he does it all the time and it never bothers him except he gets really bad breath from drinking all that Mountain Dew…people are different.*"

She was holding her head in her hands. "Oh, my God. You're a moron."

"I mean, don't get me wrong." He could hear himself talking fast and faster, almost babbling, but it was impossible to stop. "You're definitely weird. I'll give you that. But the stuff you can do, it's all within the realms of good old *homo sapiens*."

"So I'm a liar? Or just crazy?"

He had no answer for that one. After a long pause, he said, "I don't know. Maybe after working for werewolves all this time you think you're…I don't know. I'm not the brains of this team."

"You got that right," she muttered.

"I just know you're not one of *them*. You're not. I won't believe it." And you can't make me, he added silently, stubbornly.

"Why?"

Because she had nothing, not one fucking thing, in common with Geraldine. Because he wanted to marry her and have kids with her and his kids weren't going to be fuzzy. Because his sister's killer was dead and he wanted to finally build a life without grief. Because.

"I just won't."

"You said you couldn't care about a werewolf," she said slowly, and now she stood, and walked to the door (*without a limp*, his mind pointed out treacherously) and turned. Her eyes shone with unshed tears. "I take that to mean you think you care about me."

"Yes." He paused. "I'm sorry. I had about a thousand nicer ways planned to tell you. I didn't mean to just blurt it out in mid-yell. I do care, Moira. From the minute you hightailed it down the road dressed in my shower curtain, I never wanted anything bad to happen to you, ever."

She winced away from him, as if his words hurt her. "You care about a lie then, Jared. There's no shame in not knowing things. But I won't be with someone who puts on blinders on purpose. And won't take them off, no matter what he hears and what he sees." She wrenched open the door and fled.

"Moira, don't go!" He slapped his hands over his eyes and writhed in agony. "Oh, God, my head...fuck."

The door slammed open, hard enough to crash against the wall and stick as the doorknob was imbedded in the wood.

A large, blonde man filled the doorway. *Filled.* His hair was the color of the sun, cut brutally short. His eyes were a deep, mesmerizing green. He was broad-shouldered and the T-shirt he wore did nothing to hide his excellent muscle definition. Given the man's ridiculously good looks and powerful build, Jared assumed he was dealing with a Wyndham werewolf.

"I'm going to shove your head so far up your ass," the man said with ominous calm, "that you'll be able to kiss your own colon."

"Go chase a mail truck," Jared snapped. "I've got bigger problems than whatever bit you on the ass today."

The man blinked. Held up one finger. Paused. Turned. Left. Jared heard a muffled sound from the hall—a snort? A chuckle? Then the stranger returned, looking stormier than ever. "You blew it, Monkeyboy."

"It's Rocke."

"Moira hasn't given a guy so much as a come-hither look in years, and you had her. She was yours, all you had to do was ask! She saves your life, helps you avenge your sister, then finally screws up her courage and tells your bigoted sorry ass the truth, and you rejected everything she is."

"Did you actually say come-hither?"

"Stop making me laugh. This is a serious thing, ape face."

"It's *Jared Rocke*, do I have to paint it on my forehead?"

"I'm going to throw you out the window." This in the same tone someone else might have said, 'I'm going to fix you a cup of coffee.' "The fall will probably kill you, but you'll be out of Moira's hair, and it'll make me feel better. Also, you deserve multiple broken bones for making my friend cry."

So saying, the man moved with that same terrifying quickness Geraldine had demonstrated. He seized the footboard of the bed and shoved. As if it was sliding across ice, the bed zipped across the carpet and slammed against the far wall...uncomfortably close to the window. But to Jared's human senses, the man had finished with "...making my friend cry." and suddenly his bed was against the window.

He supposed he should have been terrified.

"Bring it on, German Shepherd!" His head pounding, Jared thrashed feebly among the blankets. "As soon as I get out of this bed, we'll see who goes out the window!"

"Crud." The man blew out his breath in disgust. "I forgot your injuries wouldn't have healed yet. You guys are made of tissue paper, I swear."

"Derik!"

"What?" The man turned. Wyndham's wife stood in the doorway, hands on her hips. Jared inwardly groaned.

"Keep your hands off him, " Jeannie warned, looking cutely threatening.

"I was only going to slap him around a little," Derik said defensively. "Wasn't even going to break the skin. Much."

"You and what army, Liver Snack breath?" Jared jeered.

"See? See? This guy's an asshole squared. *And* he made Moira cry." Derik kicked the footboard. Jared heard the 'crunch' of splintering wood. "For which he will bleed and puke and beg."

"Moira would jam your ass up to your shoulderblades—"

"Worth it," Derik said stubbornly.

"—and you know it. Besides, that's why *I'm* here. Ole Rockhead's got a concussion, so I figured I'd shriek at him for half an hour or so until he agreed to go after Moira."

At last the bickering couple had his attention. "Go after her? Where's she gone?"

"You think she was going to stay *here*? Tonight? She's out of here, pal. I doubt she'll be back until she gets word that you've moved on. Let me know," Derik added with a giant, toothy, terrifying smile, "if you need help packing."

Jared threw back the bedcovers again and stood. Instantly, the floor rushed up to his head. "What the—?"

Jeannie and Derik were bending over him. "You can't go anywhere," she informed him, while he tried to get up off the floor. "Geraldine really rattled your cage. You've got a bad concussion and about a zillion minor injuries."

"My knees work," he said through gritted teeth. Slowly, painfully, he rolled over onto all fours and started crawling for the door.

"Aw, nuts," Derik sighed.

"What?"

"I could get to like this puke."

Hand, hand, knee, knee. Hand, hand, knee, knee. What the hell had they done with his clothes? Oh, well...Derik could use a good mooning. Hand, hand, knee, knee.

"What if one of you guys gave him a transfusion?" Jeannie asked.

"It'd probably work," Derik replied indifferently. "Speed up his healing for a day or so. Enough to fix him up."

"Well, let's give him some blood, then."

"Forget it. He's too stupid to let you help."

"Hello?" Jared called irritably. He kept his gaze fixed on the bedroom door, which was now a mere eighteen miles away. "I can hear you two."

"I disagree," Jeannie said. "Not about him being stupid—"

"And me without my gun," Jared muttered.

"—but he'd probably do it if it meant he could get to Moira that much sooner. And Derik, it's really important he get to her before sundown. *Isn't it?*"

"Don't yell, I'm standing right in front of you. And I'm telling you, he won't do it. His tiny little mind can't get around the idea, and even if it did, he's a bigot. He's a—an anti-werewolfite!"

"Dammit, you two, am I even in the room?"

"Shut up," they said in unison. Then, from Jeannie, "No, wait. Derik, pick him up, would you?"

At once Jared felt himself effortlessly lifted and scooped into Derik's arms, as if he were a baby. A big, scowling, hairy baby. "I have to go," he nearly shouted, "and you two aren't helping." Moira was out there alone, thinking God knew what...because he was a jackass. He had to fix it right away. The thought of her unhappiness tormented him. He'd rather swallow a wasps' nest than be responsible for her pain.

Derik placed him on the bed, and Jeannie slapped her palms against his chest to keep him from rising. "Jared, if we give you a pint of werewolf blood, your injuries will be healed within the hour."

He stared at them.

"I told you," Derik said triumphantly. "Too dumb. He has no idea what you're talking about. Look, any minute he's going to start drooling."

There was a 'thud' as Jeannie's sneakered foot landed on Derik's instep. The smile on her face never wavered. "What do you say, Rocky?"

"I say you guys better not let word of this get out," he replied slowly. Thinking: I'm going to pay a high price for my foolishness...but if it'll get Moira back, it's worth it. "People will hunt you down just for the properties in your blood. You'd be werewolves and we'd be...vampires, I guess."

"Okay," Derik muttered, "*not* so dumb."

"Let's do it," he said firmly. "Right now. I gotta find Moira. She made me care and by God, she's stuck with me."

Jeannie pretended to wipe away a tear. "That's so beautiful."

"What are we standing around for? Make a fist, Lassie Boy. Somebody get a needle," Jared ordered.

Derik snorted. "A) I wouldn't piss down your throat if your heart was on fire..."

"Gross!" Jeannie cried.

"...and b) I'm not giving you shit. Besides, we keep some blood on hand in case Jeannie gets hurt, or one of our other human friends."

"Derik," Jeannie said reprovingly, "you shouldn't—"

"Back off, blondie. I've known Moira my whole life. I'm not much interested in helping someone who makes her feel the way Fucko did today."

"Fucko is going to try to make things right," Jared said. "So get me that blood—"

"Don't say it," Derik warned.

"Fetch!"

Chapter Twelve

Jared ran. He ran past the rose garden, into the woods. His headache was gone. His pain was gone. He felt like he could jump over the mansion. He felt like he could defeat an army. All this, from a pint of werewolf blood.

He understood the pack's secrecy, the way they kept to themselves. And he respected their discipline in a way he never could have before. What was to stop werewolves from taking over the world? From slaughtering humans like cattle? Wyndham, of course. Wyndham kept them in line. And dealt with the rogues, when he had to.

He'd never love them, Jared thought, leaping over a felled tree trunk, nimble as a gazelle. Or a wolf. But he could sure learn to respect the hell out of them.

He turned his thoughts away from the pack, toward Moira. He could actually smell her…her light, flowery scent, like spring violets, called to him. He had thought finding her would be tricky in the woods, the dark. About as tricky as tying his shoes. Jeannie had warned him the effects of the blood—the heightened senses— would wear off by daybreak, but he didn't care. He only needed a little more— there!

He burst into a clearing and saw her. She was nude, kneeling on the grass. She was crying, he saw with dismay, and soothing herself by rocking back and forth.

They all have their favorite places, Jeannie had said. *Places they go when they don't want us to see them. Or hear them. Moira's is the clearing just past the orchard. She'll be there, Jared, and you'd better be nice to her when you find her.*

He had promised. He would have promised anything. And now here was Moira, so upset she hadn't spotted him. Here was Moira, sobbing so hard her back shook with it. He had done this. Through stupidity or willfulness or plain Rocke stubbornness, he had wrought this.

He had no idea how to fix it.

He took a slow step forward just as Moira threw her head back. "Oh!" she cried, almost screamed. "Oh! Ohhhh…ohhhhhhhhhhhh…ouuuuuuuhhhhhhh… ooooooooooooooo!"

One minute he was watching her cry, helpless. The next—and it was that fast, that quick, if he'd blinked he'd have missed it—she was standing on four paws. Her champagne-colored fur riffled in the brisk wind. The moon came out from behind the clouds and still she cried up at the moon, a wolf who dreamed she was a woman, or a woman who dreamed she was a wolf.

He sat on the ground. He hadn't thought to, but really had no choice…his knees unhinged and bam! He was on his ass in the leaves. Suddenly, he was very glad—*very* glad—he didn't have his gun. He didn't want his hands anywhere near a weapon right now when he was so terrified. And fascinated.

He'd seen a werewolf change before, of course. Had been revolted, of course. But that had been a thug, someone he used for information. It hadn't been someone he cared about. Someone he'd held, kissed, made love to in the dead of night. Showered with. Cooked breakfast for. Oh, hell, it wasn't Moira.

And he'd denied her. Told her she couldn't be a werewolf. Shrugged off her confession, turned his back on what she was. For what? For vengeance? Renee *was* revenged. For his stupid, human sense of the way things should be? Or simply because he didn't know how to open to her?

"Moira," he said, but what came out was a whisper.

She turned and looked at him. In the moonlight, her eyes were dark purple. She was as gorgeous a wolf as she was a woman.

She stepped away—no, *cringed* away, and he felt his face get hot with shame. He had done that. Taken a fearless, gorgeous creature and made her cower like a whipped hound. In a flash of understanding, he realized Moira was all the things he cared about—good, intelligent, strong, willful, charming—because of her heritage, not in spite of it.

Too bad he hadn't figured that out a little earlier.

"Moira," he said again, just as the wolf—just as *his* wolf spun and ran out of the clearing.

He sprinted after her. "Wait! I get it now! You're a werewolf! Great! Good! I figured it out!" And all she had to do was change right before his eyes because he was so fucking stupid. But he wouldn't say that…not when she already knew…

"It's okay! The kids can be furry! I don't care, I swear!" Could she even understand English in her wolf form?

A tree branch swiped him across the cheek, hard enough to make his eyes water. He plunged ahead, ignoring the pain. "Moira, come back! I don't care that you've got more chest hair than I do!"

He was glad Jeannie had insisted he borrow a pair of Wyndham's sweatpants. They afforded his legs some protection, but the branches were scratching the shit out of his arms, chest, and face. It didn't matter. He had it coming, anyway.

Tripping over an exposed root, he went sprawling, sliding on his stomach across the forest floor. Gasping, he rolled to his feet and saw another wolf, one much bigger, with fur the color of sunlight and eyes so vividly green they were nearly hypnotic. The wolf's paws were as big as each of Jared's hands. Muscles flexed and bunched beneath the luxurious pelt as the wolf started toward him, laughing.

Laughing?

Yes. A wolf-laugh—Jared hadn't imagined such a thing was possible. The wolf made chuffing noises in its throat, and there was definitely an amused gleam in its eyes. Still, as it crossed in front of Jared, the wolf let out a warning growl and Jared realized that although the wolf didn't like him, it couldn't keep from laughing.

Derik.

And, on the heels of that thought, Jared realized he was in the middle of a forest filled with werewolves.

"I don't care," he said out loud, but of course he did care. He cared a shitload. "I'm not leaving without Moira."

He saw her, peeking at him from behind a tree. She had stopped running, then. Or…maybe heard him and came back? His heart pounded giddily at the thought.

"Moira, I'm sorry. I'm about ten thousand kinds of fool. Don't run anymore, and don't be afraid."

Slowly, the small, light-colored wolf came forward, staring at him. He couldn't read her expression as he could Derik's. In this moment, he had no idea if that was a good thing, or a bad thing.

She scratched at the dirt with her paw. Even her paws were small and delicate; the claws looked like mother-of-pearl. Scratching at the dirt…symbols?

Letters.

He went down on one knee to look. The moon was riding high, so bright it was hard to look at, lending more than enough light so he could see…

I-D-I-O-T.

He grinned down on her. "Oh, baby," he said, and gently reached out to touch her thick, glorious fur. "It must be love."

Chapter Thirteen

Moira moved silently through her room. Jared was asleep in her bed in the mansion, but she was too tired to be surprised. Sunrise after the moon had ridden her always left its mark; all she wanted was a quick shower and a ten-hour nap.

She remembered last night fairly clearly. Of course she didn't process information the same way as a human and a wolf. But she remembered seeing him in the clearing, knowing he had watched her Change. She remembered her hot shame, and running.

And then he'd come after her, Moira recalled.

She turned on the shower and stepped inside before the water had time to warm. He had come, had run after her yelling the silliest things, and making as much noise as a herd of rhinos on speed. Derik had actually rolled onto his back and waved all four paws in the air; it had been just too funny.

And despite his feelings on the subject of Jared—his loudly voiced feelings— Derik, a creature of irresistible curiosity, had gone *back*. He always liked a good show. Moira had followed, more concerned that Jared would trip and drive a branch through his eye than anything else.

And there he had been, scratched, bleeding from half a dozen places, and smelling strongly of the werewolf blood Jeannie had no doubt transfused into him. He hadn't flinched from her wolf form, hadn't pulled a gun on her.

Instead, he had told her the most amazing things. And touched her fur with a child's wonder. Even now, she could hardly believe he'd done that.

But now what? Happily ever after? Was it possible? More, was it what she wanted?

She finished showering, toweled herself dry, then slipped into bed. Beside her, Jared didn't even stir. She wasn't surprised; he was likely more tired than she was.

Time enough to worry about their future *(what future?)* later.

She woke, practically purring. Flexed, hard. Gasped. And came, her orgasm a sweet surprise, like peeling an orange and finding a chocolate inside.

Jared's head was between her thighs, his fingers held her apart as he slowly and steadily licked, licked, licked. Given how wet she felt—how terrific she felt!— he'd obviously been at this for a few minutes at least.

"Jared…" A groan.

He laughed against her flesh. "Shut up, darling." His tongue, inside her. Now gone, and lightly stabbing her throbbing clit. His fingers, inside her, now gone. Rubbing, getting slick with her juice.

She could smell his arousal, violent and sharp, like cedar on fire. His need kindled her own; she realized she wasn't gasping, she was panting, heaving for breath, desperate to have him inside her.

And part of her, the fraction of the one percent of her concentration not focused on coming again, thought this was just fine. *He wouldn't be here with me, touching me, if he didn't still want to be with me.* She felt the sweet spasms of another orgasm ripple through her, and moaned.

"Jared," she said again, and reached for him.

"Moira, sweetie, I'm going to need a little help here." He was moving up her body, touching her everywhere with hands that smelled like sex. "Also, you're going to marry me."

"I—"

"But just so there's no doubt. I mean, I get that you're ten times stronger than me and twice as smart. No problem. But between us, sugar, there's never going to be any doubt about who wears the pants in the Rocke family."

"Can't you stop talking," she groaned, wild with impatience, "and fuck me?"

"Sure thing." He had crawled up far enough so that he was crouching over her chest, kneeling on her hands. The pressure was firm, but not painful. Her leverage, however, was for shit. "But first I need your mouth."

"Wha—" Then his hot, hard length was pushing past her lips, his musky scent was in her nostrils, her throat. He throbbed between her cheeks. She shifted her weight to take more of him, and realized she couldn't move.

Not that this was such a problem. But still. The idea. Jared had her pinned and despite her strength, there (was his cock, thick and rude) wasn't much to be done about it. Not that Jared (was rocking back and forth, pushing himself in and out of her mouth) would ever hurt her, but the fact was, she was giving him a blowjob whether she liked it or not. She (could feel her jaws forced wide, to accommodate him, could taste his saltiness) happened to like it. But wasn't that beside the point?

Then he was pulsing and her mouth was flooded with that bitter sweetness so peculiar to semen. He groaned as she swallowed, and his hands were in her hair, roughly caressing her curls.

He pulled out, and away, and collapsed beside her. "Definitely not the most PC moment of my life," he sighed, and pulled her into his arms.

"Do you even know what that stands for?" She tried to be irritated, but in truth, felt almost indecently satisfied. She could still taste him in her mouth.

"Perfect Cookies. You are, you know."

"What?" She cuddled against his side, ran her fingers gently over the scratches on his chest.

"Going to marry me."

"Gosh, Jared, are you *sure*? I mean, I'm *so* demented about being a werewolf and all…"

He squinched his eyes shut. "Okay, okay, I deserved that, have mercy. I suck, all right? Although, not as well as you do…"

She poked him in the ribs, hard. "Pig. And excuse me, but I can't help being astonished at how easy this is. I mean…Jared…I'm one of the monsters. The creature you sought for years."

"Nope. Geraldine…*she* was the creature. You're the woman I love."

She digested that in silence, absently toying with the hair on his chest.

"I mean, Geraldine was just one person in the…the group. Pack. Whatever. *One* person…she didn't define the pack. I can't paint all the other werewolves with the same brush." He paused expectantly.

"What do you want, applause?" She smiled and rolled her eyes at him. "You're not telling me anything I don't know."

"All I'm saying is, werewolves are like anybody else. They're some really fabulous ones—" He squeezed her. "—and some major assholes, but most of them are in between." Another expectant pause.

"Jared, I know all this. I've been trying to get this idea through your head for days."

"Well," he said tentatively, "what kind of werewolf do you think I'll be?"

She went up on one elbow; stared at him. "What?"

"Jeannie gave me a whole pint of werewolf blood…"

"I know; I smelled it on you last night."

"…so I could get healed and go after you. I guess I'll get pretty hairy in a month or so." He contemplated his chest a little worriedly. "Hairier, I mean."

Astonishment left her wordless for a long moment. "You thought that the transfusion would make you pack…and you did it anyway. So you could find me." She could feel her face get hot; her eyes filled. "Oh, Jared…"

"Don't cry, babe. You can show me all the werewolf tricks. It'll be fine."

"…you're such an idiot."

One golden eyebrow went up. "That's not very romantic."

"I told you before," she explained, laughing through her tears, "being a werewolf isn't something you can catch. You either are one, or you aren't. You could have a transfusion every day for a year, but you'd never howl at the moon." She kissed him on the mouth, a hearty smack. "But to think that you didn't know…and you did it anyway…I love you. For all sorts of reasons, but most of all for this."

"Hey, it was nothing," he bragged. "And I love you, too. And you *are* going to marry me."

"Yes, so you keep telling me."

He showed her his vulnerable side as he squeezed her again. "Yeah, but you haven't answered."

"Of course I'll marry you. I've been waiting for you…" She thought back over the vista of lonely years. "…for a long time."

He kissed her again, a hearty smack on the mouth. "I've got about a million questions. Like, if you shave your legs when you're in your human form, will your wolf form have bare legs? And how much Nair do you go through in a month, anyway?"

She closed her eyes. "I think I liked it better when you refused to see the truth."

"And what if we're making love and the moon comes up? I mean, I'm an open-minded guy, but—"

"Jared," she groaned, "you're killing me. And you'd better be teasing, because that's both ridiculous *and* disgusting. I can see I'm going to have to get you some books."

"So, how strong are you? Can you lift a car up over your head?"

"Jared…"

"Not a serious car, like a Cadillac…how about a Volkswagon, could you lift a Volkswagon?"

"Jared!"

"Quick! Let's arm wrestle. Winner has to do all the dishes for life."

She poked him in the shoulder, hard. "I can't believe I yearned for the day you'd accept the truth."

"Be careful what you wish for, bay-bee." His teasing grin faded and he looked at her anxiously.

"Can we have kids? I mean…can you…with a regular guy?"

"Yes." *And they'll be very special.* You never knew what you got when a human mated with a werewolf. You might get a werewolf. You might get a human. You might get a human with extraordinary strength and agility. You might get a werewolf who could control their Change. It was always a toss of the dice. It was always exciting.

"What will they be?" His gaze was curious, wondering. His fingers moved softly over her belly, as if already feeling for the life within. She could feel him against her thigh, already hard again, and hot. Wanting her as badly as she wanted him.

"They'll be whatever they want to be," she said, and kissed him again, pulled him to her, and opened herself to him. Body and soul.

About the author:

*MaryJanice Davidson has written over a dozen books across a variety of genres. Her last **Secrets** novella,* Love's Prisoner, *was a P.E.A.R.L. finalist and won the Sapphire Award for best science fiction romance. She has since been nominated for another P.E.A.R.L.* (Naughty or Nice, *www.ellorascave.com) and is currently working on another Wyndham werewolf story. Her latest book, **Undead and Unwed**, is the story of Betsy Taylor, reluctant vampire queen (www.ellorascave.com). Visit MaryJanice's website to check out her published work and upcoming books: http://www.usinternet.com/ users/alongi/. And please drop her a line at alongi@usinternet.com. She loves to hear from readers!*

My Champion, My Love

by Alice Gaines

To my reader:
Passion isn't only for the young, and good guys don't always
finish last.

Chapter One

Upstate New York, 1888

The woman didn't strike Robert Albright as deranged. But the staff hadn't dressed her—or allowed her to dress herself —and now she was forced to greet him, a perfect stranger, in the middle of the afternoon wearing her dressing gown. If, indeed, she'd been sent to the Wainwright Asylum unjustly, he'd do what he could to have her released. If the patients here were mistreated, he'd look into that, too. Right now, his main concern was Mrs. Celeste Broder and her sanity.

She appeared more restless than insane. She'd paced from the window to Dr. Wainwright's desk and then back again as though measuring the dimensions of her prison in footsteps. Yards and yards of the best Belgian lace flowed and rustled behind her as she went. She stopped her meanderings at the window this time and turned to him, causing the sunlight to cast shadows from the iron bars onto her face and the length of her throat.

"Xenobia sent you?" she asked.

"She did."

One eyebrow rose as she studied him. "Do you know her well?"

"We met only once, when she asked me to check on you."

"Is she here? Now?"

"She went back to Manhattan," he answered. "She seemed to think that her friendship had gotten you into your present predicament somehow. She kept her visit to me a secret."

"Yes, of course. Dear Xenobia," she said, twisting her fingers together. "Still, I wish she could have come herself."

Mrs. Broder renewed her prowling. All long limbs and simmering impatience, she walked back and forth with her robe rustling around her ankles. But then, he'd no doubt act the same if he'd been locked away in this place for weeks.

He might have expected impatience from her, but he hadn't expected such beauty. Xenobia Stewart hadn't warned him that he'd be rescuing a tall, graceful woman with raven-black hair and limbs long and slender enough to belong to an angel.

Beauty or not, the woman needed his help, and he'd best remember that. Too many people in her life had taken advantage of her, if Mrs. Stewart's story was correct. He wouldn't add his own lust to those wrongs, no matter how deeply his own urges ran in those directions. But, damn, what a vision she made in all that lace. He couldn't have taken his eyes off her if his life had depended on it.

"What did Xenobia tell you about me?" she asked.

"That you'd been sent here unfairly. That you're perfectly sane, and that you needed someone to get you released."

"And why did she choose you, I wonder?" she said. "Do you regularly champion women you don't know, Mr. Albright?"

No, he didn't. In fact, he rarely spoke to women as beautiful as this one. He didn't find it entirely comfortable doing so now. "I imagine that Mrs. Stewart called on me because of my stature in the community."

"You're the mayor of that pretty town I passed on the way here," she said.

"Connogua Springs," he answered. "As the mayor, I'm concerned if anything improper goes on in this institution."

"This institution?" she repeated with a none-too-ladylike laugh. "Don't you mean this asylum? This haven where my tortured mind can find peace?"

"I'd be very interested in how you've been treated here," he answered.

"My mind's been treated well, I suppose. My body is quite another matter, but I don't suppose you want to hear about that, do you?"

His face heated to the roots of his hair. He didn't dare think about her body— tortured or not. He was already more aware than he should be of the curves under her gown that promised no corset but only more silk and lace. And skin—soft, warm skin.

The room felt hot suddenly, the air thickening until he had to think to breathe. He was having a very male reaction to Celeste Broder's presence, a reaction that would prove embarrassing in another moment. Curse his nature—he'd always been that way. Hot blooded. He needed to get away from her. Clear his head. He could work on her behalf from a distance. Investigate why she'd been imprisoned here and how she'd been treated. But from a distance, not so close that she overwhelmed his senses.

"I think I've heard all I need to for now," he said. He reached into his pocket and pulled out the note. Even after the days since Xenobia Stewart had given him the envelope, her perfume still wafted from the heavy vellum. Hideously expensive, if he was any judge, and too strong for a modest woman's taste. The scent hung all around him as he walked toward Mrs. Broder, his hand outstretched. "I'll deliver this to you and leave."

"No, please." She caught his hand, clutching both it and the envelope between her fingers. "Forgive me. I'm not at my best here. Kindness is so scarce. No one's very gracious within these walls, I'm afraid."

"I only want to help you, Mrs. Broder." But did he really? Or did he want something else entirely? Something sweet, but forbidden.

"Yes, of course. Please stay while I read the letter."

He shouldn't stay. If he had any sense, he'd leave. But the look of desperation in her eyes tore at him, so he nodded.

She went to the chair in front of Wainwright's desk and sank onto it, tearing open the envelope as she sat. She inhaled the perfume briefly and then read—her flush deepening over the patch of flesh revealed by the open throat of her robe. Her breath caught, so quietly he would have missed it if she hadn't held his attention so completely. She stopped reading for a moment and glanced up at him with the strangest expression in her eyes. Curiosity, definitely, but there was more, as well. Desire? Damn him for an idiot, but Robert could have sworn that look meant she wanted him.

She went back to reading the letter, and he did his best to control his imagination. He'd been without satisfaction too long. Since Millie's death. Hell, he'd been without complete satisfaction his entire life, despite Millie's good intentions. No wonder his mind wandered when he met a beautiful woman in her dressing gown. No wonder his member stiffened when she looked at him the way a woman looks at a lover.

She finished reading the letter, folded it carefully, and slipped it into the pocket of her robe. "Do you have any idea what this letter says?"

"I didn't read it, Mrs. Broder."

"That isn't what I asked. Did Xenobia tell you what her letter said?"

"No."

"Did you two discuss me?"

"Mrs. Stewart only said that you'd been put here against your will." He walked to the doorway and picked up his hat from its peg on the wall. "Now that you've read her note, I'll be on my way."

Mrs. Broder rose and reached out her hands toward him. "Please, don't go."

"I'll do what I can to have you released. You have my promise."

"But you don't know why I'm here. How can you release me if you don't even know why I'm here?"

"I won't tolerate sane people being locked away here, and it's clear to me that you're sane." He could hardly say the same thing about himself as he stood there, his hand hovering over the doorknob. He ought to leave. He ought to take his rapidly swelling erection and escape as quickly as possible. The woman held some sort of power over him—could seduce him with a mere look. If she continued to entreat him, her arms outstretched as though asking him for comfort, he'd surrender. He'd take her in an embrace, and then he'd be lost.

"I'll speak to the board of directors. I'll find you a lawyer," he said, finally clasping the doorknob in his hand. "I'll do whatever I have to to ensure your freedom."

"Please, Mr. Albright, stay. A few minutes longer. Please."

"Is that really necessary, Mrs. Broder?"

"Yes," she answered. "I want to tell you about myself before you hear about me from someone else. They'll make it all sound ugly." Her voice trailed off, and her chin trembled for a moment, but she took a few breaths and straightened her shoulders.

"They?" he asked. That seemed a safer question than what she meant by "hear about me."

"The doctors here. My husband's children—especially them." She walked toward the window and curled her fingers around the bars as she gazed out. "I have appetites, Mr. Albright. Appetites that might be tolerated in a man but not in a woman."

He removed his hand from the doorknob and dropped it to his side. "You needn't explain yourself to me."

"If I don't, someone else will, and then you'll think I'm unnatural just as the others do."

"No, I assure you..."

"This is perfectly humiliating," she muttered and resumed her pacing. She took angry steps, this way and that, as her fingers tangled with each other in front of her. "But, if I don't tell you, someone else will, and you'll think me disgusting."

He ought to do something to calm her, to comfort her. But what? He'd always felt helpless where women were concerned, and this one bewildered him completely.

"I have no choice in this, no choice at all." She stopped walking and turned to face him. "I like sex."

His jaw dropped, and he stood, gaping at her while every word he might have said flew directly out of his head. Had she really said that she liked sex?

"Frigging, swiving, tumbling," she continued. "Whatever you call it, I like it." She paused for a moment, still twisting her hands together in front of her dressing gown. "At least, I think I do. I haven't really been given a chance to find out."

"Mrs. Broder..."

"I think about sexual congress constantly. I dream about it at night. What it would be like to be held in a lover's arms—not for simpering declarations of affection. And not for chaste, little kisses, either."

Her skin had taken on that flush again—the same livid rose she'd shown after reading Mrs. Stewart's letter. Could it be nervous distraction? Could the woman be mad, after all? If so, she had some contagious sort of hysteria—something that could reach right out to him and catch him up in the insanity. With his member fully erect and throbbing now, he needed to get the hell out of here before he disgraced himself.

"These are things you should discuss with a husband," he muttered.

"My husband is dead," she answered. "And it was pointless trying to talk to him when he was alive."

"You have my condolences, but still..."

"The idea that I might require more physical attention than he gave me repulsed him. The mere thought that I might want more than his late night gropings made me avoid me for weeks."

"Please," he said, "I don't want to hear any more of this."

"Until he could no longer control his 'animal nature,' as he put it and he had to satisfy himself inside me in the least amount of time possible."

Robert put his hand back on the doorknob and turned it. "I have to leave."

"Don't go." She rushed to him and placed both her hands on his arm. "I'm sorry. I am distraught. Anyone would be in my place."

The door moved open, pushed from the other side. The matron who'd been assigned to guard the doorway stuck her head inside. "Time to go back to your room, Mrs. Broder."

Mrs. Broder forced a smile that wouldn't fool a child. "But Mr. Albright and I haven't finished chatting, have we?"

The matron harumphed. "This wasn't a good idea. Dr. Wainwright and I told you as much, Mr. Albright."

"Please, just a few more minutes."

The matron crossed her arms over her chest and glared out of narrowed eyes. Mrs. Broder's chin began to tremble again, and her eyes turned liquid with the threat of tears.

"I remember well what you told me," Robert said, pushing the door closed again. "I'll call you when we're through."

"The very idea." The matron harumphed again. "I have other things to do besides stand in this hallway all day, Mr. Albright."

"I'm sure," he said as he guided her the rest of the way out of the room and closed the door behind her.

"Thank you." Mrs. Broder gave a sigh of relief. "I'm sorry to have been so crude with you, but I wanted you to understand why I'm here. How I feel."

Unfortunately, he knew too well how she felt. But, he'd never told anyone that. Never. And out of respect for Millie, he never would. "You have my sympathy,

Mrs. Broder," he said. "I'll do whatever I can to get you released."

"You'll visit again, won't you?"

"I don't think that would be wise," he answered.

She held out her arms to him again in that gesture of vulnerability that tore at him. "Please."

"There's nothing I can do for you here that I can't do from the outside."

"But there is. Maybe they'll let me walk outdoors if you agree to take me."

That stopped him. "They won't let you go outside?"

"Not once since I've been here."

That shouldn't have surprised him. They wouldn't let her dress herself properly. How could they let her go outside? Curse Wainwright and his demand for utter control over his patients.

"I miss the sunshine," she continued. "I want to breathe fresh air again. Please say you'll come back and take me outdoors."

Damn, how could he refuse her? Even a beast of burden got to feel the sun on its face. He stood, staring at the doorknob for a moment. "All right," he said finally. "I'll be back."

"When?" she demanded.

"Soon," he answered. He'd pay a price for spending more time in her company, no doubt. The woman would drive him mad with longing. But, God help him, he couldn't let her stay caged up like an animal.

⁂

Celeste sat on her narrow bed and read Xenobia's note for the third time.

My dearest, it said.

Thank heaven I've found you. The moment I discovered where the children had you sent, I rushed to Connogua Springs myself to get you freed. Fate delivered me to the gentleman bearing this letter. Mr. Robert Albright is the mayor of Connogua Springs and of quite some upstanding reputation in the community. When I learned that he might be willing to investigate the practices of that den of vipers where you're imprisoned, I knew I had found the perfect champion for you.

By all accounts, Mr. Albright is discreet and unusually shy for a man in his position. In all, he's a wonderful fellow, and everyone who knows him adores him. But, there is one more bit of information you should have. Word has it that Mr. Albright is quite well endowed in the male drives and the machinery with which to set them into motion, if you catch my meaning. This news comes to me second hand, but Mr. A's late wife is said to have complained endlessly to her lady friends about his insatiable needs in their marriage bed. According to her, she could never satisfy him, and when she tried, she invariably found herself severely weakened from having to accommodate the considerable bulk of his sex.

The story from some loose tongues in Connogua Springs—Mr. A being far too sensitive to breathe a word of such things himself—is that the demands of the marriage bed drove Mrs. A to an early grave. Pity. I'm sure that under such circumstances you or I would perish from an excess of bliss.

In any case, I'm certain that the man will not only manage to release you from your captivity, but will make you an excellent lover as well. Take him to your bed at the first opportunity.

Forgive me for running away again to Manhattan, but I suspect that if your children were to discover my efforts to free you, they'd have you sent someplace farther away and even less appealing. I trust you'll be back with me soon, I want to hear all the details of how you get along with Mr. Albright and his considerable bulk.

As always, your devoted,
Xenobia.

Oh, thank heaven. Celeste raised the paper to her face and breathed in the scent of Xenobia's perfume. She didn't dare keep the letter with privacy so impossible in this damnable place. And yet, how could she destroy her first ray of hope, her lifeline to the outside world? She'd read it again later. She'd memorize every word and then tear it up. Truly, she would. Later. For now, she folded the letter and slipped it back into its envelope. She slid the envelope underneath her pillow and rested her palm on top as though she could feel the paper through the thickness of fabrics and goose down. Xenobia had found her, despite Young Horace and Violet—her "children"—packing her away in the middle of the night. Xenobia had not only found her, but she'd sent someone to rescue her.

Rescue. Finally, rescue. Not just from the asylum, but from all the restrictions and duties. All the obligations and fashions—corsets, teas, monogrammed thank-you notes to people she despised for gifts she couldn't bear to look at. Years of it all, first as a daughter and then as a wife. *Sit up straight, shoulders back. Speak when spoken to. Don't laugh, don't cry, don't breathe. Don't touch, don't touch, don't touch.*

Thirty-five years of living, and she still didn't dare touch anyone except herself, and that only in deepest secrecy. She wrapped her arms around her ribs and took a few deep breaths. How many times had she sat exactly like this, holding the anger inside? The frustration, the fear—no, the terror—that in the end life might have nothing more to offer. That the tiny triumphs of a new flower in her conservatory, a few moments of peace in her garden, a private dream of someplace better might be all the joy the world would ever hold for her.

She rose and walked to the window to gaze out across the long gravel drive where she'd just caught a glimpse of Mr. Robert Albright's modest gig leaving the grounds. Out of breath from having raced up the stairs to get one more look at him, she'd stood here—that dreadful Morton woman tsking her disapproval from behind—reassuring herself that he did exist. She hadn't imagined him.

Robert Albright didn't look like a rescuing knight. With his soft voice and thinning hair, he didn't even resemble the man of her fantasies. From the first day she'd become aware of the differences between men and women, she'd dreamed of one particularly handsome devil with strong arms and a wicked gleam in his eyes. Marriage had burned away the mysteries of what happened after ardent kisses and heated sighs, leaving a reality scarcely worth the grunting and sweating involved. If only marriage had satisfied a little of the hunger, too, she might have found some peace. Perhaps she wouldn't be standing here now, staring out a window and wishing that a prefect stranger would reappear on his charger to take her away.

Foolish woman. Was this what unsatisfied passions made of you? And yet...

She closed her eyes and did her best to recreate every detail of Robert Albright from memory. Had she imagined the breadth of his shoulders? The man hadn't spoken one unnecessary word, yet those he did he'd uttered in such a soft voice they might have whispered in on a breeze. As quiet as he'd been, he ought not to have dominated Wainwright's sterile office, but he had. He'd filled the room with those shoulders of his somehow. He'd brought in the smell of sunshine. And warmth, such heavenly warmth.

Saints above, such fancies. Celeste opened her eyes, turned, and stared at the blank walls around her.

Robert Albright had smiled at her, nothing more. But then, she wasn't used to people smiling at her. Certainly no one expressed any mirth in this place. Horace had only smiled when he'd bested some unfortunate soul at business. And the children…the children—best not to think of them and their insincere smiles or she'd start screaming.

Robert Albright had given her a smile that started in his eyes before it even got to his lips. A shy, uncomplicated smile she just knew she could trust, foolish woman that she was. Foolish, desperate woman.

Of course, none of those things had caused Xenobia to send Robert Albright to her. Xenobia didn't take flights of fancy when it came to men and their smiles. Mrs. Xenobia Stewart knew what went on between men and women, and she'd chosen Robert Albright for Celeste. What had the note said? *"Well endowed with the male drives and the machinery with which to to set them in motion"*? *"You or I would expire from an excess of bliss"*? The mere idea that such a man might have been created for her sent a shock of pleasure through her.

Celeste turned back to the window. Gripping the rails and staring blankly outside did nothing to relieve the tension in her chest, just beneath her breasts, so she walked toward the center of the room and stared up at the ceiling, her hands in fists by her side. She'd almost learned something of her own nature before the children had her sent here. She'd read some books, finally. She'd come to realize that the lust that captivated the men in those stories burned just as fiercely in her. She'd finally understood the ache between her own legs and found the spot where she could rub to give herself some pleasure. She'd been on the threshold of more discoveries, so many more, when the children had found her books and brought all the discoveries to an end.

Now Xenobia had sent her Robert Albright, he of the endowments and drives. She shouldn't concentrate so wholly on his smile and his gentleness—as miraculous as they were—and neglect those other aspects of him. They were kindred spirits in matters of the flesh. Xenobia had said so.

What details did she have about her champion? He was an upstanding citizen—mayor of his little town. Did small town mayors indulge themselves with inmates of institutions like this one? Most likely not. Still, she'd spoken to him frankly enough about herself. She'd told him things no decent woman even told her husband. He'd flushed and stammered in response, but he hadn't run, bless him. Perhaps he'd pitied her—who knew?—but he hadn't run.

What else did she know about him? He'd been less than satisfied in his own marriage. If what the man's own wife had said served as Xenobia's source for that little bit of information, it could hardly be doubted.

What else? Nothing, really. Only his appearance—the long fingers that had played so seductively with the brim of his hat, the kind, amber light in his eyes. His lips. He had a beautiful mouth, or maybe she'd only imagined that. No, he had a very tempting mouth, with ample lips that curved in ways that would haunt her dreams. Men shouldn't have mouths like that if they didn't know how to use them to give a woman pleasure. Had Robert Albright tried to use that mouth to love his wife? Had the unfortunate woman denied him? Celeste wouldn't deny him, if only she could have the chance to know him so intimately.

Some women might find fault with his thinning hair, but honestly, what good could hair do in the heat of passion? If he made love to her, she'd cling to those shoulders as he rode her, not to his head.

Just the idea, the mental picture of him making love to her, sent her pulse to racing. He'd kiss her, shyly at first until she encouraged him. He'd touch her with his graceful fingers. She'd show him all the right places to touch her, and he'd smile as he did it. She'd touch him, too, and kiss him. Somewhere she'd find the knowledge of how to do that to drive him past any silly objections. Then, when neither of them could stand another moment of separation, she'd take that part of him deep inside her. His cock—that was what Xenobia called it—his rod, his member, all those other words for that glorious, hard, throbbing maleness she craved.

Oh, Lord, she'd begun to throb herself. Her poor sex—cunt, she needed to say the right word—her cunt ached, and moisture had pooled between her legs. Damn, now what was she to do?

She could spend the rest of the day in this state, pacing her room near climax. Ha, the pacing itself might make her come. As hot as she'd grown, the orgasm could double her over or send her crashing to the floor. Then, they'd all come running in to see what had set their most depraved inmate off this time. Thank you, but no.

Or, she could climb onto the bed and hope for a few minutes of privacy to put out the fire between her legs. No dignity was assured here, but maybe she'd be lucky.

She walked carefully to the bed, becoming more and more aroused with each step. Once there, she sat and listened for any sound from the hallway outside that might indicate Morton's presence. Nothing but silence answered, so she lay on her stomach and breathed deeply a few times. Slowly, she inched her gown up in front, taking the lace in fistfuls until it cleared the tops of her thighs. She closed her eyes and pictured Robert Albright and his broad shoulders and long fingers as she reached into her drawers and parted the lips of her sex. She imagined his touch as she found her already hardened pearl and began to stroke it.

Chapter Two

"How good of you to visit me again, Mr. Albright, and so soon." Celeste knew very well that she was talking too much and far too fast, but she couldn't help herself. Her heart hadn't stopped its fluttering since the news that she had a visitor. She'd done her best not to hope that her caller was Robert Albright as her fingers had fumbled with the laces of her corset. But once her spirit had been set free, she hadn't managed to bottle it up again. And then, she'd seen him—so tall and handsome with his shy smiles and blushes—and her hopes had soared.

He'd come back to see her as he'd promised, and on the very next day.

Could his haste in coming back mean he'd lain awake thinking of her the night before, as she'd done thinking of him? He'd allowed her to take his arm as soon as they'd left the main hospital building. But then, he could hardly have refused that small gesture of intimacy without rejecting her outright. He wouldn't do that, would he? He might have if he thought her a true degenerate after her confessions of the day before. No, not even then. The man was far too kind to shun her so obviously. Or was he?

If only she knew more about him. If only she knew more about men in general.

"It's such a lovely day, and I've been inside for too long," she said for lack of anything better. He'd scarcely spoken three words since he'd escorted her onto the grounds. But he'd come back for her—that spoke volumes, didn't it?

"Why didn't they allow you more freedom, Mrs. Broder?" he said after a moment.

Celeste did her best to laugh lightly. "I'm sure I don't know why they do what they do here."

"I had quite some argument with Dr. Wainwright about your treatment," he said. "He claims you've been a very difficult patient."

"I suppose I haven't been completely agreeable with the staff," she answered. He said nothing but glanced at her, raising an eyebrow.

"I suppose I've been rude to some of them," she admitted. "On occasion."

He smiled—just a slight crinkle to his eyes and a soft light of amusement. She took the opportunity to lean toward him to bask in the warmth of his body.

"Being locked away doesn't do good things for my temperament," she said.

He stopped walking and turned toward her. The action separated their arms, but Celeste let her fingers rest against the wool of his coat.

"How did you get here?" he asked softly.

"What have they told you?"

"I want to hear the story from you."

She gazed up into his face and found nothing to fear, at least not that she could read in his expression. He seemed only concerned, or perhaps, just receptive. Willing to listen. And his height, combined with the strength of his shoulders, seemed to offer comfort. Here she might find shelter, a safe haven for the battered ship she'd become since the children had stolen her freedom.

"Mrs. Broder?" he prompted.

"Yes, I'm sorry," she muttered. "I must seem quite distracted. It's just that you…"

"I?"

Dear heaven, she really had to stop dithering, or he would think her feeble-minded. Only, how could she stop imagining him as a champion and lover long enough to have a civil conversation with him?

"Might we sit down, do you think?" she said finally.

"Of course. There's a bench over here." He indicated a copse of yew trees with his arm.

She walked in front of him toward the bench, enjoying the crunch of gravel under her slippers. She hadn't lied when she'd told him that she hadn't been allowed outdoors since her arrival. The smell of lush grass and flowers, the sounds of birdsong, the feel of the sun on her shoulders—it was all so seductive. So delicious. And now she'd sit for as long as he'd accompany her in the shade of the yews, obscured from everyone. None of the staff—not Wainwright nor Morton—and none of the inmates could see them here. The mere thought of privacy, with this man, made her lightheaded. Her pulse beat at the base of her throat, and the skin at the back of her neck tingled. In another moment, she'd find herself swooning from all the stimulation if she didn't gather her wits.

She sat on the bench and patted the marble beside her. Albright gave her another smile—a shy one this time—and blushed, but didn't join her. A disappointment, but she would be patient if it killed her.

Resting her hands in her lap, she looked up at him. "My husband owned several newspapers and a publishing house," she began. "He was already quite wealthy when his first wife died."

"You were young when you married him," Mr. Albright said.

"Dr. Wainwright told you that?" she asked.

"Mrs. Stewart did."

"Ah yes, Xenobia," Celeste said. "I was past prime marriage age when Horace approached my father, but I was young enough to be stupid. Young, hopeful, and stupid."

"Insulting yourself won't accomplish anything."

"No, I suppose not." She sighed. "I don't know what I expected from marriage, really. I craved excitement, I know that much. I thought Horace's money would buy that for me."

Mr. Albright said nothing but just stood, his hands behind his back, regarding her. From his appearance and what she knew of him, he had to have passed his fortieth birthday. And yet, his physique measured favorably against a younger man's, even the pirate of her youthful dreams. The modest but flattering cut of his suit outlined the breadth of his shoulders and the length of his legs. If not for his shy manner, she could easily picture him lifting her in his arms and carrying her off to someplace sinful.

She sighed again. "Horace's children, Young Horace and Violet, were in school in Geneva. I pictured us joining them there, stopping in Vienna, and then continuing to the Orient. He quickly informed me that Europe was too full of `damned Frenchmen' for his taste."

"He didn't like the French?"

"He thought even less of Italians," Celeste answered. "And the Orient was out of the question."

"Marriage wasn't what you'd expected."

"I don't suppose marriage is what anyone expects it to be, Mr. Albright. Weren't you surprised in your own marriage?"

"Yes…um…well…" His voice trailed off, and his cheeks flushed a lovely rose that crept up past his thinning hair line. His embarrassments were almost as endearing as his body was tempting.

"Must you really stand all the way over there?" she asked. "I have to twist my neck to look at you."

"Mrs. Broder…"

"Please call me Celeste."

"I shouldn't," he stammered. "That is, it isn't correct. We only met yesterday."

"And yet, I feel I know you." Such a silly cliché, and yet she meant it. She did feel as if she knew him, or would soon. If only he could allow himself to trust her. She smiled at him and patted the bench next to her again. "Please do sit down," she said. "You can always call for help if I try to molest you."

That got her a smile from him, a real one. "Are you that dangerous?"

"Absolutely. I'll steal your soul if you're not careful."

His smile grew broader. "I believe that."

He walked to the bench and sat beside her. She took the opportunity to wrap her arm around his again, and when he didn't pull away, she leaned against him. "Your marriage, Robert."

"We were talking about yours," he corrected.

"Oh, very well. My marriage." She let her fingertips travel the length of his sleeve, down to his wrist and back up. "When I learned that I wasn't to travel, I decided I'd have children and devote myself to them, but Horace didn't want any more. He had a very effective way for keeping me from getting in the family way. He avoided me."

Robert tried to pull away, but she held him fast. "I'd had urges for years— unmet cravings. I thought that at least marriage would bring me some relief from those. I thought men were slaves to their baser natures—perfect beasts. But it appeared that Horace had his own desires well under control, if he had desires at all."

"I don't think I should hear this."

"But you have to if you're to understand how I got here. Robert, please."

She reached down and intertwined her fingers with his. He seemed surprised at first, staring down at their hands as if no one had ever touched him that way before. Then his features softened, and he stroked her palm with his middle finger. The contact sent a tiny jolt of heat through her, from the underside of her wrist to the crook of her arm.

"Go on," he murmured.

Go on? When she could hardly catch her breath? And yet, it was so desperately important he hear her story and understand.

"Horace didn't want me that way," she continued, her voice unsteady. "From time to time his baser nature got the better of him, and he took his pleasure as quickly as he could in my bed. Even as rushed and unpleasant as those times were,

I knew I wanted more. I needed it, Robert. Oh, how I needed it, and he denied me."

She stopped, and a little sob caught in her throat. She ought to hate herself for using tears to gain his sympathy, but she couldn't help herself. "You must think I'm unnatural. You must be thoroughly repulsed."

"Not at all, Mrs…" He squeezed her fingers. "Not at all, Celeste."

Dear heaven, could the man be any more dear? That soft rendering of her name would have won him a spot in her heart if his kindness hadn't already. Xenobia had sent her a fine champion, indeed. If she weren't careful, she'd find herself in love with the man after knowing him for less than a day.

Love? Maybe she belonged here, after all. Only a madwoman contemplated love with a man on their second meeting. And yet, the feel of his hand in hers, the scent of his shaving soap, the tempting curve of his lips, how could any sane woman resist such things?

He studied her face, his gaze wandering gently over her features in a manner that could only be called a caress. "If your husband didn't want you, why did he marry you?"

"I always wondered about that. I asked him more than once, but he wouldn't tell me. I finally learned that he had political ambitions and needed a wife. He died before he could realize his goals, and I ended up a very rich woman."

"That still doesn't tell me how you got here."

"The children disapproved of me," she answered. That was an understatement. "I'd tried to befriend them. Honestly. But I'm afraid they always resented my marrying Horace. So, as soon as their dear father was safely dead and buried, they hurried home from Europe to protect his interests."

"His interests?" Robert repeated, one eyebrow rising. "What interests could he have once he'd died?"

"His money, of course."

"Ah, yes."

"I was so naive. I had no idea how vicious people could become when a large inheritance was involved. And by the time they returned to New York, I'd already made a fatal mistake. I'd begun to enjoy myself."

Celeste sat in silence for a moment. If the next part of her story didn't frighten him off, she could hope for an end to her imprisonment. She might even dare hope for happiness.

"I'd met Xenobia Stewart before at some dinner party or other. Alone among all the people in New York society, she seemed to see my restlessness. She alone seemed to understand that the trappings of wealth can't satisfy all of human hunger." Celeste took a breath. "She offered me friendship."

Robert looked into her eyes briefly. "Friendship."

"She offered more than friendship, actually." Celeste blushed and gripped his hand. "I turned that offer down. It's always been my blessing—or curse—to desire men exclusively."

He sighed—in surprise? relief?—if only she could tell. But, he still didn't pull away.

"So, when Horace died, I sought Xenobia out. She has…um…private evenings at her home. Soirées for intimate friends and intimate activities."

His cheeks turned a deep rose color. "I've heard of such things, although I've never met anyone who indulged in them."

"I didn't indulge," she added quickly. "I attended. I listened and learned, but I never…um…surrendered myself to…well…any of it. Not really, not in the flesh."

"It isn't my place to judge."

"I'd like your good opinion, Robert. I'm not without scruples. I'm not promiscuous. I'm only…" What? She was only what? Lonely? Craving human contact? How could she put a name to the ache inside her?

"Shhh," he whispered, quieting her.

"Xenobia gave me some books," she continued. "Voluptuous reading, things no decent woman should know about. Those I devoured as if I'd been starved for them all my life. They explained so much about how I felt. They felt like a lifeline to sanity. How ironic they'd prove my Achilles' heel."

"Your children found them," he said.

"My virtuous, upright children thought nothing of searching my room. Conventional morality doesn't extend to respecting privacy, it appears."

"I'm sorry."

"So," she said, gesturing around her, "those books and the fact that I'd attended several of Xenobia's parties were all Horace and Violet needed to prove I'd lost my reason. They had a judge friend of my husband's commit me here against my will. I suspect some money changed hands in the transaction."

"That's outrageous," he said. "Are you sure?"

"I had a great deal of their father's money. With me 'insane' and locked away, the children control my inheritance."

"Damn," he said. "That's unconscionable. I've never heard of such injustice."

Celeste took the first deep breath she'd managed since she'd begun her story. He was angry on her behalf, not repulsed by her history. The dear man, the precious, perfect man. She could dare to hope now, for freedom and more. With Robert Albright she might dare hope for so much more.

He rose from the bench, his hands clenched into his fists, and paced a few feet. "How could you be confined for mere reading when Mrs. Stewart is allowed to have her parties?"

"Xenobia's fabulously wealthy and answers to no one. I had to contend with the children and Horace's friend, the judge. Powerful enemies."

"And you had to face them alone." He straightened his shoulders. "Now you have an ally. Me."

She stood, walked to him, and took his hands in hers. "Then you will help me, Robert?"

He gave her fingers a gentle squeeze. "Of course."

"The accusations against me aren't entirely groundless. I did read those books. I did attend Xenobia's parties."

"You're as sane as I am," he declared.

"But I am a voluptuary. I do lust." *I lust for you, Robert. I want you.*

"All of us lust," he answered. "Only few of us will admit it."

She leaned toward him, tipping her face up. His breath caught, and a tiny tremor ran through him.

"Do you lust?" she whispered.

"All of us lust," he said.

She rested her palms against his chest and did her best to feel through all the layers of his clothing to sense his heartbeat. That didn't work, of course, and his expression gave nothing away. But a muscle near his mouth jumped, parting his lips no more than a feather's breadth.

Those lips had taken possession of her dreams, had occupied her thoughts until they'd nearly driven her frantic with wondering about the taste of them. Now, here they were, parted and only inches from her own. Did she dare to sample them?

Slowly, she rose toward him. When she wavered, he caught her elbows in his hands and steadied her. He was welcoming her, the dear man.

"May I kiss you, my precious Robert?" she heard her own voice ask. "May I touch my mouth to yours?"

"Celeste, I…" His voice came out unsteadily, but his hands held her firmly against his chest.

"Will you indulge me?" she breathed against his mouth. "Poor, sad sinner that I am?"

"Oh, yes." He said the words so softly they almost didn't register in her ears. But her heart heard them.

She moved the scant distance between them and pressed her lips to his. Neither of them moved for a long moment. They simply stood as before, Celeste leaning into the strength of his body while his hands supported her. She let her mouth rest against his softly, barely touching.

Such delicious textures, his lips. Soft, firm, sweet. She sampled the lower one, taking it between both of hers and nipping. He groaned deep in the back of his throat but didn't move. He held perfectly still and allowed her to explore him. She kissed him more fully, letting her mouth travel over his and then to his chin. She trailed kisses across the length of his jaw and rubbed her nose against the faint stubble on his cheek. She found his earlobe and nibbled on that until he trembled against her—his strong body shuddering.

She blew hot breath into his ear and followed that with the tip of her tongue, and something snapped inside him. With a growl, he pulled her against him, cupping her buttocks with his hands as his mouth sought hers and plundered it.

Over and over he kissed her, as if only her lips stood between him and hell. He devoured her upper lip and then the lower one. Thrusting his tongue between them, he probed her mouth until she couldn't breathe but could only gasp and return his passion with her own.

She'd lived for this her entire life. His kiss took her from dull non-being to brilliant, buzzing reality. She answered his fervor with passion she hadn't known she had. She slipped her arms around his neck and pulled herself fully against him until her breasts crushed against his chest—another set of sensations, almost painful in their erotic beauty.

On and on he went, merciless, generous, demanding. He trembled and moaned her name and held her against him with an almost frightening strength. She'd never felt the power of a man's body unleashed before. She'd never lived until this very moment. Her heart might burst with all the joy.

Then, suddenly, he stopped. He brought his hands up to her face and pressed her head to his chest, stroking her skin as though to comfort her.

"I'm sorry," he said in a rusty whisper.

"I'm not," she answered.

"I was taking advantage of your situation."

"It wasn't any advantage I didn't encourage."

"Still…" He held her gently, stroking her face. The tenderness of the gesture almost made her weep until she noticed something else. Something hard was pressing into her belly. His hardness, no doubt. His sex, his member, felt perfectly huge, impossibly long and thick. If only she had the courage to press her hand against the front of his pants, she'd get some better idea of his dimensions. But she'd spoil the moment if she did that. He'd given her so much this afternoon—his acceptance, his promise of support, the joy of his caress. So much. She'd have to be satisfied with all those gifts for now. Lovemaking would come later. One way or another, Robert Albright would be her lover, and she'd be the happiest woman in the world.

"I'm a gentleman, Celeste," he murmured after several heartbeats had passed between them. "I hope."

"I hope not," she answered. "My husband was a gentleman."

"Your husband was an ass."

She laughed. Oh, Lord, how long had it been since she'd really laughed? Robert laughed, too, and the sound echoed through his chest into her, such music.

She leaned back and gazed up into his face. She found him smiling at her, that expression of uncomplicated acceptance that had so endeared him to her on their first meeting. Dear Robert. Beloved Robert.

"So, will you help me?" she asked.

"Yes."

"And you'll come back to see me again?"

His smile broadened. "Certainly."

And will you be my lover? she added silently.

Of course, she heard him answer in her mind.

Robert drove home with a rock-hard erection that throbbed in his pants. Every jolt of the wheels traveled through his bones right to his cock, and no number of deep breaths brought him any relief. This was torture, pure torture. If he so much as touched himself, he'd spend, howling out his lust like a crazed animal. He might do that yet. He might have no choice. But right now, he'd torment himself with the image of Celeste Broder and what he'd almost done with her among the yews at the Wainwright Asylum.

Millie had never excited him like that. As much as he'd wanted his wife, as many hours as he'd spent lying next to her, aroused and aching, Millie had never sent him into such a frenzy. And to think, he'd only kissed Celeste. True, he'd brought her hips up hard against his rod and held her there, but truth be told, Long Tom had been ready for a coupling from the moment they'd entered that copse of yews. Just being alone with his raven-haired temptress was enough to make him as randy as a callow boy.

And he was going to do it again. God help him, he was going to get her someplace private and frig her until neither of them could stand.

Damn, when had his thoughts become so foul?

He pulled on the reins, bringing his horse to a halt. Sienna whinnied and shook his head, impatient to get back to the barn and some oats, no doubt. But much more jostling, and Robert's cock would spew copious amounts of sperm into his trousers.

He closed his eyes, counted to ten and then to twenty. Anything to get some control. But he'd never get control of his body if he couldn't control his mind. The images of Celeste wouldn't leave him—how her lips had felt under his, soft, pliant, and yet demanding. How her skin had flushed and her breasts had risen and fallen under her bodice as she'd worked to catch her breath. All that, and the shy way she'd asked permission to kiss him. *She'd* asked for *his* consent.

Why shouldn't he consent? Why shouldn't he consent to anything she asked of him? They were both grown and unencumbered with other attachments. He wouldn't be taking her innocence. Hell, he wouldn't be taking anything from her that she didn't freely offer. If she wanted him to take her to his bed, why shouldn't he? She did want him. He couldn't doubt that any longer. She wanted him. Mrs. Celeste Broder—wealthy, beautiful, passionate beyond any measure he'd ever hoped to find in a woman—wanted him.

He laughed out loud as the pure absurdity of it hit him. Robert Albright—a lad too shy to approach any girl he admired, a man too timid to propose marriage without sweating and stammering, a husband too frightened to speak to his own wife about his needs—that Robert Albright would soon enjoy the pleasures of the flesh with a voluptuous creature like Celeste Broder. He'd spend hours, longer if he could manage, in rapture, exploring every inch of her. He'd try every caress, every maneuver he could think of to satisfy her. And somewhere he'd find the courage to tell her what pleased him. If the words wouldn't come, he'd take her hand and show her. Damn, but he'd do it. All of it.

Millie's parents would never approve. The City Council would never approve. No one in town would approve. Fine, they'd never know, and if they did find out, they could keep their opinions to themselves.

Millie wouldn't approve. Dear Millie—his little love, his wife. But she'd died and left him. Would she expect him to remain celibate for the rest of his life? She'd never enjoyed sexual relations herself, but surely, even she would understand that a man needed that, needed to satisfy his sex between a woman's legs, as much as he needed to breathe. He'd kept a tight rein on his desires for all the years they'd been married, despite what it had cost him.

He was forty-five years old and had never had full satisfaction. He'd bed Celeste Broder and give her whatever else she needed—freedom, affection, his highest esteem—anything. He'd need some time to arrange all the details for their lovers' tryst, but arrange them, he would.

He'd approach the board of directors of the asylum and work for her release. But before he could gain her complete freedom, he'd beg for a few precious hours in his custody. He'd convince them that an afternoon at his home would help her mind to heal.

Ha, a glorious bit of irony there. Nothing in her mind needed healing, but her body did, and so did his. Eros would be their doctor and his bedroom their sanitarium. And if The Almighty had any sense of justice whatsoever, he'd make the encounter magnificent enough to make up for two lifetimes of deprivation.

Chapter Three

Celeste seemed calm enough as she crossed the threshold into Robert's house. God knew he was in enough turmoil for both of them. He'd never invited a woman to a tryst before, let alone in his own home. He'd done his damnedest to make everything perfect, but what if he'd failed? Celeste Broder was used to the finest of Manhattan society. When the time came for him to offer his hospitality—himself, his own person—would she find him lacking?

"May I take your wrap?" he asked, extending his hand toward her.

"It's lovely." She crossed the entryway into the sunlit foyer. Spinning in a near-circle, she took in the curving formal staircase, the rosewood center table with the bouquet he'd arranged himself, the antique clock against the wall. "Your home is utterly charming, Robert."

So much for his fears that she wouldn't like his house. For the first time that day, he managed to breathe deeply. "Thank you."

She handed him her shawl and scowled in a way that was more flirtatious than angry. "I should be furious with you for leaving me in that dreadful place for two full weeks with no word."

"I'm sorry you had to wait," he said, but didn't add that he'd also spent the past two weeks in an agony of anticipation and longing. "I had to go before the board of directors of the asylum to get you an afternoon free. They only meet once a month."

"But you did it, Robert," she answered. "Thank you."

He also didn't mention that he'd had to plead Celeste's case in full view and hearing of Wainwright and that matron, who'd glowered at him the whole time. He'd made enemies there, no doubt about it. He'd have to work through the board of directors in the future to win even the smallest concessions.

"Wainwright warned the board that you might try to manipulate the situation," he said.

"Did he?"

"Oh, yes." In fact, Wainwright had called her hysterical and devious.

"The pompous, old goat," she said.

"He especially advised me to keep clear of your machinations."

She laughed for a moment and then gave him a wickedly seductive smile. "And do you plan to heed his advice?"

"That depends on what your machinations are."

"My champion," she cried as she rushed to him, laughing, and threw her arms around his shoulders. "You've given me an afternoon of freedom, and I don't care what they said about me."

Still holding her shawl in one hand, he caught her in an embrace and held her against him. He'd probably regret that, having spent the entire day in a state of arousal in anticipation of her visit. Sensing that his satisfaction was near, Long Tom thickened and hardened at even this modest contact with her body. His poor cock would have to wait. He still had to get through checking that Francie had left and then tea before he found satisfaction.

Just then his two Afghan hounds burst into the room. Traveler and Georgette spotted Celeste and headed toward her, their paws slipping on the polished wood floor. Before Robert could stop the dogs' approach, Celeste squealed and dropped to her knees.

"Dogs!" she proclaimed, extending her arms to encircle the animals. "Your company, an afternoon free, and dogs, too. What a lucky woman I am."

"Get back, you two," he ordered the dogs.

"Don't you dare go." She buried her face into Traveler's fur. "I haven't played with a dog for years."

"I'm afraid their idea of play isn't ladylike."

"Good, because I don't want to be a lady this afternoon." Georgette licked Celeste's face as though they were old friends, and Celeste laughed with more abandon than he could remember since he'd met her. "I don't know if I should let you do that," she said to the dog. "Your master may not want to kiss me when you're done."

"Always," he said. "I always want to kiss you, Celeste."

She glanced up at him and smiled shyly. His member hardened further, almost jerking in his pants. Damn, but he wanted this woman.

A throat cleared at the threshold to the solarium.

"Ah, there you are, Francie," he said.

"Mr. Albright." His part-time maid nodded to him and then looked pointedly at Celeste, who rose and folded her hands together in front of her skirts.

"Mrs. Broder is my guest for tea," he said. That little bit of news would find its way all over town by morning, but he could do nothing about that now. "Would you see that it's set out, please?"

"Already done, sir."

"Good. Then thank Mrs. Kenny for me and head off for the day."

"She's gone, sir," Francie answered. "You told her to go home some time ago."

Celeste lowered her lashes, and one corner of her mouth lifted no more than a fraction of an inch. Just enough to express her approval.

"Thank you, Francie. I'd forgotten," he said. "Take the dogs with you and then run along."

Francie came just far enough into the foyer to grasp the dogs by their collars and take one more questioning look toward Celeste. With Traveler and Georgette under control, the maid turned and headed toward the back of the house.

Robert gestured toward the solarium. "Would you join me for tea, Mrs. Broder?"

"My pleasure, Mr. Albright." She went in the direction he'd indicated. He paused only to drape her shawl over the banister. As he did, the sound of the back door closing floated softly through the house. They were alone. Smiling, he followed Celeste.

She stood next to his prized white cattleya orchid, her nose no more than an inch from one of the flowers.

"That one isn't scented," he said.

"As beautiful as it is, it doesn't need perfume."

"The same's true of you," he said. He hadn't lied there. The mere sight of her—the soft flush to her skin, the length of her throat, the swell of her breasts bound deliciously by her corset—was enough to drive any man past the breaking point. He must have passed that point, though, because he thought he could make out the scent of her. Not rose water or some other pretense, but a hot, musky scent that invaded his nostrils and clouded his brain. The fertile aroma of his plants, combined with something else essentially hers.

She turned and smiled at him. "You enjoy horticulture?"

"It's one of my passions," he answered. His only passion until two weeks ago.

"I used to have a garden I loved," she said. "Horace didn't like my fingers dirty, but I insisted."

"I'll show you my garden in a bit."

"I'd like that."

"But first, let's have our tea." He gestured toward the whitewashed, cast-iron table where Francie had set the teapot and the shortcake Mrs. Kenny had made that morning. Chilled bowls of strawberries and whipped cream stood nearby—only inches from her plate and the gift he'd wrapped that morning.

He pulled out her chair. After she sat, he let his fingers drift along the length of her throat. Her pulse beat rapidly just under her skin. Apprehension? Anticipation? Impossible to tell, but once she'd opened her present, she'd have no doubt what he intended for the rest of the afternoon.

She picked the parcel up and toyed with the ribbon. "For me?"

"A small gift to replace the one you lost."

She gave him a questioning look, but he just smiled and took his own seat while she unwrapped the package. When she saw the book, she let out a little gasp of surprise. "*The Pearl.* Wherever did you find this?"

"An obscure bookshop got it for me." A bookshop in a different town, three towns over, where no one knew him.

"You know what's in here, don't you?" she asked.

He did. In that book and four other erotic ones he'd bought and read himself in the past week. "I know."

"Are Lady Pokingham and her amorous adventures your standard reading?"

"They are now."

She put down the book and stared into his face for a long moment. "I don't think I want any tea, Robert."

Rejection. His heart stopped beating, and his chest suddenly felt empty. She was rejecting him, after all. "Do you want to go back to the asylum?"

"Of course not," she answered softly.

"Then, what?"

Under the table, she reached out a hand and pressed her palm against his erection. "This. This is what I want."

A jolt of pleasure shot through him—so powerful he jumped in his seat, nearly knocking the table and its contents into her lap. "Dear God, Celeste."

"Don't deny me, my darling. Please."

"Deny you?" he croaked. "Never."

She stretched out her fingers, as though measuring the length and width of him. If she was going to become frightened of his size, she'd do it now, because his member was fully engorged under her touch.

She showed no fear, though, but only smiled. "I've dreamed of you for two weeks now. Like this. Just like this. Does that shock you?"

"No." It did shock him, although he'd never tell her that. She might remove her hand if he did. "But I need to warn you that I won't last if you continue to do that."

She squeezed him, and his cock responded, growing longer and harder, although he would never have believed that possible.

"Mercy," he cried.

"None," she answered. "I want to look at you."

"We have all afternoon," he said. "I want to pleasure you first."

"Later. Please, Robert, show yourself to me."

He groaned and turned in his chair so that the front of his pants was exposed to her view. He couldn't have stood. He wouldn't have found the strength.

She gently spread his legs apart and dropped to her knees between them. In that position, she placed her mouth against the fabric of his pants, her hot, and moist breath seeping through to his flesh. His hips jerked, pressing his throbbing member against her lips. He reached out blindly with his hands, grasping for anything to use as an anchor, anything to distract him from her assault on his control. His fingers found the curving bars that held the seat of his chair, and he clung to them while his cock swelled and threatened to explode under her touch.

She stroked his length and then slowly unfastened the buttons of his fly to free him. When she had him fully exposed, she gasped. "She was right. Oh dear heaven, Xenobia told the truth."

"Xenobia?"

"Oh…yes. Xenobia told me that a man was beautiful when aroused. She didn't exaggerate."

Celeste closed her fingers around his shaft, and the sight of her white gloves against the livid purple of his cock sent him past any wonder of what Xenobia Stewart might have said. He was going to come, any moment now. Nothing on Earth could stop him.

Celeste stroked him, down to his sac and then back up. "How should I do this?"

"That's it…doing…fine," he managed between clenched teeth.

"What about the tip?" she murmured. "It's so large."

She flicked her thumb along the underside of the swollen head and then rubbed until a drop of fluid appeared. Gripping the rungs of the chair until his palms hurt, he fought the urge to surrender. *Going to come, going to come. Must…make…it …last.*

She squeezed again and stroked and stroked. Faster. Firmer. No hope. No hope to resist. He felt the climax starting and gave in to it. He watched his own cock jerk upwards—now, now, now—as his essence spurted out of him. He hung suspended in time while his semen sprayed all over her hand and her bosom. Finally, he collapsed against his seat and closed his eyes. In the peace that followed, even consciousness slipped away from him.

Celeste watched Robert's face as he closed his eyes and drifted off into some private heaven. For now, she couldn't imagine anything more fascinating than the expression of joy on his features. Despite the urgency of her own arousal, she'd wait happily for Robert to recover. She sat up in her chair and basked in the sight of him.

Xenobia hadn't lied about his dimensions. Celeste had had no experience with men's members other than Horace's, which was to say almost no experience at all. She'd wondered often about how that part of a man was built, but she'd never imagined that one could be at once so large and so beautiful. Even in repose, it made her shiver with anticipation.

Robert opened his eyes finally, sighed, and smiled at her. She'd loved his smile since the first moment she'd seen it. Now it made her heart burst with happiness and pride.

His smile turned to an embarrassed grin, though, as he quickly picked up a linen napkin from the table and swiped at the white droplets that still adorned her bodice. "I am sorry."

"I'm not." The pressure of his hands against her breasts felt so blessedly good, she could hardly feel sorry about anything.

"I've never lost control like that," he said. "My lust may have ruined your dress."

"I don't care, as long as I pleased you," she said.

"Pleased me?" He laughed deep in his throat, a delicious, wicked sound. "Dear Celeste. You nearly killed me."

"I'll take that as a compliment."

He reached across the table and took her hand. "Oh, my darling."

"I've never done that to a man before. Reading about something is quite a different thing from doing it."

"My angel, I hope I do half as well for you."

Her heart thudded at that statement. What would he do for her? Would he touch her the same way, the way she'd imagined him stroking her while she pleasured herself? Would he drive her wild with his fingers and then let his enormous sex finish the job? When she next spent, would she do so all around his hardness? The mere thought stole her breath.

"Do you know what that does to me?" he asked.

"What?"

"The way your skin flushes. You did it the first day we met. I had to get away from you before the swelling in my pants became too obvious to miss."

She put her fingers over her mouth. "That day? In Wainwright's office? You were…that way?"

"I'm always 'that way' around you, sweetest. I'm getting 'that way' again right now."

She glanced quickly at him. He'd turned in his seat, but she could still make out the state of his member. It was swelling already and lengthening.

"Will you make love to me now?" she asked.

"Soon," he answered. "But first, I want to make you come the way you did me."

The throbbing accelerated between her legs, now so fast and hard she could feel it beating in rhythm with her heart. Moisture pooled there until her drawers were quite saturated. She had to work for breath, and the effort left her dizzy and weak.

He rose from his chair and helped her up. She watched his elegant fingers as he removed her gloves. For a moment, he stood and stared at the one that had stroked his member and still bore the evidence of his ejaculation. He slipped that into the pocket of his coat and smiled at her. "I'll treasure this always."

Such a sweet declaration almost brought tears to her eyes, but she fought them back and returned his gaze, putting every bit of her love into it. Gently, he turned her around and started undressing her. Her hat went first, landing on the tabletop, followed by the pins from her hair. While her curls fell all around her shoulders, his fingers worked on the fastenings of her dress. Layer by layer, the fabric fell away—first her bodice, then her skirts. Cool air washed over her as the warmth of his hands sank through her skin and into her bones. Petticoats came off and then her corset cover, and finally the corset itself, freeing her breasts from their confinement.

He reached around her and squeezed her breasts. She rested back against him and whimpered.

"My darling," he whispered against her throat. He kissed her there, nipping her skin to the edge of her shoulder as he eased her chemise down her arms. "My dear Celeste. My beautiful Celeste."

The cotton caught on her erect nipples, torturing the over-sensitive flesh. He pushed the chemise down and over her hips until it fell in a pool at her feet and then took her breasts in his hands again.

"Oh, Robert." She pressed back against him, against the renewed hardness of his member. If she didn't have him inside her soon, she'd die of frustration.

He touched her then. He slipped his hands over her belly and down into her drawers to stroke her sex. She shuddered and cried out as his fingers moved gently over the center of her arousal.

"Sweet," he murmured against her shoulder. "Hot, so hot. Wet and sweet."

"I can't bear it," she moaned. "Hurry. Please. Give me release."

But, instead of pushing her past the edge, he slid her drawers over her hips and helped her to turn and sit down. Breathing heavily, beyond mere torture now, she sat and watched as he dropped to his knees before her as she had done with him. He pulled the drawers over her feet and tossed them aside, leaving nothing on her body but her slippers and hose. Then he spread her legs.

Now, surely now he would touch her and end this agony. In another moment, she'd climax whether he touched her or not. But oh, how much more glorious it would be to feel his fingers on her as she came. She stretched forward, pushing her hips toward the edge of the seat. Toward him.

He still denied her, though. From under heavy eyelids, she watched as he reached to the table and dipped his finger into the whipped cream. That, then, he finally brought to her aching sex. With the other hand, he parted her lips, and he pressed the cream against her pearl. The coldness sent a jolt through her, shocking her out of her languor.

His touch gentled as he continued to rub the rapidly warming cream against her. Nothing had ever felt like this, even in her most heated dreams. Higher and higher she floated—so close to completion her whole body tensed and readied itself.

He reached for the cream again. This time she tried to steel herself for the cold, but nothing could save her from its icy burn. He rubbed it in again, at first slowly and then faster until she hovered right at the edge of sanity. Through a reddish haze of lust, she watched as he removed his finger and covered her throbbing sex with his mouth.

The instant he touched her with his tongue, she came. Throwing back her head, she cried out as the spasms raced through her. Over and over. Quicker. Harder. Each stronger and faster than the last until she lost all connection to reality and fell back against the chair. Spent. Drained. And yet, as the drowsiness enveloped her, her inner muscles still clenched and unclenched, reluctant to surrender the last bit of sweetness.

She sat that way, absolutely motionless, for what seemed like forever. Slowly, consciousness of her own being returned and with it sounds. Birdsong—lovely and distant. A rustling of leaves. The beat of her own heart.

And breathing. Robert's breathing.

She opened her eyes and found him. His head rested, cheek down, on one of her thighs as he gazed up at her. The fingers of one hand were still splayed over her other thigh, making tiny indentations in her flesh.

The image of him looking at her that way—as if she were the most perfect woman in creation—made her chest hurt and her eyes burn. In just a scant hour—less—he'd taken something ugly and made it beautiful. He'd taken a gift that Horace had scorned and elevated it to a miracle.

She lifted an impossibly heavy arm and stroked the side of his face.

"Did I please you?" he asked.

She let out a sob. What other answer could she make to a question like that? Had he pleased her? Did the sun brighten the heavens? Did she love him with every bit of her heart and soul? Yes, yes, yes.

Love. She loved Robert Albright. First, her champion. Then, her lover. Now, her soul mate. He was her world. Whatever misery had driven her to this room at this moment, she blessed it now. She'd found love, finally—the only real reason to exist.

"Here," he said, as he rose on his knees and rubbed a tear away from her cheek with his thumb. "There's no reason to cry."

She laughed, even while the tears continued to come.

"I may not be much of a lover, but I don't think I'm that bad," he said.

That little bit of absurdity made her laugh even harder. "Not much of a lover?"

"Well, you're still sitting at the tea table, wearing nothing but shoes and hose." He cleared his throat. "And I...well, my pants are undone."

Glancing down, she discovered that his pants were, indeed, still open. He'd grown hard again, and his member stuck straight out from the opening in front. Her earlier teasing and caresses hadn't diminished him in the least. If anything, he looked thicker and harder and more beautiful than ever. Her pulse quickened to think how he would feel inside her.

She rested her arms around his neck and kissed him, for the first time that afternoon and all the sweeter after what they'd given each other since her arrival. Now, she wanted more.

"Mr. Albright," she murmured against his lips. "Are we going to have to sit through several cups of tea while trying to choke down that whipped cream? Or are you finally going to make love to me?"

He laughed and scrambled to his feet, scooping her up in his arms as he rose. "To hell with tea, and to hell with the whipped cream."

Chapter Four

Celeste covered her lover's face with caresses as Robert nudged a door open with his foot and carried her into a sun-drenched bedroom as lovely as any she'd ever seen. She stopped kissing him and clung to his neck. This was what she'd dreamed of when she pictured her wedding day and initiation into womanhood— to be swept up into the arms of the man she loved and to be carried to bed as though she were some delicate treasure. Instead, she'd lost her virginity, and her innocence, with Horace in a darkened hotel room after a long and tiring wedding reception. Nothing like this little piece of Paradise.

An open window let in a warm breeze along with the sunlight and the scent of roses and green earth. More flowers like the ones in the front hallway stood in an antique ewer on the bedside table. The bed itself had ornate wooden posts at each corner, topped by a canopy of eyelet lace. The comforter and coverlets had been turned down to expose dazzling white sheets.

Robert had planned their afternoon of lovemaking well. She'd suspected as much when he sent his servants home. The dear man. Could she possibly love him any more than she did right at this moment?

He walked to the bed and set her onto the crisp sheets as gently as if she were made of butterflies' wings. After sitting beside her, he took her hand and brought her fingers to his lips. She ought to have found the image strange—a large man kissing her palm and then the inside of her wrist, while his manhood projected from his pants, fully erect and perfectly enormous. Nothing seemed the least bit odd, though. This was Robert, her shy lover and champion of contradictions.

He leaned over and kissed her. First on the forehead and then the tip of her nose. Finally, he pressed his lips to hers and teased them apart. She took his face in her hands and answered with every bit of passion and love in her. His breath was sweet, his sighs even sweeter. She opened her mouth and grazed his lips with her tongue. He groaned, invading her mouth and sending a spiral of heat from her belly upward. As he ravished her mouth, the fabric of his vest rubbed against her nipples.

She grasped the lapels of his jacket and pushed the garment over his shoulders. "You're wearing entirely too many clothes."

He sat up and smiled at her. "So are you."

"I'm only wearing shoes and stockings," she answered.

"Far too many clothes." He lifted one of her feet, removed her slipper, and dropped it to the floor. He did the same for the other and then slid his fingers under the garter that held her stocking. The feel of his hand against her inner thigh brought back sensations of how he'd driven her mad earlier. She let him stroke her there, his gentle touch sending a flash of heat through her breasts. He slipped one stocking down her leg and then reached to the other garter. By the time he'd removed that stocking, too, her bosom rose and fell as she struggled for air.

This time, though, she'd take him with her into madness.

As much as she hated pushing his hands away, she managed to sit up and maneuver his jacket the rest of the way over his shoulders and then off his arms. After that, she started in on the buttons of his vest.

"I never saw my husband naked," she said. "It didn't matter with him, but I want to see all of you."

"I'm not young anymore," he answered. "I hope you're not disappointed."

She reached down and curled her fingers around his engorged sex. It thickened even further against her palm. "I won't be disappointed."

He gave her a devilish grin. He was getting good at those. The man who'd seemed almost frightened of her the first time they'd met now became the wicked pirate of her dreams. Now, this afternoon, in this bed with the smells of sunshine and roses wafting through the window and the pristine canopy overhead, she'd finally have her pirate.

She unbuttoned his vest and took that off him. Next went his shirt, so that he was naked from the waist up and she could finally gaze at his chest and the broad shoulders she'd admired since the first. Running her palms over him, she caressed his flat nipples with her thumbs. He trembled but kept his gaze evenly on her face.

"So beautiful," she whispered, as she traced his collar bone and dipped her fingertips into the hollows at the base of his throat.

"Hardly beautiful." He took her hands in his.

"More beautiful than beautiful."

He bent and removed his shoes and hose and then stood by the side of the bed. It took only an instant to slip his pants and drawers off, and finally he was naked.

Nature could scarcely have made a more perfect creature than Robert Albright. He might no longer have been young, but he stood straight and tall. Lofty brow, strong jaw, finely muscled neck leading to a broad chest with nothing to interrupt its classic lines. His belly looked firm for the stroking, and below lay the curling hairs that concealed the base of his sex—a base as thick as her wrist. The organ itself jutted a full nine inches from his torso, if she was any judge.

For the first time, the full impact of his size hit her. What would she do if she couldn't take all of him? She'd never had any man other than Horace, and he'd never presented this kind of problem.

"Frightened?" he asked.

She opened her mouth, but no sound came out. She moistened her lips and tried again. "A little."

"I'll be gentle with you," he answered. "I might not have been capable of gentleness before you...um...gave me some relief. But I can now."

"You'd never hurt me."

"No, I wouldn't."

She raised her arms. "Then, come to me, my lover."

He eased himself onto the bed and took her into his arms. Such joy to be with him this way—flesh to flesh, with not a scrap separating them. She rested back and welcomed his weight on top of her as he claimed her mouth in a kiss like none she'd ever experienced.

He held her under his solid length while his lips and tongue explored her on their own. He teased and cajoled her mouth while the heat of his body wrapped all around her. She answered with her own kisses, but no matter how she tried, she couldn't get enough of him. She let her hands travel over his back, testing his muscles as they bunched under her palms. He touched her as he kissed her. His fingers moved along her sides, now tracing her ribs and then sliding under her hips to pull her up and against his sex. She moved, parting her legs until the tip of him rested against the entrance to her core.

"Not yet," he gritted. "Ah, my love, not yet."

She shifted again, and the head of his member pressed against the throbbing nub between her legs. She couldn't stifle a cry as sheer pleasure knifed through her. Again, she moved against him, and again a shock of arousal followed, sending her close to oblivion.

He pulled back and gazed into her face while she whimpered in disappointment.

"Soon, my darling," he whispered. "First, let me worship you."

His body slid over hers as he nipped along the length of her throat. He didn't stop there, but moved his face into the cleft of her bosom while he gathered her breasts in his hands to nuzzle them with his nose. The fire in her belly burned hot in anticipation of what would come next, but nothing prepared her for the feeling of his lips on her nipple as he took the swollen flesh into his mouth and suckled.

When he'd finished teasing that nipple into a state of ecstasy almost too intense to bear, he switched to the other. She cradled his head, holding his face to her breast as she clasped her legs together and felt herself growing wet for him.

He placed a palm against her belly and stroked her there. Close to what she needed, but not close enough.

"Soon, my love," he whispered. "Soon."

"Robert," she gasped, breath all but impossible. "Please, Robert."

"First, I want to sip your nectar."

Oh, dear heaven. He meant to put his mouth between her legs again. "But, I want you inside me when I next spend."

He chuckled against the skin of her stomach. "Then, you'll have to resist coming while I feast on your cunny, won't you?"

"I can't," she cried. "You'll make me climax. I know it."

"Climax or not, as you want. But, I will have the taste of you again."

With no further warning, he moved lower and urged her knees apart. Too weak to resist, she parted her legs and allowed him to cover her sex with his mouth. Resist, he'd told her. Impossible. His tongue slid between the petals of her sex and found the exact spot to drive her mad. She squirmed to get free, but the action only brought her harder against his mouth and the flicking of his tongue.

"Please, Robert," she said. "I can't resist it."

He didn't stop, so she grabbed fistfuls of sheets and twisted them. She bit her lip until it hurt, but nothing could keep her from spending. She couldn't hold back, not another minute. He had to stop.

"Now," she shrieked, while she still had a tiny scrap of sanity. "Please, oh please. Take me now."

He rose above her, finally, and positioned himself between her legs. Reaching down, she grasped his sex to guide it to her. The tip of him slid inside her, bringing with it a set of sensations beyond description. Large, smooth, as hard as steel, it stretched her until she could take no more and she sobbed with frustration.

Too big. He was too big. An orgasm like none she'd ever had lay just out of her reach, and his cock was too big.

"Push, Robert," she said.

"I can't hurt you," he whispered into her ear.

"I don't care if you split me in two."

"Oh, God. Agony," he said.

"Please!"

"Wait." He took a few gasping breaths. "There's another way."

"Anything."

He rolled onto his back, his sex standing straight up and out from his body. She ran her fingers down it, measuring its incredible size. No wonder she hadn't been able to accept him all. What would they do now?

"Lower yourself onto me slowly," he said. "I'll help you."

She sat up and swung a leg over him, positioning her hips so that he could drive himself into her. If they couldn't do this easily, he'd have to use pressure. One way or the other, she would have all of him inside her.

Sinking his fingers into her hips, he guided her onto him. Once again, the head of his sex entered her, and the throbbing in her own sex almost sent her spinning out of control.

This time she stretched to take more of him, and she almost wept for joy as she watched that magnificent instrument begin to disappear inside her wetness.

"That's it," he said. His face contorted in pleasure. "Easy now. More. A little at a time."

"Yes," she crooned. "Yes. Yesssssss."

She sank lower and lower onto him, slowly, loving every inch of his hardness as it entered her. She watched his face as she did. His total concentration went to the place of their joining, pure rapture on his face, and then his hips began to move. Gentle thrusts, up and into her. The movement helped her to accommodate him, as she grew wetter and hotter in response. Her own sex was on fire between her legs, and only a fierce struggle kept her from coming before he'd totally buried himself inside her. Biting her lip again, she pushed down and down onto him. Heaven. Hell. Bliss. Torture. She couldn't fight it any longer. Another moment. Just a little harder. Push.

He released her hips and placed his thumb over her pearl and rubbed. She gasped and held on. He stroked and rubbed and teased and rubbed some more, and she felt herself flying free from Earth. One last upward thrust of his hips buried him in to the hilt. Completion. She let herself come. She pushed herself forward, bringing her pearl against his thumb as it feathered madness over her. She screamed in her pleasure, and the spasms started. Gripping his shaft with each contraction, she shouted out her passion. When it was done, she fell against his chest, his cock still buried deep against her womb.

❧❀⦅♡⦆❀☙

Robert let Celeste rest for as long as he could, but in the end, he couldn't wait for her to recover. He was too hard, too hot, and much too aroused to put off his own orgasm. During his marriage, he'd managed—with a great deal of effort—to make Millie come a few times. But she'd never done it with such abandon, and she'd never done it with him inside her. The sensation was indescribable. Even now, moments after Celeste's release, her cunny still clutched at him in rhythmic spasms. She'd milk him dry in a moment, even if he just lay here in total inaction. Inaction wasn't how he planned to end this interlude.

Her face lay against his chest, and he brushed the curls from her forehead and pressed a kiss there. "Celeste, my darling?"

"Hmmmm," she answered.

There had to be gentle ways to rouse her, but Lord help him, he couldn't wait for those. He raised his hips, moving himself inside her, showing her that he was still rock hard.

"Oh!" She raised her head and looked into his eyes. "That is the most extraordinary feeling."

"This?" he said, as he thrust again, harder and deeper this time. The movement almost cost him what little control he still had.

"Oh, yes," she said, tipping her head back in what looked like pure bliss. "I could happily let you do that all day."

"Not much chance of that, I'm afraid."

"You tire of me already?" The question sounded petulant, but she smiled and began to move her hips so that her sex gripped his with a sweetness he'd never dared to dream of.

"Tire of you?" He laughed, but the sound came out forced. "It's only…" He moved again, starting a rhythm that would be the end of him. "Long Tom's waited as long as he can. He needs his reward."

She rose up, placing her hands on either side of his waist, closed her eyes, and answered his movements with her own. "I sympathize completely."

She took him easily now. Her cunny still gripped him tightly, but he slid in and out of her in fluid, maddening movements. He grasped her hips and pushed up into her with all the passion inside him. "Then, you'll understand…"

"Understand what?" She rocked forward and back, squeezing him.

That was all it took. He could stand no more. He flipped her onto her back and buried himself so deeply in her he lost his very identity. He rested his face at the base of her throat and moved inside her with a mindless violence. Over and over—he couldn't help himself.

Instead of crying out in pain, she wrapped her legs around him and met his thrusts. Lusty, loud cries issued from her throat. Or maybe they were his. Or theirs. He didn't know. His passion claimed him—white-hot and undeniable. The pressure built at the base of his spine, and the orgasm was on him. Wild now, he thrust and thrust and thrust.

Just as he sent the first stream of sperm into her, she tensed all around him and then burst into her own climax. Her spasms sent him even higher, drawing him out into one explosion after another. Finally, his body could give no more, and he went limp, sobbing his rapture into her shoulder.

Until this moment, he'd never lived. Forty-five years of existence, and he'd never been truly alive. He ought to find that sad, but right now he couldn't manage to feel anything but utter peace. Repletion, fulfillment, peace. And love. Yes, love.

He loved this woman who now lay beneath him, her body a warm haven for his own. He'd loved her from the moment he first set his gaze on her radiant face. Now, he'd love her for the rest of eternity, because she completed him, made him whole in ways he'd never imagined. And he'd keep her with him, happy and safe from anything that could hurt her. If only she'd grant him that right.

He found the strength to sigh. That done, he reached deep into his reserves and commanded his muscles to roll off her.

Celeste whimpered at the separation from her lover's body. Her eyes still closed in bliss, she turned toward him and circled his neck with her arms.

"Did you really have to leave me?" she whispered into his chest.

"Only for now."

"Don't let now last too long."

He laughed. "You really will kill me."

He rolled onto his back, pulling her with him until her head rested on his shoulder. In that position, his fingers naturally fell onto the skin of her back, and he stroked her gently, sketching circles around and over her spine. She stretched like a cat and then settled her whole length against him, casting her leg over his.

"I've never experienced anything like that," she said. "Have you?"

"Never."

"Never with your wife?"

"Never," he repeated. "I wouldn't have thought it possible. Until now."

"What was she like?" Celeste asked. "Your wife."

"Millie was…" He sighed and stroked Celeste's shoulder. "She was delicate. Small. She died very young."

Ah, yes. She died having succumbed to Robert's demands in bed, according to Xenobia's note. The poor woman couldn't have appreciated what she had. She couldn't have realized what joy could be found in the arms of a lover like Robert. Celeste would certainly never make the same mistake, so she snuggled even closer to him.

He kissed her forehead and then moved briefly away from her to open the drawer of the bedside table. After a moment, he turned back and handed her a miniature portrait. "This was Millie shortly before we were married."

She glanced at the portrait briefly and then at Robert's face. The expression she found there tore at her heart. Sadness, love, longing, and something else— regret? Could he honestly feel that he'd contributed to his wife's death?

Life and love hadn't dealt with the darling man fairly. First, he'd had a wife who couldn't cherish the gift of passion he'd had to give her. Then, he'd been left alone by her death. Xenobia hadn't treated him fairly in writing that note and revealing his secrets. Celeste herself had taken advantage of his loneliness and all that wonderful passion inside him by not telling him honestly of Xenobia's plan for him to be her lover. She'd make that up to him somehow. She'd make him happy if it killed her.

"My father-in-law had this painted for me," he was saying. "The miniaturist is quite famous now."

"It's lovely," she murmured, although she could scarcely bring herself to look at the thing, she was that jealous of the woman who'd been lucky enough to call Robert husband.

He pulled her back against his chest and handed the painting to her. Millie had been blond and perfect, with a tiny, bow mouth and upturned nose.

"She was very beautiful," Celeste said.

"No more beautiful than you," he answered. He took the painting from her and returned it to the drawer. Then he rolled over, squeezed her shoulders, and pressed a kiss to her forehead. "To me, you're the most beautiful woman in the world."

"That's because you're uncritical and generous with your feelings, Robert. I don't deserve you."

He pulled back and looked down into her face. "What an odd thing to say."

"It's true," she said. Oh, for heaven's sake, what was wrong with her? She hadn't done anything so terrible by not telling him the truth. But she had kept Xenobia's letter hidden in her room at the asylum. He'd not only be angry with her if that note came to light, he'd feel humiliated. First by his dead wife, then by Xenobia, now by her. She'd been stupid to keep the thing, of course. It could only cause the two of them misery. She'd destroy it the minute she got back to her room. And then, maybe some time in the future, she'd confess everything to him. Much later, after their love had had a chance to deepen and mature. Right now their new-found happiness was far too fragile to risk confession.

"You're not having regrets, are you?" he asked, his expression turning from one of puzzlement to outright concern. "I know this isn't the way these things are supposed to happen."

She grasped his face in her hands and stretched upward so that she could place a kiss on his lips. "I regret nothing. This has been the most wonderful afternoon of my life."

He smiled and blushed. "You flatter me."

"Not at all."

He took one of her hands in his and tangled their fingers together. "Good, because I know how I can make everything right."

"But it is right."

"I can make it even more right," he answered.

She laughed. "How could you possibly make this afternoon any better?"

"By making you my wife."

His wife? An audible gasp escaped her before she could stop it. She'd never dared to hope for anything so wonderful as a proposal from Robert. "You want to marry me?"

"If you'll have me," he answered. "I've earned a substantial amount of money of my own. I have a few good years left in me, and I'm an agreeable enough soul, or so I've been told."

"Agreeable?" She had to laugh at the inadequacy of the word. "Oh, Robert, you're wonderful. Perfect. Divine."

"And there is one extra benefit of marrying me," he said. "As your next of kin, I can have you signed out of the Wainwright Asylum, even over your children's objections."

"You can?"

"I consulted a lawyer. The children can try fighting me, but I'd win."

"Oh, Robert, I do love you so," she said. No other words would do. She threw her arms around his neck and covered his face with kisses. She'd be free. She'd have her lover, only he'd be her husband. If she'd known that her imprisonment would lead to such happiness, she would have thanked Horace and Violet for sending her away. She'd felt so desperate and trapped, and now Robert Albright was about to make her the luckiest woman alive.

He was laughing now, too, and nuzzling her neck with his nose. "I'll resign from the bank and turn Connogua Springs over to the town council. We'll travel, go anywhere you'd like."

"All I need to see with you is the inside of a bedroom," she answered.

"We'll have a harem all to ourselves in Baghdad. We'll share a tent on the Serengeti. We'll make love on the back of an elephant in India."

"That sounds bumpy," she said.

"We'll manage." He placed a hand over her breast and flicked at the nipple with his thumb.

"Mmmm," she crooned as she stretched, giving him easier access to her bosom, her belly, and anything else he cared to stroke.

"I love you, Celeste. I'll make you happy."

"You already have."

"Marry me," he said, as his fingers found their way between her thighs to start the fire inside her all over again.

"Yes," she whispered, as he touched the most intimate part of her. "Oh, yes. Yessss."

Chapter Five

Wainwright summoned them into his office the minute they returned to the asylum. Celeste could tell from the look of utter triumph on Morton's face that something unpleasant awaited them. The doctor's expression held more than a little smugness, too, badly disguised behind his normal air of arrogance and authority. The two of them appeared to think they'd caught Robert and Celeste at something. As if Wainwright and Morton knew how they'd spent their afternoon. The whole atmosphere in the room gave Celeste a sick feeling in the pit of her stomach. Nothing good was going to happen here.

Robert glanced at her out of the corner of his eye, concern plainly written on his face as if he felt the same foreboding she did. Please, Lord, let this be no more than one of Wainwright's lectures about her disordered state. Let her get through the interview and go upstairs to destroy that letter and plan her future life far away from here.

"Please sit down," Wainwright said, indicating two chairs that had been set in front of his desk.

"Is something wrong?" Robert asked. "I had the board's permission to take Mrs. Broder to visit my home."

"Very much against my clinical judgement," Wainwright said. "Boards of lay people shouldn't involve themselves in the care of patients. They have no expertise."

"No harm was done," Robert answered. "I've brought Mrs. Broder back, safe and sound."

"I'll be the judge of what's best for my patients," Wainwright said, his face positively livid with righteous indignation. "I can only imagine what went on during your 'harmless' visit."

What in heaven's name was the man talking about? He couldn't possibly know how she and Robert had spent the afternoon. She still glowed inside, despite some soreness, but she'd see these two in hell before she gave them any inkling of her joy. Pearls before swine.

"What's this all about?" she asked. "What do you want from us?"

"Sit down, Mrs. Broder," Wainwright ordered like the autocrat he was.

She glanced at Robert who gave her a tiny nod. To reassure her, no doubt. But how could he do that if they didn't know what they were facing? She sat and watched as he took the other chair. So near—near enough that she could reach out and take his hand if she dared. Instead, she twisted her fingers together and waited.

Wainwright cleared his throat—another one of his annoying habits. "While you were gone today, Mrs. Broder, an alarming discovery came to light."

"What discovery?"

The man opened a desk drawer and pulled out a piece of paper. No, not a piece of paper, but an envelope. He tapped it against the desk and studied Celeste. The scent of French perfume reached her. Xenobia's perfume. Dear God, he held Xenobia's note in his hand.

She shot out of her chair. "You searched my room."

"The maid found it when she was cleaning," Morton replied.

"That's a lie." No maid could have happened on that note where she'd buried it under her small clothes in a drawer. "You searched my room."

Morton didn't answer but only gave Celeste the same self-satisfied smile she'd worn when they first entered the office. Damn the woman, and damn that smile.

"You had no right," Celeste said, as she reached for the envelope in the doctor's hand.

He pulled back, yanking the envelope out of her reach. "Calm yourself, Mrs. Broder."

"Calm myself?" she repeated. "When you allowed that woman to search my room?"

"It's not *your* room," the doctor said. "It's part of this institution, and we're only trying to help you."

"Celeste, please," Robert said so softly the other two might not have heard him. But they did. At the use of her Christian name, the two of them looked knowingly at Robert and then back at each other.

Dear Lord in heaven, what if they meant to show him the note? Anything but that. If he read what Xenobia had written about him, he'd completely misunderstand. Everything would sound so contrived—as if she'd planned to use him for something ugly. Xenobia had even included intimate details of his body. If he read that, he'd realize that Xenobia had put it all down—even the dimensions of his sex—where people like Wainwright and Morton could find it and cluck their tongues. She couldn't let him know that. Above all, he must not read that note.

She took a deep breath and did the best she could to appear calm. Unfortunately, she'd begun to tremble. Badly. Her hand shook as she held it out to Wainwright. "Please, may I have that note? It's silly and embarrassing, really. Everyone knows how Mrs. Stewart is. No one takes anything she says seriously."

Wainwright's eyebrow came up. "Is that so?"

"Well, yes." Celeste did her best to laugh lightly. It came out desperately dishonest even to her own ears. "Xenobia gets such ideas into her head. She'll have forgotten them completely within a week."

Wainwright turned toward Robert. "I have to assume you delivered this note, Mr. Albright."

"Yes, I did."

"Do you have any idea what it says?" the doctor asked.

"No."

"I thought as much."

"I didn't see any harm in delivering a letter to one of your patients," Robert said.

"Mr. Albright," the doctor said in the tone he used to promise a scolding, "the layman can hardly imagine what goes on inside the brains of the insane."

"I'm not insane," Celeste shouted. The trembling grew even worse, until she shook with fear and rage. In another moment, she'd look like a madwoman. Robert knew better than to believe that, of course. But Lord only knew what he'd believe about her once he'd read that note.

"Our patients often appear rational, just as normal as you or me," Wainwright continued. "But underneath…ah, underneath…the perversions we have to contend with—it would shock you, sir."

"Don't listen to him, Robert," Celeste said. "It's a silly note, that's all. Not a word of it means anything."

"You're upset." Morton placed her hands on Celeste's shoulders. "Perhaps you'd like to go to your room."

Celeste shook off the woman's grip. "Of course, I'm upset. But, it isn't my room, and I don't want to go there."

Robert rose and looked into her eyes, silently offering his support and love. Love. She'd finally found love, and these two bastards were going to take it away from her.

"Please remain calm, Mrs. Broder," Robert said softly. "Whatever this is about we can settle it easily."

Morton put her hands on Celeste again, but Robert waved her away.

Celeste took a deep breath. Calm. She had to calm herself somehow, but the more she tried, the harder she trembled. "You must believe me, Robert," she said. "I didn't know you when I read that note. Everything's changed. I feel…"

Damn, but she couldn't get the words out, not in front of the doctor and his hired harpy. A sob rose in her chest before she could stop it. "This afternoon…oh heaven, this afternoon…"

"This afternoon?" Wainwright demanded. "What have you two been doing?"

"Nothing," she snapped. "We had tea. Strawberries. Whipped cream." This was coming out all wrong. She had to convince Robert that she loved him—deeply and truly. Instead, she sounded irrational.

"What happened this afternoon?" Wainwright asked again, this time addressing Robert.

Robert's skin turned a violent pink. "We had tea. As Mrs. Broder said."

"Tea." Wainwright practically snorted the word. "Then, perhaps you should see what sort of woman you took into your home, Mr. Albright."

"No." Celeste lunged for the envelope again, but Morton caught her from behind and held her back. She watched—oddly disconnected, as if from a distance—as Wainwright put the envelope into Robert's hand.

He opened the envelope, unfolded the paper, and began to read. After only a moment, he stopped reading and looked into her face. "What is this?"

"I'm sorry," she whispered. "Things aren't the way they sound in there. Please understand."

He didn't answer but went back to reading, his face falling with every new revelation. She could almost imagine each word hitting him like a blow. Such pain. She'd never meant to hurt him, but she'd caused him such pain.

After a moment, he fell back into his chair, elbows resting on his knees, head down. The note still rested in one hand. "Oh, God, Celeste…"

"Robert, listen to me, please."

"I regret having to show you that, Mr. Albright," Wainwright said. But he didn't regret it, not one tiny bit, the bastard. She'd happily scratch his eyes out, but Morton still held her firm.

Robert straightened in his chair, and his fingers crumpled the note into a mass in his palm. "I understand."

"You see now, finally, that I know what I'm doing with Mrs. Broder. You can have no more delusions about her character."

Delusions? Oh, God, it wasn't a delusion. Their lovemaking wasn't a delusion. The sweet way he looked at her—as if she were the most delicate, most treasured person on Earth—that wasn't a delusion. The way she loved him, with every part of her heart and soul—that wasn't a delusion.

"Patients like Mrs. Broder are the most deceptive," Wainwright continued. "They appear so earnest, they can often fool even the most highly trained professional."

"Stop talking about me as if I weren't here," she said.

Robert glanced up, his expression so full of hurt and anger she could hardly bear to look at him.

"I'm sorry," was all she could manage to say to him. Sadly inadequate, but the only words that came to mind. *I love you. I'm sorry. Forgive me.*

"Under the circumstances, there won't be any more afternoon visits," Dr. Wainwright said. "Mrs. Broder will remain here, where she belongs."

"I suppose so," Robert answered, his voice little more than a whisper.

No! "But you'll come back, won't you?" she said. "You have to come back."

"Mrs. Broder," Morton said, "don't make a spectacle of yourself."

"You don't understand." Celeste broke free of the woman and dropped onto her knees in front of Robert. "I can explain everything. Just give me a chance."

She reached for his hands, but he stiffened, pulling away from her. Then, slowly and carefully, he put the note into her hand and rose. "I have to go."

"You can't leave, not like this."

Morton caught her arms and pulled her to her feet and away from Robert.

He straightened his shoulders, brushed his coat, and looked around him as if seeing the room for the first time. "I apologize for any trouble I may have caused you or your staff, doctor."

"No need," Wainwright answered. "I think we understand each other now."

"Yes."

"Please." Celeste struggled in Morton's grip but couldn't get free. The trembling returned and with it, tears. Hot and wet, blurring her vision until she couldn't even see her beloved clearly.

"Take care of her, will you?" Robert said.

"Rest assured, Mr. Albright," the doctor answered.

Then Robert was gone. He simply opened the door and left, taking her hope, her happiness with him.

Nothing about Xenobia Stewart's manner nor her dress suggested she was anything other than a respectable widow approaching her middle age. Nor did the furnishings of her house—at least the ones Robert had seen so far—indicate what sort of parties she threw. Everything around him spoke of wealth, from the upholstered mahogany furniture to the statuary to the thick Oriental carpets. All in impeccable taste, all quite understated.

The woman herself made the perfect picture of petite, graying respectability as she indicated a chair in her drawing room overlooking Central Park and then took a seat nearby.

"So, you've seen Celeste?"

"Yes."

A wicked gleam entered her eyes. "More than once by now, I imagine."

He didn't answer. This woman and her meddling had brought him nothing but misery. She'd given him the illusion of love and then had torn that illusion from him. He had no obligation to supply her with information. He wanted only two things from her, and then he'd leave.

"How is Celeste?" Mrs. Stewart asked.

"I haven't seen her for several days." Several long days of missing her and wanting her with every fiber of his being. Several nights of lying in his empty bed, remembering the feel of her body next to his. And then remembering her face the last time he'd seen her in Wainwright's office. Her desperation, how she'd begged him to understand, to allow her to explain the unexplainable.

Mrs. Stewart cocked her head and studied him for a moment. "You haven't seen her for several days?"

"That's correct." Ten days, twenty-two hours, and some minutes, to be exact.

"What a pity," she said. "I thought the two of you would become great friends."

"So your letter to Celeste said."

The smile quickly disappeared from her face, as she paled. "You read that?"

"It was my misfortune."

"Celeste can't have shown it to you."

"Dr. Wainwright did."

"Wainright. The head of the asylum?" she exclaimed. She rose from her chair and paced across the carpet. "I never meant for…oh, dear Lord. The things I wrote in there, about you, about your…"

"Exactly."

She turned and looked at him, her hand at her breast, her eyes wide. "I'm so terribly sorry. I had no idea that would happen."

"One can hardly expect any other outcome in a place like that. Wainwright knows everything that goes into and out of there."

"Oh, dear." She walked back to her chair and dropped into it. "I'm sorry. I don't know what to say, Mr. Albright. I've wronged you terribly."

"I'd like to know how you got the information about my late wife." He took a breath. This whole issue disgusted him, but he had to know the truth. "I'd like to know how many people in Connogua Springs know about my private life."

"Oh, dear."

"How many people discuss my intimacies with my wife behind my back?" *How many discuss my sex drive, the size of my cock?*

"Hardly anyone. Truly," she answered. "The person who told me claimed it was a secret—not at all the subject of ordinary conversation. Dear Lord, I'm so sorry."

He'd accomplished his first objective in coming here, it appeared. She seemed to realize at least a small part of the harm she'd done. He'd keep to himself that, thanks to her, he'd fallen hopelessly in love only to discover that his happiness was founded on a sham. He wouldn't tell her how devastated Celeste had been the last time he'd seen her. Celeste, oh God, Celeste.

"I just thought I'd bring the two of you together," Mrs. Stewart said. "You seemed so perfect for each other."

His mind wandered back to exactly how perfect they'd been together. If only he could get those images out of his mind. How her body accepted him so completely, how she moved beneath him. He'd never find that sort of perfection again.

"You did enjoy each other, didn't you?" she said. "You did become involved."

He could hardly deny it, so he didn't answer, but he felt his skin heat. The color of his face would answer for him. Damn his tendency to blush.

"I knew it," she said. "I made a terrible mistake in writing that note, but I wasn't wrong about you and Celeste. You two were made for each other."

He most assuredly didn't intend discussing how he'd lost his heart to Celeste, so he'd best accomplish his second objective and go back to Connogua Spring.

"You'll have to get Celeste released on your own," he said. "I can't possibly fight Wainwright now. I'm sure you understand why not."

"He'd reveal your personal information," she said.

"I wouldn't put it past him."

"I've already taken steps to get Celeste free. I know more judges than her children do. I know a few judges rather intimately."

He blushed again, not at all interested in knowing what she meant by intimately. "Then, you can get her out of that place."

"It'll be tricky," she said. "I'm not a family member. But I think I can manage."

"Good. That's all I need to know." He rose. "I'll see myself out."

"Mr. Albright, wait." She got to her feet. "I know I've treated you badly, but you shouldn't punish Celeste for my mistakes."

"I don't care to discuss my personal life any further with you."

"I understand after the trouble I've caused you."

"Madame, you have no idea." He'd most likely never recover fully, not as long as his memories of making love to Celeste haunted him. He'd probably take those memories to his grave.

"You mustn't pass up a chance at happiness," she said. "When the Almighty creates that one, special love for you, it's a sin to toss that love aside."

"You don't know what you're asking."

"Don't I?" She reached out and placed a hand on his arm. "My Harold and I had our bad spots together, but he was the love of my life. I'd give up everything to have him back for one night."

"I really must go now."

He tried to pull away, but her grip on his arm tightened. "I mean it, Mr. Albright. I'd give up everything—absolutely everything—for one more night in Harold's arms."

"I'll bear that in mind," he answered.

"You do that. You'll see that I'm right. You and Celeste belong together."

❦

The sun warmed Celeste's skin. Warmed it too much, actually. She should have brought a parasol. Last week, all the skin had peeled off the end of her nose from sunburn. When she got back to Manhattan—if she ever did get back to Manhattan—she'd be a very unfashionable shade of brown. She ought to care about that, really. But she'd earned her walks outdoors, and she'd take every bit of heat that the sun cared to give her. At least that way she felt something.

Oh Lord, what disgusting self-pity. She deserved all the misery she'd endured in the last two weeks. She might as well just wallow in it and get the job over and done. Then she could go back to convincing Wainwright that he'd "cured" her, get a lawyer, and get herself out of this institution—which was what she should have done in the first place. Not involve an innocent person like Robert.

Robert. Oh, my poor, darling Robert. She clenched her eyes shut, held her breath, and waited out the pain. There. In a minute it was gone again, and she could open her eyes.

That seemed shorter than the last time. And the interval between the stabs of longing and shame a bit longer. Maybe in another week she'd be able to go five minutes without picturing Robert's face as he finished reading that note. Maybe by the time she got back home she'd be able to go an hour without thinking of his smile, the warmth of his eyes, the feel of his hand stroking her breast.

"I'm sorry, my darling," she whispered. "I'm so sorry."

"So am I," a soft voice said from behind her.

She turned and raised a hand to shade her eyes. That was Robert's voice, and surely this must be Robert standing just behind her. But she couldn't make out his face, with the sun in her eyes. And the tears. She hadn't even known she was crying again.

"Tell me it's really you," she said. "I couldn't bear it if you were a mirage."

"You shouldn't be sitting in the sun like this," he answered.

His voice again. Did she dare to hope? "You came back, after all."

Robert, or the figment of Robert—her vision still wouldn't clear—held out a hand to her. "I know a more sheltered place to sit."

She rose and took his hand. That felt real enough—solid and warm. She swayed, leaning into him. He caught her elbow and steadied her, a slight smile curling his lips. Lord, but she'd never expected to see that smile again. Maybe she'd imagined it. Maybe she'd imagined this whole encounter.

Before she could say anything, he linked her arm through his and guided her toward the yews where they'd strolled on the first day he'd taken her out. Toward the spot where he'd first kissed her.

"They allow you out on the grounds now?" he said.

"Once I started obeying the rules," she answered. "There seemed no point in defying them any longer."

"That doesn't sound like the Celeste Broder I know."

"That woman was a fool."

He covered her fingers with his own as they continued walking. She ought to say or do something. Ask why he'd come. But she had the warmth of his body now and the gentle pressure of his fingers on hers. Selfish to the end, she'd allow herself to enjoy every minute of his presence and suffer the consequences later.

They came to the little copse of yews finally, and he gestured to the bench they'd shared on their first walk. She sat and waited for him to join her. He did but didn't touch her again. He only looked off into the distance. She let her gaze linger on his features. If this was all she'd have of him, she'd store away as many memories as she could.

"That letter," he said finally.

"I should have destroyed it," she said. "I should have known they'd find it. It was entirely my fault."

He didn't say anything—didn't berate her, although she deserved it. But still, he'd come back to see her. That spoke of forgiveness, even if he could never trust her enough to love her again.

"You mustn't blame Xenobia for this, either," she said. "Xenobia is what she is

—an utter hedonist. I should have known better."

"Why talk of blame?" he asked. "Do you regret that afternoon we spent together?"

"No," she answered. "Oh, heaven, no. I'll always cherish those hours."

He studied her from the corner of his eye. "Then, what would you have done differently?"

How many times she'd asked herself the same question. "I don't know. I could have taken responsibility for getting myself out of here instead of acting like a spoiled child. I could have been honest with you."

"Honesty would have been nice."

"I could have given you the note to destroy. I've been looking inside myself quite a bit this past week, and I don't much like what I've found."

"Tell me, Celeste."

She looked down at her hands. "I shouldn't have married Horace if I didn't at least care for him. I could have found my own way in life. After he died, I could have used his money to do some good in the world instead of feeling sorry for myself."

"And give up your sensual nature?" he asked.

"A fine lot of good that nature did me," she replied. "Or you."

They sat in silence for a long time. She could have said so many things to him. That she was sorry, but that would sound hollow. That she loved him, but that would sound self-serving. That he was the finest person she'd ever known, but would he believe her?

Finally, after several moments, he sighed. "Let me ask you just one thing."

"Anything."

"And I want the truth."

"I'll never lie to you again, Robert."

He sat for a moment, his jaw clenched. "During our brief time together. Did you ever care for me? At least a little?"

"Care for you?" she repeated. "I loved you with all my heart. I still do. I always will."

He turned to her, his amber gaze staring into her eyes. "Truly?"

She put her palm against the side of his face and returned his gaze. "Truly, Robert Albright, and any woman who doesn't love you is a fool."

He placed his hand over hers as tears filled his eyes. "I've searched my own heart this week, and I discovered a few things, too."

"Yes, my darling."

"Mostly, that I was hurt at what Millie had said about me. I loved her so much. I thought she was happy with me."

"I'm sure she was. Don't trust those stories. Things get so distorted when they become gossip."

"I felt betrayed," he said. "First by Millie and then by you."

"I know, Robert. I'm so sorry."

"I've struggled with those feelings. I even went to visit Mrs. Stewart."

"Xenobia?" Celeste said. "What did she tell you?"

"She told me that love was more important than anything else. She told me I'd be a fool to lose you because of my hurt feelings." He brought her hand to his mouth and rubbed his lips over the knuckles. "She was right."

He looked at her with such adoration, her heartbeat jerked and stuttered in her chest. "Really?"

"I decided I won't let my pride make us both miserable. Not when we can share so much happiness," he said. "Marry me, Celeste. Forgive my stubbornness in running away from you and agree to be my wife."

"Are you sure you want me?"

"I only feel alive with you. Only you make me whole. Tell me you could learn to feel the same way."

"I do." She ran her arms around his neck and pressed her face against his. "Love me, Robert. Always."

He hugged her against him as if he'd never let her go. An unspoken promise she meant to hold him to. "We'll go to New York and spend all of Horace's money on making it a better place."

She laughed. "We'll stay here and be mayor and first lady of Connogua Springs."

"We'll explore the world and make love on the back of that elephant."

"The elephant. I'd forgotten the elephant."

"I haven't. I'm going to make love to you every way known to man." She kissed him briefly. "And we'll make up a few new ways, too."

He smiled at her, that beloved and beautiful smile. "You'll marry me, then?"

"Take this for your answer, my champion, my love," she said, as she pressed her lips to his and gave herself up to his love.

About the author:

Alice Gaines lives in Oakland, California with her husband of 23 years, 100 or so orchids, and one Carolina corn snake named Sheikh Yerbouti. She also writes for Leisure Romance as Alice Chambers. Feel free to email Alice at **algaines@pacbell.net** *or write to her at PMB 197; 5111 Telegraph Avenue; Oakland, CA 94609.*

Kiss or Kill

by Liz Maverick

To my reader:
He's part man, part machine with his life on the line. She's the woman who must decide his fate. How would you try to figure out if a man...was man enough?

$$\mathscr{Chapter\ One}$$

Washington DC, 2043

Camille Kazinsky stood in the doorway of her apartment, shaking her head in disbelief. "*That's* the robo?"

"Yeah, and if you're Kazinsky, print here." The government rep handed her the sign-in machine, and then pushed a military-issue duffel bag toward her with his foot.

Camille absently supplied her fingerprint, staring up at the robo in fascination. He waited handcuffed and silent, towering over the man at his side. The only robos she'd seen before were the ones she'd shot at from a distance during live-fire training at the academy. Trainees were taught to think of robos as targets; objects. Now, Camille couldn't imagine thinking in terms of 'it' instead of 'he.' Of course, that was just the kind of sentiment she was supposed to avoid. The robo looked like a man, but he wasn't...was he?

'He' wore short black leather gloves that contrasted oddly with the tan fitted T-shirt and camouflage pants of his dingy summer fatigues. Above the gloves, red welts from the restraints covered his forearms. His gloved fingers moved slowly, restlessly, as if he felt pain although no discomfort showed on his face.

In fact, nothing showed on his face at all. His eyes were glazed over. Built like a tank, but nobody home. On the other hand, even if he did have the intelligence of a pea, he probably had a cock the size of what used to be Texas.

Camille suppressed a laugh and moved her gaze upward. He looked like he hadn't had the opportunity to get neat and clean in a while. Greasepaint and dirt from a former assignment still smeared his face and arms. His buzz cut had grown out, and dark dirty locks of hair curled slightly at the neck and fell in disarray over his forehead.

Suddenly, the robo clenched his gloved hands then released them, flexing the muscles in his arms. The obvious power in his body made Camille wonder what kind of mayhem he was capable of, what he'd done while in service, and why they thought he wasn't capable of doing his job anymore.

The robo turned his head a fraction and looked directly at her. He blinked a set of outrageously long lashes over crystalline green eyes before returning his glazed stare to the front. Camille swallowed and stepped backward, her heart pounding in her chest. For those few seconds they'd made eye contact, he'd pierced her with a look that spoke of intelligence and understanding. The government could simulate skin and cover mechanics with life-like prosthetics, but it was hard to fake the look in a man's eyes.

Curious, Camille reached out and pressed her fingers into the skin of the robo's forearm. The pads of her fingers skidded along his warm, slippery flesh. A wry smile twisted her lips; from what she could recall, he felt exactly the way she remembered a man's sweating body felt under her hands. Now *there* was an interesting way to try to tell the man from the…machine.

The government rep looked up from the sign-in machine. "What's so funny?"

"Nothing. It's just not what I expected." She slid her palm up to the vulnerable skin at the bend in the robo's elbow. Although his face remained expressionless, a muscle in his forearm pulsed to her touch, and Camille felt a hot prickle trail down her spine in response. "Shit," she murmured and pulled her hand back, flushing.

"Hey, sweetheart, you sure you can handle it?" the rep asked, giving her a long look up and down. "They can be unpredictable."

Camille killed her smile and turned cold eyes on him. Chauvinistic prick. Could she *handle* it? It wasn't the first time she'd heard that question, and she ought to be used to it by now.

She was tall enough, but her willowy frame, blue eyes and fine blonde hair never failed to give the impression that she was somehow unable to take care of business. The girls in her unit used to tease her that in any other occupation, her baby-doll looks would be an asset. Camille frowned, reminded that her friends weren't in the unit any more. Well, she might not be as strong as most of the men, but she was a hell of a lot smarter, and that's what was supposed to count in military intelligence.

She flipped the Class II automatic weapon slung down her back around to the front, then turned her ankle to reveal the knife clipped to the side of her combat boot. "It's no problem."

The rep shrugged and tossed her the restraint punch. "So, what'd you do wrong?"

Camille clenched her jaw. He obviously knew robo evaluation was the kind of assignment an academy trainee would get only if placed on disciplinary probation. Not that it was any of his business. She certainly wasn't looking for pity.

"I think we're done here," she said. Camille pointed her Class II at the robo. With her other hand she grabbed a handful of T-shirt and pulled, jerking him over the threshold. "Inside. Let's go."

The robo stepped forward into her living space and walked into the center of the room. It suddenly seemed a lot smaller than usual. Camille sighed as she heaved the duffel bag after the robo and closed the door. She spent so little time at home, there was no point in a bigger place. Her apartment was the low-end model, perfect for a single member of the military.

Not that she completely ignored the luxuries. She'd ponied up for a subscription to the region's hot water supply, plus two additional nozzles for total body coverage in the shower. After all, a girl had needs. Camille smiled to herself. Until returning home this morning with her probation papers in hand, she'd been in the field in close quarters with thirty antagonistic, hygienically-challenged male trainees for the last four months. It was good to be home. Unfortunately, this homecoming wasn't quite like being on holiday.

Camille turned back to the robo and chewed on the broken edge of her thumbnail as she tried to decide how to proceed. She'd skimmed the procedural manual, but it wasn't too helpful. She was expected to file either a termination or reclassification report on him, solely based on behavioral observation. Supposedly, the government would simply follow the recommendation in her report. Of course, she'd heard of people getting into serious trouble after a seemingly docile robo reclassified into civilian life later became violent. The last thing she needed now was more trouble.

Just how human did one of these things have to be, to be considered human enough? How much was too much? And how could you tell one way or the other if the damn thing refused to *do* anything?

"I'd appreciate your cooperation," Camille finally said to the robo. "We're stuck with each other until I make my decision about you, but I'd like to get back to my unit ASAP."

The robo blinked, his long eyelashes batting downward.

"Hello? This is about reclassification or termination. Life or death, here. That's what robo evaluation is…are you going to talk to me?"

Camille pressed her fingertips against the dull pain in her left temple. "This is like babysitting a piece of meat. What did I do to deserve this, huh, *Meat?*" But she already knew the answer: nothing. Her partner Danny had made the 'mistake,' killing a civilian during a training exercise, but she was paying for it.

Academy life was full of strange alliances and underhanded deals as the trainees jockeyed to climb the rankings and graduate. This was one tradeoff Camille could only sit back and hope would be worth it. She'd take the fall now, if it secured her future. Anyway, Danny hadn't really given her a choice.

The robo's fists clenched and released, reminding Camille she ought to check for injuries. She drew the restraint punch from her pocket, uncuffed the robo, then pulled off his T-shirt and tossed it toward her laundry. Then, she quickly recuffed his wrists and walked around him, trailing her hand over his warm skin. He was sleek, muscular, smelling of musk and gunpowder. Camille ducked her head a little closer as she circled and breathed him in, unnerved by her attraction to him but not wanting to move away.

The robo shifted his weight. He flexed his fingers again, this time with greater agitation. Camille unzipped the neck of her training suit to get a little more oxygen. She could feel the charge in the air, the increased tension in his stance, the impact of her touch on his body…and on her own. "Damn. Twice the cock, half the brain, and zero bullshit coming out of your mouth. I should be down on my knees thanking my lucky stars."

She came around to face him and shivered as the robo stared straight down into her training suit. She knew he could see her hard nipples rubbing against the inside of the thick fabric, and the thought made her instantly wet. It shocked her a little to think this robo could get to her so quickly. But then again, it had been a while. She'd made the mistake of hooking up with a fellow trainee only once.

Clenching the muscles of her thighs to ease the ache there, she swallowed hard and looked into the robo's eyes. Watching him closely, she moved one hand down, pausing over the cold metal of his belt buckle before turning her hand and sliding it down to the long, hot ridge straining at the tan fabric of his fatigues.

The robo sucked in a breath, a quiet, excited sound as she stroked her hand over his length. "This turns you on," Camille murmured. She licked her dry lips and unzipped the fly, taking him in her hand. Maybe Old Texas had been an exaggeration, but he was beautiful; hot and sleek like titanium. As she ran her thumb over the moisture on the engorged head, the robo bucked slightly, but still never said a word. Suddenly, Camille felt strange about handling him and let go.

She stared at his throbbing cock, the wet tip thrusting upward. She wanted to take him in her mouth, run her tongue around his tip and taste him, make him admit she turned him on. But she just looked away and cleared her throat. "You follow me with your eyes but you don't really see anything. It's obvious you like it when I touch you, but you don't know what to do with feelings, do you?"

Still no answer. Frustrated, she walked toward the manual on the multi-purpose table, more to cool off than anything else. "It's going to be lonelier with you than—" On instinct, she swung around to face him.

He was watching her with the same sharp, piercing gaze she'd caught a glimpse of when she'd first taken custody of him. Of course, his expression faded the minute she walked back up to him.

"I saw that," Camille said, angry heat rushing into her face. "There's more going on in there than you want me to know, and I don't like being tricked. React to me. Right here, right now."

She searched his face for a crack in that blank expression, pissed that she'd doubted the initial signs and underestimated him. Snatching her knife off her boot clip, she launched into him, slammed one foot down on his boots and pressed the blade against his temple. Wrapping her free hand around his windpipe, she began to squeeze. "I'm going to terminate you," she growled, and waited for a reaction.

His restrained hands jerked up between them. Camille flinched but held her ground. She moistened her lips and looked into his eyes, mentally calming herself in preparation to kill him if necessary. His hands suddenly stopped short. Very slowly, he moved them toward his own throat and clamped down on Camille's wrist at his windpipe.

His eyes locked with hers, and she could see a very clear survival instinct in those green, green eyes.

"Man. Machine. Animal. Vegetable. What are you really?" Camille taunted him, testing him further. She gritted her teeth and cut the very tip of the blade into the flesh at his temple. A surge of adrenaline pumped through him. His body jerked with primal fury, his cock rock-hard against her.

Camille inhaled sharply, dizzy for a moment. Sweat slid down the side of her face, stinging her eyes. She watched the robo try to read her the way she was trying to read him. She struggled to control her response to him but knew he was taking it all in. Her breath coming out in harsh pants, the fresh sheen on her skin, the instinctive shift of her legs to get more of him against her before she caught herself. He read her well, and thrust his erection against the center of her spread legs. A wave of pleasure rocked her body as he pressed against her clit.

Her senses swamped by lust and fear, Camille shivered but refused to lose focus on the subtext, noting the subtle tightening of his grip around her wrist. Whether he was asking her not to kill him or suggesting that he might kill her if she tried, she couldn't say. Either way, Camille had to assume that he hadn't already tried to snap her wrist for a good reason.

She cut him deeper to remind him who was in control and a trickle of blood slid down the blade. The robo got the picture and released her wrist, never breaking eye contact.

"Damn," Camille breathed and pushed backwards off him, turning away. Her hands were shaking; she felt panicked, aroused and pissed all at once. "What the hell am I doing? This can't be normal. I'm getting hot for a fucking piece of machinery. Camille, you are totally self-destructing."

A low, intense voice spoke out from behind, the words breathed deeply into her left ear. "I think you need to relax."

Camille froze. *Holy shit.* Her sweating palm tightened around the knife in a death grip, and she slowly turned around. She found herself staring directly into green eyes that finally admitted to total comprehension. The robo's body language was non-threatening, but she backed up to a safe distance anyway, shifting her gaze down to the thick shaft still standing erect through the fly of his fatigues.

"Let me guess," the robo said quietly. "You're thinking, 'If I make him lie down and take him from the top, he's strong enough to roll me over and take the advantage.' And you lying down with me on top is obviously out of the question from a security point of view. If you go down on me, besides the fact that it's probably not what you had in mind, I could break your neck, even in handcuffs. That leaves only one option for you...am I close?"

Too close for comfort, but she wasn't about to admit it. Camille concentrated on breathing and sounding as normal and in control as possible. Coolly, she said. "How about a little more talk and a lot less action." She took her knife and threw it tip down into the tabletop. It hit the wood with a hollow sound, tiny red specks of his blood scattering out from the blade onto the surface.

The robo looked at the knife then turned back to Camille, running his gaze down the length of her body. "When was the last time someone did something nice for you?"

Camille eyed him suspiciously. He didn't know anything about her, so what was his game? "Well, *Meat*, I don't really know. Depends on what you mean by, 'nice.' Why don't you give me an example?" She pulled the knife back out of the wood and pretended to inspect it, watching him from the corner of her eye.

"Well...*Camille* is it? Why don't I just get down on my knees," he said pointedly, "and thank my lucky stars."

Camille stared at him in shock, realizing that on a fairly high level, he'd understood everything, from the moment she'd opened the door. She tried to remember everything she'd revealed while she was talking aloud, thinking *he* was the resident idiot.

"Lean against the table." The robo gestured behind her.

"What?"

"The edge of the table. Lean against it." He swiped a black-gloved thumb across his lower lip, the corner of his mouth quirking up in the hint of a smile. "You can leave your boots on."

Camille hesitated. "You're kidding." Suddenly, she laughed. "I think you're missing the big picture here. If you hurt me, I'll kill you myself, right now. Even if you don't hurt me, I might have you killed."

He took a step toward her, and Camille flashed the knife in his face. He eyed the knife and reached around the weapon with his bound hands to grasp the zipper tab of her training suit, slowly pulling it down, the zipper rasping and humming until he reached the bottom and brushed against her crotch with his knuckles.

She gasped, and he crowded her against the edge of the table, moving his thigh between her legs and pressing upward until Camille moaned.

"Take it off," he said.

Damn. He wasn't kidding. This rated right up there with some of the crazier things she'd ever gotten herself into...but she wanted this. She definitely wanted this. And why not? It wasn't every day you had a man going down on his knees for you. Volunteering, without even getting his first. A nice change.

The robo stepped back and moved his hands to the exposed skin where the two sides of her suit fell open. Camille swallowed hard as she watched the black leather massage her pale skin, his fingers tangling in the fine curls at the bottom of the gaping vee in her training suit. His erection brushed against her leg, and she squirmed at the thought of that gorgeous cock sliding between her thighs into her slick, aching heat.

Logic, Camille. Think. She was armed, she wouldn't have to let her guard down to get satisfaction...and didn't she deserve a little satisfaction after everything that'd happened?

Pulling her arms out of her suit, she pushed the material past her knees then looked back up at the robo with a challenging smirk. He hooked a black leather-clad forefinger into the string low on her hip and pulled her panties down so fast, it took her smirk along with them.

She could see in his eyes, gone dark liquid jade, that he wanted to fuck her badly. Too bad they both wanted that because that wasn't going to happen.

"Sit down," he said, his voice thick. He kneeled on the floor, and Camille sat on the edge of the table. She parted her legs until she was completely exposed to him, unbelievably wet, the aching throb at the center of her cunt matching her heartbeat in double-time. Vulnerable, were it not for the knife she held out at arm's length next to his face.

He lifted his cuffed hands above his head, used his elbows to keep her legs apart and licked her slick folds. Camille shuddered, straining to keep her eyes open and watch.

The greasepaint on his face smeared warm and thick across the inside of her thighs as he entered her with his tongue, gently drawing himself in and out. Camille gasped and arched up to him, spreading her legs wider, giving him total access.

He sucked her clit, and she nearly lost it. He licked her there again, once, twice, three times...it happened so fast. Camille cried out and threw her head back as she came, slamming backwards on the table. Unable to speak and unwilling to move as pleasure coursed through her body in tiny aftershocks, she just stared at him through a flurry of white as the scattered pages of the manual fell to the floor. *Damn. I think I just made a terrible mistake.*

Meat stood up and awkwardly thrust his erection back into his fatigues, then rolled his shoulders, whipped his head to one side and cracked his neck. He looked Camille straight in the eye, flashing a wicked smile with all the male arrogance of a job well done, and said, "*Now* we talk."

Chapter Two

The girl stared at him in shock for a moment, then burst into peals of laughter. "A guy who wants to talk after sex."

Meat blinked in confusion. He wiped the sweat off his forehead with his shoulder and turned away from the sight of her lithe body disappearing once more into the severe gray uniform.

"That was very impressive," she said. "I'm looking forward to seeing what other programming is available."

Meat's eyes narrowed. "I'm happy to oblige," he snapped. Nothing pissed him off faster than cheap shots about his non-human qualities. He strolled casually to the other end of the room, needing to cool off both his temper and his own unsatisfied needs.

The exhaustion built up over the last few weeks was catching up to him, dulling his wits and emphasizing his baser needs. Food, water, sleep, and something to calm the lust that burned low in his groin.

He glanced back at the girl. She sat on the table swinging her legs, tossing her knife from hand-to-hand, and watching him examine her living space.

She'd left the neck of her uniform half-zipped, showing off the smooth swells of her breasts, a hint of rosy nipple. He'd be willing to bet she'd done it on purpose, and had to admit it was a power play he was particularly susceptible to at the moment. He gazed at what she'd left open for him to see and chuckled softly. Point to Camille Kazinsky. Whatever he'd been expecting, it wasn't this.

"What's so funny," she asked, smiling back.

"Nothing. I'm merely enjoying the scenery."

Her smile vanished, and she stopped tossing the knife. "You sound like a Brit. Like an educated Brit. What's that all about? Is that part of the program?"

All business again. He'd thought he'd had her pegged in the few minutes it took to detect the undercurrent of desperation that ran through her. And he certainly thought he'd figured out his strategy. He might not be in the battlefield anymore, but seduction was a weapon he could definitely still wield...and one she definitely responded to.

But it wasn't as simple as that, was it? Her unpredictability had him way off-balance, making first one assumption and then another. "One of my trainers was a Brit. The other sounded like you."

"I'm surprised you even speak in complete sentences."

He snorted disdainfully and her eyebrows flew up, emphasizing the feline shape of her blue eyes. Truth be told, he'd never even seen anyone remotely like this Camille Kazinsky before. Her delicate kitten looks warred with everything else about her.

Sure, the legs, tits and blonde hair got his attention, but what kept it were those eyes, and a lush pair of full lips, burnt fuchsia from dehydration. She licked them constantly, her tongue flicking out like a cat lapping milk.

No, he'd certainly never seen a woman like Camille before; he'd certainly never touched one like her either. When he'd dipped his tongue between her legs and took in her taste and scent, he'd felt a desire so vicious it clouded any sense of manipulation or strategy.

He needed a better overall read. Maybe she got off on being ordered around. Maybe she'd like to take out some aggression on him. Maybe she needed a confidant. Maybe she just needed a daily fuck.

He circled the perimeter of the room, trying to keep his mind focused on the end goal. Not many additional clues to be gained from her living space.

Central living room, appearing to fan out in the standard layout to bathroom, kitchen, bedroom, and equipment room. Sparsely furnished with only the necessary furniture all color-coordinated in beige. A bookshelf next to the communications system, filled with academy manuals and a few random objects that seemed placed almost self-consciously, in a deliberate attempt to camouflage the general sterility of the place.

You had to play it safe at first, play dumb. Hang back and observe to determine what characteristics your evaluator liked about you…and then give them more of the same until the only option that makes sense to them at the end is reclassification.

"Meat? Hello? I thought you said you were ready to talk."

And if they wanted to call you Meat, you let them call you Meat. He'd been called a lot worse, and his real name had never really mattered anyway.

She shrugged when he didn't answer, and tidied up the papers still on the table. He noted that her eyes flickered in his direction every now and again. She was always aware of where he was, always aware of the distance between them.

He was aware, too, by how the overwhelming desire that should have subsided by now gnawed at him even as he watched her from the other side of the room.

"What exactly would you like to know?" he asked woodenly, unwilling to let his voice reveal his growing excitement as she suddenly knelt down on her hands and knees, her body rocking as she reached out to collect scattered sheets of paper.

"Let's start with why you were deactivated. Did you…I don't know…'break down?'"

Meat laughed, a hollow sound. He needed her to see his human qualities first, his robotics a distant second. "I'm not a toaster or a fastcook. I'm a man." He moved casually to the bookcase, watching her through his lashes as he pretended an interest in what she displayed there.

"A *man*, huh? I almost believe that you believe it. But what's important is whether I believe it." She looked over her shoulder at him, her sleek back arching slightly. "Why don't we go with that assumption for the moment. Tell me why you were deactivated."

Her back would be the same delicate pale color as her creamy white thighs; her ass would be as smooth and tight as the rest of her body. He glanced down as a sharp pain raced through his hand, drawing his attention to the rough piece of crystal he held tightly in one fist. Meat carefully released the jagged purple rock and put it back on the bookcase. "I don't know."

"They just one day up and said, okay, you there, your service is over?"

He swallowed hard, a little dizzy on his feet, suddenly, desperately thirsty. He looked down at Camille still on the floor, imagined kneeling down behind her and stripping the training suit off her body all over again, imagined himself without restraints running his palms delicately down her back, so delicately it didn't hurt him, it didn't burn her.

Releasing his rigid cock and sliding it along the narrow well of her satin-covered cheeks; taking himself to the edge by pressing his throbbing erection between two handfuls of that perfect ass and then slowly grazing over the smooth blue fabric of her panties down and under her body until they both moaned.

He'd keep those panties on, and pull the silky scrap of material aside just enough so he could watch as he sheathed himself inch-by-inch into the moist pink opening of her beautiful cunt, then bury himself to the hilt and thrust into her over and over again until they both cried out their release.

Suddenly, Camille stood up and brushed off her hands. "I'd appreciate an answer."

Meat shuddered as the image faded of his hands on her slim hips, his body crouched over her, impaling her from behind. "Sorry. Tired. Could you repeat the question?"

She gave him a funny look, and moved the stack of papers from the ground to the table. Then she walked to the recliner by the fireplace and plopped down into the chair, curling up with her head resting on the arm. "Why do you think they deactivated you?"

The human commanders became afraid because I was not so different from them. "They didn't say anything. As far as I can tell, nothing is different about my physical or mental capabilities now compared to my last campaign a month ago."

"Mmm," she said, looking him up and down. "So, what robotic parts do you have? I guess the obvious question is, what makes you different from a man?"

Meat walked up to the recliner and gazed down at her. "What do *you* think makes me different?"

She shifted back in the chair, putting more distance between them. "If you make me feel like a woman does that necessarily make you a man?" she asked with a smirk. "Maybe they programmed you especially well."

Meat stiffened at the insult but simply smiled as seductively as he could manage. "I don't think they could program what I'm thinking about right now. Would you like to find out?"

Camille tossed her hair back over her shoulder and laughed. "Evasion tactics. What's your game?"

He shrugged. "No game. I'm curious. I enjoyed giving you pleasure, and I'd like to get to know you better."

"That's lovely, but maybe flattery is part of a giant piece of software in your head. I have no idea just how human you really are. That's what I'm interested in finding out."

She flinched as he crouched down suddenly and moved his shackled hands toward her cheek, relaxing again in a moment when he simply brushed his knuckles against her skin. "I'd be willing to bet I'm at least as human as some of those men you work with. Maybe more." Her jaw tightened and he guessed he'd hit a sore spot.

"Believe me, I know how it is out there. You feel empty inside. It's like you against the world, sometimes." He spoke slowly, gauging her reaction. "It's…lonely, isn't it?"

She didn't speak at first, then suddenly cleared her throat. "Yes, well. Life's a bitch and then you die. Some of us sooner than others. Tell me what makes you a robo."

She was a tough one. Or at least that was what she wanted him to believe. He took his hands from her face and held them out to her, palms down. "Take off one of my gloves."

She hesitated, then climbed out of the chair and stood up, taking hold of his right wrist with one hand and slowly peeling the leather off with the other. Her touch was so gentle it tickled, a funny little feeling that charmed his senses in one instant and made him doubt his sanity in the next.

He quickly made a fist, then brought it up in front of her face. "Sorry to disappoint you, but this is all there is. Both hands."

Camille's eyes widened as he unclenched his fist and revealed the flexible metal plates implanted into his flesh from the tips of his fingers to the top of the palm of his hand. He waited for her expression to change to disgust or fear, but it never did. Instead, she simply examined him with an almost respectful curiosity.

"There's nothing robotic inside you?"

"No."

She looked at him suspiciously, but didn't say anything.

Meat could feel the metal in his hand heat up as she swept her fingertips against his palm, skin on skin, with a featherlight touch as erotic as the violent sexuality she'd displayed earlier.

She took his wrist and pulled his hands back up to her face, inhaling roughly as she placed his palm against her cheek and the metal made contact.

The rapid rise and fall of her breasts and the peaked nipples under the gray fabric of her training suit encouraged him, and he ignored the spiraling of his own desire to focus all of his attention on her.

"Whatever you like," he murmured. "I'll give it to you."

He ran his thumb across her mouth, and she tipped her head back slightly, parting her lips. He swallowed hard to control himself against the pleasure of her mouth gently closing around him, sucking at the hot, pulsing current.

She took him with half-closed eyes, like she'd probably suck his cock, running her tongue over and around the tip, encircling him with those lush lips and taking his entire length inside her down to the palm.

He snatched his thumb from her mouth and looked away, his mind confused, a jumble of unfocused images and thoughts clouding his mission.

She licked her bottom lip and watched him. "The metal's warm."

He nodded. "It tends to heat up when I'm experiencing extreme emotions."

A little breathlessly, she asked, "So you're experiencing extreme emotions, now?"

"Yes."

"Which ones? You don't look angry to me."

"Excitement. You excite me."

She looked surprised by his honesty. "What happens when you're angry?"

"At some point, the metal can burn."

"What happens when you're scared?"

"I don't get scared."

"Is that so?"

She likes vulnerability, Meat thought suddenly. And she responds well to the facts of my robotics. "Well, that's not true actually. Perhaps I'm scared that the more I tell you about robotics, the less you'll be inclined to recognize my human qualities."

"The more I know about you, the more I'll want to kill you?"

He nodded and she picked up his hand again, swirling her index finger delicately in his palm. "The less I know about you, the easier it will be to kill you without a qualm."

He took a chance. "Don't."

"Don't what? Touch you?" she teased.

"Kill me."

She inhaled quietly, like a whisper, but he heard the sound, and he could have sworn it was the sound of compassion.

Camille had cut her questioning short in favor of a meal, which Meat gratefully accepted although it took some skill to prevent himself from falling face first into the food tray with exhaustion.

She took the hint, and Meat thanked his good fortune when she grabbed one of her own pillows and tossed it to the floor onto the pallet she'd made up for him across the room from her bed.

Quickly, he held out his hands, thinking to take advantage of her mood.

"Nice try, Meat. I'm not stupid enough to try and sleep with you running around unchained. Lie down with your hands above your head."

Without a word, he did, and Camille clipped a second chain to the middle of his restraints and strung it to the metal pipe that ran from floor to ceiling. She obviously wanted him where she could see him and hear him. Smart. She'd wake up immediately if he tried anything.

She turned the lights off and changed before he could get accustomed to the darkness, but he could tell from the sound of the fabric against her bedcovers that she wore something silky.

He grinned into the darkness as she got into bed, biting his lip to keep from laughing at the sound of the safety latch clicking against her Class II weapon. She was sleeping with her gun when she could have been sleeping with him.

Interesting choice.

"Good night," he finally said. It seemed a little awkward, but hell, a little friendliness couldn't hurt matters.

She didn't answer, and then suddenly she got back out of bed. Meat tensed, instinctively preparing himself for an attack.

A shard of moonlight slipped through the drapes and illuminated her body as she walked across the room, the hem of her white silk nightgown swirling around her thighs, her blonde hair splayed down her back. She seemed fragile at first glance, but a second look revealed a covered field knife strapped to her bare leg, nearly camouflaged in the dim light.

His senses on the alert, Meat didn't move as she crouched down by his head and pulled the knife from its sheath, the fabric of her nightgown shifting to his advantage in every way.

Who's trying to seduce who? Meat wondered grimly. He waited with a guarded stare, unsure of her intent. If he had the use of his hands, he'd take the gorgeous breasts revealed by the dip of her neckline in his hands and suck on those tight peaks until she begged him for something even better.

"Kiss me," she said, simply. "I'm curious. I want to know what it's like with one of you."

Meat frowned, confused by her request. He adjusted his body, positioning his face on level with the blonde curls peeking out from between her legs as the hemline crept farther up her thighs.

She pressed her knees together and swung them to the side, looking at him strangely. "I just said, 'kiss.'"

Meat tried to think how he could fake his way through this.

She moved closer and put her hand on the back of his neck, lowering her mouth down to his level, her lips curved in a delicate smile. "It's just a kiss. Don't tell me I've found your Achilles' Heel."

"I don't have an Achilles' Heel," he said automatically, staring down the front of her nightgown. She smelled incredibly clean. That stuff he'd seen in the bathroom. A sweet scent...jasmine. Definitely a smell that never floated across any of the battlefields he'd ever fought on.

Pressing her lips against his, she swiped her tongue across his lower lip and finally pressed her moist warmth inside. Such a strange sensation. Meat suddenly had to suppress an inexplicable impulse to weep.

He followed her lead, copying her movements until instinct took over in a wave of lust. He plunged into her mouth with his tongue like he wanted to plunge between her thighs, imagining her urging him on, his free hands full of her curves.

He sucked on her tongue, and he could feel her lose herself a little, her hands skittering blindly across his overheated skin.

"You taste so sweet," he murmured, the metal chain above him clanking as the restraints hit their limit and he was left straining to reach her body with his cuffed hands.

She pulled away and stared at him, wrapping her arms against her body in a protective motion. "We could both use some sleep." She turned and climbed back into bed with her arsenal.

Meat touched his forearm to his lips and tried to get control of himself. Humans had brought him and his friends nothing but pain. He'd do well to remember that.

Camille manipulated him in a way he had no experience with. And he couldn't for the life of him see the point. She had nothing to lose in all this. All she had to do was decide whether or not he deserved to die. But if he couldn't understand, he couldn't defend himself...and he couldn't plan a proper counterattack.

He just needed sleep. Tomorrow he could reassert his dominance. He'd stay focused and detached, but encourage her attachment to him.

It would be a lot easier to stay focused and detached without aching balls and a rock-hard cock. Meat curled his knees up to his body in the dark and pressed his face down into the pillow to stifle his groan.

Chapter Three

Camille lay on her bed fully clothed, listening to Meat's breathing over the faint patter of rain outside.

He didn't look rested, and she guessed neither of them had slept much last night. She remembered the look on his face after their goodnight kiss, and suspected she'd been closer to the truth than she realized. Meat definitely had feelings, but he just as surely didn't know what to do with them. Odd that he'd never kissed before. Of course, once he'd gotten the hang of it, it'd been like turning on the ignition.

She'd wanted him badly. She'd wanted to take those damn cuffs off and let him have at her. She dreamed about him ripping the pipe out of the wall just to get to her, pulling her on top of him with her nightgown sliding up around her waist and ordering her to ride him with that stormy, arrogant look on his face. Camille pressed her face into the comforter and giggled.

That was the problem. She understood her feelings exactly. A *big* problem considering this was an assignment that inherently required objectivity.

Meat's eyes flew open and he blinked a couple of times and then tried to stretch his arms. "Son of a bitch!" He looked at the restraints around his wrists and then turned and focused on Camille stretched out on the bed. "Camille Kazinsky."

She gazed at him. "Yeah?"

"I want to…I need to get cleaned up."

"Well, it's your lucky day. Water's finally back on." She got off the bed, then walked over to his pallet and unlocked the restraints from the pipe, her damp hair swinging around her shoulders. "Besides, it's important that you look nice for Danny. Ha-ha."

He quirked an eyebrow. "Who?"

"My partner. It's protocol to visit your partner when they're on probation, and I'm sure Danny wouldn't miss this opportunity to show a little sympathy."

Meat eyed her with a curious expression. Indicating with his chin the Class II lying on the bed next to her, he asked, "Is that for him or for me?"

She let out a short laugh. "I'm prepared to use it on either of you. In any case, before he gets here, you and I should have a talk about behavior."

"I'm an adult. An adult *man*."

Camille looked at him sharply. "Watch the attitude. I'm totally serious. Danny's got connections."

"If your partner has connections, why didn't he get you out of probation?"

"It's not exactly in his best interest." She frowned. "Look, the bottom line is that when Danny gets here, if anything happens to make me look like I don't have everything completely under control…you get what I'm saying."

He didn't answer.

"Okay, let's go," Camille said, grabbing her weapon and urging him forward with a palm on his back. "I already put a change of clothes in the bathroom."

Meat looked over his shoulder at her. "You're coming with me?"

"Uh, yeah. Just like last night."

His shook his head slightly, eyes narrowed, but led the way to the bathroom.

She took his hands and unpunched the restraints, her gaze lingering on the raw welts revealed when she took the metal cuffs off. Snatching his hands away, he moaned in pleasure over his temporary freedom, the muscles in his back rippling as he stretched out and shook his cramped limbs.

She leaned against the door, thoroughly enjoying the scenery. "Go ahead, do what you gotta do."

"Are you going to watch everything I do? Are you going to watch me every time I take a piss? Would you like me to jerk off in front of you?"

Camille snorted, moving her hand subconsciously to the barrel of her Class II in reaction to his rising temper. Was he actually expecting her to blush? She didn't shock that easy. "I just took you out of restraints. You think I'm going to turn my back on you now?"

"I'm quite serious. I'd like some privacy."

Man, he was cocky. He'd never been anybody's property before, that was for sure. Everything he said, he said with that same voice. Quiet, urgent, deep, a little dangerous, meant to intimidate. Almost nothing he asked was really a question, what with that clipped speech at the ends of his sentences. Camille could tell he was used to giving orders, not so much taking them.

In truth, she wished he had a robotic monotone instead of that rich, seductive voice. She wished he had metal all over his body and that he moved in jerky fits and starts like the droids in those old-fashioned movies. It was starting to bother her that the only thing that seemed different about him from the full human guys back in the field was the way he made her feel inside.

"Sorry." She motioned in the direction of the toilet. "It's all yours."

"Suit yourself," he snarled. He turned the other way and stepped into the shower, very pointedly shifted his stance, and pissed into the drain.

Camille gaped and looked away, curling her lip in disgust. "This isn't the field."

He shut the door to the shower with a flourish. Camille rolled her eyes. The door was glass from top to bottom; completely transparent. He was just trying to get under her skin. Since he wasn't using it, she crossed over to the toilet and sat down. *Christ. Well, this was just great. A robo with attitude.*

Meat turned on the water and worked quickly to wash and rinse his hair.

From her morning shower, Camille knew just how cold the water was today. Meat muttered some obscenity or another but didn't say a word about the temperature. She didn't say a word either, she just pressed the button on the wall and turned on the hot water.

The hotpipe cables were always slow to kick in the first few times after restarting a subscription, but Meat still didn't complain about the goosebumps all over his body. When the heat finally hit, he looked at her suspiciously. Then, after a few more seconds, a smile bloomed across his face, and he put his hand out to the water, watching it collect in his palm like rain as the steam began to rise.

When was the last time someone did something nice for you, he'd asked. The real answer was that it seemed like forever. And equally as long since she'd gotten any pleasure out of the reverse.

He was chuckling now, obviously as thrilled with the heated water as Camille always was coming straight from the field. She opened the door of the shower to reach in and press the button for the surround spray. He just stood there in the middle, the hot water sluicing over his body from all sides. He tipped his head back, a look of ecstasy on his face that made Camille's nipples harden.

She'd seen him naked before bed last night, but here in the daytime, with the water streaming down his muscular body, well, he was spectacular. All this power and beauty in one man. She crossed her arms over her chest and looked away.

"Thanks."

She looked back up at Meat, and he was just standing there, staring at her, with a raging hard on and a look of such pure sexual frustration she almost had to laugh.

He must have seen the laughter in her look, because he answered with an intense stare and the hint of a smile. Then his lips parted, and he wrapped one hand around the head of his stiff cock. Camille dropped her arms to her sides, her pulse racing.

He swallowed hard and moved the circle of his fist down to the base of his cock, using his free hand to swipe the steam off a length of glass in one fierce motion.

She walked up to the clear streak to press her palms against the glass, grateful for how cool it felt under her hands, while the rest of her seemed to burn under his gaze.

Meat pumped his hand up and down more urgently now, and Camille slid her hands down the humid glass as if she were actually touching the body she only looked at.

With a gasp of pure pleasure, he tipped his head back, and his hand rammed down hard a few more times. Yelling out his relief like an animal, he looked directly into Camille's eyes, and came into the water at his feet.

Camille could hardly breathe by the time he closed his eyes and dropped his hand. She moved her shaking hands away from the glass and held them against her chest.

The door sensor sounded, jolting Camille back to reality. She had no clue how many times it had already rung.

Shit, Danny was here. Early.

She cleared her throat, wishing she could clear her head as easily, and said, "Remember, I'm armed and don't try anything while he's here."

Meat stepped out of the shower, naked and dripping wet. She grabbed his bare hands, shut the restraints around his wrists, and tossed him his pants. "And put these on, will you?"

≈≈(ᘓ)≈≈

Danny Dietrich stood on the threshold looking the same as usual; like he'd never sweat a day in his life.

While Meat had the powerful build and demeanor of a true fighter, Danny looked prettier, more like the politician he aspired to be. Even with a buzz cut and military uniform, he carried himself as if he wore an expensive business suit.

Posture really made a difference, thought Camille, standing up a little straighter. Not to mention, he probably would have looked even better to her if she didn't dislike him so much.

"'Morning, Cami," he said cheerfully and stepped inside. "Protocol visit."

"I've been so hoping you'd come over today," she said in deadpan.

"I'm sure."

Still holding the door, she answered, "Well, it's been great. Thanks for stopping by."

Danny looked around the room. "So, how's it going?"

Camille rolled her eyes. "Look, I'm on assignment as we speak. So, if you don't mind..."

"Actually, I do. So, where is it? I'm dying to see one up close."

She went for the jugular. "Can't you just call Daddy and have him arrange a special tour of the robo training facilities for you?"

Anger flickered in Danny's eyes for just a moment. "I don't ask my father for favors like that. You know that."

Camille held up her hands in mock defense. "No, of course not. God forbid anyone should accuse you of moving up the ranks because of nepotism. Not to mention, you certainly wouldn't want a big government official like your dad to know you've had a few...difficulties, should I say, during training."

Danny eyed her as he rubbed the monogram on his signet ring, his expression equal parts charming and sinister. "You, of all people, should be glad I don't waste my connections on the small favors. That way, when it's do or die, I can get what I need."

He ran his hand along the smooth skin of his square jaw and added meaningfully, "Or what I need for someone else. Just remember, you keep your mouth shut, and I'll do my part to keep the other guys at bay until you graduate. You know you're on the edge as it is. And if it looks really bad for you, I might just call in a...Real. Big. Favor."

"I get it, Danny. Okay? My mouth didn't open when you were busy passing me the blame. I don't see what I gain by trying to convince anyone otherwise at this point. You know I want to graduate. That's what this is all about."

"Good, then."

"You'd just better keep your side of the bargain," she mumbled under her breath.

Danny looked at his watch. "Now as soon as you show me the robo, I'm out of here. Everyone's curious, and I want to tell 'em all what one's like up close."

Camille laughed and shook her head. "That will be nice for you. You'll be the center of attention."

"I'm glad you understand. Okay, show 'n' tell."

Camille was in no hurry to oblige. "You make him sound like an art project, or something."

Danny looked at her sharply. "Mmm. You make 'him' sound like you're one day into your assignment and already in danger of losing your elusive objectivity. Not exactly surprising."

He put his finger under Camille's chin and lifted her face to his. "My, my, Cami, your soft underbelly is showing again."

Camille knocked his hand away.

"Is he bothering you?"

Meat stood in the doorway, water from his hair dripping down his naked chest, his pants only partially buttoned. He looked big, strong, and threatening. And he was on her side.

Danny looked over his shoulder and then wheeled around, his jaw dropping. "Holy shit…This thing's built." A slow smile spread across his face. "I wish the others were here right now. Are the robotics inside?"

Meat ignored Danny's rude perusal and continued to look directly into Camille's eyes. "Because it seemed like he was bothering you."

Camille couldn't help but smile. "No, he's not bothering me. Danny wouldn't bother me, because Danny knows I know something that he wishes I didn't know."

Danny slowly approached Meat with his weapon at the ready, a look of awe on his face. "Check this thing *out*." He stretched his free arm out and snapped his fingers in front of Meat's face.

Camille swallowed nervously as Meat balled his hands into fists.

"Leave him alone, Danny."

Danny whipped his head around and then walked back up to Camille. He tipped his head to one side and gave her a sympathetic smile. "Does Cami have a new best friend? Does Cami feel *sorry* for the robo?"

"Obviously not. I'm beginning to feel sorry for you because if anyone heard you talking like this, they'd have you committed. Feeling sorry is not the issue. Acting like an ass is the issue."

Meat snorted, and Camille shot him a warning look before continuing. "So, now you've stopped by, you can go back to the unit and tell them what a team player you are, standing by your shamed partner and all."

Danny shrugged. "Yeah, I plan to do that. But what's the rush? I've never seen a robo close-up." He walked around Meat, poking him and touching him as he moved. "This thing's pretty solid."

Camille tried to affect a confident nonchalance to distract Danny from taunting Meat. "Haven't you had enough? This isn't a social call."

"Isn't it? We were social once, weren't we?"

"For about five minutes in the back of a modified Humvee, I think. But the entire episode isn't particularly memorable."

"You slept with this guy?" Meat asked, looking Danny up and down with ill-concealed distaste.

Danny's eyebrow quirked up. "Oh, man, now it's jealous. This just gets better and better."

"Okay, you know what? Testosterone overload. Danny, you saw what you wanted, so why don't you leave."

Danny leered at Meat. "Yeah, sure. I ought to give you two a little privacy, eh, tough guy? You'd like that, wouldn't you? But Camille's hard to please, let me warn you." He moved his gaze to Camille. "Are you sure it understands all this?" He turned back to Meat, enunciating carefully, "Hard. To. Please."

Camille pressed at the headache throbbing just above her left eye as Danny walked around to Meat's back and ran his palm over the scars. "Jesus, look at these."

Meat stiffened, a look of revulsion on his face.

Time for this visit to end. "Danny, stop. I'm serious. Don't make me do something we'll both regret."

"You seem unusually on edge. Are you having trouble with the killing part of your assignment?"

Meat looked sharply at Camille, but held his tongue.

Danny caught the look. "Don't worry, robo. Nobody thinks Camille has what it takes. Of course, I could kill you for her, and no one would have to know." He swung his Class II into position, pointing it at Meat. "Now that would be a favor."

Camille pushed the barrel of Danny's gun away. "You and your favors," she said with disgust. "This situation is in *my* hands."

"Your hands," Danny said. "One little fingerprint to file that report. If the robo had any brains at all, it'd cut off your finger and take care of business. Funny. One little finger is all it takes to live…"

Danny raised the tip of his Class II up to the side of Meat's head. "And one little finger is all it takes to die." He slowly unclipped the safety.

Camille felt Meat tense beside her. She caught the way he stared at Danny with unveiled hostility, like a chained dog straining at its leash. She almost wished she hadn't made such a big issue of Meat controlling his behavior.

Danny fought hard and he had a strong bloodlust, but she could tell at a glance he didn't have Meat's strength, and she knew from experience he didn't have her agility.

Danny tilted his head and chuckled. "I think it's mad."

Camille could feel the heat coming off of Meat's body; she sensed he was about to jump out of his skin. If he made a move on Danny, two possible things could happen. Danny would report the incident, and she'd look like she was unable to control the robo. Or Danny would kill Meat, and she'd look like she was unable to control anybody.

Fact was, Danny looked like he'd truly relish blowing Meat's brains out all over Camille's living room, and his trigger happy ways were what got them both in this situation in the first place.

Camille shot a warning look at Meat, even as she struggled with her own temper. She gripped her Class II up at the shoulder pointedly and said, "Leave him alone. This is my assignment, and I'm prepared to defend my position."

"'Leave him alone.'" Danny laughed. "You *are* soft, aren't you, Camille? Just like all the other girls."

Camille gritted her teeth. "Get. Out. I've had enough."

"I'm going, I'm going…" Danny sighed loudly and backed up across the room and pressed the door release. "…but it's *so* tempting." He paused on the threshold, looking at them with a boyish lopsided smile, like a guilty schoolboy about to steal candy out of the teacher's drawer.

And in one smooth movement, he swung his weapon up, pointed it at Meat, and pulled the trigger.

Chapter Four

Meat hit the ground, the sound of Camille's scream ringing in his ears. She'd lunged toward him, knocking him down as she tried to shield him with her body.

Danny stared down at them incredulously. "It's not loaded, Cami. Man, you *are* soft. It's just a robo." In two strides he was out the door and gone.

Camille shifted her body to straddle Meat on her hands and knees while he lay face up beneath her on the floor. She looked down at him blankly through a tangled mass of gold hair.

Meat stared up at her in shock. "I think you would have just taken a bullet for me. Or at least shared one."

"God *damn* him." Camille sat back on his thighs and looked down at him, fists curled. She clearly wanted to punch something…or someone.

"He has something on you, doesn't he?" There was something strange going on here. The way she let him fawn and insult her. He knew that she had more of a spine than that, but she let him get away with it. "Does he have something on you?" Meat repeated.

Camille wasn't listening. "I let him get to me, every *god damn time*."

Meat searched her face, unsure what his tactics should be. Not entirely clear at the moment about the difference between his strategic tactics and his personal preference. "Even without a weapon, I'm more useful without the handcuffs."

"You think I trust you that much?" she spat out.

"Take them off, Camille," Meat said softly. "I'm not going to hurt you. By now you've got to know that I'm not some mindless robot with a kill reflex. And it's certainly not in my interest to hurt you." He hesitated. "I don't *want* to hurt you. I'd never hurt you. Take them off, and I'll prove that you can trust me. These hands will only give you pleasure."

She looked wild, a stormy expression on her face.

Meat replayed the scene in his mind. No wonder she was in trouble at the academy. There was obviously something wrong with her self-preservation instinct. He sure as hell wouldn't take a bullet for someone he didn't really know. They were all trained that way. Robos and humans alike. It's probably why she was so angry at herself now. He'd be smart to make her feel better about having done it.

He must be making Camille care about him, on some level, at least. How strange that her regard for him should feel so good, when it wasn't supposed to really matter at all.

"What you did there…" He hesitated, then stopped short of reminding her that she'd been kind to him. "Just take off the restraints, and I'll give you whatever you need."

She turned to look at him with eyes bright, almost feverish. "Go to hell, you manipulative shit."

Meat kept his mouth shut.

"You're trying to play me just like Danny. You're nothing more than a collection of metal parts and computer chips. And I'm messing up my situation just to save your ass. One small thing I asked of you. Don't do anything to make it look like I don't have total control. I wish Danny had blown your sorry head off."

It was irrational for her to blame him for this, and Meat guessed they both knew it. "So, hit me."

"What?"

"Hit me. You're pissed, go ahead and take it out on me. I can handle it."

"That's not what I want."

"What do you want, then?"

"I don't know."

"Don't you?" Meat locked his legs around her body and rolled her over, trapping her underneath him, his cuffed hands above her head.

She didn't struggle, which surprised Meat a little. She just eyed him angrily. "You're nothing but trouble for me."

"Nah. I don't think you mean that, Camille. I think you're just pissed as hell. I think you've been pissed as hell for a long time now, with no way to show it without getting yourself in trouble."

"What is that supposed to mean?" she ground out between her teeth. "I knew what I was getting into when I sat for the academy entrance exam. I can take it."

"Sure, you can take it. But why bother?"

She stared at him in confusion and anger, almost as if this was the first time it had occurred to her that she really had a choice in the matter. "Excuse me?"

Meat shrugged. "You heard me."

"I *like* my job," she said, sounding like she was trying to convince herself as much as him.

"If Danny is a prime example of who you spend your time with on the job, I'm surprised you manage to use as much restraint as you do. As you said, you let him get to you every single time."

Her eyes narrowed, and she twisted her legs, trying to drag her body out from under him. "I like to think holding back is a positive. It's as difficult a skill to master as kicking ass. That's something Danny's never figured out."

"Then why does he always win?"

Camille stopped moving for a moment as she stared at him in shock, then just as abruptly pushed at his chest with fisted hands. "He doesn't. Get the hell off me."

Meat let more of his body weight press down against her. "If I get the hell off you, what are you going to do with all these 'feelings'?"

"You don't know anything about feelings, mine or yours. That's obvious."

Not nearly as obvious as the pounding of her heart against his body. "Mmm. I know a little, at least. I know you don't really want me to get the hell off you." He leaned down and licked her hard nipple through the fabric of her shirt. She arched underneath him in surprise and he immediately pulled his mouth away. "If you don't want to punch me in the face, I can think of other ways to ease your frustration...let me help you."

"Let you *help* me? Are you kidding? You just want me to set you free."

Meat winced internally at the well-aimed retort. "Obviously, in the big picture. I don't pretend otherwise. Right now I just want you to give me back my hands so I can fuck you properly like I know you want me to."

"You can fuck me from here to next Tuesday but it won't affect my decision about whether you live or die."

We'll see about that. He moved his hands from over her head down to her breasts, and massaged her nipple with the pulsing heat of his bare thumb.

Camille was panting now. "Who says you need your hands back?"

"Ripping our clothes off with my teeth will take too long."

"Figure something out. You're trained to solve tough problems under difficult conditions." She grabbed at his waistband, yanking the two sides of his fly apart. The zipper whizzed down, her mouth already pressed hot and wet to his chest, her hand moving inside to his balls.

His body instinctively jumped, giving Camille an in. She scrambled out from under him and flipped their positions, grabbing his bound hands and thrusting them above his head. She straddled him again, grinding his pulsing cock against the center of her thighs.

Meat thrashed his head to the side, and growled, "Give me my hands, or I swear to God…"

"What would you do? Huh? What?" Camille stripped off her shirt and bra and tossed them away. She bent down over his body, her breasts shifting down in front of his face and undid her fatigues. "What are you going to do? Huh, Meat? What are you going to do *now*?"

He took her breast in his mouth, sucking and pulling first at one nipple, then the other as she pressed his cock up to her clit and squirmed, building a frenzy inside him that made him crave even more.

She let go of him suddenly, and leaped up, thrusting one boot square on his chest while she pulled off the rest of her clothes and tossed them inside out across the room. When she was through, she took her foot off his chest, knocked the unlaced boot away and lowered herself back down, cunt to cock. "It's a real bitch not to be in control, I completely—"

He sat up, swinging the arc of his arms up and over her head, his bare hot cock brushing heavily against the moist center of her thighs.

"Oh, *god*." She arched her back, running her palms over his back.

"What would you do if you were me? You let my arms go for this, and I swear you will not be sorry."

"I'm already not sorry," she gasped, biting her lips as she thrust back and forth, sliding the wet lips of her cunt along the surface of his cock.

Meat couldn't take it anymore. He was nearly out of his mind with the need to bury himself in her. He took the advantage as soon as he could get it, rolling them over, tackling her to the ground, pressing her naked body down into the carpet with his own. Desperate with lust, he plunged deep inside.

Tossing her head from side to side, Camille wrapped her arms tightly around his body, arching her body up to meet him and forcing him into her deeper and deeper until she screamed in climax.

"Go ahead and fuck me hard," she murmured into his ear, giving him free rein to let himself go.

And he did let himself go, slamming his bound fists into the floor above her head each time he rammed his cock deep inside her tight, slick passage, his frustration at not being free and his lust for her taking him to the boiling point.

She kissed him deeply as he came, swallowing his groan as his hot seed shot deep inside her body.

And then silence. Nothing but the faint smell of burning fiber from the singed carpet above her head where he'd grabbed fistfuls of the pile.

He rolled off her and they lay side-by-side on the carpet, staring up at the ceiling, Meat unwilling to break the spell.

Camille had no such reservations. "Do all robos have these hands?"

"What? Are you kidding me?"

"I need to ask you some more questions."

"Don't you ever give it a rest?"

"Why should I?" she asked curtly. "This is my assignment. If you're just fucking me so that I'll stop doing my job, you'd better think of a better strategy."

He gazed at her for a moment in silence, then answered in monotone. "Only a few of us have these hands. The DOD develops robos in small batches, to experiment for desirable combinations."

"What else is robotic in you?"

"Nothing. Other than my hands, I'm clean."

"What do your hands do?"

"If you're ready for another round, I'm happy to show you," he murmured suggestively.

"I'm waiting for a real answer."

He paused. "Not a whole lot anymore."

"Not a whole lot."

"They were created for special weaponry, and I don't have access to that equipment anymore."

"What do they do with weaponry?"

"They can act as a wireless device, transmitting third-party information to the weapon during the heat of battle. One man, one weapon, multiple forms of destruction on call."

"Very impressive."

"But as I said, I don't have access to that arsenal anymore, so my robotic abilities are irrelevant."

"They used you like a thinking remote control." She studied him. "And nothing's wrong inside you?"

"Nothing's wrong inside me," he said, somewhat testily. "I'm not saying all robos are this low-grade. But many are. I am."

She cocked her head and gazed at him, and Meat could almost see her wondering if this entire dialogue was part of some pre-written script. "Does it hurt?" she asked.

He shrugged. "They're mostly just ultra-sensitive."

"When did they do this to you?"

"After puberty."

"Do you have any family?"

"I was born in a government facility, educated, and trained there, then sent out to the field. There's no other family."

Camille stared at him. "Doesn't that bother you?"

"Not particularly."

She seemed concerned by that answer. Maybe he ought to have manufactured a past and a family to make his plight more sympathetic. It never occurred to him to bother. "Do you have a family?"

"They're dead now. Both were in government jobs." She smiled wistfully. "My mother wanted to be miltel, but they wouldn't let her in. Everything has to be so hard." She didn't speak for a long while, then yawned and said, "God, sometimes I feel like no matter how long I sleep, I'll always be tired."

"Camille."

She turned her head and looked at him.

"Whatever it is that…" He reached out his arms, hesitating for a moment, but she nodded just slightly and he pulled her on to his lap and put his arms around her, rocking her. "It's all going to be fine."

"Of course," she murmured, and leaned back, resting her full body weight against him. In another moment she was asleep.

She was naked, three feet from her nearest weapon, and now dozing off guard in the circle of his bound arms. And what bothered Meat most was that *he* felt vulnerable. His motives were confused, his mission clouded. It was hard to separate what he wanted to do from what he thought he was supposed to do.

Camille whimpered, and Meat held her closer. "Shh, kitten…"

She snuggled into his arms and smiled.

An hour later she sat up with a start and looked wildly around her. Meat watched her warily as she absorbed the fact that she'd left herself unguarded.

She shook her head in disbelief and reached out and slowly dragged her weapon toward her. She held it loosely in her hands and looked at Meat, deep in thought. Finally, she said a little too brightly as she stood up, "My back is killing me. Why don't we ever do this sort of thing in my bed?"

"You haven't invited me into your bed," he said simply.

She took him by the hand, running her fingers lightly over the metal pads. Then she slid her hand up to his wrist and pulled him up from the floor. "I'm inviting you now." She stood up and left the room, returning a moment later with the restraint punch. "Come on."

A funny look came over his face. "No," he said and stood stubbornly in place. "No?"

"Sleeping with my arms chained to the bed would be more uncomfortable than the set up I've already got." He frowned. "Or did you just mean for one go-round?"

Camille looked ashamed. She held out her hand again.

Meat stepped backwards. "If it means you're going to start back at square one in terms of trusting me not to hurt you, I'd rather keep them on."

"I trust you," she blurted out.

He slowly held his hands out to her, half expecting her to laugh in his face at the last minute.

She punched the lock and the restraints fell open with a whizzing sound. Meat moved his hands apart. He took a deep breath, flexing his arms, and swinging them apart. "I feel like a new man."

She didn't answer. Just smiled and would have turned away, but he took her face in his hands and kissed her, the swirl of his tongue against hers making him want to start all over again. "Thank you. You have no idea how good this feels. I swear, I'm not going to give you trouble."

Chapter Five

For the next two weeks, trouble lurked in the back of Camille's mind.

Turned out Meat had a thing for the game of chess, and so Camille set up a board on a side table between the two recliners. Each night they played the game in front of the fire while it rained sheets of ice outside, and he waited for her to file the report that determined whether he would live or die.

Every time they sat down to play, the entire scenario struck Camille as perverse. She'd come to accept the fact that she cared about him a great deal. The reward of that unguarded smile that appeared whenever she did something nice for him that she didn't have to do, made her feel good.

Not that she'd said anything to him about her feelings.

The problem was that as she came closer to the filing deadline for his report, there was still a nagging detail, an unease that never went away, no matter how many times they made love.

"It's your move," Meat finally said in a grumpy tone.

Camille looked down at the board and grinned. "Checkmate! And it's about time." She looked up at him quickly. "You didn't just let me win, did you?"

Meat leaned back in his chair. "I don't 'just let people win.'"

The sharp tone caught her by surprise, and she looked up, but couldn't detect anything unusual about his expression.

But there it was. A comment, a tone, an expression, an odd movement. It was the possibility that everything he did and everything he said was carefully calculated to lead her to filing a reclassification report.

To think that after all this time, after everything she'd come to feel for him, that it could all be a lie was a concept that made her nearly sick to her stomach.

"I'd say best of three but I don't want to be here all night." He reached over and smoothed a hand along her thigh. "One more?"

"Sure."

Truth was, she'd taken this damn long making the decision because she'd never been happier. Odd in a way, because she'd always imagined graduation day would be the happiest time in her life. Or maybe that was just what she'd convinced herself to believe.

Camille put the last few chess pieces back in place and stared down at the board. No, she didn't want things to change, but there was some relief as the report-filing deadline loomed at the end of the week.

She knew she could only rest easy about how he honestly felt about her if his life wasn't at stake. When she did reclassify him as she planned, he wouldn't need her anymore. And she'd finally know the truth. Would he still want to be with her?

What they shared had to be real. It had to be. No man had ever held her in his arms and whispered in her ear that everything would be okay. No man could be programmed to know what the perfect thing to say would be, to know how each individual woman wanted to be touched. The way she felt had to be real. Didn't it?

Meat claimed the only thing he had were special implants in his hands. But he'd also admitted that most robos weren't as low-grade as that. Most had more robotics and some of them had internal components. And that was her dilemma. He could be lying about how human he really was, but if he was as human as he seemed, terminating him would be nothing less than murder.

"What did he do to you?"

"What?" Camille asked, startled.

"What did Danny do to you that put the wedge between you?"

The last person she wanted to talk about was Danny. "Danny's not unique. None of the guys are too friendly with me. Some are worse than others and because Danny's my partner, things with us are that much more complicated."

"What about the girls?"

"There aren't any girls in the unit anymore."

"They died?"

Camille choked in surprise. "No. They just didn't make it through training." She paused, unsure of how much to say. "I haven't seen any of them in months. I'm not supposed to be around those girls anymore. They say it reflects on me."

"What does?"

"Their weakness. The term used at the academy is 'soft.' We're not supposed to be soft."

"And that's why they failed out of the academy? Because they were soft?"

"That's right. Well, that's what they say. But it was pretty much fixed anyway."

Meat studied her face. "If you're the only woman in the unit who's made it this far, the other men should have a great deal of respect for your abilities."

"You'd think."

"With robos, no one cares if you're male or female. It's all about abilities and implants. But then again, our training might be a little different since we're assumed to have no emotions and you're assumed to have too many. If you're the only one left, you must be very good at what you do."

Camille shrugged. "I've worked really hard. This is what I've spent my whole life working toward. My mother wanted to be in miltel. They still weren't letting any women into the unit at that time, so it's a point of pride on her behalf as well as mine." She paused to make her next move, and then looked up at him. "By graduating I'll fulfill her dream."

"*Her* dream?"

"And mine. I meant mine, too. After all, I'm the only female left in my class, so I must want it pretty badly." Camille felt her face flush over the hesitation in her words. Obviously, she wanted it badly, or she wouldn't be doing this.

Quickly she added, "Maybe I just want to succeed more than some of the others that didn't make it through. But as you know, it ain't over 'til it's over, and they don't want me to graduate. Which is why this probation is particularly bad timing. There's just one more module in the training, and if I don't make it through that, it's over for me. So what's your story?"

"My story? There's not much to tell and you already know what that is."

"Well, you told me you've pretty much grown up in a military training environment. I can imagine what that's all about. But what about after?"

"That depends on you, doesn't it?"

Her heart pounded in her chest. "Let's forget that for a moment," she said quickly.

"I want what everybody wants. The ability to live my own life on my own terms. I want freedom."

"What would you do with freedom?"

"Play chess and fuck."

Camille burst out laughing. "The last couple of weeks must have been like heaven."

He stared at her, then looked down at the board.

Camille cleared her throat. "How would you make money?"

"I'd go freelance mercenary. I have some connections to help set me up."

"Reclassified robos, I'm guessing."

He nodded without looking up from the board.

"Freelance mercenary. Fair enough. A nice way to get people to leave you alone." She laughed and added, "Not to mention, no one tells you what to do…you have to be good to get enough contracts, though. And develop enough of a name to get passes into all the different territories." She watched him consider his next move. "I think you'd do very well going solo."

Meat moved his knight then looked up and said, "I can already tell that *you* are going to *lose*."

Camille gaped down at the board. "You take all the fun out of the game if you think that far ahead. This isn't the World Chess championship."

"But that's why I love playing. To be successful, I need to think long-term. Every move is deliberate, every move is planned. Keeps me sharp for the real world."

"Who'd've thought? Robos playing the cerebral game of chess between battles."

"All the time. Bullets versus rocks." He picked up his black knight and studied the piece, slowly turning it between his fingers. "The more plays you can anticipate, the more plays you can imagine in your head, the more successful your end result. A small move now may seem to be irrelevant or have no consequence, and only in the end can you see that the entire strategy depended on it."

Camille's smile faded.

"So…checkmate, it is," he said, as he knocked her white queen over with his knight. "Sorry about that."

He chucked her gently under the chin, and Camille grinned, her doubts fading away. "You're not sorry one bit."

"Uh-uh. Nevertheless, I still get the prize."

"Come and get it."

"You know I will." He stood up and scooped her out of her chair, carrying her into the bedroom.

I'm going to reclassify you, tomorrow, Meat, she said silently as he hovered over her and stripped off her clothing. *And when I do that I'm going to have my proof. Because you won't need me any more after that, and I'll know the truth.*

He laid her gently on the bed and slowly unbuttoned her shirt, leaving a trail of fire along her skin as he worked.

"You won the game, so why are you doing all the work?"

"This isn't work."

Camille smiled and stretched her legs out fully on the bed. Meat stripped everything else off her body except her panties, this time pink and lacy. He slipped his hand under the lace and Camille arched her back in pleasure as the warm metal and bare skin slid through the slickness.

"God, you're wet," he said, on a labored breath.

His words made her more so. She watched his face, his lips parting as he followed the movement of his hand underneath the pink fabric. He reflexively pressed his hips forward against the side of the bed as he made love to her swollen clit with his fingers, groaning at the contact.

When he took his hand away, Camille almost cried out in disappointment until she saw him remove his clothes. He lay down next to her, the muscles in his arms leaping as he moved over her in a push-up stance and then lowered his body over hers.

His erection grazed the sensitive skin between her thighs, and Camille arched up again to press up around him but he was too fast. He pushed himself back up, wearing an arrogant grin that didn't hide his obvious desire.

Once more he lowered his body down to hers, this time slipping the head of his cock just inside her. Camille writhed against him. "More. Give me more of you."

He leaned forward and swirled his tongue around her hard nipple, gently taking the tip between his teeth, until she shuddered.

"I want you *now*." Camille slipped her hands between them to push at his chest. Meat kissed her breast and moved back, once more finding her opening with his warm fingers, and running the faint current in his fingertips over her sensitive bud until she moaned for more. At last he pressed his thick shaft into her tight cunt, inch by slick inch until her moan became a scream of pure pleasure.

He looked into her eyes and there was no way Camille could believe this wasn't for real, his lips hovering a whisper away from her own as he slowly pumped his engorged cock between her thighs. He moved deliberately, pausing after pulling back to drive her desire as high as he could, forcing an anticipation that made them both crazy with want, and then sliding back inside and gently pressing on her clit with one hand.

He pulled back once more, and she reached down and took his balls in her hand, massaging them even as the tension built up inside her. He went a little wild, pumping into her faster, until the rhythm was in her blood, and the hot metal of his hands streaking over her body pushed her over the edge.

She came, a lightning bolt of pleasure rushing through her. Arching her back to milk the sensation for as long as she could, both hands at the base of his cock, holding his balls, and Meat bucking like a stallion as he worked to hold out for her.

"Camille!" He buried himself into her one last time and roughly pulled her body to his.

Camille could smell her jasmine scent all over his shuddering body, and she felt a sense of possession. "I'm falling in love with you," she whispered.

Meat stiffened, and she glided her hand down his back, slick with sweat, to smooth out the muscles that were already tensing up again.

She probably *was* in love with him, already, but that big question mark still stood between them. Well, she'd have her answer soon enough. And he'd have his. Smiling into his shoulder, she said, "It's okay if you don't understand yet. You will."

Camille rose from bed, then slipped on her robe and padded out to the living room. In the quiet of the morning, she turned on her computer and called up her project file. Her heart raced as she entered the disk and pressed the button to file the report.

With trembling fingers she selected 'Reclassification,' and pressed her index finger into the touchscreen. With a shiver of excitement, she keyed in the security code upon request and waited for confirmation.

It took her five minutes to comprehend the significance of the return message flashing on the screen:

Request for Reclassification On Hold. Please Report to Headquarters Immediately.

On hold? Camille stared at the screen, then finally collected herself long enough to redo all the steps. Same result.

Either something was wrong with her system or the government wanted Meat to die.

She threw her robe to the floor and dashed into the equipment closet, pulling on a clean training uniform and fastening her body armor with sweating hands.

Camille stood stiffly at attention in the center of the commander's office, amazed at how easily it all came back to her after so much time away. And at how the dread that lived with her here at the academy had disappeared over the past month.

"At ease, Kazinsky. We've been following your progress for some time now. You operate at an above-average level in many areas, but there is concern that you don't fit the profile of the elite unit we strive to develop."

The commander folded his hands on the desktop and smiled warmly at Camille. "Fit is extremely important. I think you know that."

"Sir, if this is your way of—"

"—I'm not finished."

"Yes, sir."

"We'd love to be proven wrong. You tried to file a reclassification report this morning, correct?"

"Yes, sir. It was rejected."

The commander pursed his lips. "The robo is to be terminated."

Camille swallowed hard, refusing to allow the panic in her heart to show. "Excuse me, sir. Robo evaluation involves an independent decision by the assigned evaluator. After deep consideration, I chose to reclassify the robo."

"Let's just say that you made the wrong choice."

Camille stared.

His tone hardened. "Terminate the robo, Kazinsky. Otherwise we'll have the answer we've been expecting. Are you soft or not?"

Camille looked down at the open file on the commander's desk; her file. "This was a set up."

The commander shrugged. "A test."

"You never meant for…the robo…" she tripped over her tongue on the term.

"You never meant for the robo to be reclassified."

"It was never a relevant question. It was deactivated for the purpose of your assignment."

"You have no idea whether he really deserves to be terminated or not, do you?"

The commander's eyes narrowed. "'He,' Kazinsky? Don't talk yourself into a corner."

Camille struggled with her temper. "This robo does not deserve to be terminated. This robo does not deserve to die simply to prove a point about me."

"That's its mission," the commander said simply. "And now its mission is over." He checked his watch and dug into his molars with his pinkie finger. "We've taken the hold off your report. You can go ahead and file. Kill it, or you don't graduate. You're dismissed."

The walls seemed to close in on her as she came to attention, saluted the commander and practically stumbled from the room in a daze.

Well done, Camille. You've finally found the physical and emotional connection you always craved in the man you must kill.

Chapter Six

Meat frowned as Danny opened the door to leave just as Camille came up the walkway. Nice timing.

Danny looked back over his shoulder at him and said, "Think about what I said. You know how to contact me." He turned back and saluted Camille cheerfully on the way out. "Been waiting awhile, Cami. Now I gotta run."

Camille watched Danny pass her on the walkway then turned to stare at Meat. She looked grim, with dark smudges under her eyes and a muscle straining at her jawline. "Why was he here?"

Meat shrugged. "He came to see you and had to settle for me."

She looked at him strangely. "I would have expected you two to try and kick the shit out of each other. I guess you made nice." She looked down at his hands. "And apparently the fact that you're not wearing restraints didn't bother him." She shot him a pointed look and stepped past him into the house, looking around curiously as if she expected evidence of a brawl. "So, what did you two talk about?"

Meat studied Camille's face. It looked like she was going to play innocent after all. "Where did you go this morning?" he asked.

"What?"

"I asked you where you went this morning."

"I asked you what you and Danny talked about." When Meat didn't answer, she crossed her arms over her chest. "You want to tell me what's going on here? I'm really not comfortable coming home to find Danny just leaving and you acting like *I'm* up to something."

He stared at the floor, his jaw clenched. "I kind of thought we were beyond the bullshit stage."

"That's what I thought, too." She wound a lock of hair around her finger then let it go, sighing. "Look, I've got a lot on my mind, and I…I'm going lie down. I just need to lie down and think."

Meat's heart dropped. Danny said she'd walk in that door with intent to terminate. He said she'd gone to HQ and when she returned, she'd begin to emotionally disconnect herself from him. Danny had said a lot of things that made him wonder if he'd been a fool to ever hope that Camille would give him his freedom. "What is there to think about, Camille? Are you having trouble making up your mind about something?"

She turned slowly and cocked her head, studying his face. "Meat, Danny had no reason to come over and see me today. If you tell me what he told you, we can clear up any misunderstanding."

"Amongst other things, he mentioned that you have no choice but to kill me to stay at the academy. He said reclassification was not an option." The metal in his fingertips burned, and he had to struggle to hide his growing desperation. "Do you deny it?"

"He knew?" she blurted out.

Meat made a choking sound. "*You* knew, obviously."

"I just found out this morning."

"You expect me to believe that?"

"Yeah, I do. Danny would sell out his own mother if he could make it look good. He obviously told you a bunch of crap and now you need to figure out who to believe. I'm not lying to you, Meat. This assignment was a setup."

"Let's say I believe you. So you learn there's an ultimatum that means I die in less than forty-eight hours. And you come home and decide to go lie down and take a fucking nap so you can think about what to do?"

Her face paled.

"You hadn't decided, had you?" His hands fisted at his sides. "*Had* you?"

Camille swallowed. "Give me a break, you son of a bitch. I tried to reclassify you this morning, even knowing that once I did, you'd have what you wanted and you could stop acting like you cared about me, if that's what all this was. An act. But it was a chance I had to take because I cared about *you*. And now I'm starting to believe that I was right to walk in this door, hesitating to sacrifice my future for yours."

She tried to walk past him into the bedroom, but Meat grabbed her by the arm and swung her around. "Listen to what you're saying. You're hesitating to sacrifice a job I don't think you even like for my *life*." Meat nodded slowly. "I see how it is. This must have been a fun fantasy vacation for you, Camille."

Her voice trembling, she said, "I suggest you get your *head* out of your ass, because we have a serious problem."

"I'll say. One of us dies today."

She flung his hand away from her arm. "I tried to reclassify you."

"You get bonus points for that, all right? But it turns out what you did this morning when you claim the stakes weren't this high is irrelevant. All that matters is what you plan to do now."

"You don't care about me at all, do you? I was right to hesitate…You and Danny…oh, God. Let me guess, he promised you reclassification, didn't he?"

She must have seen the answer in his eyes, because she gasped and added, "I'm right! What the hell do you have that he wants? Don't tell me he offered to trade your freedom for my life…He has to know I'll keep my mouth shut. I can't believe…"

Meat wiped the sweat off his forehead with his sleeve. It wasn't her life Danny wanted, it was the videodisk showing Danny's part in the training accident. The only proof of his mistake. "Let me put it this way. Danny wants a sure thing. And he knows he can't control you absolutely."

The robos used in live-fire exercises were video-equipped. Danny realized that he couldn't go into a classified robo facility without raising suspicion. But another robo could, so he came to Meat to cut a deal. A deal Meat was willing to completely ignore if Camille hadn't still had doubts about reclassifying him when she'd walked through that door.

It was just as well she'd made it unnecessary for him to feel bad about choosing himself over her. All Meat wanted was reclassification. It really didn't matter how he got it. And he wasn't interested in wasting any more time.

He pulled Danny's pistol out from his back waistband and held it out in front of him at the ready.

Camille looked stunned. She gasped, her eyes tearing up. "Damn," she muttered. "And to think I almost missed the pleasure of seeing your true colors come out."

Meat heard the hint of panic in her voice. He could sympathize. He'd felt the same way when he realized she'd decided to terminate him. He didn't blame her. He'd do the same if the places were reversed.

He backed her up against the wall, and she put her hand up lightly against his chest. "You don't understand," she said softly.

"Yes, I do. You're going to have to terminate me to get what you want, and I'm not going to let that happen. Where's the report disk?"

Her expression hardened and her gaze moved to the knife on her bootclip. His pistol was up to her temple in an instant. "Don't even think about it."

He held the gun on her and carefully bent down and snapped off the knife.

Camille's eyes narrowed. "I thought you were something special."

"Now, there's a line. The report disk. Where is it?"

"You'd cut off my finger to file that report, wouldn't you?"

"Yeah, I would." He switched weapons and stuck the pistol back in his waistband, then grabbed her arm and bent it behind her back. He winced at her yelp of pain, pushing the thought to the back of his mind that he actually did have a problem with the idea of cutting off her finger. "I'm going to ask you for the last time. Where's the disk?" He applied more pressure to her arm, then eased up just as suddenly when he remembered that she was as much of a soldier as he was, and she'd never give him what he wanted for the cheap price of a broken arm.

He held her up against the wall, silently cursing that it had all come to this.

"You have no qualms betraying me to get what you want," she said, eyeing the knife nervously. "I'm just glad I didn't betray myself to give it to you. You're not worth it. You're just a fake, after all. Nothing about you is real or even remotely human."

"I *am* human," he ground out. He slammed her back against the wall and kissed her roughly, taking her mouth like a possession. She let him, her body unable to resist reacting to his. He pulled away, and wiped his mouth with the back of his hand. "Not that it matters anymore, but don't tell me that it isn't real on my side. You're the one who let me whore for you with your true intentions written out from the very beginning."

"You must be kidding me. Making an alliance with Danny makes you a fool *and* an asshole. You should have tried to work something out with me."

"There's nothing to work out. It's simple. Only one of us gets the prize we want."

"And you never let anyone win."

He held the knife between his teeth as he roughly patted her down, running his hands over the curves of her body and lingering more than necessary. Finally, he felt the disk and grabbed it from one of her inside pockets.

"So easy." Meat plugged the disk into the computer, called up Camille's file, then took a calming breath and turned back to her. "It's your turn." He grabbed her hand by the wrist and moved it to the touchscreen. "Do it."

"No." She was shaking, now.

"Do it, Camille."

She didn't answer, and he grabbed her hand and shoved it against the touchscreen. Her fingerprint triggered, and the computer requested the security code.

He held on to her with one hand and pressed his palm flat against the wall with the other, reveling in the pain of his implants, staring at the screen.

"This requires more than a fingerprint to file. You have to give me a code." He laughed in disbelief.

Camille didn't say a word.

"Fuck! Fuck, Camille!" The desperation he heard in his own voice shamed him. "What do you want from me? I don't want to die, can't you understand that?"

Tears slipped down her face, but she didn't make a sound.

He struggled to regain his self-control. "Can't you understand?"

"I understand everything," she said, her mouth a grim slash. "You screw me blind, and I'm supposed to do whatever the hell you want."

"Are you trying to turn me on?" he said sarcastically.

"Are you turned on? Does the idea of hurting me turn you on?"

"No, it doesn't," he said, his voice like ice. "But some other things do." He whipped her around and shoved her face first against the wall, forcing her hands up against the wall in an imitation of a de-arming procedure.

He could hear her breathing start to come in pants. "Are you excited or scared?"

At first she didn't answer, but then she looked over her shoulder. "I can't believe you could fake it that well. Last night was…last night I saw the look in your eyes. There's no way you don't care about me."

"You make the mistake of equating sex with caring. I don't think it makes a difference. You're excited, and so am I. You're excited," Meat repeated, wanting her to admit it.

"So. What." she spat out. "Apparently, it doesn't mean anything."

He placed the palm of his hand over the tops of hers against the wall and ran his other hand down her arm. He moved his hands down in front and placed them over her breasts, squeezing them and running his hands over her nipples until there was no question of her arousal.

"Do you want me to stop?" he asked.

"I want you to…I want it like it was."

He just grabbed the two sides of her shirt and ripped it off her body. She was panting now, and he moved to her waistband, running the edge of the knife down the seams and cutting the fabric away from her body.

She pulled her hands off the wall and tried to turn around, but he caught her hands. She struggled like a wildcat, her eyes revealing all the same confusion and anger he felt in the second before he turned her back around and pressed her against the wall with his body.

He moved her arms back up above her head, then took his knife and snapped the strings of her bra and panties until she was naked in front of him, save for her boots. So beautiful. So, so beautiful. Why did it have to end like this? Why did it have to end at all?

He ran his thumb down that well, running it down over the tight pink opening of her beautiful ass, underneath, where it skidded across the creamy wet truth of how badly she wanted him. Camille made a sound, obviously angry that her desire should be obvious to him at a time like this.

"You still want me," he whispered into her ear, as he unzipped his pants and let his rigid cock rest against the pale skin of her ass.

She slammed her forehead against the wall. "Damn you."

"Tell me you still want me." He had no idea why he would beg her to say this, he just knew he wanted to hear the words.

Her voice thick with tears, she said, "*I'm no liar. I still want you.*"

He lifted her right leg up under the knee, folding it against the wall, opening her to him. He knelt down and flicked his tongue over her sweet little asshole and then swept it to her wet cunt.

"Oh, God," she moaned. "This is how we started, and I guess it's how we'll end."

He didn't like thinking about the end. He stood up and thrust his cock deep inside her.

She gasped, pressing back against his groin, and he fucked her hard and fast, almost daring her not to come.

When she cried out, he himself released. He let go of her, his heart pounding against her back, unsure of what he wanted to do.

She stayed up against the wall while he zipped up and sat down in the chair to watch her put her ripped shirt back on.

Meat put his head in his hands. "I'm supposed to hurt you now, do you get that? That's what makes sense here. That's what a smart soldier would do to get the code. I know what all the training guides say *you're* supposed to do in this situation, so I know how to trick you. I know all the psychology. Do you get what's supposed to happen here, now?"

He was definitely losing it. He could barely speak above a hoarse whisper. He didn't even want to look at her.

"Supposed to?" she asked, her voice choked with tears.

"That's what a smart soldier with a good sense of strategy would do," he said woodenly. "A soldier who hadn't lost objectivity."

He sat there, harsh breathing the only sound in the room. Suddenly, he stood up and took her hand, dragging her to the pallet he'd slept on in those first few nights. He took the restraints and bound her hands together, then chained her to the same metal bar. "Goodbye, kitten."

She stared at him, her eyes huge in her pale face.

He tossed the restraint punch across the room and walked out.

Moving quickly to her equipment room, he stuffed a handful of dry rations, a blanket, the knife, and Danny's pistol into his duffel bag before heading for the door.

He hit the door release, and a pain deep inside took root as he paused on the threshold of Camille's apartment without really knowing why.

She didn't call out to him, and he stepped out into the cold.

Tears streamed down Camille's face as she reviewed her options. The son of a bitch. "You're bigger than me and stronger than me and you've clearly got more field experience than me, but I'm not going down without a fight."

Chapter Seven

Meat couldn't have hurt Camille any more than he had. What he'd done made him feel sick enough. He cared too much to do what he should have done, and the only option left was to run as fast and as far as he could before someone let her loose and she sent the marshals after him.

The rain hit the streets in slushy waves. Meat looked around him, the acrid odor of the wet cement almost comforting, the urban battlefield solid and familiar under his feet.

He only had Danny's pistol and the knife, and he felt strangely unarmed in this familiar setting without the normal accoutrements of battle. He looked down at the metal in his hands; useless, without the right equipment.

He felt unprepared, unsure for the first time since he'd dreamed about freedom, what it might mean for a renegade robo flagged in all the systems as an escapee marked for termination.

Meat's eyes had grown accustomed to the dark now. He stepped out from the overhang into the mist of his breath and took up at a jog toward the city gates.

The way the cold seeped into his skin disoriented him. He'd been in worse conditions during weeks of fighting for oil rights in the Siberian Territory, but he couldn't remember the cold ever cutting into him so mercilessly.

He was getting soft. Too much time around Camille had changed him. He could only hope the change would prove to be for the good, because right now this was pretty miserable, slogging through the deserted streets.

He needed to keep his mind off Camille, that was—

The image of Camille in his mind shattered as the broad side of a Class II smashed into his shoulder and arm. He lost his footing on the frozen street and went down, letting go of the duffle bag to concentrate on absorbing the fall by curling his body. He took it on a roll with his arms curled around his head as he hit the street corner, the concrete curb taking his breath away.

"Do you think I'm stupid?" Camille's voice hit him along with a wave of jasmine perfume.

"I realize I have shortcomings. I never said I was perfect. I'm too *nice* to be a good miltel soldier, for one thing. They've been trying to tell me that for months. Years, really. 'You're too likely to empathize with the enemy,' they said. We'll that's all too true, isn't it? But one thing in my favor is that I'm not stupid."

Breathing better now, he tried to roll into a sitting position, but she slammed her boot on his chest. He groaned as the side of his head fell backwards into the cold water pooling at the side of the gutter, a cold stream seeping into his ear.

"I know how to track down one *super-size* guy running through the streets toward the border during *curfew*, wearing a *T-shirt* in freezing weather. It's really not that hard." She paused. "What's the matter, Meat, cat got your dick? You should be trying to seduce me about now to get out of this mess."

"Why delay the inevitable," he said grimly. "Are you going to do it yourself? Right here? Now?"

His betrayal sparked in her eyes as bright and clear as the raindrops on her lashes. "I can't believe you think I'd let you get away." Her mouth twisted. "Losing a robo in my custody would kill my career forever." She looked directly at him for just a moment, enveloping him in the ice-blue stare of her eyes, then shifted her gaze just slightly to the side as if she couldn't bear to look at him.

The frigid water slapped against his cheek as he lay on his side in the street with Camille standing over him, and he welcomed it; reminded him of how she'd made him feel, and he'd almost lost his freedom because of it.

He knew that time was running out. His mind switched back into battle mode with so little resistance it was almost frightening.

"Toss out the pistol," she said.

"What?"

"I know you have it." She crushed down on his bent knee with her boot. Meat grunted, quickly working through the pain and rolled off the pistol he was concealing underneath his body.

Camille moved off his knee and took the pistol, the look in her eyes one of resigned and unflinching duty.

And as she straightened up, their eyes met, hers revealing a searching look that asked him to prove her wrong, to prove he hadn't betrayed her, worked her over, played her for a fool.

He didn't beg; he just watched. She lifted the pistol and moved her finger to the trigger in what seemed like slow motion.

The curve of her delicate forefinger against the black metal. The last second of indecision where she seemed to change her mind, and he leapt toward her as the clip unloaded, her body jerking at the recoil. The tang of gunpowder in his nostrils and the terrible pain that spread like an ocean tide across his body. The sound of the gun clattering down on the pavement.

He pulled Camille down with him as he fell forward, both weapons falling to the pavement, her scream bouncing off the empty alleys in the silent streets.

She struggled to recover her weapons as he held her around the legs.

The killer instinct, they called it. Ah, Camille, your so-called friends are right. You really don't have it, do you? But I still do. In spades. I can almost taste the metal in my blood. And the gunpowder...these are my triggers.

She thrashed in his grip as he dragged himself up her body, blood running down his arm over his hand as he moved above her.

"The patrol will be by here any minute," she gasped out. "Let me go. You know I could have killed you." She struggled for another moment, then let her upper body rest back on the ground, leaving her white throat exposed as she looked left and right, scrabbling around helplessly in the dim light with her hands for one of the weapons. She looked terrified.

"You should have shot me through the head, but you couldn't do it. I made you care about me and you couldn't do it."

She just stopped moving entirely, the futility of her efforts seeming to crash down around her. She lay on the pavement, his weight binding her to the cold stone, her eyelashes fluttering as the rain picked up again.

She was waiting for him to kill her, gasping in tight intermittent breaths like a fish running out of oxygen.

Brave Camille. He knew she wouldn't beg for her life either.

"I can't believe I thought I could love you," she said suddenly, between gulps of air. And then she reared up, and backhanded him across the face.

Without a second thought, Meat knocked her back onto the pavement, watching her beautiful face as she lost consciousness.

He stared at her, half-wishing she'd wake up and fight back. He wiped a streak of grit from her cheek and held her face in his hands. She was so pale, her lips turning a faint blue around the edges from the cold, and even though he knew what he'd done couldn't possibly have killed her, his heart nearly jumped out of his throat.

He dragged himself off her and slid a hand behind her head to check for blood, nearly insane with relief to pull back his fingers wet only with rain.

As he kneeled down with his head bowed over her to protect her face from the hail that began to pelt from the sky, he cried for the first time.

He cried thinking that he could still save himself if he ran, but now realizing that he'd never leave her like this, hurt, alone and cold in the dirty streets.

She said he'd understand and he did. He loved her. More than the dream of freedom.

Sirens sounded in the distance, reminding Meat of reality. The metal in his hands was beginning to freeze, but he ignored the pain, awkwardly searching the duffelbag for a blanket.

He wrapped Camille in the blanket and looked around carefully as the sirens drew closer. Then, he picked her limp body up in his arms and turned for home.

Chapter Eight

In five hours he would be a dead man.

Meat had given Camille a mild sedative before leaving the house again. It hadn't taken him long to track down what Danny wanted, but he didn't like the idea of her waking up while he was gone and needing something for the concussion.

When he returned, he wrote a quick note and tucked it along with the small black videodisk containing Danny's training accident under the chunk of crystal on the bookcase, then nearly jumped out of his skin to find Camille standing in the door of the bathroom.

"Whatever you gave me, I feel like crap. We need to talk."

Meat frowned. "I want you back in bed." He turned her around, put his hand on her back and pushed her back into the bedroom.

"I've been out of bed since you've been gone." She rubbed the back of her head, frowning.

"Back in bed. Now."

"But—"

He shushed her with a finger to her lips. "There will be time later." He didn't like lying, but it was better than saying goodbye.

"I need to talk to you. It's about your status. Hey, don't you walk away from me!" From behind the bedroom door, Camille yelled, "Fine! I'll just go back to bed, then."

He smiled in spite of himself and checked the time as he went back into the bathroom to get cleaned up. He changed out of his wet uniform, lingering in the shower, ignoring the sting of the hot water in the bullet wound in his arm.

Once out, he pulled on fresh fatigue pants and boots, shaved, then gave himself the best buzz cut he could manage, lowering his razor just as Danny Dietrich's reflection appeared in the mirror.

"The door was open," Danny said.

Meat nodded, and carefully wound a fresh bandage around his upper arm.

"Did you get it?" Danny asked.

Meat could see the strain in his face. He reached around Danny to pull his clean shirt off the hook. He put the T-shirt on and turned back to the mirror, carefully smoothing the fabric over his chest. "Let's move into the living room. I don't want to bother Camille."

Danny nodded and disappeared.

Meat pulled Danny's pistol from under the bathmat piled up on the floor, and checked to make sure it still had clips. He pulled one of the black leather gloves from his pocket and slid his right hand into it, then wiped the gun all over with a towel and stuck it behind him in his waistband. He was as ready as he'd ever be.

He joined Danny in the living room.

Danny stood up immediately. "Did you get the videodisk?"

Meat folded his arms over his chest. "How's my reclassification coming along?"

Danny glanced nervously in the direction of Camille's bedroom. "Fine, fine. It's looking good."

"But it's not settled, is it?"

"It will be. Give me the videodisk, and I'll make it happen."

"If I believed that, I wouldn't have run. You're a liar, Danny," Meat said softly.

Danny rubbed his fingers together at his sides. He must be sweating.

"I'm the only chance you've got if Camille doesn't come through. And if she hasn't done it by now, buddy, it's not looking good, is it?"

"No, it's not looking good at all. For either of us." Meat pulled the pistol out of the back of his waistband and pointed it at Danny.

Danny swallowed but didn't lose his cool. "You're making a big mistake."

"I don't think so." He cut through the distance between them in an instant, grabbing Danny's throat with his bare hand. "It's only going to get worse; I get angrier than this."

Danny struggled, panicking in Meat's grip as the implants heated up. It wouldn't be too long before the metal could burn.

"Take the gun," Meat said.

"Wha?"

"Take the gun. It's yours."

Danny took the gun from Meat's gloved hand, and Meat released Danny's neck to avoid making burn marks, but he left his palm hovering close to his skin.

Danny looked down at the gun, wobbling in his hand. "I get it. You want my fingerprints on this thing."

"That's right. And now I want you to shoot me. Aim true on the first shot if you're feeling generous."

"Jesus! Are you crazy?"

"Shoot me, or I'll kill you."

"Fine," Danny said. A single bead of sweat trickled down his temple, and he wiped it away with his uniform sleeve. "With you this close I'll be able to claim self-defense."

"It will look curious given what's on the videodisk. Either way, you'll still have the scandal."

"You *do* have the video. Shit!" He looked helplessly around the room. "Where is it?"

Meat shrugged. "It's safe for now. Could we get on with this?"

"You *are* crazy. You're willing to die for Camille's career?"

Meat was quickly losing his patience. "Yes. Let's get this over with."

Danny just stared at him, so he pressed the hot metal in his hands against Danny's skin.

Danny swallowed and raised the gun; his hand was shaking so hard, Meat figured he'd better not count on a quick and painless death.

And then, just like that, a shot rang out. Easy. Too easy.

Meat waited for the pain to hit, but there wasn't any pain. Just Danny standing there staring off beyond Meat's shoulder with a glazed look on his face and a tiny trickle of blood running down the thumb of his empty hand.

Meat could hardly think over the pounding of his heart. He looked down at his body; couldn't see anything but the bandage wrapped around his arm and Danny's gun lying on the carpet.

"Camille," Danny said in a voice so tiny it was hardly there at all. Meat turned and looked behind his shoulder where Camille stood in the doorway, wiping her pistol off on her white silk robe.

Camille stopped cleaning the pistol and took a couple of slow, deep breaths to calm her rapid breathing. That had been uncomfortably close.

"Camille?"

She looked up, fixing Danny with blazing eyes. "Are *you* still here? Get the fuck out."

Danny picked up his gun and backed up, looking like he wanted to puke. His heel struck the door, and he stumbled, then turned and ran without another word.

She turned to Meat, undone by the sight of the bandage around his arm. Leaning her shaky weight on the doorjamb, she swallowed hard and stared at the carpet under her feet. "I really shot you. I can't believe it. I mean, I can believe I *shot* you, because I'm obviously capable…but I shot *you*…I…"

Meat walked up to Camille and took the gun out of her hands, his chest heaving from the adrenaline in his system. He tossed the gun on the nearest recliner, then grabbed her by the shoulders. "Are you crazy? Are you fucking insane? You could have had everything! What were you thinking?"

He was undone; his eyes burning into hers, fierce and wild. He couldn't get any more words out so he just shook her, his fingers digging into her shoulders.

Camille raised her chin, her trembling voice giving her false bravado away. "Now wait just one minute. I didn't think you even cared about me. Technically, you deserved to be shot, when it gets right down to it."

He let one of his hands drop, the fist clenching and unclenching as he worked to come down from the intensity of his emotions. "I'm not talking about then. I'm talking about now. I left the videodisk for you. You'd have him under your thumb, with no more problems at the academy. You'd have graduation and your career. You should have let Danny kill me."

Camille pushed angrily against his chest, gaining a little space as she caught him off balance and he stepped back. "You big idiot. I mean, I realize I shot you, but tell me you never really believed I could let you die." She shook her head in disbelief. "I reclassified you when you were out this morning. My career's over."

Meat's mouth opened in shock, but no sound came out. Finally, he managed one word: "Why?"

"Why do you think?" Camille asked, near tears, inexplicably angry. "I can't believe you. You almost went and got yourself ki—"

"—Camille?"

"Yeah?"

"Shut up." Meat placed his bare hand behind her neck and kissed her hard, pressing roughly into her mouth, his tongue sweeping against hers as if he'd been kissing her his whole life. He pulled her body up against him, as close to him as he could get her, his hands strong and possessive.

He kissed her as if he needed her heat, her touch to burn off the raw emotion that threatened to overwhelm him, and when he finally broke away, he rested his hot, wet mouth to her cheek and quietly exhaled. And just before he released her, Camille could feel his lips curve against her in a smile.

She swallowed, her heart racing. "I think I get what you're trying to say."

He held her out at arm's length and said, "I knew you were something special from the moment you stuck your knife into the side of my head. A real sense of style. That's my girl."

It was a relief to hear his cavalier tone once more. Camille stroked her fingers over his palm and said, "That job wasn't really my dream, you know. I don't need it anymore. I have you."

"Yeah, you do. So, quit thinking there's a problem somewhere." His hands slipped beneath the white silk, sliding it off her shoulders to pool at her arms.

"What are you doing?" Camille asked innocently.

Meat put his hand on her thigh, sliding his palm slowly up the curve of her body, leaving a trail of warmth in his wake. "First aid. I'm making sure that concussion didn't have any lasting effects. I'm sorry I hurt you." He stroked the side of her neck with his warm fingertips, his mouth pressed hot and greedy to her collarbone.

"You think you can accomplish anything with a little seduction, don't you?" she accused, not minding one bit.

He gave her an unintelligible response, then pressed a kiss between her breasts. Camille smiled as her knees went weak. She leaned back against the wall again, running her fingers through his newly-cropped hair. A girl could get used to this sort of treatment. "Meat?" she said softly. "I really am sorry about the bullet in your arm."

"A nice clean hole. Stop thinking about it. I already picked the bullet out and dumped some antiseptic in. I'm fine."

He swirled his tongue around the tight pink tip of one breast, then the next, gently biting her nipples until Camille shivered from the sensation. "In fact, I think I told you earlier everything was going to be fine."

"Yeah." She took his hand and threaded her fingers through his. "You were right."

He bent down and trailed his tongue down the middle of her body, the robe falling to the ground in a whisper as his tongue found the soft skin of her stomach.

"You're right about something else," she said. "I should really be in bed right now."

He smirked and scooped her up in his arms, carrying her into the bedroom. He laid her down on the bed and kneeled above her on his hands and knees, trying to pick up where he'd left off, but Camille wasn't having it.

She scooted down underneath him, between his legs until she could practically feel the heat at his groin on her face. She unfastened his fatigues. The muscles in Meat's abdomen contracted as she pulled his fatigues down his lean hips, teasing the hot shaft that jutted out to her with tiny licks of her tongue.

"Camille, you need to rest," he ground out. "Let me...oh, *man*...you don't have to do this. Don't want to get too rough."

"Oh, but I want to. And I like it rough. Don't you start thinking I'm too delicate."

She played with him, sucking the head of his cock, flicking over the moisture at the tip. Running her hand up the length of him, and then moving down to stroke his balls with her tongue, his unbridled reaction building up tension in her own body.

She took him deep in her throat and he growled, arching his back, his muscles jerking as she sucked on him harder.

"Stop!" He pulled away from her, panting and wide-eyed for a moment. "Come here," he said, his voice low and silky with want. Camille lowered herself down, his cock sliding thick and slow up between her drenched cleft. She rode him, the hot metal in his fingers caressing the insides of her thighs.

He swore under his breath, lifting his hips up from the bed to press himself even farther inside her. She tilted her head back, and he grasped a handful of her hair, wrapping it around his fingers, and pulling her head back gently as she moved faster and faster.

He moved his free hand to her clit, letting his fingers play against the wetness there. Looking into his eyes she gasped, and leaned forward with a wild toss of her head. Her hair whipped out his grasp in a wave of gold as she came, calling out to him. The she lifted up from his body and plunged back down on his cock, and he followed her over the edge, roaring out his climax.

Camille held him inside her for a while, with her head resting over his heart. Finally, she slid off him onto her side and ran her hand over his chest, tracing a long scar with her finger. "Why did you…I mean, when did you…"

Meat rolled over onto his side to face her, his head leaning on his hand. "When you love someone, you give up total self-preservation."

Camille chuckled. "Who'd have thought you'd turn out to be the romantic in this relationship."

Meat watched Camille barrel through the tinted glass doors of the academy. She stood at the top of the long set of stone steps and looked down toward the transport where he waited.

She still wore her body armor, but the insignia was missing from the arms of her training suit and she wasn't carrying any weapons.

He stuck his head out of the window of the transport. "Hey, kitten, look sharp! The road awaits. I have this whole wide world to see."

She cocked her hip and looked up, holding her hand out for signs of rain.

Suddenly she let out a little shriek of joy and ran down the steps to the transport. She opened the driver's side door. "Move over," she said. "You don't have your license yet."

"Fine with me, the steering wheel bothers my hands. So, we're all done?"

Camille nodded. "I gave Danny his video—or a copy of it anyway—he finally sucked it up and called Daddy to make it so I wasn't going to be kicked out…and then I quit."

"You sure that's what you want?"

"Are you kidding? Let's go." She slid into the driver's seat, then turned once more to Meat with a grin. "One more thing. If I'm going to be your girl, maybe I should use your regular name instead of 'Meat?'"

Meat frowned. "I like it."

"Excuse me?"

"You gave it to me. It means I belong to you."

"That's absurd. It was an insult."

"Not anymore."

"Tell me your real name."

"Mattheson."

"What? That's your last name, right?"

"Yeah."

"What's your first name?"

He paused. "My first name?" He had to smile. "No one's ever asked me my first name before. It's Peter."

Camille started to laugh.

"What the hell is so funny about 'Peter?'"

"I don't know. It just doesn't suit you. Now that I've been calling you Meat since I've known you."

"My point exactly. Kitten, you can call me whatever you want."

She covered her lips with her fingertips, choking back giggles. He'd never seen her look so happy. He never thought he'd feel this way either.

"Do we have enough supplies?" she asked as she punched the ignition. "It might be a while before we get our first contract."

"Don't you trust me?" he asked. "Your clothes, my clothes, a small arsenal, and two months' worth of frozen meals. What more could a girl want?"

Camille gave him a seductive little grin as she eased the transport away from the curb and turned toward the Northern horizon. "I'll fill you in when we get to our first overnight."

About the Author:

Unfortunately, Liz Maverick is not one of those lucky authors who could spell five-syllable words as a young babe and write fully plotted stories before she could walk. However, what she lost in time, she made up in enthusiasm.

After exhausting her left-brain in pursuit of an MBA degree, this former dot-commer chucked it all and found her true calling (and luckily rediscovered all that dormant right-brain matter in the process) as a writer. Kiss or Kill *is her first published work. You can visit her at* www.lizmaverick.com.

Dear Reader,

We appreciate you taking the time out of your full and busy schedule to answer this questionnaire.

1. Rate the stories in **Secrets Volume 8** (1-10 Scale: 1=Worst, 10=Best)

Rating	Taming Kate	Jared's Wolf	My Champion, My Love	Kiss or Kill
Story Overall				
Sexual Intensity				
Sensuality				
Characters				
Setting				
Writing Skill				

2. What did you like *best* about **Secrets**? What did you like *least* about **Secrets?**

3. Would you buy other volumes?

4. In future **Secrets**, tell us how you would like your *heroine* and your *hero* to be. One or two words each are okay.

5. What is your idea of the ***perfect sensual romantic story***? Use more paper if you wish to add more than this space allows.

Thank you for taking the time to answer this questionnaire. We want to bring you the sensual stories you desire.

Sincerely,
Alexandria Kendall
Publisher

Mail to: Red Sage Publishing, Inc.
P.O. Box 4844
Seminole, FL 33775

If you enjoyed Secrets Volume 8 but haven't read other volumes, you should see what you're missing!

Volume 1:

In *A Lady's Quest*, author Bonnie Hamre brings you a London historical where Lady Antonia Blair-Sutworth searches for a lover in a most shocking and pleasing way.

Alice Gaines' *The Spinner's Dream* weaves a seductive fantasy that will leave every woman wishing for her own private love slave, desparate and running for his life.

Ivy Landon takes you for a wild ride. *The Proposal* will taunt you, tease you, even shock you. A contemporary erotica for the adventurous woman ultimate fantasy.

With *The Gift* by Jeanie LeGendre, you're immersed in the historic tale of exoctic seduction and bondage. Read about a concubine's delicious surrender to her Sultan.

Volume 2:

Surrogate Lover, by Doreen DeSalvo, is a contemporary tale of lust and love in the 90's. A surrogate sex therapist thought he had all the answers until he met Sarah.

Bonnie Hamre's regency tale *Snowbound* delights as the Earl of Howden is teased and tortured by his own desires—finally a woman who equals his overpowering sensuality.

In *Roarke's Prisoner*, by Angela Knight, starship captain Elise remembers the eager animal submission she'd known before at her captor's hands and refuses to be his toy again.

Susan Paul's *Savage Garden* tells the story of Raine's capture by a mysterious revolutionary in Mexico. She quickly finds lush erotic nights in her captor's arms.

Volume 3:

In Jeanie Cesarini's *The Spy Who Loved Me*, FBI agents Paige Ellison and Christopher Sharp discover excitement and passion in some unusual undercover work.

Warning: This story is only for the most adventurous of readers. Ann Jacobs tells the story of *The Barbarian*. Giles has a sexual aresenal designed to break down proud Lady Brianna's defenses — erotic pleasures learned in a harem.

Wild, sexual hunger is unleashed in this futuristic vampire tale with a twist. In Angela Knight's *Blood and Kisses*, find out just who is seducing who?

B.J. McCall takes you into the erotic world of strip joints in *Love Undercover*. On assignment, Lt. Amada Forbes and Det. "Cowboy" Cooper find temptation hard to resist.

Volume 4:

An Act of Love is Jeanie Cesarini's sequel. Shelby's terrified of sex. Film star Jason Gage must coach her in the ways of love. He wants her to feel true passion in his arms.

The Love Slave, by Emma Holly, is a woman's ultimate fantasy. For one year, Princess Lily will be attended to by three delicious men. She delights in playing with the first two, but it's the reluctant Grae that stirs her desires.

Lady Crystal is in turmoil in *Enslaved*, by Desirée Lindsey. Lord Nicholas' dark passions and irresistible charm have brought her long-hidden desires to the surface.

Betsy Morgan and Susan Paul bring you Kaki York's story in *The Bodyguard*. Watching the wild, erotic romps of her client's sexual conquests on the security cameras is getting to her — and her partner, the ruggedly handsome James Kulick.

Volume 5:

B.J. McCall is back with *Alias Smith and Jones*. Meredith Collins is stranded overnight at the airport. A handsome stranger named Smith offers her sanctuary for the evening — how can she resist those mesmerizing green-flecked eyes?

Strictly Business, by Shannon Hollis, tells of Elizabeth Forrester desire to climb the corporate ladder on her merits, not her looks. But the gorgeous Garrett Hill has come along and stirred her wildest fantasies.

Chevon Gael's *Insatiable* is the tale of a man's obsession. After corporate exec Ashlyn Fraser's glamour shot session, photographer Marcus Remington can't get her off his mind. Forget the beautiful models, he must have her — but where did she go?

Sandy Fraser's *Beneath Two Moons* is a futuristic wild ride. Conor is rough and tough like frontierman of old, and he's on the prowl for a new conquest. Dr. Eva Kelsey got away once before, but this time he'll make sure she begs for more.

Volume 6:

Sandy Fraser is back with *Flint's Fuse*. Dana Madison's father has her "kidnapped" for her own safety. Flint, the tall, dark and dangerousmercenary, is hired for the job. But just which one is the prisoner — Dana will try *anything* to get away.

In *Love's Prisoner*, by MaryJanice Davidson, Jeannie Lawrence experienced unwilling rapture at Michael Windham's hands. She never expected the devilishly handsome man to show back up in her life — or turn out to be a werewolf!

Alice Gaines' *The Education of Miss Felicity Wells* finds a pupil needing to learn how to satisfy her soon-to-be husband. Dr. Marcus Slade, an experienced lover, agrees to take her on as a student, but can he stop short of taking her completely?

Angela Knight tells another spicy tale. On the trail of a story, reporter Dana Ivory stumbles onto a secret—a sexy, secret agent who happens to be a vampire.She wants her story but Gabriel Archer believes she's *A Candidate for the Kiss*.

Volume 7:

In *Amelia's Innocence* by Julia Welles, Amelia didn't know her father bet her in a card game with Captain Quentin Hawke, so honor demands a compromise — three days of erotic foreplay, leaving her virginity and future intact.

Jade Lawless brings *The Woman of His Dreams* to life. Artist Gray Avonaco moved in next door to Joanna Morgan and now is plagued by provocative dreams. Is it unrequited lust or Gray's chance to be with the woman he loves?

Surrender by Kathryn Anne Dubois tells of Free-spirited Lady Johanna. She wants no part of the binding strictures of marriage to the powerful Duke. But she doesn't realize the Duke wants sensual adventure, and sexual satisfaction.

Angela Knight's *Kissing the Hunter* finds Navy Seal Logan McLean hunting the vampires who murdered his wife. Virginia Hart is a sexy vampire searching for her lost soul-mate only to find him in a man determined to kill her.

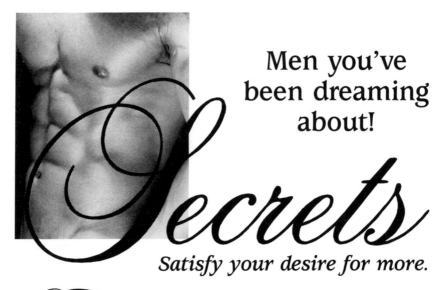

Men you've been dreaming about!

Secrets

Satisfy your desire for more.

*F*eel the wild adventure, fierce passion and the power of love in every *Secrets* Collection story. Red Sage Publishing's romance authors create richly crafted, sexy, sensual, novella-length stories. Each one is just the right length for reading after a long and hectic day.

Each volume in the *Secrets* Collection has four diverse, ultra-sexy, romantic novellas brimming with adventure, passion and love. More adventurous tales for the adventurous reader. The *Secrets* Collection are a glorious mix of romance genre; numerous historical settings, contemporary, paranormal, science fiction and suspense. We are always looking for new adventures.

Reader response to the *Secrets* volumes has been great! Here's just a small sample:

> *"I loved the variety of settings. Four completely wonderful time periods, give you four completely wonderful reads."*

> *"Each story was a page-turning tale I hated to put down."*

> *"I love Secrets! When is the next volume coming out? This one was Hot! Loved the heroes!"*

Secrets have won raves and awards. We could go on, but why don't you find out for yourself — order your set of **Secrets** today! See the back for details.

Secrets, Volume 1

Listen to what reviewers say:

"These stories take you beyond romance into the realm of erotica. I found *Secrets* absolutely delicious."

—Virginia Henley,
New York Times Best Selling Author

"*Secrets* is a collection of novellas for the daring, adventurous woman who's not afraid to give her fantasies free reign."

—Kathe Robin, *Romantic Times* Magazine

"...In fact, the men featured in all the stories are terrific, they all want to please and pleasure their women. If you like erotic romance you will love *Secrets*."

—*Romantic Readers* Review

In *Secrets, Volume 1* you'll find:

A Lady's Quest by Bonnie Hamre

Widowed Lady Antonia Blair-Sutworth searches for a lover to save her from the handsome Duke of Sutherland. The "auditions" may be shocking but utterly tantalizing.

The Spinner's Dream by Alice Gaines

A seductive fantasy that leaves every woman wishing for her own private love slave, desperate and running for his life.

The Proposal by Ivy Landon

This tale is a walk on the wild side of love. *The Proposal* will taunt you, tease you, and shock you. A contemporary erotica for the adventurous woman.

The Gift by Jeanie LeGendre

Immerse yourself in this historic tale of exotic seduction, bondage and of a concubine's surrender to the Sultan's desire. Can Alessandra live the life and give the gift the Sultan demands of her?

Secrets, Volume 2

Listen to what reviewers say:

"*Secrets* offer four novellas of sensual delight; each beautifully written with intense feeling and dedication to character development. For those seeking stories with heightened intimacy, look no further."

— Kathee Card, *Romancing the Web*

"Such a welcome diversity in styles and genres. Rich characterization in sensual tales. An exciting read that's sure to titillate the senses."

— Cheryl Ann Porter

"*Secrets 2* left me breathless. Sensual satisfaction guaranteed ... times four!"
— Virginia Henley, *New York Times* Best Selling Author

In *Secrets, Volume 2* you'll find:

Surrogate Lover by Doreen DeSalvo
Adrian Ross is a surrogate sex therapist who has all the answers and control. He thought he'd seen and done it all, but he'd never met Sarah.

Snowbound by Bonnie Hamre
A delicious, sensuous regency tale. The marriage-shy Earl of Howden is teased and tortured by his own desires and finds there is a woman who can equal his overpowering sensuality.

Roarke's Prisoner by Angela Knight
Elise, a starship captain, remembers the eager animal submission she'd known before at her captor's hands and refuses to become his toy again. However, she has no idea of the delights he's planned for her this time.

Savage Garden by Susan Paul
Raine's been captured by a mysterious and dangerous revolutionary leader in Mexico. At first her only concern is survival, but she quickly finds lush erotic nights in her captor's arms.

Winner of the Fallot Literary Award for Fiction!

Volume 2

Secrets
The Best in Women's Sensual Fiction

Doreen DeSalvo
Bonnie Hamre
Angela Knight
Susan Paul

"Novellas to titillate and satisfy the adventurous woman."
— Romantic Times Magazine

Secrets, Volume 3

Listen to what reviewers say:

"*Secrets, Volume 3* leaves the reader breathless. A delicious confection of sensuous treats
awaits the reader on each turn of the page!"
>   —Kathee Card, *Romancing the Web*

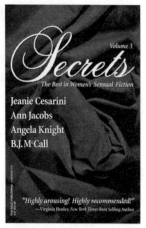

"From the FBI to Police Dectective to Vampires to a Medieval Warlord home from the
Crusade—*Secrets 3* is simply the best!"
>   —Susan Paul, award winning author

"An unabashed celebration of sex. Highly arousing! Highly recommended!"
>   —Virginia Henley, *New York Times* Best Selling Author

In *Secrets, Volume 3* you'll find:

The Spy Who Loved Me by Jeanie Cesarini
Undercover FBI agent Paige Ellison's sexual appetites rise to new levels
when she works with leading man Christopher Sharp, the cunning agent
who uses all his training to capture her body and heart.

The Barbarian by Ann Jacobs
Lady Brianna vows not to surrender to the barbaric Giles, Earl of
Harrow. He must use sexual arts learned in the infidels' harem to
conquer his bride. A word of caution—this is not for the faint of heart.

Blood and Kisses by Angela Knight
A vampire assassin is after Beryl St. Cloud. Her only hope lies with
Decker, another vampire and ex-mercenary. Broke, she offers herself as
payment for his services. Will his seductive powers take her very soul?

Love Undercover by B.J. McCall
Amanda Forbes is the bait in a strip joint sting operation. While she
performs, fellow detective "Cowboy" Cooper gets to watch. Though he
excites her, she must fight the temptation to surrender to the passion.

Winner of the 1997 Under the Covers
Readers Favorite Award

Secrets, Volume 4

Listen to what reviewers say:

"Provocative … seductive … a must read!"
—*Romantic Times* Magazine

"These are the kind of stories that romance readers that 'want a little more' have been looking for all their lives…."
—*Affaire de Coeur* Magazine

"*Secrets, Volume 4* has something to satisfy every erotic fantasy … simply sexational!"
—Virginia Henley, *New York Times* Best Selling Author

In *Secrets, Volume 4* you'll find:

An Act of Love by Jeanie Cesarini
Shelby Moran's past left her terrified of sex. International film star Jason Gage must gently coach the young starlet in the ways of love. He wants more than an act—he wants Shelby to feel true passion in his arms.

Enslaved by Desirée Lindsey
Lord Nicholas Summer's air of danger, dark passions, and irresistible charm have brought Lady Crystal's long-hidden desires to the surface. Will he be able to give her the one thing she desires before it's too late?

The Bodyguard by Betsy Morgan and Susan Paul
Kaki York is a bodyguard, but watching the wild, erotic romps of her client's sexual conquests on the security cameras is getting to her—and her partner, the ruggedly handsome James Kulick. Can she resist his insistent desire to have her?

The Love Slave by Emma Holly
A woman's ultimate fantasy. For one year, Princess Lily will be attended to by three delicious men of her choice. While she delights in playing with the first two, it's the reluctant Grae, with his powerful chest, black eyes and hair, that stirs her desires.

Secrets, Volume 5

Listen to what reviewers say:

"Hot, hot, hot! Not for the faint-hearted!"
—*Romantic Times* Magazine

"As you make your way through the stories, you will find yourself becoming hotter and hotter. *Secrets* just keeps getting better and better."
—*Affaire de Coeur* Magazine

"*Secrets 5* is a collage of lucious sensuality. Any woman who reads *Secrets* is in for an awakening!"
—Virginia Henley, *New York Times* Best Selling Author

In *Secrets, Volume 5* you'll find:

Beneath Two Moons by Sandy Fraser
Ready for a very wild romp? Step into the future and find Conor, rough and masculine like frontiermen of old, on the prowl for a new conquest. In his sights, Dr. Eva Kelsey. She got away once before, but this time Conor makes sure she begs for more.

Insatiable by Chevon Gael
Marcus Remington photographs beautiful models for a living, but it's Ashlyn Fraser, a young corporate exec having some glamour shots done, who has stolen his heart. It's up to Marcus to help her discover her inner sexual self.

Strictly Business by Shannon Hollis
Elizabeth Forrester knows it's tough enough for a woman to make it to the top in the corporate world. Garrett Hill, the most beautiful man in Silicon Valley, has to come along to stir up her wildest fantasies. Dare she give in to both their desires?

Alias Smith and Jones by B.J. McCall
Meredith Collins finds herself stranded overnight at the airport. A handsome stranger by the name of Smith offers her sanctuaty for the evening and she finds those mesmerizing, green-flecked eyes hard to resist. Are they to be just two ships passing in the night?

Secrets, Volume 6

Listen to what reviewers say:

"Red Sage was the first and remains the leader of Women's Erotic Romance Fiction Collections!"

—*Romantic Times* Magazine

"*Secrets Volume 6* is the best of *Secrets* yet. ... four of the most erotic stories in one volume than this reader has yet to see anywhere else. ... These stories are full of erotica at its best and you'll definitely want to keep it handy for lots of re-reading!"

—*Affaire de Coeur* Magazine

"*Secrets 6* satisfies every female fantasy: the Bodyguard, the Tutor, the Werewolf, and the Vampire. I give it Six Stars!"

—Virginia Henley, *New York Times* Best Selling Author

In *Secrets, Volume 6* you'll find:

Flint's Fuse by Sandy Fraser
Dana Madison's father has her "kidnapped" for her own safety. Flint, the tall, dark and dangerous mercenary, is hired for the job. But just which one is the prisoner—Dana will try *anything* to get away.

Love's Prisoner by MaryJanice Davidson
Trapped in an elevator, Jeannie Lawrence experienced unwilling rapture at Michael Windham's hands. She never expected the devilishly handsome man to show back up in her life—or turn out to be a werewolf!

The Education of Miss Felicity Wells by Alice Gaines
Felicity Wells wants to be sure she'll satisfy her soon-to-be husband but she needs a teacher. Dr. Marcus Slade, an experienced lover, agrees to take her on as a student, but can he stop short of taking her completely?

A Candidate for the Kiss by Angela Knight
Working on a story, reporter Dana Ivory stumbles onto a more amazing one—a sexy, secret agent who happens to be a vampire. She wants her story but Gabriel Archer wants more from her than just sex and blood.

Secrets, Volume 7

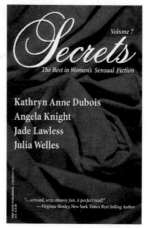

Listen to what reviewers say:

"Get out your asbestos gloves—*Secrets Volume 7* is ... extremely hot, true erotic romance ... passionate and titillating. There's nothing quite like baring your secrets!"
—*Romantic Times* Magazine

"... sensual, sexy, steamy fun. A perfect read!"
—Virginia Henley,
New York Times Best Selling Author

"Intensely provocative and disarmingly romantic, *Secrets Volume 7* is a romance reader's paradise that will take you beyond your wildest dreams!"
—Ballston Book House Review

In *Secrets, Volume 7* you'll find:

Amelia's Innocence by Julia Welles
Amelia didn't know her father bet her in a card game with Captain Quentin Hawke, so honor demands a compromise—three days of erotic foreplay, leaving her virginity and future intact.

The Woman of His Dreams by Jade Lawless
From the day artist Gray Avonaco moves in next door, Joanna Morgan is plagued by provocative dreams. But what she believes is unrequited lust, Gray sees as another chance to be with the woman he loves. He must persuade her that even death can't stop true love.

Surrender by Kathryn Anne Dubois
Free-spirited Lady Johanna wants no part of the binding strictures society imposes with her marriage to the powerful Duke. She doesn't know the dark Duke wants sensual adventure, and sexual satisfaction.

Kissing the Hunter by Angela Knight
Navy Seal Logan McLean hunts the vampires who murdered his wife. Virginia Hart is a sexy vampire searching for her lost soul-mate only to find him in a man determined to kill her. She must convince him all vampires aren't created equally.

Secrets, Volume 8

Listen to what reviewers say:

"*Secrets Volume 8* is an amazing compilation of sexy stories covering a wide range of subjects, all designed to titillate the senses. ... you'll find something for everybody in this latest version of *Secrets*."

—*Affaire de Coeur* Magazine

"These delectable stories will have you turning the pages long into the night. Passionate, provocative and perfect for setting the mood...."

Escape to Romance Reviews

"*Secrets Volume 8*, is simply sensational!"

—Virginia Henley, *New York Times* Best Selling Author

In *Secrets, Volume 8* you'll find:

Taming Kate by Jeanie Cesarini
Kathryn Roman inherits a legal brothel. Little does this city girl know the town of Love, Nevada wants her to be their new madam so they've charged Trey Holliday, one very dominant cowboy, with taming her.

Jared's Wolf by MaryJanice Davidson
Jared Rocke will do anything avenge his sister's death, but ends up attracted to Moira Wolfbauer, the she-wolf sworn to protect her pack. Joining forces to stop a killer, they learn love defies all boundaries.

My Champion, My Lover by Alice Gaines
Celeste Broder is a woman committed for having a sexy appetite. Mayor Robert Albright may be her champion—if she can convince him her freedom will mean a chance to indulge their appetites together.

Kiss or Kill by Liz Maverick
In this post-apocalyptic world, Camille Kazinsky's military career rides on her ability to make a choice—whether the robo called Meat should live or die. Meat's future depends on proving he's human enough to live, man enough...to makes her feel like a woman.

It's not just reviewers raving about *Secrets*. See what readers have to say:

"When are you coming out with a new Volume? I want a new one next month!" via email from a reader.

"I loved the hot, wet sex without vulgar words being used to make it exciting." after *Volume 1*

"I loved the blend of sensuality and sexual intensity—HOT!" after *Volume 2*

"The best thing about *Secrets* is they're hot and brief! The least thing is you do not have enough of them!" after *Volume 3*

"I have been extreamly satisfied with *Secrets*, keep up the good writing." after *Volume 4*

"I love the sensuality and sex that is not normally written about or explored in a really romantic context" after *Volume 4*

"Loved it all!!!" after *Volume 5*

"I love the tastful, hot way that *Secrets* pushes the edge. The genre mix is cool, too." after *Volume 5*

"Stories have plot and characters to support the erotica. They would be good strong stories without the heat." after *Volume 5*

"*Secrets* really knows how to push the envelop better than anyone else." after *Volume 6*

"*Secrets*, there is nothing not to like. This is the top banana, so to speak." after *Volume 6*

"'Would you buy *Volume 7*?' YES!!! Inform me ASAP and I am so there!!" after *Volume 6*

"Can I please, please, please pre-order *Volume 7*? I want to be the first to get it of my friends. They don't have email so they can't write you! I can!" after *Volume 6*

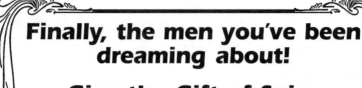

Finally, the men you've been dreaming about!

Give the Gift of Spicy Romantic Fiction

Don't want to wait? You can place a retail price ($12.99) order for any of the *Secrets* volumes from the following:

① **Waldenbooks Stores**

② **Amazon.com** or **BarnesandNoble.com**

③ **Book Clearinghouse (800-431-1579)**

④ **Romantic Times Magazine**
Books by Mail (718-237-1097)

⑤ Special order at other bookstores.
Bookstores: Please contact Baker & Taylor Distributors or
Red Sage Publishing for bookstore sales.

Order by title or ISBN #:
Vol. 1: 0-9648942-0-3
Vol. 2: 0-9648942-1-1
Vol. 3: 0-9648942-2-X
Vol. 4: 0-9648942-4-6
Vol. 5: 0-9648942-5-4
Vol. 6: 0-9648942-6-2
Vol. 7: 0-9648942-7-0
Vol. 8: 0-9648942-8-9

Secrets Mail Order Form:
(Orders shipped in two to three days of receipt.)

	Quantity	Mail Order Price	Total
Secrets **Volume 1** *(Retail $12.99)*	_____	$ 8.99	_____
Secrets **Volume 2** *(Retail $12.99)*	_____	$ 8.99	_____
Secrets **Volume 3** *(Retail $12.99)*	_____	$ 8.99	_____
Secrets **Volume 4** *(Retail $12.99)*	_____	$ 8.99	_____
Secrets **Volume 5** *(Retail $12.99)*	_____	$ 8.99	_____
Secrets **Volume 6** *(Retail $12.99)*	_____	$ 8.99	_____
Secrets **Volume 7** *(Retail $12.99)*	_____	$ 8.99	_____
Secrets **Volume 8** *(Retail $12.99)*	_____	$ 8.99	_____

Shipping & handling (in the U.S.)

US Priority Mail
1–2 books .... $ 5.50
3–5 books .... $ 8.50
6–8 books .... $11.50   _____   _____

Media Mail/Book Rate
1–2 books .... $ 5.00
3–4 books .... $ 7.00
5–6 books .... $ 9.00
7–8 books .... $10.00   _____   _____

UPS insured
1–3 books $15.00
4–7 books .... $22.00   _____   _____

SUBTOTAL   _____

Florida 6% sales tax (if delivered in FL)   _____

TOTAL AMOUNT ENCLOSED   _____

Name: (please print) _____

Address: (no P.O. Boxes) _____

City/State/Zip: _____

Phone or email: (only regarding order if necessary) _____

Please make check payable to **Red Sage Publishing**. Check must be drawn on a U.S. bank in U.S. dollars. Mail your check and order form to:

Red Sage Publishing, Inc.   Department S8   P.O. Box 4844   Seminole, FL 33775

Or use the order form on our website: www.redsagepub.com